BREVERTON'S
PHANTASMAGORIA

Breverton's
Phantasmagoria

A Compendium of Monsters, Myths and Legends

Terry Breverton

Quercus

CONTENTS

INTRODUCTION

In every culture across the world, we grow up believing in certain things that we gradually stop believing as we grow older. In Western culture, for example, most nations have a St Nicholas, or Santa Claus or Father Christmas, whom we only believe in as children. Other concepts, such as angels and demons, are discarded by many of us as we grow older, while friends and associates may remain believers. For some, the 'fear of the bogeyman' and fear of darkness are correlated throughout life. Many religions share the same stories and some of them, such as a 'great flood', are based upon actual happenings thousands of years ago. The belief held by many gardeners that

plants react to speech and music was held by our animistic ancestors. Many stories, such as the Arthurian legends and the *1001 Nights* tales, cross different cultures and may recur in modern fiction as the basis for new plotlines. Some fabulous monsters were based upon travellers' tales, but turn out to be real animals. Others, like giant birds, are probably based upon extinct species. Humans have always been fascinated by their forefathers, and have passed on elaborate stories from the earliest days of speech and writing. There is a cornucopia of legends about monsters, ghosts and the strange creatures which transfer across many cultures. Today, with our instant access to information and a far, far greater factual knowledge about different countries, animals and natural wonders, we can still be entertained by and learn from our forefathers.

'Phantasmagoria' is the art of creating supernatural illusions, the gathering of phantoms or fantasies. The name was given to a projection ghost show in the 18th century in which a modified magic lantern projected frightening images of demons, skeletons and ghosts onto walls, smoke or semi-transparent screens, sometimes using a technique of rear projection. Multiple projection devices allowed for quick switching between different images. Today we realize that

some of our ghosts and demons are based on events in real life or in past experiences, and that our forebears, with less knowledge or information, rationalized things that they could not understand by means of myths, legends and religions. This book is intended to be entertaining, and is written in the full knowledge that in 3000 years time our descendants will view us as just as primitive and non-rational as we regard our early ancestors. However, some beliefs, places, people and animals are 'magical' and 'mysterious' in so many ways. To lose our sense of wonder at the diversity of life and how history has shaped us, is to lose sight of the purpose of life. This is a magical, exciting planet, which has always been full of wonder and it always will be.

The book firstly describes strange and interesting people who have affected our perceptions throughout history. They are followed by mythical monsters and ghosts from across the world. Then there are mysterious places that people have sought out or found especially powerful. The legends of flight, from angels to strange beings, form the next chapter, and then come mysteries of the deep seas and flowing water, followed, appropriately enough, by tales of hidden treasure. Strange and mystical artefacts of the past and present come next, and they are followed by an account of those 'monsters' and myths which have a basis in reality. Above all, the book is meant to be entertaining. I hope that it will encourage readers to investigate further the strange world in which we live.

CHAPTER I
Mysterious, Magical *and* Weird People

ADAM AND EVE The zoologist Richard Dawkins, in his book *River Out Of Eden* used a complicated mathematical model to trace us all back to one common female ancestor, a woman who lived in Africa around a quarter of a million years ago. He noted, *'There has to be a woman of whom this claim can be made. The only argument is whether she lived here or there, at this time rather than at that time. The fact that she did live, in some place and at some time, is certain.'* Dawkins is a noted atheist, but this scientific proof of an 'original woman' or African Eve can also be used by those who believe in God to justify their beliefs.

ALCHEMISTS Many 'alchemists' (as we term them) were not simply involved in trying to transmute base metals, such as copper and iron, into silver and gold, but in genuinely trying to understand chemical processes. Most alchemists sincerely believed that mankind had lost the 'secrets of the ancients', and looked backwards in order to rediscover their skills. Many espoused the Aristotelian theory of the four elements of matter. All matter was assumed to have arisen from prime, chaotic material, which might only come into actual existence if impressed by 'form'. This 'form' arose out of the chaos of prime matter creating the four elements of Fire, Air, Water and Earth. The result of blending these 'simple bodies' together in different proportions produced the infinite variety of life and matter. Each element possessed two of four prime 'qualities'. Fire was hot and dry; Air was hot

and fluid; Water was cold and fluid; and Earth was cold and dry. In each element, one quality predominated over the other: heat in Fire; fluidity in Air; cold in Water; and dryness in Earth. By 'transmutation', any element might be transformed into another, through the quality which they had in common. Air could become water through the medium of fluidity, and fire can become air through the medium of heat etc. Attempts to transmute materials were made by burning, calcination, solution, evaporation, sublimation and crystallization. If copper and gold were metals consisting of fire, air, water, and earth in differing proportions, then changing the elemental proportions of copper could give the elemental proportions of goal. Alchemists thus wished to alter the elemental proportions of base metals, to make rarer ones such as silver and gold. Alchemists were bound by secret oaths and wrote down their formulae in complex codes. Not until the end of the 16th century did alchemists begin moving away from classical theory and become what we today call chemists. However, even in the 18th century, eminent scientists such as Isaac Newton were studying alchemy.

ALIENS FROM OUTER SPACE

Astronomers estimate there are millions of billions of stars in the universe and the likelihood is that many of them are orbited by planets. We know there are eight main planets in the Solar System, a handful of dwarf planets (including Ceres, Pluto, Sedna, Eris and a few others), and 429 extra-solar planets in the nearby portion of our own galaxy. Now, NASA has announced that its Kepler probe has found another 700 suspected new planets, including 140 of a similar size to Earth. We are lucky that the UN has chosen a '*Leader*' to represent us Earthlings in any communication or visit that may emanate from any of these planets. Like all massive, unelected organizations reliant on public money, the UN has a large number of committees of which the purpose and use is obscure. One such is the United Nations Office for Outer Space Affairs (UNOOSA), headed by a female Malaysian astrophysicist, Mazlan Othman, who has in 2010 now officially been delegated as the Earth 'leader' to negotiate any dialogue with aliens. UNOOSA actually oversees the *Outer Space Treaty* of 1967, whereby UN members agreed to protect Earth against contamination by alien species by 'sterilizing' them. For over four decades this has been Earth's

official policy to visitors from outer space, although two *Voyager* spacecraft launched in 1977 carried a message saying: '*We step out of our Solar System into the universe seeking only peace and friendship.*' Unfortunately the message was recorded by the then UN Secretary-General Kurt Waldheim, subsequently disgraced, and once stationed with the Nazis just outside Auschwitz where sterilization and worse was taking place. Professor Stephen Hawking has warned of the dangers of humanity trying to seek out alien life: '*I imagine they might exist in massive ships, having used up all the resources on their home planet. The outcome for us would be much as when Christopher Columbus first landed in America, which didn't turn out very well for the native Americans.*'

ARCHIMEDES (*c.*287 BCE – *c.*212 BCE) – THE MECHANICAL GENIUS

Archimedes was born in the Greek colony of Syracuse in Sicily and educated in Alexandria in Egypt. He returned to Syracuse, where he spent most of the rest of his life devoting his time to research and experimentation in many fields. There is a possibility that Archimedes built a steam cannon to fire incendiary projectiles against the Roman fleet which was besieging Syracuse. There are drawings by Leonardo da Vinci in which a steam cannon is described and attributed to Archimedes. One of Archimedes's war machines to defend Syracuse against the Romans was supposed to consist of large concave mirrors to concentrate solar rays and set fire to Roman ships. This so-called 'heat-ray' has been reconstructed using highly polished copper shields to set fire to small wooden ships coated with tar. In 2010 Cesare Rossi, an Italian professor,

Archimedes is quoted in later Arabic texts in relationship to advances in mathematics and mechanics, including the construction of hydraulic devices, such as water-clocks. His treatise '*On Floating Bodies*' established the physical foundations for the buoyancy and stability of ships. It was long lost, and it was many centuries before his brilliant insights were actually applied in ship design and ship safety assessment. Archimedes was also the greatest mathematician of his age. His contributions to geometry revolutionized the subject and his methods anticipated integral calculus 2000 years before Isaac Newton and Gottfried Leibniz. His practical inventions included a wide variety of machines including pulleys and the *Archimedean screw* pumping device. In mechanics he defined the principle of the lever and is credited with inventing the compound pulley and the hydraulic screw for raising water from a lower to a higher level. He once said of his work with levers: '*Give me a place to stand on, and I will move the Earth.*' He is most famous for discovering the law of hydrostatics, sometimes known as '*Archimedes' principle*', stating that a body immersed in fluid experiences a buoyant force equal to the weight of the amount of fluid it displaces. When Syracuse was captured, Archimedes was killed by a Roman soldier. It is said that he was so absorbed in his calculations that he admonished his killer not to disturb him. Cicero visited the tomb of Archimedes, which was surmounted by a sphere inscribed within a cylinder. Archimedes had proven that the sphere is two-thirds of the volume and surface area of a cylinder that circumscribes it, and he had regarded this as the greatest of his mathematical

argued that these two inventions, the solar heat ray and the steam cannon, were one and the same device. Rather than reflecting sunlight directly onto moving ships, he thinks that Archimedes used mirrors to heat 'kettles' of water to power his prototype artillery. Curved mirrors concentrated the Sun's rays on a tank filled with water. The water boiled and the trapped steam would have fired the gun, sending flaming cannonballs towards the Romans, 1500 years before gunpowder was used in Europe. Rossi designed his own version and stated that a heated cannon barrel would only need to convert just over an ounce of water into steam to hurl a 13-pound (6-kg) projectile a distance of 500 feet (150 m). Rossi thinks the cannonballs were made of clay and filled with the incendiary mixture known as '*Greek Fire*', a lethal combination of sulphur, bitumen, pitch and calcium oxide which would have exploded like a firebomb on the tarred wooden decks of the Roman galleys.

Arthur – The Most Potent Legend in Europe

The time of Arthur is one of the most debated areas of British history. It is termed 'The Age of Saints' in Wales, yet known as 'The Dark Ages' across the rest of Europe. Arthur was a sixth-century Celtic warlord, around whom the mythology of Camelot, Guinevere, Merlin, Lancelot, The Holy Grail, the Fisher King, Sir Galahad, Morgan le Fay, the Black Knight and the Round Table gathered. He repulsed the Saxon threat from the east, and the Pictish threat from the north and west. Until the 19th century Arthur was always identified as a real person, Prince Athrwys, or Arthmael – the Bear Prince (Arthwyr ap Meurig ap Tewdrig). His son Morgan became king of Glamorgan. This author has written more than 20 books on Welsh history, and considers that other claimants to be Arthur can be dismissed. Arthwyr ap Meurig ap Tewdrig lived in Glamorgan-Gwent and was a documented son and grandson and great-grandson of kings of the region which had been controlled by the Celtic tribe of the Silures. Boverton in Glamorgan is suggested as the site of one of his courts. There are more than 100 sixth-century Welsh saints with Arthurian connections, and also with connections to the ruling kings of Glamorgan-Gwent, which are described in stories that predate the medieval romances.

achievements. Space here does not permit the full description of his dozens of inventions, which ranged from odometers to block-and-tackle pulley systems, but after the capture of Syracuse the Roman general Marcellus took two mechanisms used as aids in astronomy, which showed the motion of the Sun, Moon and five planets. These were mechanical planetariums or orreries, and to work they would have needed differential gearing like the *Antikythera Mechanism* (q.v.), which Archimedes may also have designed. In 1906, a 174-page, 13th-century goatskin parchment of prayers was found in Constantinople. It was discovered to be a palimpsest, where ink had been scraped from an earlier work before the parchment was reused. The older document was shown to contain tenth-century copies of seven unknown treatises by Archimedes, including the only surviving copy of '*On Floating Bodies*' in the original Greek.

THE BABUSHKA LADY In analysis of the film footage of the assassination of John F. Kennedy in Dallas, Texas in 1963, a mysterious woman was spotted. She was wearing a brown overcoat and a scarf on her head. She wore it in a similar style to Russian grandmothers – also called babushkas. She appeared to be holding something in front of her face which is believed to be a camera, and can be spotted in many photos of the scene. When most people had fled the area, she remained and continued to film. Shortly after, she was seen moving away up Elm Street. The FBI publically requested that the woman should come forward and gave them the footage that she shot, but she never did so. No one knows who the Babushka Lady was, what she was doing there or why she did not come forward to give evidence.

THE BALDLANDERS OF BALDLAND AND THE ONE-EYED ARIMASPI Around 450 BCE, the Greek historian Herodotus wrote: *'As far as* [the Scythians'] *country* [modern Turkmenistan], *the tract of land whereof I have been speaking is all a smooth plain, and the soil deep; beyond you enter on a region which is rugged and stony. Passing over a great extent of this rough country, you come to a people dwelling at the foot of lofty mountains, who are said to be all, both men and women, bald from their birth, to have flat noses, and very long chins. They live on the fruit of a certain tree, the name of which is Ponticum; in size it is about equal to our fig-tree, and it bears a fruit like a bean, with a stone inside. When the fruit is ripe, they strain it through cloths; the juice which runs off is black and thick, and is called by the natives "aschy". They lap this up with* their tongues, and also mix it with milk for a drink; while they make the lees, which are solid, into cakes, and eat them instead of meat; for they have but few sheep in their country, in which there is no good pasturage …Thus far, therefore, the land is known; but beyond the bald-headed men lies a region of which no one can give any exact account. Lofty and precipitous mountains, which are never crosssed, bar further progress. The bald men say, but it does not seem to me credible, that the people who live in these mountains have feet like goats; and that after passing them you find another race of men, who sleep during one half of the year. This latter statement appears to me quite unworthy of credit. The region east of the bald-headed men is well known to be inhabited by the Issedonians, but the tract that lies to the north of these two nations is entirely unknown, except by the accounts which they give of it…The regions beyond are known only from the accounts of the Issedonians, by whom the stories are told of the one-eyed race of men and the gold-guarding griffins. These stories are received by the Scythians from the Issedonians, and by them passed on to us Greeks: whence it arises that we give the one-eyed race the Scythian name of Arimaspi, "arima" being the Scythic word for "one", and "spü" for "the eye".'*

BANSHEE This is a supernatural being in Irish and other Gaelic folklore, sometimes called 'the woman of the fairies'. Her screaming or lamentation in the night is thought to presage either the death of a family member or of the person who heard the banshee's cries.

Sometimes the banshee takes the form of an old woman who walks under the windows of the house of the person who is soon to die. In Ireland it is believed that banshees only warn families of pure Irish descent. The Welsh counterpart, the '*gwrach y Rhibyn*' (the Rhibyn witch), visits only families of pure Welsh stock.

BASIL THE BULGAR-SLAYER

Basil Bulgaroktonos ruled the Eastern Roman Empire from Byzantium from 976–1025 CE. Basil oversaw the expansion of the Byzantine empire's eastern frontier, and the final and complete subjugation of Bulgaria, the empire's foremost European enemy. At his death, the empire stretched from southern Italy to the Caucasus, and from the Danube to the borders of Palestine, its greatest territorial extent since the Muslim conquests of four centuries earlier. The Bulgars began raiding Byzantine lands on Basil's accession in 976. Basil permitted the escape of his captive, Boris II of Bulgaria, hoping that the resulting internal power struggle would weaken the Bulgars. Basil then invaded in 986, besieging Sofia, but retreated and was badly defeated at the Battle of the Gates of Trajan. Samuel I of Bulgaria consolidated his victory, taking lands from the Adriatic to the Black Sea and raiding Greece. From 1000, Basil was able to focus entirely upon the Bulgarian threat, and from that year onward was continually fighting in Bulgarian territories. Samuel became isolated in his core territories in the mountains of western Macedonia, and was defeated in 1009 near Thessaloniki. In 1014, after 15 years of war, Basil outmanoeuvred the Bulgar army at the Battle of Kleidion, and Samuel only just escaped. Basil was said to have captured 15,000 prisoners and blinded 99 of every 100 men. This left just 150 men to lead them back to their ruler. Samuel was physically struck down by the sight of his blinded army, and he died two days later after suffering a stroke. This incident gave rise to Basil's nickname of Bulgaroktonos, 'the Bulgar-slayer'. Because of Basil's cruelty, the Bulgars fought on for four more years but finally submitted in 1018.

BÁTHORY, COUNTESS ELIZABETH - THE BLOOD COUNTESS (1560-1614)

Countess Elizabeth Báthory de Ecsed is remembered as the 'Bloody Lady of Čachtice', so named after her castle in Slovakia. The countess was said to have been very beautiful in her youth, but as time ravaged her features she turned to 'witchcraft' to retain her youth. Her assistant, Dorka, told her that she would regain her beauty if she bathed in the blood of virgins at the 'magical hour' of 4 o'clock in the morning. The remedy did not work, so Dorka told the countess that she should torture the girls and let their blood splash over her face for the spell to work. Locals girls were abducted, tortured and killed. The people of the village below her castle lived in fear of the countess, but were too frightened to take action. Her assistants were brought to trial, and found guilty of torturing and murdering 80 young girls. Two of the countess' female servants were sentenced to have their fingernails ripped out and then be burned at the stake. Elizabeth Báthory, however, because of her lineage, was neither tried nor convicted but remained under house arrest walled up in a set of rooms in Čachtice Castle, where she was found dead four years later. Since then she has been identified with Vlad the Impaler and been called 'Countess Dracula', the 'Blood Countess' and the like. She was one of the leading nobility of Transylvania, and as a Protestant was opposed to the Catholic Habsburg Holy Roman Emperor. Emperor Matthias had pressed for a death sentence, as he owed her family money, and upon her death he was able to confiscate her possessions and wealth.

BOA SR - THE LAST OF AN ANCIENT TRIBE

The last member of a unique tribe which had inhabited the Andaman Islands 750 miles (1200 km) off India for 65,000 years died in February 2010. Boa Sr was the last member of the Bo, one of the ten Great Andamanese tribes considered indigenous inhabitants. Aged 85, she was the last speaker of the Bo language, which was distinct from those of the other Great Andamanese tribes, but had been unable to converse in her own language for some years since the penultimate Bo survivor had died. The last king of the Bo died in 2005. Boa Sr had survived the 2004 tsunami, which killed over 3500 of the islanders, and felt jealous of the neighbouring Jarawa tribe who lived in the forest away from settlers. The 200-300 Jarawa live in nomadic

Sawney Bean

One of the strangest stories in Europe – but a true one – concerns a cannibal family which terrorized part of the Ayrshire coast in Scotland in the 15th century, committing mass murder on a terrible scale. The family of some 48 members, headed by Sawney Bean, practised incest, and also captured and ate passing travellers. They were found hiding in a sea cave full of pickled body parts and booty they had taken from their victims. The family members were taken to Edinburgh, where the men were burned alive without trial. The women and children had their hands and feet cut off and bled to death. Their victims may have numbered over 1000 people.

bands hunting pigs and lizards, with little contact with the outside world. The Onge of Little Andaman Island number only around 100 people. The Sentinelese live on their own island of North Sentinel and have no contact with outsiders. After the 2004 tsunami they were photographed firing arrows at a helicopter that was trying to assist them.

BOGEYMEN AND BLACK MEN AND LULUS AND COCOS

In many countries the 'bogeyman' or 'boogyman' is a ghostly monster of which children are scared. He is imagined as hiding behind a bedroom door or under the bed. In Holland he is thought to hide under water. The term has become a metaphor for something or someone of which we have an irrational fear. Even sports fans refer to a '*bogey team*' which their side always has difficulty in beating. Parents often use the bogeyman as a way to discipline misbehaving children, or children who bite their nails, suck their thumbs etc., telling them that '*The bogeyman will get you!*' Some believe that the word originated with a fear of '*Old Boney*', Napoleon Bonaparte, who was nicknamed the '*Boneyman*' by the British. Others believe that its origin lies in the Middle English '*bugge*' or Scottish '*bogle*' or Welsh '*bwg*' meaning hobgoblin or ghost. Again, the *Bugis* pirates of the Straits of Malacca may have been called '*bugismen*' by returning sailors. The most accepted origin for bogeyman as a devil links it to the Slavic '*bog*' (god).

English cognates were *bugabow, bugaboo, bugbear* and *boggle-bo*, names that used to designate the pagan image carried in a procession to the Maypole (q.v.) for May Day games. '*Humbug*' came from the Norse '*hum*' (night) and bog or bogey, originally meaning a night spirit. If you do not believe in something fantastical, you may say '*Humbug!*' The word 'bug,' from the Welsh *bwg* (spirit), was applied to insects because of the belief that insects were souls in search of rebirth. Other words derived from bog are the Scottish *bogle*, Yorkshire *boggart*, English *Pug, Pouke* and *Puck*, Irish *Pooka* and Welsh *Pwcca*. From the Danish derivation *Spoge* and Swedish *Spoka*, we have *spook*.

In Germany the bogeyman is known as *der Schwarze Mann* (the Black Man), as he hides in dark places like forests at night, or in a bedroom cupboard or under the bed in the dark. In Italy, the bogeyman's equivalent is also '*l'uomo nero*' (the black man), a tall man wearing a heavy black coat, with a black hood or hat which hides his face. Sometimes, parents will knock loudly under the table, pretending that someone is knocking at the door, and saying: '*Here comes l'uomo nero! He must know that there's a child here who doesn't want to drink his soup!*' *L'uomo nero* is not supposed to eat or harm children, but rather takes them away to a mysterious and frightening place. In Iran, naughty children are warned to be afraid of the *Lulu-Khorkhore* (the bogeyman who eats everything up) to make them finish their meals. The Spanish bogeyman is known as *El Cuco* or *El Coco*, a shapeless figure, sometimes a hairy monster, that eats children who misbehave when they are told to go to bed. Parents will sing lullabies or tell rhymes to the children warning them that if they don't sleep, El Coco will come and get them. The rhyme originated in the 17th century and has evolved over the years, but it still retains its original meaning. The term is also used in Spanish-speaking Latin American countries. In Sweden the bogeyman is referred to as *Monstret under sängen* which essentially means 'the monster under the bed'.

BOYLE, ROBERT (1627-91) AND PREDICTIONS OF THE FUTURE

A founder member of the Royal Society in 1660 and a contemporary of Isaac Newton, this remarkable scientist asked an assistant to write down his hopes and predictions for the future. At a time when the average lifespan was 40, Boyle forecast far greater longevity, and '*the Recovery of Youth, or at least some of the Marks of it, such as new Teeth, new Hair coloured as in Youth.*' Almost all of his 24 predictions have come true, such as '*A Ship to sail with All Winds, and A Ship not to be Sunk*'; '*Freedom from Necessity of much Sleeping exemplified by the Operation of Tea and what happens in Mad-Men*'; '*Potent Drugs to alter or Exalt Imagination, Waking, Memory, and other functions, and appease Pain, procure innocent Sleep, harmless Dreams, etc.*'; '*The making Armour light and extremely hard*'; '*The Acceleration of things out of Seed*'; '*The practicable and*

certain way of finding Longitudes'; '*The Art of Flying*'; and '*The Cure of Diseases at a distance or at least by Transplantation.*'

THE BRAHAN SEER (c.1650-c.1677)

The Brahan Seer from Uig on the Isle of Lewis was probably known in Gaelic as Coinneach Odhar. He is thought to have been a Mackenzie, born on lands owing to the Seaforths. Having become famous as a diviner, he was invited to work as a labourer for the 3rd earl of Seaforth, Kenneth Mackenzie, at Brahan Castle near Dingwall. He is thought to have used a stone with a hole in the middle to conjure up his visions. He was said to have predicted the bloody Battle of Culloden. He foresaw that Strathpeffer would be full of crowds seeking health and pleasure. With the discovery of mineral springs in 18th century, it did indeed became a popular spa. According to one source, the Brahan Seer predicted that Bonar Bridge over the Kyle of Sutherland would be '*swept away under a flock of sheep*'. On 29 January 1892 the bridge was swept away by a flood. Eyewitnesses '*likened the foam-current to a densely packed flock of sheep*'.

He said that if five churches were built in Strathpeffer, ships would anchor themselves to their spires. Shortly after the First World War, an airship's grapnel became entangled in a spire, fulfilling that prophecy. The Seer forecast that when five bridges spanned the River Ness in Inverness that there would be worldwide chaos. In August 1939 there were five bridges over the Ness and the Second World War started.

He also predicted that when there were nine bridges that there would be fire, flood and calamity. The ninth bridge was built in 1987 and in 1988 the Piper Alpha oil rig disaster occurred. His most remarkable prediction seems to be, '*One day ships will sail round the back of Tomnahurich Hill*'. In his day, there was already a passage for shipping using the River Ness, but it was on the opposite side of the hill from today's great Caledonian Canal which bisects Scotland and which was completed in 1822. The Seer made four prophecies regarding Fairburn, at least three of which are reputed to have been fulfilled. According to one prophecy, '*The day will come when the Mackenzies of Fairburn shall lose their entire possessions; their castle will become uninhabited and a cow shall give birth to a calf in the uppermost chamber of the tower.*' This apparently heralded the demise of the Mackenzies of Kintail and Seaforth. In 1851, the now-ruined Fairburn Tower was being used by a farmer to store hay, and a cow gave birth in the garret. It is believed that the animal, following a trail of hay, entered the tower, climbed to the top and got stuck. Both the cow and the calf were taken down five days later, allowing enough time for people to come and see the prophecy fulfilled. Unfortunately he further predicted that the absent earl of Seaforth was having extramarital sex with one or more women in Paris. Lady Seaforth was incensed, and had the Seer burnt to death in a spiked tar barrel at Chanonry Point. The date of the execution may have in 1677 as a 'Keanoch Odhar' was prosecuted for witchcraft in that year, and the 3rd earl of Seaforth died in 1678. From the barrel he shouted to the crowd that the line of the Seaforths would come to an end with a deaf earl whose sons would die before him. He yelled that the gift lands of the estate would be sold and the line become extinct when there were four great contemporary lords with certain physical defects. The four were Sir Hector Mackenzie of Gairloch (buck-toothed); Chisholm of Chisholm (hare-lipped and squint-eyed); MacLeod of Raasay (who stammered) and Grant of Grant (half-witted). Lord Seaforth's last surviving son died in 1814, around the time that the earl sold certain gift lands.

CAGLIOSTRO, COUNT (1743-95) – THE 'DEMON OF HELL'

The Comte de St-Germain (q.v.) called Cagliostro '*the demon of hell*'. Cagliostro's biographer Iain McCalman (2003) noted Cagliostro's enemies: '*Casanova, the greatest lover of the age, was bitterly jealous of him; Catherine the Great, Empress of Russia, wanted to strangle him; Johann von Goethe, the most revered of Germany's writers, was driven almost mad by hatred of him; King Louis XVI of France persecuted him as a dangerous revolutionary; Queen Marie-Antoinette wanted him locked permanently in the Bastille for involving her in a diamond necklace swindle; and Pope Pius VI accused him of threatening the survival of the Catholic church.*' He was born Giuseppe Balsamo in Palermo, Italy. In a Benedictine monastery he discovered a talent for medicine and chemistry, but later ran away and joined a band of 'vagabonds'. Aged 17, he became interested in the dark arts of alchemy and the occult. He convinced a goldsmith named Marano that he could transmute base metals, and asked for 60 ounces of gold to prove it. Cagliostro's colleagues beat up the goldsmith and the newly rich Cagliostro took the money and travelled throughout the world, visiting Egypt, Greece, Persia, Rhodes, India and Ethiopia, studying the occult and acquiring alchemical knowledge. Back in Naples in 1768 he opened a casino in order to cheat rich foreign travellers out of their money, but he was forced to leave the city. In Rome, he became a doctor but was suspected of heresy by the Inquisition and forced to decamp to Spain with his new wife. Returning to Palermo, he was arrested for cheating the goldsmith Marano, but after defrauding an alchemist of a huge sum of money, he escaped to England. Here he met the Comte de St-Germain, who initiated him into freemasonry and gave Cagliostro recipes for the elixirs of youth and immortality. Cagliostro now established Egyptian Rite Masonic Lodges in England, Germany, Russia and France. He went to Paris in 1772, selling medicines and elixirs and holding séances. Louis XVI became interested, and was entertained by the count who held magic suppers to please the court at Versailles. Cagliostro was a favourite of the French court, but in 1785 he was involved in the Affair of the Diamond Necklace, one of the major scandals that led to the French Revolution in 1789. The scandal concerned a plot to defraud a jeweller of the price of a hugely expensive necklace, and it involved Marie-Antoinette, Cardinal de Rohan and Cagliostro who was held in the Bastille for nine months. Acquitted, he was banished from France and left for England. Here Cagliostro was accused of being Giuseppe Balsamo, which he denied in his published '*Open Letter to the English People*', forcing a retraction and apology from his accuser. Cagliostro left England for Rome with his wife in late 1789, taking up the practice of medicine and séances once more. However, he attempted to found a Masonic Lodge in Rome, so the Inquisition arrested him in 1791. He was imprisoned in the Castel Sant'Angelo in Rome (a wonderful circular tower, which was originally the tomb of Roman Emperor Hadrian) and was tried for the crimes of heresy, magic, conjury and freemasonry. After 18 months of deliberations, the Inquisition sentenced Cagliostro to death, but his sentence was commuted by the pope to life imprisonment.

Cagliostro attempted to escape, so was sent to solitary confinement in the castle of San Leo near Montefeltro, one of the strongest castles in Europe, where he died on 26 August 1795. The reports of Cagliostro's death were not believed throughout Europe and only after a report commissioned by Napoleon did people accept the fact of his death. He was an extraordinary forger. In his autobiography, Casanova wrote of an encounter in which

Cagliostro was able to forge a letter by Casanova, despite being unable to understand it. Once considered one of the greatest figures in occult, since the late 19th century he has been dismissed by academics as a charlatan.

CASSANDRA'S PROPHECIES

She was the daughter of King Priam of Troy and was loved by the god Apollo, who gave her the gift of prophecy. In return, he expected her favours but she refused him, so he determined that although her prophecies would come true, no-one would believe her. Despite her warnings, Priam allowed her brother Paris to sail for Greece. There he took Helen, wife of Agamemnon, and shipped her back to Troy, so precipitating the terrible Trojan War. Cassandra warned the Trojans not to allow the Trojan Horse into the city, but was again ignored. This led to the destruction of Troy. Sheltering from the Greeks in the Temple of Athena, she was raped on its altar by Ajax, then was taken as a slave and concubine by Agamemnon. According to Aeschylus, just before her death she pronounced a curse of bloodshed to overtake the royal line of Agamemnon, the so-called '*Curse of the House of Atreus*'.

DEE, JOHN (1527-1608) - THE ORIGINAL 'BLACK JACK', 'THE MAGUS OF HIS AGE'

Ieuan Ddu, John Dee, Black Jack, the man who became Elizabeth I's tutor, was a respected figure at court who was also a noted mathematician, antiquary, astronomer, philosopher, geographer, propagandist, astrologer and spy. John Dee was better known in Wales as a magician and practitioner of the Black Arts than as a court adviser to Queen Elizabeth. Dee moved to Louvain (Leuven) in Flanders as he believed that the discipline of English humanism was not scientific enough, and he made contact there with some of the finest minds in mathematics and geography, such as Mercator, Ortelius and Gemma Phrysius. He then lectured in mathematics at Paris 'to enormous acclaim' when he was 23, and in 1551 returned to the court of Edward VI.

Cambyses II and the Lost Army

This King of Persia conquered Egypt in 525 BCE. Herodotus records that he sent an army of 50,000 men to take the Oracle of Amun at the Siwa Oasis in western Egypt. When they were halfway there, it appears that there was a great sandstorm, and no trace of the army has ever been found.

'An astounding polymath… the lectures of this twenty-three-year-old at Paris were a sensation; he was to be courted by princes all over Europe. He returned to England with navigational devices like the balestila or cross-staff, was taken up by the Queen, the retinue of the Earl of Leicester and the Sidneys, and was at the heart of the Elizabethan Renaissance.' By the skin of his teeth he escaped the Marian persecution of Protestants. Upon the accession of 'Bloody Mary' in 1553 Dee was accused of *'using enchantments against the queen's life'* and imprisoned at Hampton Court. Dee noted in his translation of Euclid's *Elements* that he was always regarded as *'a companion of the hellhounds, a caller and a conjurer of wicked and damned spirits'*. In 1555 Dee was freed by an act of the Privy Council and was taken into the heart of Queen Elizabeth's court. He is said to have been the model for both Shakespeare's character *Prospero* and Marlowe's *Faust*. *'With his remarkable library at Mortlake,* [Dee] *became the thinker behind most of the ventures of the English in their search for the North-East and North-West Passages to Cathay, pouring out treatises, maps, instructions, in his characteristic blend of technology, science, imperialism, speculation, fantasy and the occult.'* Dee invented the term 'the British Empire' for Queen Elizabeth in 1576 to prove her right to North America, which had been 'discovered' by the Welsh prince Madog ap Owain Gwynedd in 1170 (i.e. the Brythonic Celts, or the British, were the founders of her empire). Dee claimed

Scandinavia, the Arctic and America for Elizabeth, using the Madoc story to justify the American claims. Dee also advised Drake upon his circumnavigation, and planned a Northwest Passage with the explorer Humphrey Gilbert.

In 1581 Dee began to search for the 'Philosopher's Stone' and to experiment with crystalomancy (crystal gazing), a mode of divination using a glass globe or a clear pool of water (the method that Nostradamus also used to compose his quatrains). According to his diary on 25 May 1581 Dee first saw spirits while crystal gazing, and during the following year he saw a vision of the angel *Uriel*, who gave him a convex piece of crystal that would allow communication with the spirit world. After developing further interests in spiritualism and alchemy, a London mob sacked his fabulous library of 4000 books and over 70 manuscripts in 1583 after denouncing it as the den of a black magician. Dee now disappeared to Bohemia, Prague and Poland from 1584–9. In 1587–8 Dee was spreading prophecies from Prague about *'the imminent fall of a mighty kingdom and fearsome storms'*. These reached the Vatican via Dee's patron, the Emperor Rudolph, and were reprinted across Holland, undermining the morale of its Spanish occupying army. Dee's exultant letter to Queen Elizabeth on the Spanish Armada's defeat in 1588 justifies his predictions. However, her successor James I later refused Dee's petition to clear him of the slander that he was '*a conjuror or caller or invocator of spirits*'. While Dee sometimes brought suspicion on himself because of his prodigious intelligence and occult practices, the whispering campaign against him arose because of a wonderful stage device in the Cambridge production of an Aristophanes play. People saw his scientific brilliance as proof of collusion with occult forces. The *Dictionary of Welsh Biography* states: '*… it would seem certain that if he had adhered to pure science and steered clear of the esoteric or occult, he would rank amongst the foremost British pioneers of science*'. Most of his 79 treatises remain in manuscript, but his works on hieroglyphics were published across Europe, and his Diary in England after his death. Dee prepared an edition of Robert Recorde's mathematical studies, Recorde being a fellow-Welshman and inventor of the 'equals' (=) sign. Dee is credited with making the calculations that would enable England to adopt the Gregorian calendar, and championed the preservation and the collection of historic documents. Dr Dee was a great astronomer and mathematician and one of the first modern scientists. Interestingly, he was also one of the last serious alchemists, necromancers and crystal gazers.

THE DOGON AND 'THE SIRIUS MYSTERY'

The Sirius Mystery is a 1976 book by Robert K.G. Temple, in which he describes the extraordinary knowledge of the Dogon tribe of Mali in west Africa. The tribe was apparently aware for centuries that Sirius, the 'Dog Star', was orbited by a white dwarf neighbour that is invisible to the naked eye, and was only recently discovered. Temple believes that this knowledge of the Dogon tribe is 5000 years old, and also was known to the ancient Egyptians in the pre-dynastic times prior to 3200 BCE, so that the Dogon people could be partially descended from them. There are about 400,000–800,000 Dogon living in Mali, south of the River Niger. They believe that the brightest star, Sirius (sigui toloor, star of the sigui), has two companion stars, Digitaria (po tolo) and Sorghum (the female star emme ya tolo). When Digitaria is closest to Sirius, it is brightest, and when at its furthest away, every 60 years, it twinkles like several stars. Sirius B is totally invisible to the naked eye, and 'digitaria' means the smallest grain of sand known to the Dogon. The existence of Sirius B had only been inferred through mathematical calculations undertaken in 1844. The Dogon's highest god is the creator, Amma, worshipped once a year (the Egyptians had a major deity called Amon). The Dogon's most important ceremony is the Sigui, which happens every 50 years, the same cycle as governs sigui toloor, the white dwarf Sirius B. Recently, some astronomers have postulated that there is a third star next to the binary stars of Sirius A and Sirius B.

DOPPELGÄNGER

This frightening image seen at a window, or caught out of the corner of your eye, could be your own. It is your 'double', or *doppelgänger* (from the German for double-goer or double-walker), the sight of which can foretell your imminent death. It is sometimes described as the soul embodied, sometimes an astral projection or an aura, and presents itself as a warning. Queen Elizabeth I reportedly saw such a vision of herself lying on her deathbed, pale and still, soon before she died. Goethe and Abraham Lincoln also claimed to have seen their doubles, and when Catherine the Great of Russia saw her own coming toward her, she ordered her soldiers to shoot at it. The poet Percy Bysshe Shelley saw his double shortly before drowning in 1822. It is recorded that Lady Diana Rich, daughter of the earl of Holland, saw her mirror-image double while walking in a garden a month before she died of smallpox. Witches, it was long accepted, could project their own doubles and set them loose to do mischief far and wide. As a result, many women were executed as witches even though it could be proven beyond a shadow of a doubt that they were somewhere else entirely when the barn burned down, the cow died or whatever else had happened with which they were charged.

An old Halloween custom holds that if a young girl lights two candles before a mirror while eating an apple, she will see in the mirror the ghostly image of her future husband, staring back at her as if from over her shoulder. If she is brave enough to venture out to a graveyard, and walk all the way around it 12 times, she will meet the double itself. The old custom of covering all the mirrors in a house where a death has just occurred is to prevent anyone from seeing the aura, or double, of the deceased. Under different names, such as the 'fetch' in England and Ireland (the double has come to 'fetch' you to death) the double is known all over the world. The Egyptians believed that the soul had a double called the *ka*. Upon death the ka resided in the tomb along with the corpse, while the soul went to the underworld. A special part of the tomb was called 'the house of ka', which was reserved for the double, where the priest ministered to it with food, drink and funerary offerings.

EARHART, AMELIA – HER MYSTERIOUS DISAPPEARANCE

The first woman to fly the Atlantic, Earhart set off on a round-the-world flight with navigator Fred Noonan in 1937, and had completed all but 7000 miles (11,265 km) of her 29,000-mile (46,670-km) journey. The next leg was from Papua New Guinea to a tiny atoll named Howland Island where a runway had been constructed and a US Navy coastguard cutter was stationed to provide radio guidance. Poor radio contact eventually broke up and the cutter headed northwest to search for the missing aircraft. For 16 days a huge search and rescue operation was mobilized by the US Navy, scouring deserted islands. The most prevalent theory is that she was operating as an American spy, passing over Japanese-held territory. Photographs of her were found on the island of Saipan in 1944, and an

Fairies

These are supernatural beings and spirits that can be either good or bad. Some think they exist in a realm between heaven and earth, and others that they dwell on earth. They appear in various shapes and are dressed in different ways. For instance, a dwarf creature might have green clothes and hair, live underground or in stone heaps and exercise magical powers to benevolent ends. A fairy might be a tiny, delicate, feminine creature dressed in white clothing, which lives in a fairyland, and has benevolent intentions towards humans.

The Irish leprechaun usually wears a cocked hat and apron and can be either good or bad. A tiny cobbler by trade, his tapping makes others aware of his presence, and he may possess a hidden crock of gold, the whereabouts of which he is not about to divulge unless his capturer threatens him with bodily harm. The belief in fairies is ancient, and their many forms include Sanskrit *gandharva* (semidivine celestial musicians), the nymphs of the Greeks, the jinns of Arabia mythology,

brownies, goblins, dwarves, elves, trolls, goblins, pookas et al.

King James I, in his book of witchcraft, '*Daemonologie*', named Diana the goddess of witches, and also the queen of fairies. Oberon, the name of the king of fairies, also was the name of a demon summoned by magicians.

army sergeant claimed he had seen US marines guarding her plane, which was later burned. A marine gunner was shown her grave on the neighbouring island of Tinian in 1944 and told that she and Noonan had been shot as spies. It is thought that rather than admit it had used this famous heroine as a spy, the US government covered up the facts. Equally the Japanese would not admit to another war crime, so complied with the cover-up. Another theory is that the plane ran short of fuel and the aviators landed on the uninhabited island of Nikumaroro, starving to death when no rescue ship could find them.

FREDERICK WILHELM II (1688-1740) AND THE 'POTSDAM GIANTS'

This king of Prussia (from 1713) built up an army of 40,000 foreign mercenaries. He loved very tall soldiers, who comprised his regiment of the 'Grand Grenadiers of Potsdam'. The grenadiers had to be at least 6 Prussian feet tall, about 6 feet 2 inches (1.88 m), and they came from all over Europe. The king needed several hundred recruits each year. The king trained and drilled his own regiment every day. He liked to paint their portraits from memory. He tried to show them to foreign visitors and dignitaries to impress them. Sometimes he would cheer himself up by ordering them to march before him, even if he was in his sickbed. This procession, which included the entire regiment, was led by their mascot, a bear. He never risked his 'giants' in battle, and told the French ambassador that *'the most beautiful girl or woman in the world would be a matter of indifference to me, but tall soldiers – they are my weakness.'*

THE GREEN MAN

This is the legendary pagan deity who roams the woodlands of Europe, possibly a remnant of the animistic beliefs of the Celts and druids. He is often depicted as a horned man peering out of a mask of foliage, usually made of the sacred oak. He is

known by other names such as 'Green Jack', 'Jack-in the Green' and 'Green George', and represents the spirits of trees, plants and foliage. It is believed he has rainmaking powers to foster livestock with lush meadows. He is sometimes seen in church decorations in Britain.

HENRI IV AND LOUIS XIV

Henri IV was the 14th king of France and Navarre (following the extinction of the family of Navarre), and he was born on 14 December 1553 (1+5+5+3 = 14). His wife Marguerite de Valois was born on 14 May 1553 (again totalling 14). There are 14 letters in his name Henri de Bourbon. He won a great victory at Ivry on 14 March 1590, but on 14 May of that year a huge demonstration was held against him in Paris. Gregory XIV placed a papal ban on the king, who was assassinated on 14 May 1610 in Paris. Louis XIV came to the throne in 1643 (1+6+4+3 = 14), and died in 1715 (=14), living for 77 years (=14). His birth date of 1638 and death date of 1715 add together to make 3353, the sum of these figures adding up to 14.

THE HOLY BLOOD

The only real evidence we have about the family of Jesus of Nazareth comes from the New Testament, and it is contradictory in places. Nevertheless, all the sources agree that the mother of Jesus was called Mary, that she was married to Joseph (although the story of the virgin birth would mean that Joseph was not the father of Jesus). We also read that Jesus had at least four brothers (James 'the Just', Joses, Simon and Judah) and at least two sisters. None of the sources (whether canonical or otherwise) indicates that Jesus was married and only a few apocryphal texts suggest that there was anything special

about Jesus' relationship with Mary Magdalene. Proponents of a bloodline stretching from Christ believe that he married Mary Magdalene. According to the historian Hegesippus (c.110–180 CE), as quoted by Eusebius (c.260–340 CE), descendants of Jesus' brothers continued to lead the Jerusalem church until the early second century CE. Any other relations named by modern authors are nothing more than speculation.

HUBBARD, L. RON AND THE BEST OPENING LINE TO A BOOK ON BELIEF

'*The creation of Dianetics is a milestone for man comparable to his discovery of fire and superior to his invention of the wheel and the arch.*' (L. Ron Hubbard, *Dianetics: The Modern Science of Mental Health*, 1950). Hubbard's first article on dianetics was published in *Amazing Science Fiction* in 1950, and the Church of Scientology disseminates his work. The best-known scientologists are Tom Cruise and John Travolta. In the above book, Lafayette Ronald Hubbard tells us: '*It is well accepted that life in all forms evolved from the basic building blocks: the virus and the cell.*' He develops this into a theory of evolution in his 1952 title *A History of Man*. Each cell in our bodies has a memory dating back to our evolutionary inception, and it remembers each trauma

of our forefathers, which is the source of our psychological weaknesses. Trillions of years ago a cosmic impact created a single-cell organism known as a *Helper*. The next evolutionary step for man was the *Clam*, a '*scalloped-lipped creature*'. Among its traumas was '*to get its shell stuck open and be unable to shut it.*' Then came another shell, a *Weeper* which had 'two pumping tubes' to allow transition from sea to land, and these tubes evolved into eyes. Next we evolved into defenceless sloths, then into Piltdown Man, and then into mankind as we know it. The next stage in the lives of believers in Hubbard's religion of Scientology is to become a *Thetan*, but I am afraid it is too late for this evolved sloth.

IBN BATTUTA (1304-68 or 1377) AND THE CHINESE DISCOVERY OF AMERICA

Abu Abdullah Muhammad Ibn Abdullah Al Lawati Al Tanji Ibn Battuta was a Moroccan Berber scholar and Sunni Islamic judge, who covered 73,000 miles (117,000 km) as a traveller and explorer. These journeys covered almost all of the known Islamic world and beyond, including Europe, Africa, India and China. His account was *A Gift to Those Who Contemplate the Wonders of Cities and the Marvels of Traveling*, often simply referred to as the *Rihla* or *Journey*. He tells of a conversation with a Chinese captain in Zanzibar, who told him that he had made in his youth a voyage to '*a land of gold… so many days east of China they were unaccountable*'. The Chinese expedition brought back gold and silver from a place of high mountains and a holy lake. This may be Peru and Lake Titicaca – where else east of China could it be?

THE IMMORTAL WOMAN

Henrietta Lacks, a 31-year-old black woman from Virginia, was killed by extremely aggressive cervical cancer in Baltimore in 1951. Unknown to her family, a piece of her tumour was given to the head of tissue culture research at the hospital. Scientists had been trying to grow human cells and had failed, but Lacks' cells grew rapidly. Under the codename HeLa, they were sent to laboratories around the world, quickly becoming a primary tool for medical research and being used for the development of cancer treatments, the polio vaccine and countless other conditions. They have been sent into space and blown up in nuclear explosions, and there are now tons of Henrietta Lacks' fast-growing cells to be found across the world.

LAZARUS - THE RETURN FROM THE DEAD

Jesus raised Lazarus from the dead, and such an occurrence is a rare but well-documented phenomenon, now known in medical textbooks as 'Lazarus Syndrome'. Its causes are not well understood, but at least 25 times since 1982 it has been recorded that a heart has spontaneously restarted after failed attempts at resuscitation. In the United States in 2008 the heart of Velma Thomas stopped beating three times, and she lay clinically brain dead for 17 hours. Her son left the hospital to make funeral arrangements. Ten minutes after her life support mechanism was shut down, doctors were preparing to remove her organs for donation when the 59-year-old woke up.

LEONARDO DA VINCI (1452-1519) - THE TRUE RENAISSANCE MAN and THE END OF THE WORLD

Leonardo di ser Piero da Vinci's achievements encompassed both the world of art and the world of the sciences. He was a painter, sculptor, architect, mathematician, botanist, geologist, anatomist, cartographer, writer, musician, engineer, inventor and scientist, the epitome of the 'Renaissance Man'. He was an illegitimate child of the Florentine notary, Piero da Vinci, and a peasant woman, Caterina. In his adolescence Leonardo became an apprentice in one of the most acclaimed studios in Italy. He stayed there until 1483, when he left for Milan. In that city he was called upon by Duke Ludovico Sforza to construct an equestrian statue in honour of Sforza's father. It was here that he completed an early masterpiece, the Madonna of the Rocks. Leonardo was also a great engineer and inventor. There were many instances when Leonardo was commissioned by the government to design elaborate state buildings or churches, or to conceive of new armaments that would take an enemy by surprise. He was also was one of the greatest scientific minds ever to have lived. Huge numbers of observations and experiments were executed and recorded in his sketches. There are elaborate, detailed drawings of bone and muscle structure, organ-system observations, and anatomical studies. He is widely revered as one of the greatest painters of all time and the most diversely talented person ever to have lived. Two of his works, the *Mona Lisa* and *The Last Supper*, are probably the most famous paintings in the world, along with his contemporary Michelangelo's Creation of Adam. His drawing of a hillside waterfall near his home in Tuscany, painted in August 1473, is the earliest pure landscape study in Western art, the first surviving example of an artist choosing the natural world as his sole subject rather than using it as a backdrop to a mythological or religious scene. Leonardo even conceptualized a design for a helicopter, a tank, the calculator, solar power, the submarine, the double hull and many other inventions of engineering.

Legend has it that King Francis I of France, who had become a close friend, was at his side when he died, cradling Leonardo's head in his arms. Twenty years after Leonardo's death, King Francis was reported by the goldsmith and sculptor Benvenuto Cellini as saying: '*There had never been another man born in the world who knew as much as Leonardo, not so much about painting, sculpture and architecture, as that he was a very great philosopher.*' Sabrina Sforza Galitzia, a Vatican researcher, believes that there are clues in Leonardo's *The Last Supper* mural that indicate that the world will end on 1 November 4006. The central half-moon window contains a mathematical and archaeological puzzle in which he foresaw the end in a '*universal flood*', which would mark '*a new start for humanity.*'

LEPRECHAUN This Irish fairy usually appears as a solitary old man, the size of a small child, dressed in a red or green coat. He enjoys making mischief. Leprechauns spend their time making and mending shoes, and store away all their coins in a hidden pot of gold at the end of the rainbow. If ever captured by a human, the leprechaun has the magical power to grant three wishes in exchange for his release. Popular depiction shows the leprechaun as being no taller than a small child. Stories of 'the little people' appear across the world, spanning the centuries since recorded history.

Until the 20th century, the leprechaun wore red, not green. Samuel Lover in 1831 wrote: '*… quite a beau in his dress, notwithstanding, for he wears a red square-cut coat, richly laced with gold, and inexpressible of the same, cocked hat, shoes and buckles.*' W.B. Yeats tells us that solitary fairies, like the leprechaun, wear red jackets, whereas the 'trooping fairies' wear green. The leprechaun's jacket has seven rows of buttons with seven buttons to each row. On the western coast, the red jacket is covered by a frieze one, and in Ulster the creature wears a cocked hat, and when he is up to anything unusually mischievous, he leaps on to a wall and spins, balancing himself on the point of the hat with his heels in the air. David McAnally gave the best description: '*He is about three feet high, and is dressed in a little red jacket or roundabout, with red breeches buckled at the knee, gray or black stockings, and a hat, cocked in the style of a* century ago, over a little, old, withered face. Round his neck is an Elizabethan ruff, and frills of lace are at his wrists. On the wild west coast, where the Atlantic winds bring almost constant rains, he dispenses with ruff and frills and wears a frieze overcoat over his pretty red suit, so that, unless on the lookout for the cocked hat, ye might pass a Leprechaun on the road and never know it's himself that's in it at all.' He also stated that the Northern Leprechaun or Logheryman wore a 'military red coat and white breeches, with a broad-brimmed, high, pointed hat, on which he would sometimes stand upside down.' The Lurigadawne of Tipperary wore an 'antique slashed jacket of red, with peaks all round and a jockey cap, also sporting a sword, which he uses as a magic wand'. The Luricawne of Kerry was a 'fat, pursy little fellow whose jolly round face rivals in redness the cut-a-way jacket he wears, that always has seven rows of seven buttons in each row'. The Cluricawne of Monaghan wore 'a swallow-tailed evening coat of red with green vest, white breeches, black stockings, shiny shoes, and a long cone hat without a brim, sometimes used as a weapon'.

WILLIAM LILLY (1602-81) AND THE FORETELLING OF THE GREAT FIRE OF LONDON

Lilly was the foremost English astrologer of the 17th century, and he began studying astrology in 1632. In 1641 he launched a professional practice and soon became heavily involved on the Parliamentary side in the English Civil War. It was said that if King Charles I could have persuaded Lilly to his side, he would have been worth a half a dozen regiments. Lilly published many astrological almanacs and in 1647 wrote *Christian Astrology*, the most definitive work on horary astrology ever produced in English. It remains popular even today and has never gone out-of-print. He is perhaps most famous for predicting in 1651 the outbreak of the Great Plague and Great Fire of London of 1666. After the Restoration, Lilly was repeatedly investigated as a Parliamentary supporter, and was hauled before a Parliamentary committee in 1666 when aged 64. He was asked 'if you can say anything as to the cause of the late fire, or whether there might be any design therein', as he was suspected of starting it. Lilly blamed 'the finger of God' for the tragedy, and was set free. He continued his thriving astrological practice and died on 9 June 1681.

LÓPEZ, FRANCISCO SOLANO (1826-70), THE MADDEST SOUTH AMERICAN DICTATOR

López succeeded his father Carlos as president, effectively dictator, of little, land-locked Paraguay. He bought himself an exact replica of Napoleon's crown, expanded his army, kitting the troops out with Napoleonic army uniforms, and brought a courtesan from Paris to live with him. In the War of the Triple Alliance (1864–70) López took on the might of neighbours Brazil, Argentina and Uruguay. After sacrificing all his best troops against overwhelming odds, he retreated into the interior with thousands of civilian refugees. In 1868, he convinced himself that his Paraguayan supporters had actually formed a conspiracy against his life. Several hundred prominent Paraguayan citizens were seized and executed by his order, including his two brothers, two brothers-in-law, cabinet ministers, judges, prefects, military officers, bishops and priests, and nine-tenths of the civil officers, together with more than 200 foreigners, among them several members of the diplomatic legations (an event known as the San Fernando massacres). During this time he also had his 70-year-old mother flogged and ordered her execution, because she revealed to him that he was born out of wedlock. López also attempted to have himself canonized by the local bishops. In 1870 he proclaimed himself a saint. Twenty-three Paraguayan bishops disputed the canonization and were executed on López's orders. By the time he was killed, over half the population of Paraguay (more than a quarter of a million people) was dead. Only 28,000 men survived the carnage of the war.

THE LOST TRIBES OF ISRAEL

In 1492 the voyages of Colombus brought news of humans not accounted for in the Bible. Europeans were puzzled where they had come from. The solution was that they were the tribes of Israel which had disappeared with the fall of the kingdoms of Israel and Judah in the middle of the 1st millennium BCE. A Spanish

priest, Bartolomé de Las Casas (1484–1566), became a champion of the Native American cause protesting against the carnage carried out by the conquistadores in the West Indies, Peru and Guatemala. Las Casas believed that the Native Americans should be converted to Christianity, as he was convinced that they had originated in Ancient Israel. He believed that the Bible contained the proof that they were members of the *Lost Tribes of Israel*. Eventually Pope Paul III declared that the Native Americans were 'fully human' in 1537.

A 1644 report (unfortunately fictional) by the Portuguese traveller, António Montezinos, claimed that there was a Jewish tribe living beyond the mountain passes of the Andes, and that he saw them practising Jewish rituals. Thomas Thorowgood's *Jewes in America* of 1650 argued for the need to convert these lost tribes. Certain Christian traditions claimed that when the Ten Tribes of Israel were found and restored to the Holy Land, the return of Christ to reign supreme would be imminent. The 'Ten Lost Tribes of Israel' disappeared from the Biblical account after the kingdom of Israel was totally destroyed, its people enslaved and exiled by the Assyrian empire. There are various ethnic claimants to be these tribes, e.g. the British/Welsh and the Pashtun. The Bene Ephraim (southern India) claim descent from the Tribe of Ephraim, and the Bnei Menashe (northeast India) claim descent from the lost Tribe of Manasseh. Beta Israel are an ancient group of Ethiopian Jews who believe they are descended from the lost Tribe of Dan. Persian Jews (especially the Bukharan Jews) claim descent from the Tribe of Ephraim and Igbo Jews in Nigeria claim descent variously from the Tribes of Ephraim, Menasseh, Levi, Zebulun and Gad. The Lemba tribe (South Africa) claim to be descendants from a lost tribe of Jews which fled from modern Yemen and journeyed south.

PRINCE MADOC AND THE DISCOVERY OF AMERICA

The Daughters of the American Revolution paid for a plaque to be erected at Fort Morgan, Mobile Bay, in 1953. The plaque read: *'In memory of Prince Madoc, a Welsh explorer, who landed on the shores of Mobile Bay in 1170 and left behind, with the Indians, the Welsh language'*. This son of King Owain Gwynedd of north Wales is claimed to have visited America, where he and his followers were assimilated into a tribe on the upper Missouri. This tribe fuelled tales of fair-haired Indians living in round huts and using round coracle-like boats, both of which were common in Wales but unheard of in America at the time. They were also said to speak a language similar to Welsh. On arrival in America, they sailed from Mobile Bay up the great river systems, settling initially in the Georgia/Tennessee/Kentucky area where they built stone forts. They warred

with the local Indian tribe, the Cherokee. When they decided to return downriver some time after 1186, they built big boats but they were ambushed trying to negotiate the falls on the Ohio River (where Louisville, Kentucky now stands). A battle took place lasting several days. A truce was eventually called and, after an exchange of prisoners, it was agreed that Madoc and his followers would depart the area never to return. They sailed down river to the Mississippi, which they sailed up until the junction with the Missouri, which they then followed upstream. They settled and integrated with a powerful tribe living on the banks of the Missouri called Mandans. In 1781-2 smallpox, reduced the Mandans, a tribe of 40,000 people, down to 2000 survivors. They partially recovered, increasing their numbers to some 12,000 by 1837, when a similar epidemic almost wiped the tribe out completely. It is recorded that there were only 39 survivors, but the Mandan-Hidatsa claim it was about 200. The survivors were taken in by the Hidatsa who had also been affected by the disease but to a much lesser extent. George Catlin, the American painter, was positive that the Mandans were originally Welsh.

Magicians and Wizards

People have long believed that some individuals were skilled in hidden or arcane arts and skills. Those who claimed secret knowledge were called magicians or wizards, and often attributed with supernatural powers. Some alchemists could be included in this characterization, dealing in 'magic', while others were simply trying to advance the science of chemistry. Magicians were respected and feared, and sometimes prosecuted, depending upon their reputation. In some cultures, they were thought of as shamans or seers. In Egypt, priests were regarded as having magical powers, overseeing the Pharaoh's passage into the next life. In their lifetimes, men mentioned in this book, the Count of St Germain, John Dee, Nostradamus and Alessandro Cagliostro were regarded as magicians and courted for their powers.

Doctor Faust The prototype for *Doctor Faust* was probably the alchemist Johann Georg Faust (*c.*1480–*c.*1540), who was accused of practising magic. From 1506 for three decades, he is recorded as performing magic tricks and giving horoscopes. He was variously accounted for as a physician, doctor of philosophy, alchemist, magician and astrologer, and was often accused as a fraud. The church denounced him as a blasphemer in league with the devil. However, in 1520, he received money for carrying out horoscopes for the bishop and town of Bamberg. In 1528 Faust was banished from Ingolstadt, and in 1532 tried to enter Nuremberg, where a junior mayor called him a necromancer and sodomite. In 1536 a professor recommended Faust as a respectable astrologer, and a physician in Worms in 1539 praised Faust's medical knowledge. Faust allegedly died in an explosion during an alchemical experiment, in which his body was 'grievously mutilated', proof that the Devil had tried to collect him.

Faust's near contemporary in Germany was Heinrich Cornelius Agrippa von Nettesheim (1486–1535). He was regarded as a magician, theologian, occult writer, astrologer and alchemist. In 1510, he finished an early draft of his masterpiece, *De occulta philosophia libri tres*, a summary of occult thought. He was advised to keep this controversial

work secret and it was not published for 20 years. Lecturing in France in 1512, he was denounced as a 'Judaizing heretic', which was probably a case of anti-Semitism. Agrippa travelled through France, Germany and Italy, gaining employment variously as a soldier, legal expert, theologian and physician, studying the occult and being constantly denounced because of his opinions. Among his sayings are: '*Nothing is concealed from the wise and sensible, while the unbelieving and unworthy cannot learn the secrets*' and '*All things which are similar and therefore connected, are drawn to each other's power.*'

Gypsy Magic Roma people are known as gypsies in Britain, stemming from the belief that they came from Egypt, and for over 1000 years they have been linked with fortunetelling, because of their relationship with nature. Romas believe that there are certain among them who possess great power through the ability to perform magic with their special range of knowledge. Such people would generally be called witches, warlocks or wizards but within Roma and gypsy society they are known as *chovihanis*. Among the chovihani there are four favourite methods of fortune telling: palm reading, tea leaves, the crystal and cards. The left hand reveals the life with which we are born while the right hand is what we make of that life. In a reading, the chovihani uses the lines, mounts, divisions and type of hand to tell of a person's past, present and future. The earliest known tarot deck came from India and the gypsies introduced them to the world. Their magical arts are almost always practised by women.

The Great Beast The most notorious magician of his time was Aleister Crowley (born Edward Alexander Crowley, 1875–1947). Crowley was brought up under the strict rules of the Plymouth Brethren, and his rebellion against his upbringing, and the fact that his own mother identified him with the *Great Beast of the Revelation*, steered his life. He was initiated into the *Golden Dawn* – the most influential occult group in Britain – was said to have summoned demons, held the black mass, and to have taken part in sexual orgies. In 1912 he visited Germany and, interested in 'erotic magic', took the magnificent title of 'Supreme and Holy King of Ireland, Iona and all other Britons within the Sanctuary of the Gnosis'. After the First World War, Crowley became known as 'The Wickedest Man in the World'. In 1916 he rose to the rank of Magus by crucifying a toad after he had baptized it Jesus Christ. In 1934 Crowley was declared bankrupt after losing a court case in which he tried to sue the actress Nina Hamnett for calling him a black magician. Crowley died in Hastings aged 72 years, still a heavy heroin user, after taking a dosage that would have killed at least five people.

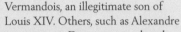

The Man in the Iron Mask

An unidentified prisoner of state was held for over 40 years during the reign of Louis XIV of France. He died in the Bastille in Paris on 19 November 1703, and was buried under the name of 'M. de Marchiel'. He was moved between prisons, never allowed to speak to anyone and wore a black velvet mask (not iron, as is shown in the movies). Some believe that he was the Duc de Vermandois, an illegitimate son of Louis XIV. Others, such as Alexandre Dumas, wrote that the masked man was Louis XIV's illegitimate older brother, the son of Cardinal Mazarin. Lord Acton thought he was Count Matiolo, a minister of the duke of Mantua born in 1640, who had been treacherous in negotiations and was originally imprisoned at Pignerol.

MARINUS OF TYRE (c.70-130 CE) AND THE FORTUNATE ISLES Marinus was a geographer and mathematician, as well as the founder of mathematical geography. He assigned to each place its proper latitude and longitude with equal spacing for lines, introduced improvements to the delineation of maps and developed a system of nautical charts. The island of Rhodes was his central point of reference for measurement of latitude. His maps were based on previous maps and the diaries of travellers, and were the first in the Roman empire to show China. Around 120 CE, Marinus wrote that the habitable world was bounded on the west by the *Fortunate Islands*. Claudius Ptolemy (90–168) adopted the Fortunate Islands as the prime meridian for his *Geographia*, written around 150 CE. This was the most famous classical map of the world, and was unsurpassed for almost 1500 years. The sources that Ptolemy cited most consistently were the maps and writings of Marinus. Some 1700 years before the modern discovery of the source of the Nile, Marinus wrote an account of a journey to the Ruwenzori in around 110 CE. A Greek merchant, Diogenes, had made a 25-day journey inland from the African east coast to '*two great lakes and the snowy range of mountains where the Nile draws its twin sources*'. Ptolemy and Marinus were major authorities used by Columbus in determining the circumference of the globe. The importance of Marinus is that he knew that there was a continent on the eastern side of the Pacific Ocean, as his maps (and those of Ptolemy, two generations later) showed the west coast of America, not the east. He mapped three prominent capes just south of the equator, namely

Cape San Lorenzo, Cape Santa Elena and Cabo Blanco. It is unsure how Marinus knew there was an American continent – the fire at the great Library in Alexandra destroyed the source books containing much knowledge of the ancient world.

MERLIN (5th-6th century CE) – ARTHUR'S WIZARD

King Arthur's advisor, prophet and magician is basically a construct of Geoffrey of Monmouth's *History of the Kings of Britain*. Geoffrey combined the Welsh traditions of the prophet-bard Myrddin with a story from Nennius, the Welsh monk and author. Geoffrey also wrote *The Prophesies of Merlin*. Merlin then became a popular figure in 13th-century French works, and Thomas Malory depicted him as Arthur's advisor in the *Morte d'Arthur*, and the creator of the Round Table at Caerleon for Uther Pendragon. Tennyson made him the architect of Camelot in *The Idylls of the King*. The earliest known reference is in the prophetic Welsh poem *Armes Prydain* (*The Prophecy of Britain*) probably dating from around 900. Myrddin Emrys, after whom Caerfyrddin (Carmarthen) was named, is the Merlin of Arthurian legend. The most famous wizard in the world, he appears in Welsh folk tales long before the Arthurian cycle, where he acts as Arthur's counsellor, and prophesies that hero's downfall. He became known as Merlin because the Latinized form of Myrddin would have been Merdinus. He was also a poet and a prophet, forecasting that one day the Welsh would once again take over the land of Britain and drive the Saxons out. This shows remarkable foresight – the east side of the British Isles is dropping into the sea at three to four times the rate of that of the west side. In future millennia, England may well have disappeared and Wales and its Cornish, Cumbrian and Strathclyde cousins – the old Britons – will once again rule the island. As a youth, Merlin was linked with Vortigern, king of Britain, who could not build a tower on Dinas Emrys. Merlin informed him that there was a problem because two red and white dragons were fighting near an underwater lake. Recent archaeological excavation has uncovered an unknown underground pool. The dragons were symbolic of the fight between the British (red dragon flag) and the Saxons (white dragon flag) for Britain.

In legend, Merlin next advised Ambrosius Aurelius, the conqueror of Vortigern, to bring back the Giant's Ring of sacred stones from Ireland and to erect Stonehenge. After the death of Ambrosius, his successor Uther Pendragon became besotted with Eigyr (Igraine), wife of Gorlois, so Merlin transformed Uther into the likeness of Gorlois and she conceived Arthur as a result of their union. After the Battle of Arturet, Merlin went insane and lived in the woods. He returned to advise

Arthur. Welsh traditions say that he lies in chains in a cave under Bryn Myrddin, Carmarthen, or in a cave near Dinefwr castle, or buried on Bardsey Island, where he took the magical item known as the *Thirteen Treasures of Britain*. He is also thought to have been imprisoned in a pool in Brittany. There were probably two Myrddins, one Myrddin Wyllt, a Celtic wizard who lived in the Scottish woods at the time of Vortigern, and Myrddin Emrys from Carmarthen, who lived at the time of Arthur. Merlin left behind a set of prophecies for the next millennium after his death. Thomas Heywood's 1812 book *The Life of Merlin* links Merlin's prophecies to major events in British history, for example the Gunpowder Plot: '*To conspire to kill the King, / To raise Rebellion, / To alter Religion, / To subvert the State, / To procure invasion by Strangers.*' A French scribe wrote in *Vita Edward Secundi* (*The Life of Edward II*) around 1330: '*The Welsh habit of revolt against the English is a long-standing madness… and this is the reason. The Welsh, formerly called the Britons, were once noble, crowned with the whole realm of England; but they were expelled by the Saxons and lost both name and country. However, by the sayings of the prophet Merlin they still hope to recover England. Hence it is they frequently rebel.*'

METHUSELAH AND THE SECRET OF LONG LIFE

According to the Book of Genesis, Methuselah lived for 969 years. He was the father of Lamech (whom he sired at age 187) and the grandfather of Noah, and he died in the year of the Great Flood. However, the prophet Enoch never died, so he is around 3000 years old.

Gilgamesh was a Babylonian king who undertook a quest for eternal life. He failed to fulfil the command to stay awake for seven days and seven nights, however, and the secret of immortality was taken from him. In the Hunza Valley, in Pakistan, it is said that the people routinely live healthily until 90, with many living as long as 120. They eat a diet primarily of fruits, grains and vegetables. Many of the inhabitants of the Vilcabamba Valley, in southern Ecuador, are reported to reach 100 and more in a state of good health. Some people attribute this longevity to the natural mineral water. The Abkhasia are a people living in the Caucasus Mountains in southern Russia who have a reputation for extremely long and healthy lives. In Soviet Russia it was claimed that Shirali Muslimov was 168 years old, and he was honoured with a special postage stamp. Japanese people have what is probably the world's longest natural lifespan, living on average to around 82 (the USA's figure is around 77). The healthiest Japanese live in Okinawa where rates of coronary heart disease, cancer and strokes are the lowest in the world. Okinawans live into their 90s and 100s, and their longevity is attributed to a diet which includes fresh fish, fresh vegetables, seaweed, tofu, green tea and plenty of exercise. Known as Longevity Island, Okinawa is home to the world's highest-known concentration of centenarians. Data reveals that Okinawans not only enjoy one of the world's longest life expectancies, but also a remarkable ability to age successfully and (significantly) disease-free. The Okinawan Centenarian Study reported that compared to North Americans, Okinawans suffer 80 per cent fewer incidences of breast and prostate cancers, and less than half the ovarian and colon cancers. In addition to extremely low rates of hormone-dependent cancers, Okinawans also have significantly lower rates of diabetes and heart disease. The traditional Japanese diet of fish and vegetables, with not too much saturated fat from meat, is followed in Okinawa – but with special Okinawan features. Okinawan and mainland Japanese cooking differ because of the climate. The warm and sunny weather in semi-tropical Okinawa allows the cultivation of fresh vegetables all year round. This makes it unnecessary to preserve vegetables by pickling them in salt, which reduces the Okinawans' sodium intake. In addition to diet, Okinawan's attitude to food plays a vital role in their longevity. Okinawans refer to their food as '*kusuimun*' or '*nuchigusui*', which means 'medicine' or 'medicine for life'. Any food that doesn't contain healthful qualities is deemed worthless and is not eaten.

There is one certain way to add to one's lifespan. In 1907, Einstein postulated in his General Theory of Relativity that time runs more quickly at higher altitudes because of a weaker gravitational force, and a century later using the most accurate atomic clocks, it was proven that time ran faster when the clocks were raised by 12 inches (30 cm). Gravitational time dilation also means that one's head ages more quickly than one's feet, and those who live in tower blocks age more quickly than those at ground level. It is now scientifically proven that if you live in a basement, this would add 90 billionths of a second to an average lifespan of 79 years.

Mister Eat-Everything

Michel Lotito (1950–2007) was a French performer, famous for being able to eat indigestibles. His stagename was *Monsieur Mangetout*. On stage he would eat metal, rubber and glass, taking items from bicycles, televisions, shopping trolleys and once even a Cessna 150 light aircraft. Items were cut up and swallowed, with the aircraft being gradually consumed between 1978 and 1980. He began eating such materials aged nine, and gave his first public performance aged 16.

He apparently suffered no ill effects, even when he had consumed items considered to be poisonous. When performing, Lotito usually ate more than 2 pounds (1 kg) of material daily, drinking considerable quantities of water with his meal. Interestingly, he claimed that eating hard-boiled eggs or bananas would make him sick. Between 1959 and 2007 it is thought that he ate about a ton of metal. He died of natural causes at a relatively young age.

Mythological Immortals of the Greek Pantheon

The Greeks passed on to the Romans and the rest of Europe lasting myths, although many of their legends and beliefs were themselves based upon those of other civilizations like the Medes, Persians, Babylonians etc.

PROTOGENOI - THE FIRST-BORN GODS

The first immortals in the Greek Pantheon were the primeval beings who created the Universe: Gaia (Earth), Ouranos (the Dome of Heaven), Pontos (Sea), Sky, Night, Day, etc. Although they were elemental divinities, they were sometimes represented in an anthropomorphic manner, e.g. Gaia might manifest herself as a matronly woman half-risen from the ground. Thalassa might lift her head above the waves in the shape of a woman formed from the sea, etc.

NYMPHAE - NYMPHS, THE SPIRITS OF NATURE

These immortals nurtured life in the four elements of nature: the Naiades in freshwater, the Dryades in woodlands, the Tritones in the marine environment and the Satyroi looked after all the animals.

DAIMONES - THE SPIRITS OF THE MIND AND BODY

The third category of immortals included Phobos (Fear), Geras (Death), Eros (Love), Hypnos (Sleep), Euphrosyne (Joy), Eris (Hate), Thanatos (Death), etc. From these words we derive the modern terms phobia, eroticism, hypnosis etc., and we sometimes hear *'He's got the demon(s) in him'* referring to someone acting strangely.

THE THEOI - THE GODS OF NATURE AND ARTS

This fourth class controlled the forces of nature and granted civilized arts to mankind. They included:

Apotheothenai (deified mortals). Some great humans were elevated through apotheosis into gods at the wish of the gods, e.g. Herakles and Asklepios.

Theoi Titanes (Titan gods). The first gods e.g. Prometheus, Kronos, Themis etc.

Theoi **Khthonioi** (Underworld gods)
e.g. Hekate, Persephone, etc.

Theoi **Olympioi** (Olympian gods) e.g.
Hebe, the Mousai etc.

Theoi **Ouranioi** (sky gods) e.g. the
Anemoi (Winds), Helios (Sun) etc.

Theoi **Halioi** (sea gods) e.g. Glaukos,
the Nereides, Triton, etc.

Theoi **Nomioi** (pastoral earth gods) e.g.
Aristaios, Pan etc.

Theoi **Georgikoi** (agricultural earth
gods) e.g. Ploutos etc.

Theoi **Polikoi** (city gods) e.g. Eunomia,
Hestia etc.

THE TWELVE GODS OF OLYMPUS - THE OLYMPIAN GODS

The fifth class of immortals was by far the most important to the Ancient Greeks. The entire Greek Pantheon was ruled by a council of 12 gods who demanded worship from all their subjects. Those who failed to honour any one of the 12 with due sacrifice and libation would be punished. The Olympians governed all aspects of the universe and human life and commanded hundreds of lesser gods and spirits. The Romans adopted the Greek gods but gave them different names.

Greek Name	Roman Name	Parents	God of	Spouse	Children
Zeus	Jupiter, Jove	Titan Kronos and Titanis Rhea	King of Heaven, Fate, Kingship, Sky, Weather	Hera	Apollo, Aphrodite, Artemis, Athene, Ares, Dionysos, Herakles, Hermes, etc.
Here, Hera	Juno	Titan Kronos and Titanis Rhea	Queen of Heaven, Sky, Women, Marriage, Fertility	Zeus	Ares, Hephaistos, Eileithyia, Hebe, Enyo
Poseidon	Neptunus, Neptune	Titan Kronos and Titanis Rhea	King of the Seas, Rivers, Horses, Earthquakes	Amphitrite	Triton, Theseus, Polyphemos
Demeter	Ceres	Titan Kronos and Titanis Rhea	Agriculture, Grain and Bread, the Afterlife	None	Persephone, Ploutos, Liber, Arion
Hestia	Vesta	Titan Kronos and Titanis Rhea	Home, Hearth, Family, Meals, Sacrificial Offerings	None	None (Virgin Goddess)
Apollon	Apollo	Zeus and Titanis Leto	Music, Prophecy, Education, Healing and Disease	None	Asklepios, Troilius, Aristaeus, Orpheus
Artemis	Diana	Zeus and Titanis Leto	Hunting, Wild Animals, Choirs, Children, Disease	None	None (Virgin Goddess)

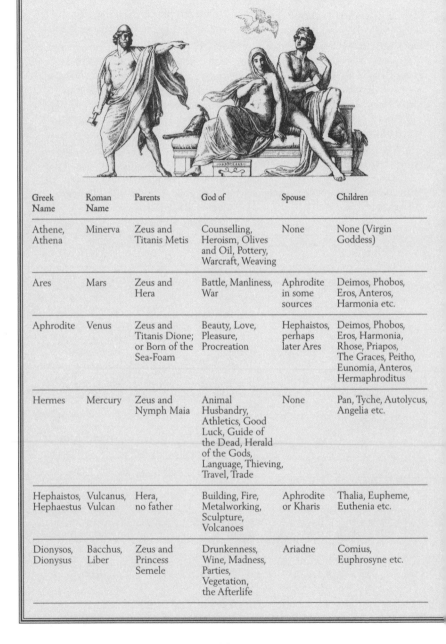

Greek Name	Roman Name	Parents	God of	Spouse	Children
Athene, Athena	Minerva	Zeus and Titanis Metis	Counselling, Heroism, Olives and Oil, Pottery, Warcraft, Weaving	None	None (Virgin Goddess)
Ares	Mars	Zeus and Hera	Battle, Manliness, War	Aphrodite in some sources	Deimos, Phobos, Eros, Anteros, Harmonia etc.
Aphrodite	Venus	Zeus and Titanis Dione; or Born of the Sea-Foam	Beauty, Love, Pleasure, Procreation	Hephaistos, perhaps later Ares	Deimos, Phobos, Eros, Harmonia, Rhose, Priapos, The Graces, Peitho, Eunomia, Anteros, Hermaphroditus
Hermes	Mercury	Zeus and Nymph Maia	Animal Husbandry, Athletics, Good Luck, Guide of the Dead, Herald of the Gods, Language, Thieving, Travel, Trade	None	Pan, Tyche, Autolycus, Angelia etc.
Hephaistos, Hephaestus	Vulcanus, Vulcan	Hera, no father	Building, Fire, Metalworking, Sculpture, Volcanoes	Aphrodite or Kharis	Thalia, Eupheme, Euthenia etc.
Dionysos, Dionysus	Bacchus, Liber	Zeus and Princess Semele	Drunkenness, Wine, Madness, Parties, Vegetation, the Afterlife	Ariadne	Comius, Euphrosyne etc.

THE KING AND QUEEN OF THE DEAD - HADES AND PERSEPHONE

The 13th and 14th of the 'great gods' were Hades and Persephone. Unlike the other 12, they were never titled Olympian, nor partook in the Olympian Feasts of Heaven. They remained in the Underworld forever.

Greek Name	Roman Name	Parents	God of	Spouse	Children
Haides, Hades	Pluto, Dis	Titan Kronos and Titanis Rhea	King of the Underworld, Death, the Dead	Persephone	
Persephone	Proserpina	Zeus and Demeter	Queen of the Underworld, the Afterlife, Spring Growth, Grain	Hades	Macaria, Melinoe, Plutus, Zagreus

THE SPIRITS OF THE CONSTELLATIONS

The sixth class of the immortals were the spirits which circled the heavenly night sky. Every constellation, including the 12 signs of the Zodiac, was possessed of one or more spirits, e.g. Sagittarius was the centaur Kheiron, Gemini was the Dioskouroi Twins, etc.

MONSTERS, BEASTS AND GIANTS

This seventh class consisted semi-divine creatures which were closely related to the gods, e.g. Drakones (Dragons), Gigantes (Giants), Kentauroi (Centaurs), Kerberos (Cerberus), Sphinx, Sirens, etc.

HEROI HEMITHEOI (Semi-Divine Heroes)

This final class was worshipped after death as minor divinities, and included heroes such as Akhilleus (Achilles), Theseus and Perseus. Heroines such as Alkmene, Helene and Baubo, and important founding kings like Erikhthonios, Kadmos and Pelops were also semi-divine. Some divinities in the Greek Pantheon fell into more than one of these categories. Tykhe (Lady Fortune), for example, can equally be classified under Class Two as an Okeanis Nymphe, Class Three as Fortune, and Class Four as a popularly worshipped goddess of Nature and the Arts.

Some Olympian Gods

Zeus (Jupiter) and Hera (Juno)

Poseidon (Neptune)

Aphrodite (Venus)

Demeter (Ceres)

Dionysos (Bacchus)

Apollon (Apollo)

Hephaistos (Vulcanus)

MOTHER SHIPTON c.1488-1561 - THE GROTESQUE SIBYL OF KNARESBOROUGH

Ursula Southeil (or Southill or Soothtell) was a soothsayer and prophetess who was said to have been born in a cave in Knaresborough, Yorkshire. It was during a thunderstorm, and her mother died to the sound of 'terrible noises'. The place is now called Mother Shipton's Cave and with its Petrifying Well it is open to the public. She was said to be hideously ugly, but married Toby Shipton, a local carpenter, in 1512 and told fortunes and made predictions throughout her life, becoming known as Mother Shipton. The first publication of her prophecies did not appear until 1641. They contained a number of mainly regional predictions, but only two prophetic verses. In Samuel Pepys's diaries, he records that while surveying the damage caused by the Great Fire of London in 1666, the Royal Family were heard discussing Mother Shipton's prophecy of the event. Many of her 'predictions', e.g. about the end of the world in 1881, were actually made by a man named Charles Hindley for an 1871 edition of her prophecies.

NEPHILIM - THE SONS OF GOD

The Nephilim were regarded as the 'ancient ones' – a superior civilization – by the Sumerians. To the Hebrews, the 'Nefilim' were a race that dominated the pre-Flood world. They are referred to in the Bible as the heroes of old, men of renown. They were reportedly the children born to the 'Sons of God' by the 'daughters of men' (as told in the Book of Enoch).

NOSTRADAMUS (1503-66)

Michel de Nostredame was by profession a French apothecary, but is most famous for his predictions which achieved real recognition after he claimed to have discovered a cure for the plague. One of his prophecies reached the ears of Catherine de Medici, the wife of King Henry II of France, who believed it was about her husband: *'The young lion will surpass the old one in national field by a single duel. He will pierce his eyes in a golden cage two blows at once, to die a grievous death.'* She summoned Nostradamus to Paris in 1555, after reading his almanacs, to explain them and draw up almanacs for her children. After Henry was killed in 1559 during a tournament when a lance pierced his eye, Nostradamus became famous, and Catherine made him counsellor and physician to the new king. By 1566, Nostradamus's painful gout had turned into dropsy (oedema), and in late June, he summoned his lawyer to draw up an extensive will. On the evening of 1 July, his assistant Jean de Chavigny found him writing at his bench and enquired *'Tomorrow, master?'* Nostradamus replied *'You will not find me alive at sunrise.'* De Chavigny left the room. When he returned the next day, he found Nostradamus dead and a note on the desk: '*Upon the return of the Embassy, the King's gift put in place, Nothing more will be done. He will have gone to God's nearest relatives, friends, blood brothers, Found quite dead near bed and bench.*' (Bernard Chevignard, *Présages de Nostradamus*, 1999). The Prophecies of Nostradamus, the first edition of which appeared in 1555, have rarely been out of print since his death. One which seems to refer to the Great Fire of London in 1666 comes from Stanza 51 of Century 2, where the 'old lady' is said to be St Paul's Cathedral: '*The blood of the just will be demanded of London burnt by fire in three times twenty plus six. The ancient lady will fall from her high position, and many of the same denomination will be killed.*'

ODD PEOPLE Around 77 CE Pliny the Elder commented on '*The Wonderful Forms of Different Nations*' in his *Natural History*: '*In the vicinity also of those who dwell in the northern regions, and not far from the spot from which the north wind arises… the Arimaspi are said to exist… a nation remarkable for having but one eye, and that placed in the middle of the forehead… On many of the mountains again, there is a tribe of men who have the heads of dogs, and clothe themselves with the skins of wild beasts. Instead of speaking, they bark; and, furnished with claws, they live by hunting and catching birds. According to the story, as given by Ctesias, the number of these people is more than a hundred and twenty thousand: and the same author tells us, that there is a certain race in India, of which the females are pregnant once only in the course of their lives, and that the hair of the children becomes white the instant they are born. He speaks also of another race of men, who are known as Monocoli, who have only one leg, but are able to leap with surprising agility. The same people are also called Sciapodæ: because they are in the habit of lying on their backs, during the time of the extreme heat, and protect themselves from the sun by the shade of their feet. These people, he says, dwell not very far from the Troglodytæ [cave dwellers]; to the west of whom again there is a tribe who are without necks, and have eyes in their shoulders…*'

PARACELSUS (1493-1541) – THE 'GERMAN HERMES'

Philippus Aureolus Theophrastus Bombastus von Hohenheim went to the university at Basle in Swizerland where he studied alchemy, surgery and medicine. Apart from his experiments in alchemy, Paracelsus is credited with the introduction of opium and mercury into the arsenal of medicine. His works also indicate an advanced knowledge of the science and principles of magnetism. He has been called '*the precursor of chemical pharmacology and therapeutics and the most original medical thinker of the sixteenth century*'. He was forced to leave Basle hurriedly after trouble with the authorities over his studies in necromancy. He began travelling through Germany, France, Hungary, the Netherlands, Denmark, Sweden and Russia, supporting himself by astrological predictions and occult practices of various kinds. In Russia, he was taken prisoner by the Tartars and brought before the Grand Cham, the emperor of China, at whose court he

As a crowning insult Paracelsus burned the works of these masters in a brass pan with sulphur and nitre. He now gave himself the Latin name of Paracelsus, meaning 'greater than Celsus'. Aulus Cornelius Celsus was one of the great encyclopaedists of the first century CE, whose medical compendium *De re mediea* was one of the first ancient works on medicine to appear in print in 1478. After assuming his new name, Paracelsus bravely announced that his medicine was greater than that of the ancient Greeks and Romans. This made him countless enemies. The fact that the cures he performed with his mineral medicines justified his teachings merely served further to antagonize the medical faculty, infuriated that their authority and prestige was being undermined by the teachings of such a 'heretic'. Paracelsus was forced once again to leave the city and take to the road in a wanderer's life. He was known to his supporters as '*the German Hermes*' after the Greek god of medicine.

became a great favourite. Paracelsus accompanied the Cham's son on an embassy from China to Constantinople, the city in which the 'supreme secret' of the universal solvent (the *alkahest*) was imparted to him by an Arab. Paracelsus returned to Europe, passing along the Danube into Italy, where he became an army surgeon. It was here that his wonderful cures began. In 1526, at the age of 32, he re-entered Germany, and at Basle university took a professorship of physics, medicine and surgery. The position was offered to him at the insistence of Erasmus and Ecolampidus. He became known as '*the Luther of physicians*', as in his lectures he denounced as antiquated the revered systems of medicine of the Roman physician Galen and his school. These teachings were held to be so unalterable and inviolable by the authorities of that time that the slightest deviation from their teachings was regarded as heretical.

POPE JOAN According to legend, Pope Joan was a female pope who reigned from 853 to 855. The *Chronicon Pontificum et Imperatum* by Martin of Opava states that, '*It is claimed that this John was a woman, who as a girl had been led to Athens dressed in the clothes of a man by a certain lover of hers. There she became proficient in a diversity of branches of knowledge, until she had no equal, and afterwards in Rome, she taught the liberal arts and had great masters among her students and audience. A high opinion of her life and learning arose in the city, and she was chosen for pope. While pope, however, she became pregnant by her companion. Through ignorance of the exact time when the birth was expected, she was* *delivered of a child while in procession from St Peter's to the Lateran, in a narrow lane between the Coliseum and St Clement's church. After her death, it is said she was buried in that same place.'* The earliest mention of the female pope was recorded in the early 13th century, and the events are set in 1099: *'Concerning a certain Pope or rather female Pope, who is not set down in the list of Popes or Bishops of Rome, because she was a woman who disguised herself as a man and became, by her character and talents, a curial secretary, then a Cardinal and finally Pope. One day, while mounting a horse, she gave birth to a child. Immediately, by Roman justice, she was bound by the feet to a horse's's tail and dragged and stoned by the people for half a league, and where she died, there she was buried, and at the place is written: "Petre, Pater Patrum, Papisse Prodito Partum"* [Oh Peter, Father of Fathers, Betray the childbearing of the woman Pope]. *At the same time, the four-day fast called the "fast of the female Pope" was first established.'* (Jean de Mailly *Chronica Universalis Mettensis*). The *Chronicon* of the Welsh bishop Adam of Usk (1404) names her Agnes, and mentions a statue in Rome which is said to be of her. By the 14th century, it was believed that two ancient marble seats, called the *sedia stercoraria* (the defecation chairs), which were used for enthroning new popes, had holes in the seats that were used for determining the gender of the new pope. It was said that the pope would have to sit on one of the seats naked, while a committee of cardinals peered

through the hole from beneath. The sedes stercoraria did indeed exist, and were used in the elevation of Pope Pascal II in 1099. One is still in the Vatican Museums and the other in the Louvre in Paris.

PRESTER JOHN - FACT OR FICTION?

The origins of this fabled Eastern Christian king are obscure. In 1122, Patriarch John of India was reputed to have visited Pope Callistus II, but there seems to be no basis in fact for the story. Next, Bishop Otto von Friesing wrote of '*Prester*' (Presbyter or Priest) John in 1145. He states that Prince Raymond of Antioch sent Bishop Hugo of Gabala (Syria) to Pope Eugene II in 1144 to report upon the pressures upon Jerusalem. Prince Raymond begged the pope to raise another Crusade to secure the Holy Land. Bishop Otto met Bishop Hugo in Pope Eugene's presence, and learned that King John and his people in the Far East had converted to Nestorianism and had conquered Persia and Media. After a terrible battle, John had led his army to save Jerusalem but had been halted by the swollen waters of the Tigris. John was said to be descended from the Three Wise Men, the Magi, enormously wealthy and possessing a sceptre of pure emeralds. Twenty years later, a series of letters were sent to the Byzantine Emperor Manuel, to Barbarossa and to princes across Europe. The letters purported to describe a lost kingdom of Nestorian Christians still existing in Asia. Many copies still exist and they are thought to be Nestorian forgeries of the time. In 1177, Pope Alexander III sent his physician Philippus to meet John to extend an invitation to join the Roman church. Alexander's letter offered John a church in Rome and certain rights in Jerusalem's Holy Sepulchre, and is still in existence, but the outcome is not known. In his 1145 letter, Bishop Otto wrote that the battle when the Christian John defeated the Persian sultan had happened *'not many years ago'*. In 1181 the *Annals of Admont* tell us: *'Presbyter John, King of Armenia and India fought and defeated the kings of the Persians and Medes.'* The only record of a battle shortly before 1145 is in 1141, when the Persian Sultan Sanjar was defeated and killed by Korkhan (Ku Khan) of China, near Ecbatana. In 1219, Damietta, a port in Egypt, was conquered by Crusaders, and in 1221 a report was circulated among them that in the east, King David, the son or nephew of Presbyter John, had placed himself at the head of three powerful armies, and was moving upon Mohammedan countries. King Frederick II eagerly awaited David's arrival at Damietta. However, this 'King David' was none other than Genghis Khan, who with three armies annihilated Islamic power in Asia. Hearing reports of the slaughter and depredations carried out by the Mongols, it was now believed that they were the 'wild hordes' mentioned in Prester John's letter to Emperor Manuel, who had risen up and killed Prester John and David. Vincent of Beauvais wrote in the *Speculum Historiale*: *'In the year of our Lord 1202, after murdering their ruler* [David] *the Tatars set about destroying the people'*.

REICH, WILHELM (1897-1957) AND THE COPERNICAN REVOLUTION

Wilhelm Reich called his theory of orgonomy *'a revolution in biology and psychology comparable to the Copernican Revolution'*. He claimed to have discovered a form of energy, 'orgone', which permeated the atmosphere and all living matter. He then built 'orgone accumulators', which his patients sat inside to harness the energy for health benefits. He died in a federal penitentiary.

ST-GERMAIN, LE COMTE DE - THE WONDERMAN

'A man who knows everything and who never dies', said Voltaire of this mysterious courtier, adventurer, inventor, amateur scientist, violinist and amateur composer. He also displayed skills in the practice of alchemy. In his life he was known as *'der Wundermann'* but we do not know his origin, and he disappeared without trace. He spoke all the major European languages fluently, had a complete knowledge of history but was most famous for his skills in medicine and alchemy. He could transmute metals into gold and had a secret technique for removing flaws from diamonds. He was also said to be the inventor of freemasonry, as he claimed to be thousands of years old. He practised the Kabbalah (esoteric Jewish teachings), hardly ever ate in public and was always dressed in black and white. The first written record is a 1743 letter by Horace Walpole describing St-Germain's presence in London at court. Shortly after, the 'count' was deported after being accused of spying for the Catholic Stuart pretenders to the English crown. St-Germain arrived in France in around 1748, and became a great favourite of Louis XV. The king employed him as a spy several times, and the count seemed to exert great influence over Louis. Louis XV must have known who he was, for he extended to him a friendship that

aroused the jealousy of his court. He allotted him rooms in the Château de Chambord. He shut himself up with St-Germain and Madame de Pompadour for whole evenings at a time; Madame du Housset says in her memoirs that the king spoke of St-Germain as a personage of illustrious birth. Around 1760 St-Germain was forced to leave France, returning to England where he met Count Cagliostro, teaching him the 'Egyptian Rite' of freemasonry. In 1762 St-Germain was in St Petersburg in Russia, where he had an important part in the conspiracy to make Catherine the Great empress of Russia. Count Alexis Orloff met him some years later in Italy and said of him: '*Here is a man who played an important part in our revolution*'.

After returning to Paris in 1770, he travelled through Germany, settling in the state of Schleswig-Holstein. Here the count studied the 'Secret Sciences' with the Landgrave Charles of Hesse Cassel. This German noble, with whom the count spent his last years, may also have known the secret of his birth. He practised alchemy with him, and St-Germain treated him as an equal. It was to him that St-Germain entrusted his Masonic papers just before his supposed death in 1784. Some people dispute this date, since he was said to have been in Paris in 1789 during the French Revolution. The official documents of freemasonry say that in 1785 the French masons chose him as their representative at the great convention that took place that year, with Mesmer, St-Martin and Cagliostro also being present. Since 1789 he is said to

have been seen all over the world, both in spirit and in the flesh. Many believe that the count was the illegitimate son of the widow of Charles II of Spain and Comte Adanero. Others think he was one of the sons of Francis Rákóczi II, prince of Transylvania. The prince's children were brought up by the emperor of Austria, but one of them was withdrawn from his guardianship. The story was that he was dead, but actually he was given into the charge of the last descendant of the Medici family, who brought him up in Italy. He is said to have taken the name of St-Germain from the little town of San Germano, where he had spent some years during his childhood and where his father had estates. The silence kept by him and by those to whom he entrusted his secret would be explained by fear of the emperor of Austria and possible vengeance on his part if the secret were divulged. However, the hardest fact to believe is his longevity. The musician Rameau and Madame de Gergy (with the latter of whom, according to Casanova, the count was still dining around the year 1775) both assert that they met him at Venice in 1710, under the name of the Marquis de Montferrat. Both of them agree that he looked around the same age. During his period of celebrity in Paris from 1750 to 1760, it was agreed that his appearance was that of a man aged 40-50. He disappeared for 15 years, and when the Comtesse d'Adhemar saw him again in 1775, she declared that she found him younger than ever. When she saw him again in 1789, after the storming of the Bastille, he still looked the same and said that he had been in China and France.

The story continues: '*I have seen St-Germain again*', wrote Comtesse d'Adhemar in 1821, '*each time to my amazement. I saw him when the queen was murdered, on the 18th of Brumaire, on the day following the death of the Duke d'Enghien, in January, 1815, and on the eve of the murder of the Duke de Berry.*' Mademoiselle de Genlis asserts that she met the Comte de St-Germain in 1821 during the negotiations for the Treaty of Vienna; and the Comte de Chalons, who was ambassador in Venice, said he spoke to him there soon afterwards in the Piazza di San Marco.

THE SILBADORES OF LA GOMERA La Gomera, 30 miles (50 km) west of Tenerife in the Canary Islands, is an extinct volcano, scarred by deep, unnavigable, mist-filled canyons called *barrancos*. Early Greek traders described the inhabitants' language as '*not the language of men, but like birds singing*'. The language, known as *Silbo Gomero*, is composed entirely of whistling. In Spanish, *silbar* means to whistle, and the language was developed by shepherds to communicate with each other up to 6 miles (10 km) away on other sides of the misty barrancos. Silbo has been postulated

The Sibyls and the Sibylline Chronicles

These female seers derived their name from Sibylla, a prophetess who lived near Troy and was given the gift of prediction by Apollo (he also gave Cassandra this gift). In the ancient world, the most famous sibyls were based at Delphi (see the Delphic Oracle on page 105), Libya, Persia, Cimmeriam, Erythrae, Dardania on the Hellespont, Samia, Phrygia, Tibur (Tivoli) and Cumae. The sibyl who inhabited a cave at Cumae near Naples reputedly lived for a thousand years. The cave, a passage 425 feet (130 m) long cut into the side of a hill, was found by archaeologists in 1932. Her prophecies were collected in 12 books which were acquired by Tarquin, the last king of Rome. The books were kept in the Temple of Jupiter but

destroyed by fire in 83 CE. Virgil said that this sibyl was Aeneas' guide to the Underworld, and that she predicted the coming of a saviour, whom Christians identify as Jesus.

to be the lost language of Atlantis, but is thought to have arrived via Berber tribesmen around 2500 years ago. A form of whistling language still exists in the mountains of Morocco. The language has four vowels and four consonants that can be whistled in rising or falling pitches to form over 4000 words. It is 'spoken' by nearly 3000 of La Gomera's 18,000 inhabitants. It is called an 'articulated speech' and fingers are placed in and around the mouth to effect different tones. The language was dying in the face of the widespread use of mobile phones, but now a programme of education has begun to teach every Gomeran schoolchild the language.

THE SIXTH SENSE Rare individuals seem able to foretell when something is going to happen – an occurrence which cannot be dismissed as merely coincidental or a chance happening. For several days, 10-year-old Eryl Mai Jones kept telling her mother that she was '*not afraid to die*' as '*I shall be with Peter and June*'. On 20 October 1966 she told her mother, '*Let me tell you about my dream last night. I dreamt I went to school and there was no school there. Something black had come down all over it!*' The next morning, a mountain of coal waste and slurry cascaded over her primary school in Aberfan in Wales, suffocating and crushing to death 116 schoolchildren and 28 adults. Eryl was buried in the same mass grave as her best friends Peter and June. Larry Dossey in *The Power of Premonitions* recorded one North Carolina mother dreaming about spinning into blackness, while hearing a man's voice repeating '*2830!, 2830!*' He also uttered a name which '*sounded like Rooks or Horooks*'.

She cancelled her family's plane tickets to Disneyland on 11 September 2001, despite her husband's protestations. The initial tally of deaths at the Twin Towers in New York was 2830 and Michael Horrocks was first officer of United Airlines Flight 175, which crashed into the South Tower. Dossey writes of another woman holidaying in Washington D.C. two weeks before the atrocity. She was dozing in the car while her husband was driving, but suddenly saw the Pentagon with billows of black smoke pouring out of it. In a panic, she became hysterical and traumatized. Two weeks later, American Airlines Flight 77 was flown into the Pentagon, killing 184 people, and billows of black smoke issued from the building. Lawrence Boisseau, who worked in the World Trade Center, dreamed that the towers were crashing around him. A few days later, his wife dreamed that the streets of Manhattan were filled with debris. A few days later, Boisseau was on the ground floor helping to rescue several children trapped in a care centre. He died there. Strangely, the occupancy rate of the four planes which crashed was only 21 per cent, a figure that was much lower than normal for commuter services, which points to many people postponing or cancelling their flights.

Famous people have had such visions as well. The financier John Pierpont Morgan had a premonition that the *Titanic* would sink in 1912 and cancelled his passage at the last minute. In November 2007, the 12-day-old twins of the actor Dennis Quaid and his wife Kimberley were rushed into a Los Angeles hospital with suspected bacterial infections, and routine antibiotics were administered. On their second day in hospital, the exhausted parents left the hospital to sleep for a few hours at their home. At 9p.m. Kimberley Quaid awoke, desperately frightened: '*I just had this horrible feeling come over me, and I felt like the babies were passing. I just had this feeling of dread.*' She was so scared that she jotted down: '*9pm. Something happened to babies.*' Dennis Quaid phoned the hospital and was told that the babies were fine, but someone went to check the children. They were fighting for their lives after accidentally being given a huge overdose of an anti-clotting drug, and had to spend 11 days in intensive care. There are also many stories of the premonition of animals knowing that the death of their master or mistress is about to occur, of flamingos on the southern coast of India fleeing before the 2004 Boxing Day tsunami struck etc. It is often forgotten that humans are animals too, and perhaps some of our senses may lie dormant within us.

SOUTHCOTT, JOANNA (1750-1814) AND THE BOX OF PROPHECIES

A farmer's daughter from Devon, she was aged 42 when she convinced herself that she had supernatural gifts of prophecy, and was the woman spoken of in the Book of Revelation: '*And there appeared a great wonder in heaven; a woman clothed with the sun, and the moon under her feet, and upon her head a crown of twelve stars…*'

She wrote and dictated prophecies in rhyme, going to London and recruiting 'the elect' of 144,000 chosen ones at a charge varying from 12 shillings to a guinea. Aged 64, she said she was pregnant and would be delivered on 19 October 1814 of the new Messiah, the Shiloh of Genesis. The Messiah did not arrive as promised and her supporters reported that she went into a trance, dying two months later. Her followers retained her body for some time in the belief that she would be raised from the dead, and only agreed to its burial after it began to decompose. Her followers, referred to as Southcottians, are said to have numbered over 100,000 on her death. She left a sealed wooden box of prophecies, usually known as Joanna Southcott's Box, with the instruction that it should be opened at a time of national crisis, and then only in the presence of all 24 bishops of the Church of England (there were only 24 at the time). In 1927 the Bishop of Grantham opened the box, which contained only some unimportant papers, a horse pistol and a lottery ticket. However, some believers protested that this was not the authentic box and are still calling for the real box to be opened.

TESLA, NIKOLA (1856-1943) - THE GREATEST INVENTOR SINCE DA VINCI

Tesla is one of the few men whose intelligence and versatility approach the level of the genius Leonardo da Vinci. A naturalized American of Serbian origin, Tesla was a mechanical engineer, electrical engineer and above all an inventor. In the 'War of the Currents' he managed to see off Edison's DC system with the AC (alternating current) system we know today, and thus was the main contributor to the birth of commercial electricity.

He is also known for revolutionary developments in electromagnetism and wireless communication. The unit of measurement of magnetic flux density, the tesla, is named after him. Tesla also worked on advances in X-rays, robotics, remote control, radar, nuclear physics, theoretical physics and ballistics. He had a photographic memory and 'visualized' his many inventions, including a 'peace ray' to prevent war. This was a type of charged-particle device that would bring down enemy aircraft at very long ranges.

THOMAS THE RHYMER – TRUE THOMAS (*c.1220-c.1297*)

Thomas Learmonth was a 13th-century Scottish laird from Earlston who lived on the Scottish Borders, and is probably the source of the *Legend of Tam Lin*. Thomas was said to have lived with the Queen of the Fairies for seven years in Elfland under the Eildon Hills. His verses predicted the death of Alexander III in 1286, the Battle of Bannockburn in 1314 and the accession of James VI of Scotland to the throne of England in 1603. He is also the protagonist of the ballad 'Thomas the Rhymer' made popular in the 1970s by the folk group Steeleye Span.

THE TIBURTINE SIBYL

Her seat was in the ancient Etruscan city of Tibur, modern Tivoli in Italy. The early Christian author Lactantius wrote: '*The Tiburtine Sibyl, by name Albunea, is worshipped at Tibur as a goddess, near the banks of the Anio, in which stream her image is said to have been found, holding a book in her hand.*' In the Sibylline Chronicle of around 380 CE, she is supposed to have prophesied the advent of the Emperor Constantine to bring Christianity to the world. She also forecast that '*the Antichrist will be slain by the power of God through Michael the Archangel on the Mount of Olives*'.

TIMUR THE LAME (1336-1405) AND THE HILLS OF SKULLS

Known as Tamerlane, he ruled from 1369–1405 and invaded lands from India to the Volga. In the cities and countries he defeated, he left towers of severed heads as a warning to others never to oppose his progress. These hills of skulls were seen in Delhi, Isfahan, Baghdad and Damascus. Although he was a Muslim and tried to restore the Mongol empire, his greatest victories were against the Islamic 'Golden Horde' of Tatar tribes. He was nicknamed 'the lame' by his enemies after a battle injury. Timur was born around 50 miles (80 km) south of Samarkand in modern Uzbekistan, one of the Barlas tribe, a remnant of the Mongol hordes of Genghis Khan. From 1360 he was involved in fighting across Asia, his success leading him to become leader of the Barlas, being crowned at Samarkand in 1369. Christopher Marlowe alludes to the event in his play *Tamburlaine the Great*:

'Then shall my native city, Samarcanda...
Be famous through the furthest continents,
For there my palace-royal shall be placed,
Whose shining turrets shall dismay the
*   heavens,*
And cast the fame of lion's tower to hell.'

In a state of constant warfare for the next 35 years, he conquered lands from the Caspian Sea to the banks of the Volga and Ural rivers, and took over Persia and northern Iraq. Isfahan in Persia surrendered without resistance to Timur in 1387 and was treated leniently. However, there was an uprising against punitive taxes and some tax collectors were killed. Timur ordered the complete massacre of the city, killing a reported 70,000 citizens. An eye-witness counted more than 28 towers of skulls, each constructed of about 1500 heads. From 1385, Timur was fighting the Golden Horde of Mongols, advancing to Moscow with 100,000 men across the steppes for 1700 miles (2750 km). The fighting continued until 1395 when the Golden Horde was broken at the Battle of the Terek River. Timur had destroyed the Golden Horde's capital at Sarai, then Astrakhan, wrecking his rivals' economy, which was based upon Silk Road trade. In 1398 he invaded India, with particular atrocities wreaked upon Hindus there. Before the battle for Delhi, Timur executed 100,000 captives, mostly Hindus.

Timur recorded in his memoirs: *'When the soldiers proceeded to apprehend the Hindus and gabrs who had fled to the city,*
many of them drew their swords and offered resistance. The flames of strife were thus lighted and spread through the whole city from Jahán-panáh and Síri to Old Dehlí, burning up all it reached. The savage Turks fell to killing and plundering. The Hindus set fire to their houses with their own hands, burned their wives and children in them, and rushed into the fight and were killed. The Hindus and gabrs of the city showed much alacrity and boldness in fighting. The amirs who were in charge of the gates prevented any more soldiers from going into the place, but the flames of war had risen too high for this precaution to be of any avail in extinguishing them. On that day, Thursday, and all the night of Friday, nearly 15,000 Turks were engaged in slaying, plundering, and destroying. When morning broke on the Friday, all my army, no longer under control, went off to the city and thought of nothing but killing, plundering, and making prisoners. All that day the sack was general. The following day, Saturday, the 17th, all passed in the same way, and the spoil was so great that each man secured from fifty to a hundred prisoners, men, women, and children. There was no man who took less than twenty. The other booty was immense in rubies, diamonds, garnets, pearls, and other gems; jewels of gold and silver; ashrafis, tankas of gold and silver of the celebrated 'Alái coinage; vessels of gold and silver; and brocades and silks of great value. Gold and silver ornaments of the Hindu women were obtained in such quantities as to exceed all account. Excepting the quarter of the saiyids, the 'ulamá, and the other Musulmáns, the whole city was sacked. The pen of fate had written down this destiny for the people of this city. Although I was desirous of sparing them I could not succeed,

for it was the will of Allah that this calamity should fall upon the city.' Timur took 90 elephants merely to carry the precious stones looted from India, and used them to finance the building of the fabulous Bibi-Khanym Mosque in Samarkand. By 1399 he had started fighting the sultans of Egypt and the Ottoman empire. He invaded Syria, sacked Aleppo and killed all the Moslem inhabitants of Damascus except the artisans who were taken back to Samarkand to work for him. Timur then invaded Christian Armenia and Georgia, capturing 60,000 slaves, and afterwards took Baghdad in 1401, killing 20,000 citizens. He ordered each of his soldiers to show him two severed human heads or face punishment. He had just ravaged western Anatolia when the Ming Emperor of China demanded that Timur should pay him homage. Timur allied with the Mongols and prepared to invade China, but he died of plague before this campaign took place. His tomb still stands in Samarkand, and when exhumed in 1941 his skeleton was found to be tall for his era and lame owing to a hip injury. Timur's tomb is protected by a slab of jade in which are carved the words in Arabic: *'When I rise, the World will Tremble'*. It is said that an additional inscription inside the casket was found reading *'Whosoever opens my tomb shall unleash an invader more terrible than I.'* Two days after the Russians had begun the exhumation, Nazi Germany launched Operation Barbarossa and invaded the Soviet Union. Ironically, had Timur not destroyed the power of the Mongols, Russia and eastern Europe would have been overrun and Islamicized. Western Europe would probably have quickly followed.

TRUTH WIZARDS There seems no doubt that certain people have different powers to others (see Sixth Sense, page 51). The Wizards Project (formerly called the Diogenes Project) was a research project that studied the ability of people to detect lies told by others. A 'Truth Wizard' is a person identified in the Wizards Project who can identify deception with exceptional accuracy of at least 80 per cent or higher, whereas the average person is only as good as evens. No truth wizard, however, is 100 per cent accurate. The term 'wizard' was defined as 'a person of amazing skill or accomplishment'. Scientists identified only 50 people as truth wizards after testing 20,000 people (1 in 400) from all walks of life, including the Secret Service, FBI, sheriffs, police, attorneys, arbitrators, psychologists, students and many others. Oddly, while psychiatrists and law enforcement officers showed no more aptitude than students, Secret Service agents were the most skilled. Dr Paul Ekman noted that they *'have found 50 who have this really nearly perfect ability to spot liars, and that's without any specialized training.'* Dr Maureen O'Sullivan stated, *'Our wizards are extraordinarily attuned to detecting the nuances of facial expressions, body language and ways of talking and thinking. Some of them can observe a videotape for a few seconds and amazingly they can describe eight details about the person on the tape.'* Truth wizards use a variety of clues to spot deception and do not depend on any one specific clue to identify a liar. They appear to have a particular knack for spotting micro-expressions and also focus with amazing skill on inconsistencies in emotion, body language and words spoken.

Mysterious People of Fact and Fable

Merlin - King Arthur's Wizard

Vlad Tepes - Vlad the Impaler

Pope Joan - the female pope

Mother Shipton – the sibyl of Knaresborough

Archimedes – the mechanical genius

Legendary Hercules

THE TWELVE LABOURS OF HERCULES

The son of Zeus and the mortal woman Alcmene, Hercules (or Heracles as he was in Greek mythology) was endowed with fabulous strength. He strangled two serpents in his cradle, and killed a lion before reaching manhood. Because of Zeus's infidelity, Hercules was hated by Zeus's wife, Hera. Hercules grew up, married and had three sons, living in peace. However, Hera made him have a terrible nightmare during which Hercules killed all of his family. Hercules was so grieved that he exiled himself. Frightened, Hercules went to the Oracle of Apollo to ask the gods what he should do to atone for his crime, and was sent as a slave to serve King Eurystheus. The king set him 12 labours which would free him from the fate of having murdered his family. Only if Hercules completed all the tasks would he be free of Hera's vengeance, and also gain his freedom once more. They were to:

1 Kill the Lion of Nemea. He strangled it without further ado.
2 Kill the Nine-Headed Hydra. Two new heads would grow on the Hydra from each fresh wound, and one head was immortal. Hercules burned the neck stumps of eight of the heads to cauterize them and secured the immortal head under a rock.
3 Capture the Ceryneian Hind. After chasing it for many months, he finally trapped it and brought it to Eurystheus.
4 Capture the Wild Boar of Erymanthus.
5 Clean the stables of King Augeas in a single day. He succeeded by diverting a nearby river to wash the filth away.
6 Kill the Carnivorous Birds of Stymphalis, with their toxic dung and metal beaks and feathers.
7 Capture the Wild White Bull of Crete.
8 Capture the Maneating Mares of Diomedes.
9 Obtain the Girdle of Hippolyta, Queen of the Amazons.
10 Capture the Chestnut Oxen of the monster Geryon.
11 Take the Golden Apples from the Garden of the Hesperides, which was always guarded by the dragon Ladon. Hercules tricked Atlas into getting the apples by offering to hold up the heavens for Atlas. When he returned with the apples, Hercules asked him to take the load for a moment so that he could get a pillow for his aching shoulders. Atlas did so, and Hercules left with the apples.
12 Bring Cerberus, the Three-Headed Dog of Hades, to the surface world.

Hercules was now free to return to Thebes and marry Deianira. Later the centaur Nessus tried to abduct Deianira; Hercules shot him with a poisoned arrow. The dying Nessus told Deianira to keep his blood, as it would always preserve Hercules's love. When Deianira later feared that she was being supplanted by

Iole, Deianira sent Hercules a garment soaked in Nessus's blood. It burned his body and poisoned Hercules, who was taken after death to Olympus and endowed with immortality.

VAMPIRE The vampire has figured in most folk cultures in the world. The word itself is derived from the Russian word *Vampir*, *pi* being the verb to drink. Some say that the Greek word *nosophoros* (plague-carrier) evolved into the Old Slavonic word '*nosufur-atu*' which became *nosferatu*, synonymous with a vampire. Vampire folklore stories occur extensively among the Slavic peoples, perhaps because of the historically high population of gypsies or Romanies in that part of the world. The migration of gypsies has been traced back to northern India, where the religion embodied many bloodthirsty deities such as Kali and creatures such as a bhutu. A vampire is supposed to be a dead person who returns in physical form and drinks the blood of animals or humans to prolong their existence. The most likely people to become vampires reputedly are magicians, people who are werewolves, the excommunicated, people who have committed suicide, murderers and those themselves attacked by vampires. From 1730–5 Hungary, the Balkans, Poland, Bulgaria and Bohemia (now the Czech Republic) suffered a *Vampire epidemic*, most possibly caused by an outbreak of cholera. Many cholera victims were buried prematurely and tried to escape from their coffin, which was interpreted as a sign of vampirism.

The United States has reported many outbreaks of vampirism in New England, as in 1854, 1888 and 1890, and all cases again were later attributed to cholera victims. The vampire's most notable features are extreme paleness, an allergic reaction to sunlight and a swollen and gorged appearance if it has just feed upon blood. There are no signs of the corruption of the body even years after the burial and rigor mortis is absent. The vampire must attack humans and drink their blood, usually biting the jugular vein in the neck and drinking much of their victim's blood from the incision. The victim of a vampire usually dies from lack of blood, but in turn becomes a vampire after death.

There are various ways to protect yourself from a vampire. The brandishing of a cross or crucifix was thought to be very powerful in the Christian countries. Garlic was the most popular natural vampire repellent, as well as hawthorn and the mountain ash (rowan). Another defence was scattering seeds – vampires were supposed to become so engrossed in counting every single seed that they would either lose interest in the victim, or be caught still counting even as the sun came up. Silver was not as traditional a protective metal as is supposed in popular fiction, as iron was the material of choice. Iron shavings were placed beneath a child's cradle or a necklace with an iron nail was worn, and other iron objects were placed strategically around the place needing protection. The most common way of killing a vampire was to take the body out of its coffin, remove and burn its heart, then behead it and impale the corpse with a stake made of any wood except pine, which is a symbol of everlasting life due to the fact that a pine never loses its leaves. Other superstitions held that a vampire could be destroyed by touching it with a crucifix, drenching it in holy water and garlic, stealing its left sock, filling it with stones and throwing it in a river, or using a '*dhampir*' (a vampire's child.) Dhampirs were allegedly the only people who were able to see invisible vampires, and they sometimes took advantage of this expertise by hiring out their services as vampire hunters.

VLAD III, VOVOIDE (PRINCE) OF WALLACHIA (1431-76) - VLAD THE IMPALER or DRACULA

Vlad's surname Drakyula means '*son of the dragon*', a reference to his father, Vlad II Dracul. After Vlad III's death, he was popularly known as Vlad Tepes (*the Impaler*). Vlad III was born in Transylvania, and at the age of five was initiated into the Order of the Dragon in Nuremberg, as his father had been some years previously. In 1436 his father was ousted from the throne by pro-Hungarian factions. In 1442 he regained control of the country with the help of the Ottoman sultan, but had to surrender Vlad and his younger brother Radu to the Ottoman court as hostages. Vlad was imprisoned there and often whipped and beaten, but his brother converted to Islam, entering the sultan's service. In 1447, Vlad's father was killed by boyars (nobles) in league with the Hungarian regent, and his eldest son and heir was blinded and buried alive. To stop Wallachia (Romania) from falling into Hungarian control, the Ottomans

invaded Wallachia and put Vlad III on the throne. However, another Hungarian invasion then took place and Vlad fled to his uncle's court in Moldavia. Upon his uncle's assassination in 1451, Vlad fled to Hungary. Hating the Ottomans he was reconciled with his erstwhile enemy the Hungarian regent. In 1453, the Ottomans took Constantinople and by 1456 they were threatening Hungary. They were laying siege to Belgrade when Vlad led an army into Wallachia, reconquering his native lands and killing its king in hand-to-hand combat.

Vlad immediately tried to strengthen his country's economy and defences. He executed many boyars by impaling them and gave lands and offices to the lesser nobility and free peasants. Because of the links of the Wallachian boyars with the Saxon leaders of Transylvania, Vlad launched attacks on Transylvania, again

impaling captives. Allied with the new king of Hungary, Vlad controlled one side of the Danube, but the Ottoman Turks sought to gain control of the river to prevent attacks from the Holy Roman Empire. In 1459, the sultan demanded that Vlad should pay him his delayed tribute of 10,000 ducats and 500 young boys, but Vlad killed the Turkish envoys by nailing their turbans to their heads. The Turks crossed the Danube to try to recruit an army against Vlad, but he impaled the messengers. The sultan now tried to capture Vlad by arranging a meeting between Vlad and the Bey of Nicopolis. Vlad discovered the intended treachery and set up his own ambush, with all 1000 Turkish cavalry being killed and impaled. In the winter of 1461, Vlad invaded the area between Serbia and the Black Sea, writing to the King of Hungary *'I have killed men and women, old and young… 23,884 Turks and Bulgarians without counting those whom we burned alive in their homes or whose heads were not chopped off by our soldiers…'* In 1462 Sultan Mehmed II sent an army of around 60,000 troops and 30,000 irregulars against Wallachia. He encountered a forest of stakes on which Vlad had impaled 20,000 of Mehmed's previous Ottoman army. However, Vlad only had between 20,000 and 40,000 men under his command, and was unable to stop the Ottomans from occupying his capital in June 1462. Resorting to guerrilla warfare, he led the best men in his army in disguise as Turks into the Ottoman army camp to try and assassinate the sultan. Mehmed II escaped but lost up to 15,000 men. After three more battles, the Ottomans escaped over the Danube. Vlad was lauded by the Pope, Italian states such

as Genoa and Venice, and in Transylvania. Now the sultan sent Vlad's younger brother Radu and his Janissaries against his enemy, but was defeated. However, many remaining disaffected boyars now joined Radu, preferring Ottoman to Hungarian protection. Vlad had no money to pay his mercenaries and asked the Hungarian king for help, but he was thrown into prison, falsely accused of high treason. King Matthias Corvinus had received from the pope massive financial support to fight against the Turks, but he had spent the money on completely different purposes. He now had the Turks at his borders, and needed to use Vlad as a scapegoat. Vlad was imprisoned for around 12 years before being released in 1474 when he married the king's cousin. In 1476, with Hungarian support, Vlad returned to conquer Wallachia but was he killed in battle near Bucharest. The Turks decapitated him, preserved the head in honey and sent it for the Sultan to display in Constantinople.

VOODOO (VODOUN) WORSHIPPERS

There are an estimated 50 million worshippers who believe in spirit possession, the process by which gods speak to devotees for a short time during ritual ceremonies. The faithful believe that the influence of the gods is present in all aspects of daily life, and that pleasing the gods will earn them health, wealth and spiritual merit. Vodoun is almost universally practised in Haiti, but also is observed in New York, New Orleans, Houston, Charleston, South Carolina and Los Angeles, being recognized as a legitimate religion. The word *vodoun* means '*spirit*' or '*deity*' in the Fon language of the West African kingdom

of Dahomey (now Benin) and some parts of Togo. Slaves transported across the Atlantic brought the religion of Vodoun to the New World from the Caribbean islands of Jamaica and Saint Domingue (now the Dominican Republic and Haiti.) White slave-owners became fearful of it and forbade religious practices and gatherings in any type of congregation. Penalties for violations or for possessing a *'fetish'* were extreme, including mutilation, sexual disfigurement, flaying alive and even burial alive. The French President Nicolas Sarkozy in 2008 demanded the withdrawal from French

shops of a voodoo doll made in his image, sold with a set of pins and a manual detailing how to put 'the evil eye' on him.

WILKINS, JOHN - THE INVENTION OF THE METRE AND THE FIRST ATTEMPT TO LAND ON THE MOON

In his 1668 *An Essay Towards a Real Character and a Philosophical Language*, the Reverend John Wilkins (1614–72), attempted to lay out a rational universal language. His language contained the traditional words for units of measure: line, inch, foot, standard, perch, furlong, mile, league and degree, but he was also trying to achieve a universal measurement standard. He decided on a method that he said was suggested by his contemporary Sir Christopher Wren, which was to base the length standard on the time standard (as is

Hugh Williams - the Luckiest Name Aboard Ship

On 5 December 1664, a ship sank in the Menai Straits off the north coast of Wales. Of its 81 passengers, the sole survivor was named Hugh Williams. On 5 December 1785 a pleasure schooner sank in the Menai Straits, with one survivor – Hugh Williams. Sixty people died, including the rest of his family. On 5 December 1860 a small 25-passenger vessel foundered in the Menai Straits. The sole survivor's name was Hugh

Williams. In a change of season, on 5 August 1820, a picnicking party on a boat on the Thames was run down by a coal barge. Of the 25 on board, most were children under 12 years old. Hugh Williams from Liverpool, only five years old, was the only survivor. On 19 August 1889, a nine-man Leeds coal barge sank. Two men, both named Hugh Williams, an uncle and nephew, were rescued by fishermen.

done today), and let the standard length be the length of a pendulum with a known 'period'. Pendulums are extremely reliable time standards, and their period depends only their length and on the local effect of gravity. Gravity varies very little over the surface of the Earth. Wilkins directed that a pendulum should be set up with the heaviest, densest possible, spherical 'bob' (weight) at the end of lightest, most flexible possible cord, and the length of the cord should be adjusted until the period of the pendulum was as close to one second as possible. However, Wilkins did not simply take the standard length as the length from the fulcrum to the centre of the bob. Instead he noted that:

'… *there are given these two Lengths, viz. of the String, and of the Radius of the Ball, to which a third Proportional must be found out; which must be as the length of the String from the point of Suspension to the Centre of the Ball is to the Radius of the Ball, so must the said Radius be to this third which being so found, let two fifths* [0.4] *of this third Proportional be set off from the Centre downwards, and that will give the Measure desired.*' For mathematicians, this can read: Let d be the distance from the point of suspension to the centre of the bob; let r be the radius of the bob, and let x be such that $d/r = r/x$. Then $d + (0.4)x$ is the standard unit of measurement. Wilkins asserted that if you follow these instructions, the standard unit of measurement '*will prove to be… 39 Inches and a quarter*', i.e. 0.997 of a metre. Wilkins called his new measurement the 'Standard'. The metre is the base unit of length in the International

System of Units. In 1791 the French National Assembly accepted a proposal by the French Academy of Sciences that the new definition for the metre be equal to one ten-millionth of the length of the Earth's meridian along a quadrant passing through Paris, that is the distance from the equator to the North Pole. Since 1983, it has been defined as the distance travelled by light in a vacuum in 1/299,792,458th of a second. Apart from his feat of inventing the standard unit of measurement of almost exactly one metre 113 years before it was officially adopted, Wilkins also decimalized his measurements of the size of a standard. He called 1/100th of a standard an inch, but actually it was a centimetre, and 1000 standards was still called a mile, but actually it measured almost exactly a kilometre. He proceeded to carry out the same decimalization with weights and measures and currencies – a man before his time and one of the greatest scientific minds of the time.

Dr John Wilkins was a founder of the Royal Society, married Oliver Cromwell's sister, and invented the first airgun, a mileage recorder, an artificial rainbow machine to entertain guests in his garden and an inflatable bladder, a prototype for the pneumatic tyre. On top of all this, Wilkins planned his own lunar mission, inspired by the great voyages of discovery around the globe by the famous explorers Columbus, Drake and Magellan, he explored the possibilities of space travel in two books. Records show he began investigating prototypes for spaceships, or *flying chariots* as he called them, to carry the astronauts. In 1638, when he was just 24, Wilkins published *The Discovery of a New World in the Moone*. He believed that the other planets and the Moon must be inhabited. He wanted to meet the *Selenites* as he named them, and even trade with them: '*So, perhaps, there may be some other means invented for a conveyance to the Moon, and though it may seem a terrible and impossible thing ever to pass through the vast spaces of the air, yet no question there would be some men who durst venture this…*' However, Wilkins had to consider how to escape from the Earth's pull almost 50 years before Isaac Newton wrote about the force of gravity in 1687. Wilkins thought that we were held on Earth by a form of magnetism. His observations of clouds suggested to him that if man could reach an altitude of 20 miles (32 km), he could be free of this force and be able to fly through space. His idea was to build a real flying machine designed like a ship, but with a powerful spring, clockwork gears and a set of wings. Gunpowder could be used to power a primitive form of internal combustion engine. The wings needed to be covered with feathers from high-flying birds, such as swans or geese. Wilkins believed that the spaceship should take off at a low angle, just like modern aircraft. He estimated that ten or 20 men could club together, spending 20 guineas (£21) each, to employ a good blacksmith to assemble such a flying machine from his set of plans. Wilkins believed that food would not be needed by his explorers, as there was already evidence of people surviving for long periods without eating. In space, free of Earth's magnetism, he reasoned that there would be no pull on their digestive organs

to make them hungry. It was known that mountaineers suffered breathlessness at high altitude, but Wilkins said that this was because their lungs were not used to breathing the pure air breathed by angels. In time his astronauts would get used to it and so be able to breathe on their voyage to the Moon. Wilkins experimented in building flying machines with another leading scientist and polymath, the great Robert Hooke, in the gardens of Wadham College, Oxford, around 1654. However, by the 1660s, he began to realize that space travel was not as straightforward as he had imagined and abandoned his flying ship into space in favour of decimalizing units of measurement.

WITCH-FINDER GENERAL MATTHEW HOPKINS (*c.*1620-47)
During the English Civil War in the 17th century, Matthew Hopkins claimed to hold the title of Witch-Finder General,

and from 1645 he conducted witch-hunts across the eastern counties of England, using torture and sleep deprivation to extract confessions from his victims. He retired and died, possibly from tuberculosis, just two years later, aged around 27. In around 14 months, he and his associates were responsible for more people being hanged for witchcraft than in the previous 100 years. It has been estimated that all of the English witch trials between the early 15th and late 18th centuries resulted in fewer than 500 executions for witchcraft, and that the efforts of Hopkins and his colleague John Stearne accounted for about 40 per cent of the total. Hopkins's witch-hunting methods were outlined in his book, *The Discovery of Witches*, published in 1647. These practices were recommended in law books, and immediately trials and executions for witchcraft began in the New England colonies across the Atlantic with the conviction of Margaret Jones obtained through the use of Hopkins's techniques of 'searching' and 'watching'. Jones's execution was the first in the series of witch-hunts that lasted in New England from 1648 to 1663. Thirteen women and two men were executed, and his methodology was used again during the Salem Witch Trials in Massachusetts in 1692–3, when there were 20 executions and 150 imprisonments.

ZHENG HE (1371–1435) – THE ADMIRAL OF THE WESTERN SEAS

A stone pillar was discovered in a town in Fujian province. It bore an inscription that described the amazing voyages of a Chinese 'eunuch admiral' named Zheng He. It related how the emperor of the Ming Dynasty had

ordered him to sail to '*the countries beyond the horizon... all the way to the end of the earth*'. His mission was to display the might of Chinese power and collect tribute from the '*barbarians from beyond the seas*'. The pillar contains the Chinese names for the countries Zheng He visited, 30 nations from Asia to Africa during voyages that covered about 35,000 miles (56,000 km). Between 1405 and 1433 he led seven Chinese expeditions to '*the Western Ocean*', to Java, Jeddah, the Arabian Sea, the Bay of Bengal, and he probably even rounded Africa 70 years before the Portuguese. His achievements show that China had the ships and navigational skills in the 15th century to explore the world. China did not follow up on these voyages of exploration, however. The Chinese destroyed their oceangoing ships and halted further expeditions. Thus, a century later, Europeans would 'discover' China, instead of the Chinese 'discovering' Europe. Chinese shipbuilders also developed fore-and-aft sails, the stern post rudder and boats with paddlewheels. Watertight compartments below decks kept the ship from sinking if it sprung a leak. Some boats were armour-plated for protection. All these developments made long-distance navigation possible. In each country that Zheng He visited, he was to present gifts from the emperor and to exact tribute for the glory of the Ming. The Chinese had a unique view of foreign relations. Because China developed its culture in isolation from other great civilizations, it saw itself as the centre of the world. The Chinese therefore called their country *'the Middle Kingdom'*. Originally named Ma He, Zheng was a Muslim from Yunnan province. When the Ming Dynasty conquered the province in 1378, he was taken to the imperial Chinese capital to serve as a court eunuch. He became a great influence at court, and was given command of the Chinese navy. In 1402 Zheng He and Wang Jinghong took a giant fleet to the Western Sea (today's Southeast Asia), initiating trade and cultural exchanges. The ships in his fleet numbered between 40 to 63 on each voyage, and many soldiers and sailors accompanied him, meaning the total party amounted to over 27,000 people. Zheng He's last expedition took place half a century earlier than the equivalent voyages of European navigators. His remarkable flagship was known as *The Treasured Ship*, whose *'sails, anchors and rudders cannot be moved without 200 or 300 people'*. Built in the early 15th century, she was said to be 500 feet (152 m) long by 207 feet (63 m) in beam, and to have no fewer than nine masts. A £2,000,000 expedition off the coast of Kenya is focusing on what may be one of Zheng's fleet, in an attempt to prove that he reached east Africa 80 years before Vasco da Gama. DNA testing of local Swahili in the Lami archipelago has revealed traces of Chinese ancestry, something that the community has long laid claim to.

ZOMBIES A zombie is a dead person who is brought back to life through means of vodoun (voodoo) or necromancy that destroys the mental powers of the person in the process. Thousands of people in Haiti are considered to be zombies, some of whom lead normal everyday lives with families, jobs and as respected citizens. The Haitian Penal Code, Article 249 reads: *'It shall also be qualified as attempted murder the employment which may be made against any person of substances which, without causing actual death, produce a lethargic coma more or less prolonged. If, after the person had been buried, the act shall be considered murder no matter what result follows.'* To create a zombie, a voodoo practitioner is said to make a potion that consists mainly of the poison of the puffer fish (one of the strongest nerve toxins known to man). This is given to the intended victim, causing severe neurological damage, primarily affecting the left side of the brain which controls speech, memory and motor skills. The victim becomes lethargic, then slowly seems to die. In reality, the victim's respiration and pulse become so slow that it is nearly impossible to detect signs of life. The victim retains full awareness as he or she is taken to the hospital, then perhaps to the morgue and finally when being buried alive. The voodoo practitioner then exhumes the victim, to become his slave. At one time it was said that most of the robot-like slaves who worked in the sugar cane plantations of Haiti were zombies.

Zoology of Human Senses

In order for us to experience a sense, there needs to be a sensor. Each sensor is tuned to one specific sensation. Traditionally, we are taught that we have five senses:

Sight (Visual sense. In our eyes, we have two different types of light sensors. One set, called rods, senses light intensity and works in low-light situations. The other type, called cones, can sense colours and require fairly intense light to be activated).

Hearing (Auditory sense from sound sensors in the ears).

Smell (Olfactory sense from chemical sensors in the nose).

Taste (Gustatory sense from chemical receptors in the mouth).

Touch (The skin senses. However, because touch involves four different sets of nerves, the skin senses are considered to be four separate types registering: heat, cold, pressure and pain. Some add 'itch-sensitive' to this list.

To these eight or nine senses we can add **Motion** (Kinaesthetic sense, where we feel we are moving) and **Balance** (Vestibular sense from sensors in your ears that let you detect your orientation in the gravitational field) making ten or more senses. In our muscles and joints, there are sensors that tell us where the different parts of the body are in relation to one another and about the motion and tension of the muscles. These senses allow us, for example, to touch the tips of our index fingers together with our eyes shut. In the bladder, there are sensors that indicate when it is time to urinate. Similarly, our large intestine has sensors that indicate when it is full. There are also the senses of hunger and thirst. The nervous system registers and determines the countless sensations that we feel all over our bodies every day. How does this work? What causes your leg or arm to tingle when it 'falls asleep'? How do you know when you're about to sneeze? Depending on how we choose to count them, there are between 14 and 20 different senses listed here. There are people who seem to have other senses as well. Some can 'see the future'. Some can 'dowse' for water, oil and hidden objects. Some can direct the police to the location of a hidden body. There are many people who can sense impending weather changes. Others feel that they can sense when someone is looking at them, or when they are not alone. This author believes that our forefathers had senses that we have lost today, for example the ability to follow magnetic lines for navigation that is still possessed by many mammals, birds and fish.

CHAPTER 2
Mythical Monsters, Ghosts *and* Things That Go Bump *in the* Night

THE ABERDEEN BESTIARY

A bestiary is a collection of short descriptions about all sorts of animals and monsters, real and imaginary, often accompanied by a Christian allegory or moralizing explanation. The *Aberdeen Bestiary* is considered to be one of the best examples of its type. The manuscript was written and illuminated in England around 1200. The recorded history of the work begins in 1542 when it was listed as No.518 *Liber de bestiarum natura* in the inventory of the Old Royal Library at Westminster Palace. This library was assembled by Henry VIII, with professional assistance from the antiquary John Leland, to house manuscripts and documents rescued from the dissolution of the monasteries.

THE AMPHISBAENA SERPENT

This was a Libyan serpent with a poisonous head at each end of its body, as shown in medieval bestiaries (See also Ouroboros). Around 150 CE Aelian wrote *'Nikandros asserts that the slough of the Amphisbaina, if wrapped round a walking-stick drives away all snakes and other creatures which kill, not by biting but by striking… The Amphisbaina is a snake with two heads, one at the top and one in the direction of the tail. When it advances, as need for a forward movement impels it, it*

leaves one end behind to serve as tail, while the other it uses as a head. Then again if it wants to move backwards, it uses the two heads in exactly the opposite manner from what it did before.' Isidore of Seville in the seventh century concurred: *'The amphisbaena has two heads, one in the proper place and one in its tail. It can move in the direction of either head with a circular motion. Its eyes shine like lamps. Alone among snakes, the amphisbaena goes out in the cold.'* The *amphisbaena* is often depicted in heraldry and medieval paintings as having wings and two feet, with horns on its head. The name amphisbaenidae is now given to a family of legless lizards that can move either forwards or backwards, though this is a relatively modern use of the name.

THE AMPHISBAENA TORTOISE
and TRANSPLANTS A similar creature to the serpent was said to inhabit the mythical Seven Isles of the Southern Ocean (the Heliades q.v.) In the first century CE, Diodorus Siculus recorded: *'There are also animals among them, we are told, which are small in size but the object of wonder by reason of the nature of their bodies and the potency of their blood; for they are round in form and very similar to tortoises, but they are marked on the surface by two diagonal stripes, at each end of which they have an eye and a mouth. Consequently, through seeing with four eyes and using as many mouths, yet it gathers its food into one gullet, and down this its nourishment is swallowed, and all flows together into one stomach; and in like*

manner its other organs and all its inner parts are single. It also has beneath it, all around its body many feet, by means of which it can move in whatever direction it pleases. And the blood of this animal, they say, has a marvellous potency; for it immediately glues on to its place any living member that has been severed; even if a hand or the like should happen to have been cut off, by the use of this blood it is glued on again, provided that the cut is fresh, and the same thing is true of such other parts of the body as are not connected with the regions which are vital and sustain the person's life.'

BASILISK (BALISKOS or COCKATRICE) - THE KING OF THE SERPENTS

The basilisk is alleged to be hatched by a cockerel from the egg of a serpent or toad, but the cockatrice is hatched from a cockerel's 'egg' incubated by a serpent or a toad. This small serpent is generally believed to be born from a spherical, yolkless egg, which has to be laid in the days of Sirius (the Dog Star). It can only be laid by a seven-year-old cockerel, and has to be hatched by a toad. One type of basilisk burns everything it approaches with its poison, while the second kind can kill every living thing with a mere glance. Both species are so dreadful that their breath wilts vegetation and crumbles rocks. Another source refers to three types of basilisk, all with deadly rock-shattering breath. The 'golden basilisk' poisoned everything by its mere look. The 'evil-eye

basilisk' terrorized and killed every creature with its third eye on the top of a golden head. The sting of the 'sanguineness basilisk' made the flesh fall off the bones of its victim. The only way to kill a basilisk is by holding a mirror in front of its eyes, while avoiding looking directly at it, so causing it to die of fright. Its natural enemy is the weasel, which is immune to its glance. If the weasel gets bitten, it withdraws from the fight to eat some rue, the only plant that does not wither under the basilisk's breath, and it returns to the fight with renewed strength. For this reason, the basilisk is often now identified with a cobra and the weasel with a mongoose. The basilisk could thus have originated with the horned adder or hooded cobra from India. Another enemy is the cock, as if the basilisk hears it crow, it will die instantly.

By the Middle Ages, it had been transformed into a snake with the head of a cock, or sometimes with the head a human. In art, the basilisk symbolized the devil and the antichrist, and to Protestants it was a symbol of the papacy. The name basilisk comes from the Greek basileus, 'king'. The

basilisk was known as the 'King of the snakes' and feared as the most poisonous creature on Earth. The Romans called it 'regulus' or little king, not only because of its crown (perhaps the hood of a cobra), but also because it terrorized all other creatures with its deadly look and poison. It was usually yellow, sometimes with a kind of blackish hue. Pliny mentioned a white spot on its head, which could be misinterpreted as a diadem or a crown, and others speak of three spikes on his forehead. His appearance has always been a matter of dispute since no-one can actually look at a basilisk and survive. In heraldry the basilisk is represented as an animal with the head, torso and legs of a cock, the tongue of a snake and the wings of a bat. The snake-like rear ends in an arrow-point.

Pliny the Elder writes in his *Natural History*: '*Anyone who sees the eyes of a basilisk serpent dies immediately. It is no more than twelve inches long, and has white markings on its head that look like a diadem. Unlike other snakes, which flee its hiss, it moves forward with its middle raised high. Its touch and even its breath scorch grass, kill bushes and burst rocks. Its poison is so deadly that once when a man on a horse speared a basilisk, the venom travelled up the spear and killed not only the man, but also the horse. A weasel can kill a basilisk; the serpent is thrown into a hole where a weasel lives, and the stench of the weasel kills the basilisk at the same time as the basilisk kills the weasel.*' The seventh-century Spanish scholar Isidore of Seville writes: '*The basilisk is six inches in length and has white spots; it is the king of snakes. All flee from it, for it can kill a man with its smell or even by merely looking at him.*

Birds flying within sight of the basilisk, no matter how far away they may be, are burned up. Yet the weasel can kill it; for this purpose people put weasels into the holes where the basilisk hides. They are like scorpions in that they follow dry ground and when they come to water they make men frenzied and hydrophobic. The basilisk is also called sibilus, the hissing snake, because it kills with a hiss.' During the pontificate of Leo IV (847–55), a basilisk reputedly concealed itself under an arch near the temple of Lucia in Rome. Its odour caused a devastating plague, but the pope slew the creature with his prayers. In Basle, in 1474, an old cock was discovered laying an egg. The bird was captured, tried, convicted of an unnatural act and burned alive before a crowd of several thousand people. Just before its execution, the mob prevailed upon the executioner to cut the rooster open, and three more eggs, in various stages of development, were discovered in its abdomen. This fact is taken from the marvellously titled 1906 book by E.P. Evans *The Criminal Prosecution and Capital Punishment of Animals*. When the parish church of Renwick, Cumbria, was torn down in 1733, a huge, bat-winged creature,

Fit For a King

Representations of a cockatrice – half-serpent and half-cockerel – were served at royal feasts. The edible cockatrice was made by sewing together half a chicken and half a suckling pig, covered in a baked case of flour and egg yolk.

supposed to have been a cockatrice, angrily flapped at the workmen. A man named John Tallantire killed it with a rowan tree branch, earning exemption from the fees due to the lord of the manor. Villagers reported that they could sense the presence of this creature due to a sudden chill in the air.

BEHEMOTH - THE GREAT MONSTER OF THE BIBLE

In The Bible, the Book of Job describes the fire-breathing sea-monster Leviathan (see Mysteries of the Deep) along with Behemoth, the unconquerable monster of the land. The author records that it is futile to question God, as he has created these monsters and he alone can capture them. In Job Chapter 40 we read of Behemoth:

40.15 Behold now the behemoth that I have made with you; he eats grass like cattle.

40.16 Behold now his strength is in his loins and his power is in the navel of his belly.

40.17 His tail hardens like a cedar; the sinews of his tendons are knit together.

40.18 His limbs are as strong as copper, his bones as a load of iron.

40.19 His is the first of God's ways; [only] his Maker can draw His sword [against him].

40.20 For the mountains bear food for him, and all the beasts of the field play there.

40.21 Does he lie under the shadows, in the cover of the reeds and the swamp?

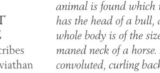

40.22 Do the shadows cover him as his shadow? Do the willows of the brook surround him?

40.23 Behold, he plunders the river, and [he] does not harden; he trusts that he will draw the Jordan into his mouth.

40.24 With His eyes He will take him; with snares He will puncture his nostrils.

BONACON, BONNACON - THE EXCREMENT HURLER

'In Asia an animal is found which men call bonnacon. It has the head of a bull, and thereafter its whole body is of the size of a bull's with the maned neck of a horse. Its horns are convoluted, curling back on themselves in such a way that if anyone comes up against it, he is not harmed. But the protection which its forehead denies this monster is furnished by its bowels. For when it turns to flee, it discharges fumes from the excrement of its belly over a distance of three acres, the heat of which sets fire to anything it touches. In this way, it drives off its pursuers with its harmful excrement.' (The Aberdeen Bestiary c.1200). Pliny the Elder tells us: 'The bonasus is found in Paeonia. It has the mane of a horse but otherwise resembles a bull. It has horns that curve back so they are useless for fighting; when attacked, it runs away, while releasing a trail of dung that can cover three furlongs. Contact with the dung burns pursuers as though they had touched fire.' Paeonia roughly corresponds to modern Macedonia. A 'cacafuego' in medieval England was a bully, braggart or 'spitfire', but the term meant literally to 'defecate' rather than 'spit' fire. The treasure ship *Nuestra Señora de la Concepcion* was pursued by Francis Drake for several days before he took it on 1 March 1579. She was the greatest prize in history, being valued at around 1.5 million ducats at the time, or around half a billion pounds in today's money. She had been given the vulgar name of the *Cacafuego*,

meaning '*shitfire*', by the chasing privateers, because she was one of the few Spanish treasure ships of that time to have cannon. Queen Elizabeth took most of the booty. A Spanish youth on the captured galleon said that his ship '*shall no longer be called the Cacafuego, but the Cacaplata* [shit-silver]', and ruefully suggested that Drake's small ship *Hind* (before she was renamed the *Golden Hind* on account of her exploits) should be renamed the *Cacafuego*.

CENTAURS (KENTAUROI) - HALF-HORSE/HALF-MAN

The Kentauroi was a tribe of savages that were half-man, half-horse in form. They inhabited the mountains and forests of 'Magnesia'. A primitive race, they made their homes in mountain caves, hunted wild animals for food and armed themselves with rocks and tree branches. The Kentauroi were the offspring of the cloud nymph Nephele, who was raped by the Lapith King Ixion. Her misshapen children were deposited on Mount Pelion, where the daughters of the centaur-god Kheiron (Charon) nursed and fostered them to adulthood. They were invited to attend the wedding of their half-brother Peirithoos, the Lapith king, but became drunk and attempted to carry off the bride and the female guests. In the battle which followed the centaurs were virtually wiped out. There was another tribe of centaurs in the western Peloponnese, where they fought the hero Herakles (Hercules). There is also mention of a tribe of bull-horned centaurs native to the island of Kypros (Cyprus). The Kentauros was depicted with the upper body of a man, from head to loins, set upon the body of a horse. Sometimes a centaur bore the facial features of a man, but at other times it was portrayed with the snub nose and pointed ears that are typical of a rustic satyr.

CERASTES - THE HORNED SNAKE

Isidore of Seville records: '*The cerastes is a snake with horns like a ram's on its head; from this it gets its name, the Greeks call horns kerata. It has four horns, which it displays as bait, and instantly kills the animals it attracts. It covers itself with sand, leaving exposed only the part with which it catches allured birds and animals. It is so flexible that it seems to have no spine.*' It is reported to have had either two horns, which are like a ram's horns, or four pairs of small horns.

CERBERUS (KERBEROS) - THE GREAT HOUND OF HADES

Kerberos was the gigantic hound in Greek and Roman mythology which guarded the gates of Hades, preventing the ghosts of the dead from leaving the underworld. Kerberos was described as a three-headed dog with a serpent's tail, a mane of snakes, and a lion's claws. Some say he had 50 heads, though this number might have included the heads of his serpentine mane.

Hercules was sent to fetch up Kerberos from the underworld as the last of his 12 labours, a task which he accomplished through the grace of Persephone. When he presented the mighty beast to King Eurystheus, the frightened monarch took refuge in a large jar and begged Hercules to return Kerberos to the underworld.

CHIMERA (KHIMAIRA) - THE MOTHER OF THE SPHINX

The daughter of Typhon and Echidna, she gave birth to the Sphinx and the Nemeian Lion. She was a monstrous fire-breathing beast which, according to Greek mythology, ravaged the countryside of Lycia (Lykia) in Anatolia (on the southern coast of Turkey). The Chimera possessed the body and head (sometimes three heads) of a maned lion, but with a goat's head rising from its back, a set of goat-udders and a serpentine tail. Homer related in the *Iliad* how Bellerophon, riding the winged horse Pegasus, slew it by driving a lead-tipped lance down its throat and suffocating it: '*First he* [King Iobates] *sent him* [Bellerophon] *away with orders to kill the Khimaira none might approach; a thing of immortal make, not human, lion-fronted*

and snake behind, a goat in the middle, and snorting out the breath of the terrible flame of bright fire. He killed the Khimaira, obeying the portents of the immortals...' Hesiod recounted in *Theogony*: '*She* [Ekhidna] *bore the Khimaira, who snorted raging fire, a beast great and terrible, and strong and swift-footed. Her heads were three: one was that of a glare-eyed lion, one of a goat, and the third of a snake, a powerful dragon. But Khimaira* [Icy Air] *was killed by Pegasos* [Spring] *and gallant Bellerophon. But she also, in love with Orthos* [Morning Twilight], *mothered the deadly Sphinx... and the Nemeian Lion.*' She served as the model for the dragon that fought St George. It seems that the Chimera was identified with the winter-rising constellation Capricorn (the serpent-tailed goat), that was driven from the heavens by the constellation Pegasus every spring. Some writers place the origin of this fire-breathing monster in the volcano named Chimaera near Phaselis, in Lycia, or in the volcanic valley near the Cragus, which is described as the scene of the events connected with the Chimera. In recently discovered Lycian works of art, she has been depicted in the simple form of a lion (she gave birth to the Nemeian Lion). The Asiatic lion once lived in Greece, Turkey and the Near East, but is now restricted to a population of just 400 in the Gir Forests of India.

CROCOTE - HALF-HYENA/ HALF-LIONESS

'*In a part of Ethiopia the hyena mates with the lioness; their union produces a monster, named crocote. Like the hyena, it too produces men's voices. It never tries to change the direction of its glance but*

Cyclops – One-Eyed Giants, the Elder Cyclops

These were the three sons of Gaia and Uranus, Brontes (Thunderer), Steropes (Lightener) and Arges (Bright). Together with their brother Titans, they were cast by their father Uranus into the dark pit of Tartarus, but, instigated by their mother, they assisted Kronus in usurping power. But Kronus again threw them into Tartarus. Zeus then released them in his war against Kronus and the Titans, and the Cyclopes provided Zeus with thunderbolts and lightning, Pluto with a helmet, Hades with a helmet of invisibility and Poseidon with a trident. Henceforth they remained the ministers of Zeus, but at least one was killed by Apollo for having furnished Zeus with the thunderbolts to kill Asclepius. Hermes killed Arges while he guarded Io for Hera.

strives to see without changing it. It has no gums in its mouth. Its single, continuous tooth is closed naturally like a casket so that it is never blunted.' (The Aberdeen Bestiary c.1200).

THE YOUNGER CYCLOPES

In the Homeric poems the Cyclopes are a gigantic, insolent and lawless race of shepherds, who lived in the southwestern part of Sicily and devoured human beings. They had no laws or political institutions, and each lived with his wives and children in a mountain cave, and ruled over them with arbitrary power. Polyphemus, the principal among them, was a son of Poseidon and is described as having only one eye on his forehead. Homer relates in the *Odyssey* how Odysseus and his men were captured by Polyphemus but Odysseus blinded him and so escaped. A later tradition regarded the Cyclopes as the assistants of Hephaestus. Volcanoes were the workshops of that god, and Mount Etna in Sicily and the neighbouring isles were accordingly considered as their homes. As the assistants of Hephaestus they were no longer shepherds, but made the metal armour and ornaments for gods and heroes; they worked with such might that Sicily and all the neighbouring islands resounded with their hammering.

DIPSA This snake is so small that it is not seen before it is stepped on, and so poisonous that anyone it bites dies before he feels the bite. It was recorded by Lucan in the first century CE and by Isidore of Seville in the seventh century.

Dragons

There are many types of dragons described in the Greek and Roman myths, for example, the Drakones Aithiopes were a breed of gigantic serpents native to subSaharan Africa. The Roman author Aelian tells us: '*The land of Aithiopia (the place where the gods bathe, celebrated by Homer under the name of Okeanos, is an excellent and desirable neighbour), this land, I say, is the mother of the very largest Drakones (Serpents). For, you must know, they attain to a length of one hundred and eighty feet, and they are not called by the name of any species, but people say that they kill elephants, and these Drakones rival the longest-lived animals.*' Aelian described the Drakones Indikoi, a race of gigantic toothed serpents that inhabited India preying upon elephants: '*In India, I am told, the Elephant and the Drakon are the bitterest enemies. Now Elephants draw down the branches of trees and feed upon them. And the Drakones, knowing this, crawl up the trees and envelop the lower half of their bodies in the foliage, but the upper portion extending to the head they allow to hang loose like a rope. And the Elephant approaches to pluck the twigs, whereat the Drakon springs at its eyes and gouges them out. Next the Drakon winds round the Elephant's neck, and as it clings to the tree with the lower part of its body, it tightens its hold with the upper part and strangles the Elephant with an unusual and singular noose.*' Among the many other different types of dragon recorded in fable can be found:

Phrygian Dragons in Anatolia, which stood 60 feet (18 m) tall. They stood upright supported by their tails, snaring birds with a magical breath.

Cetea, huge serpentine sea dragons.

Scolopendra, a gargantuan sea-monster with hair extending from its nostrils, a flat crayfish-like tail and rows of webbed feet lining each of its flanks.

Colchian Dragon, which never slept and guarded the Golden Fleece.

Cychreides, driven out of Salamis to become an attendant of Demeter.

Hesperian Dracon, a 100-headed dragon which guarded the golden apples of the Hesperides and was killed by Hercules.

Hydra, a nine-headed water dragon killed by Hercules.

Nemean Dragon, which guarded the sacred groves of Zeus.

Python, used by Gaia to guard the Delphic Oracle.

Trojan Dragons, a pair of dragons sent by Poseidon to destroy Laocoön of Troy and his sons, when he attempted to warn his people of the threat posed by the Wooden Horse. There is a fabulous monumental statue of Laocoön and his sons fighting the serpents in the Vatican Museums, probably sculpted in Rhodes around 40 BCE.

There was also a type of dragon called the *Dracaena* or '*She-Dragon*', which had the upper body of a beautiful nymph and the body of a dragon or sea-monster in place of legs.

Campe was a monstrous she-dragon which guarded the prison gates of Tartarus. She had the body of a serpent, 100 serpent 'feet' and a fearsome scorpion's tail. Campe was slain by Zeus when he rescued the Cyclopes and Hecatoncheires from their prison.

Ceto was a monstrous marine goddess with the body of a sea-dragon in place of legs. She spawned Echidna, the Hesperian dragon and a host of other monsters.

Echidna was the she-dragon wife of the serpent-giant Typhon, who spawned many of the dragons of mythology.

Scylla was a marine she-dragon which haunted the Straits of Messina between Sicily and Italy, snatching and devouring sailors from passing ships. She was a nymph with the tail of a sea-monster in place of legs.

Sybaris was a she-dragon which haunted a mountain near Delphi devouring shepherds and passing travellers. She was pushed off the cliff by the hero Eurybarus.

Mythical Monsters

Hydra

Dragon

Basilisk

Bigorne, a medieval monster that lived on a diet of faithful men

A hydra with a dragon's body

ETHIOPIAN (AFRICAN) MONSTERS

Pliny, in his *Natural History* tells us: '*Aethiopia produces Lynxes in great numbers, and Sphinxes with brown hair and a pair of udders on the breast, and many other monstrosities – Winged Horses armed with horns, called Pegasoi Aithiopikoi; Crocotas* [Hyenas] *like a cross between a dog and a wolf, that break everything with their teeth, swallow it at a gulp and masticate it in the belly; tailed Cercopitheci* [Monkeys] *with black heads, ass's hair and a voice unlike that of any other species of ape; Boves Indici* [Indian oxen or Rhinoceroses?] *with one and with three horns; the Leucrocota, swiftest of wild beasts… the Yale… the Tauros Silvestres* [Forest bulls, with a red hide impervious to weapons]*… the Mantichora… In Western Aethiopia there is a spring, the Nigris, which most people have supposed to be the source of the Nile… In its neighbourhood there is an animal called the Catoblepas… the Basilisci Serpentis… is a native of the province of Cyrenaica.*'

THE FATES

The Moirae, Moerae or Moirai (in Greek, the apportioners) were in Greek mythology the three white-robed personifications of destiny. They were the daughters of Zeus and the Titaness Themis, or of the primordial beings Nyx (Night), Chaos or Ananke (Necessity). They controlled the metaphorical thread of life of every mortal from birth to death. They appeared three nights (some say seven) after a child's birth to determine the course of its life.

Clotho (Spinner) spun the thread of life from her distaff onto her spindle. Lachesis (Drawer of Lots) measured the thread of life allotted to each person with her measuring rod. Atropos (Inevitability) was the cutter of the thread of life, and chose the manner of each person's death. When their time was come, she cut their life-thread with '*her abhorred shears*' as Milton imagined it in his poem '*Lycidas*'. Perhaps the cloaked figure of Old Father Time with his scythe stems from this legend.

GHOULS

Ghouls have their origin in the Arabic, Persian and Indian tales which were compiled in Arabic and translated into English in the 19th century under the title *The book of the Thousand Nights and a Night*. Sir Richard Burton, translator of the tales, has several footnotes referring to the male *Ghul*, a creature who eats human flesh: '*Arab. "Ghul", here an ogre, a cannibal. Ghuls in the "Nights" are rather fearsome, and do not seem to prey on humanity mearly through necessity. Their appetite is nearly insatiable… "Allah ease thee, O King of the age even as thou hast eased me of these Ghuls, whose bellies none may fill save Allah!"…*' Even their names are fearsome, such as '*The-Ghul-who-eateth-man-we-pray-to-Allah-for-safety*'. Burton noted female ghuls and origin of the word ghul: '*The Ghulah (Fem. of Ghul) is the Heb. Lilith or Lilis: the classical Lamia; Etymologically "Ghul" is a calamity, a panic fear; and the monster is evidently the embodied horror of the grave and the graveyard.*'

HYDRUS (HYDROS) - THE CROC-KILLER

Hydrus is a snake said to be found in the River Nile, which would swim into the mouths of crocodiles, and, after being swallowed, would eat its way out of the crocodiles' sides, thus killing them. Isidore of Seville noted *'The enhydros is a small animal; it gets its name because it lives in water, specifically the Nile river. If it finds a sleeping crocodile, it first rolls in mud, then crawls into the crocodile's mouth; after eating all of the crocodile's inner parts it comes out of the beast, killing it... The hydros is a water snake; its bite makes the victim swell up. The disease caused by the bite of this snake is sometimes called boa because it can be cured with ox dung.'* The hydrus was sometimes confused with the Hydra which Hercules slew; some texts saying that it was a many-headed water dragon living in the swamp of Lerna, that could grow new heads. The mid-12th-century Icelandic manuscript *Physiologus* portrays the hydrus as a bird, with feathers in the crocodile's mouth and a bird's head emerging from its side. However, the hydrus is almost always illustrated as a serpent with its tail sticking out the crocodile's mouth and its head emerging from the crocodile's side.

JINN - THE UGLY FIRE DEMONS

Jinn are ugly and evil demons in Arabian and Muslim folklore, having supernatural powers which they can grant to people who possess the powers to call them up. The singular of jinn is *jinni* or *djinni*, and in the West they came to be called *genies*. In legend, King Solomon had a ring with which he called jinn to assist his armies in battle. In Islam, jinn are fiery spirits associated with the desert. While they are disruptive of human life, they are considered worthy of being saved. A person dying in a state of sin may be changed into a jinni, in the period of separation between this world and the next. The greatest jinni is *Iblis*, who used to be known as *Azazel*, the Prince of Darkness, i.e. the Devil. The jinn were thought to be lower-ranking spirits than angels, because they are made of fire and are not immortal. They can take on human and animal forms to influence men to do good or evil. According to Persian mythology, some of them live in a place called Jinnistan, but others relate that they live with other supernatural beings in the Kaf, mystical emerald mountains surrounding the Earth. The Arabic origin of the name means 'hidden'.

In the *Qur'an* (Koran), there are three sentient beings: angels, humans and jinn. Two of these creations have free will: humans and jinn. The *Qur'an* mentions that jinn are made of smokeless flame, living in a parallel world to mankind. Their form can be similar to humans if they choose to spiritually possess a human body. Jinn can be good, evil or neutrally benevolent.

In 1998, Pakistani nuclear scientist Sultan Bashiruddin Mahmood stated in an interview with the *Wall Street Journal* that jinn could be tapped to solve the energy crisis, as they were made of fire: *'I think that if we develop our souls, we can develop communication with them... Every new idea has its opponents, but there is no reason for this controversy over Islam and science because there is no conflict between Islam and science.'* A *New York Times* headline of 2 November 2001 reads: '*A NATION CHALLENGED: NUCLEAR FEARS; Pakistani Atomic Expert, Arrested Last Week, Had Strong Pro-Taliban Views.'* The report says: '*Sultan Bashiruddin Mahmood, a nuclear engineer who was one of three Pakistani scientists arrested last week because of their suspected connections with the Taliban, is an expert on nuclear weapons production, but also a fundamentalist Muslim with unorthodox scientific views, scientists familiar with the Pakistani scientific circles said today.*

During more than 30 years in Pakistan's nuclear program, he pioneered construction of plants to produce enriched uranium and plutonium for Pakistan's small but growing arsenal of atomic weapons. But as a subscriber to a brand of what is known to practitioners as "Islamic science", which holds that the Koran is a fount of scientific knowledge, Mr. Bashiruddin Mahmood has published papers concerning djinni, which are described in the Koran as beings made of fire. He has proposed that these entities could be tapped to solve the energy crisis, and he has written on how to understand the mechanics of life after death.' In August 2001, the sultan and a colleague met Osama bin Laden and his deputy, Ayman al-Zawahiri, in Afghanistan. The *New York Times* reported '*There is little doubt that Mahmood talked to the two Qaeda leaders about nuclear weapons, or that Al Qaeda desperately wanted the bomb.'* On 8 January 2009, again in the *New York Times*, we read: '*... "This guy was our ultimate nightmare," an American intelligence official told me in late 2001,*

when the New York Times *first reported on Mahmood. "He had access to the entire Pakistani program. He knew what he was doing. And he was completely out of his mind."'* The sultan has written 15 books, the most well-known being *The Mechanics Doomsday and Life After Death*, which is an analysis of the events leading to doomsday in light of scientific theories and Qur'anic knowledge. In it, the sultan made it clear that he believed Pakistan's bomb was '*the property of the whole Ummah*', referring to the worldwide Muslim community. The US Institute of Historical Biographies presented him with a gold medal in 1998, and the sultan has also been awarded a Gold Medal by the Pakistan Academy of Sciences.

THE KERES - SHE-DEMONS OF DEATH While the spirit Thanatos was the god of peaceful kinds of death in Greek mythology, the Keres were demons or female spirits of violent or cruel death, accident, murder or ravaging disease. They were agents of the Fates, who measured out the length of a person's life when they first entered the world, and Doom

(Moros), the demon god who drove people towards their inevitable destruction. The Keres craved blood and feasted upon it, after ripping a soul free from the mortally wounded bodies of soldiers on a battlefield, and sending it on its way to Hades. Thousands of Keres haunted the battlefield, fighting amongst themselves like vultures over the dying. The Keres had no absolute power over the life of men, but in their hunger for blood would seek to bring about death beyond the bounds of fate. Olympian gods are often described as standing by their favourites in battle, beating the clawing death spirits away from them. Some of the Keres were personifications of epidemic diseases, which haunted areas of plague. The Keres were depicted as fanged, taloned women dressed in bloody garments. They seem to have been some of the evil spirits that escaped from Pandora's Jar to plague mankind. According to the ancient Greek poet Hesiod in the seventh or eighth century BCE, they are the daughters of Nyx and sisters of the Moerae, and punish men for their crimes: '*And Nyx [Night] gave birth to hateful Moros [Doom] and black Ker [Violent Death] and Thanatos [Death], and she gave birth to Hypnos [Sleep] and the tribe of Oneiroi [Dreams]. And again the goddess murky Nyx, though she lay with none, gave birth to Momos [Blame] and painful Oizys [Misery], and the Hesperides… Also she gave birth to the Moirai [Fates] and the ruthless avenging Keres [Death-Fates]… Also deadly Nyx gave birth to Nemesis [Envy] to afflict mortal men, and after her, Apate [Deceit] and Philotes [Friendship] and hateful Geras [Old Age] and hard-hearted Eris [Strife].*'

LEONTOPHONE - LION-KILLER

The leontophone is a small animal that is deadly to lions. To kill a lion, the flesh of a leontophone is burned and its ashes are sprinkled on meat, which is placed at a crossroad. Even if a lion eats only a small amount, it dies. Lions hated leontophones and hunted and killed them, tearing them apart with their claws rather than biting them.

THE MINOTAUR - THE CRETAN BULL AND THE MAN WHO FELL TO EARTH

This bull-headed monster was born to Queen Pasiphaë of Crete after she had coupled with a bull. He lived in the twisting maze of the labyrinth, built for King Minos by Daedalus, where he was offered a regular sacrifice of youths and maidens to satisfy his cannibalistic hunger. He was eventually destroyed by the hero Theseus. His proper name Asterion (the starry one) suggests that he was associated with the Taurus constellation. Pseudo-Apollodorus wrote in the second century CE: '*Minos aspired to the throne [of Crete], but was rebuffed. He claimed, however, that he had received the sovereignty from the gods, and to prove it he said that whatever he prayed for would come about. So while sacrificing to Poseidon, he prayed for a bull to appear from the depths of the sea, and promised to sacrifice it upon its appearance. And Poseidon did send up to him a splendid bull. Thus Minos received the rule, but he sent the bull to his herds and sacrificed another… Poseidon was angry that the bull was not sacrificed, and turned it wild. He also devised that Pasiphaë should develop a lust for it. In her passion for the bull she took on as her accomplice an architect named Daidalos [Daedalus]… He built a wooden cow on wheels… skinned a real cow, and sewed the contraption into the skin, and then, after placing Pasiphaë inside, set it in a meadow where the bull normally grazed. The bull came up and had intercourse with it, as if with a real cow. Pasiphaë gave birth to Asterios, who was called Minotauros. He had the face of a bull, but was otherwise human. Minos, following certain oracular instructions, kept him confined and under guard in the labyrinth. This labyrinth, which Daidalos built, was a "cage with convoluted flexions that disorders debouchments"* [i.e. with complex bends and turns which frustrated ways of getting out].'

It seems that the Athenians had killed the son of King Minos, Androgeus, at a time when there was Cretan supremacy in the Aegean and Athens was still a fledgling state. Minos then defeated the Athenians in revenge, and, according to Catullus, Athens was *'compelled by the cruel plague to pay penalties for the killing of Androgeos'*. King Aegeus of Athens could only avert the plague caused by his crime of killing Androgeus by sending *'young men at the same time as the best of unwed girls as a feast'* to the Minotaur. King Minos demanded seven Athenian youths and seven maidens, drawn by lots, to be sent every ninth year (or every year according to other sources) to be devoured by the Minotaur. When the third sacrifice approached, Theseus, the son of King Augeus, volunteered to slay the monster. He promised his father that he would put up a white sail on his voyage home if he was successful, but would have the crew put up black sails if he was killed. In Crete, Ariadne, the daughter of Minos,

fell in love with Theseus and helped him to navigate the labyrinth, which had a single path to its centre. In most accounts she gave him a ball of thread to unwind behind him, allowing him to retrace his path. Theseus killed the Minotaur with the sword of Aegeus and led the young Athenians back out of the labyrinth. However, Theseus forgot to put up the white sail, so when his father saw the ship he presumed that his son was dead and threw himself into the sea, committing suicide. The massive ruins of Minos's palace at Knossos have been found.

Daedalus, a talented Athenian craftsman, tried to escape from his exile in the palace of Crete, where he and his son Icarus had been imprisoned by King Minos. Daedalus was under house arrest because he gave Minos's daughter, Ariadne, clues to help Theseus, the enemy of King Minos, find his way through the labyrinth and defeat the Minotaur. In order to escape, Daedalus made two pairs of wings out of wax and feathers for himself and his son. Before they took off from the island, Daedalus warned his son not to fly too close to the Sun, nor too close to the sea. Overcome by the thrill of flying, Icarus soared up into the sky, but flew too close to the Sun, which melted the wax. Icarus fell into the sea in the area which now bears his name, the Icarian Sea, southwest of Samos, and was drowned. There are later variants on the legend, in which the escape from Crete was actually by boat, provided by Pasiphaë, for which Daedalus invented the first sails, to outstrip Minos' pursuing galleys. In this version Icarus falls overboard en route to Sicily and is drowned.

MUSCALIET - SIX ANIMALS IN ONE

This animal, which appears in the *Bestaire* of Pierre de Beauvais, is said to have a body like a rabbit, legs and tail like a squirrel, the ears of a weasel, a snout like a mole, hair like a pig and teeth like a boar. It climbs trees and jumps from branch to branch by the strength of its tail. When it climbs a tree it devastates the leaves and fruit. It makes an underground nest in a hollow below the tree, and its body heat causes the tree to dry up and die.

ONOCENTAUR - THE SYMBOL OF MALE LUST

The onocentaur has the upper body of a man and the lower body of an ass. The upper part is rational, but the lower part is exceedingly wild. The two-part nature of the beast symbolizes the hypocrite who speaks of doing good but actually does evil. Philippe de Thaon, a medieval Anglo-Norman poet, noted that man is rightly called man when he is truthful, but an ass when he does wrong.

OUROBOROS - THE CIRCULAR SERPENT

Depictions of a serpent or dragon eating its own tail can be traced back to Egypt around 1600 BCE. Even earlier, hieroglyphs in the sarcophagus chamber of the Pyramid of Unas (*c.*2350 BCE) read: '*A serpent is entwined by a serpent... the male serpent is bitten by the female serpent, the female serpent is bitten by the male serpent, Heaven is enchanted, earth is enchanted, the male behind mankind is enchanted*'. The Greeks gave this creature the name Ouroboros (tail-devourer). In Gnosticism, this circular serpent symbolized eternity and the soul of the world. The Chrysopoeia Ouroboros of Cleopatra is one of the oldest images of the Ouroboros, which has inspired alchemists, masons and esoteric sects throughout history. The Ouroboros has many meanings interwoven into it. Foremost is the symbolism of the serpent biting and devouring its own tail. This symbolizes the cyclic nature of the Universe: creation coming out of destruction, life out of death. The Ouroboros eats its own tail to sustain its life in an eternal cycle of renewal. In the natural world, the armadillo lizard or typical girdled lizard (*Cordylus cataphractus*) is around 7.5 inches (19 cm) in length and is endemic to areas of southern Africa, and it could be the origin of the Ouroboros. It possesses the anti-predatory mechanism of taking its tail in its mouth and rolling into a ball when frightened. In this shape it is protected by the thick, squarish scales along its back and the spines on its tail. This behaviour resembles that of the armadillo, from which the lizard gets its name.

The 19th-century chemist August Kekulé dreamed of a ring in the shape of the ouroboros, which inspired him in his

discovery of the molecular structure of benzene. In 1865 he wrote that the structure contained a six-membered ring of carbon atoms with alternating single and double bonds. The new understanding of benzene, and hence of all aromatic compounds, proved to be so important for both pure and applied chemistry that in 1890 the German Chemical Society organized an elaborate appreciation in Kekulé's honour, celebrating the 25th anniversary of his first benzene paper. The cyclic nature of benzene was finally confirmed by crystallography in 1929.

PLAINS DEVILS William Clark, of the Lewis and Clark Expedition which set out in 1803 to explore the western part of the United States as far as the Pacific coast, wrote in his journal on 25 August 1804 about the plains devils:

'In a northerly direction from the mouth of this creek, in an immense plain, a high hill is situated, and appears of a conic form, and by the different nations of Indians in this quarter, is supposed to be the residence of devils: that they are in human form with remarkable large heads, and about 18 inches high, that they are very watchful, and are armed with sharp arrows with which they can kill at a great distance. They are said to kill all persons who are so hardy as to attempt to approach the hill. They state that tradition informs them that many Indians have suffered by these little people, and, among others, three Maha men fell a sacrifice to their merciless fury not many years since. So much do the Maha, Sioux, Otos, and other neighbouring nations, believe this fable, that no consideration is sufficient to induce them to approach the hill.'

Parandrus – Master of Camouflage

'The parandrus is the size of the ox; its head is larger than that of the stag, and not very unlike it; its horns are branched, its hoofs cloven, and its hair as long as that of the bear. Its proper colour, when it thinks proper to return to it, is like that of the ass. Its hide is of such extreme hardness, that it is used for making breastplates. When it is under threat, this animal reflects the colour of all the trees, shrubs, and flowers, or of the spots in which it is concealed; hence it is that it is so rarely captured.' (Pliny the Elder, *Natural History*). The beast is described as coming from Ethiopia, but Pliny also mentions the *Tarandrus* from Scythia which can change colour, which some think must represent a reindeer or elk.

POLTERGEISTS - THE KNOCKING SPIRITS

The German words *poltern* (to knock) and *geist* (spirit) describe a phenomenon which involves strange noises and/or moving of objects. Poltergeist activity has been reported across many cultures, and in the past it was variously blamed on the devil, demons, witches and ghosts of the dead. Scientists have tried to explain the phenomena as due to earth tremors, gusts of air etc. Common types of poltergeist activities include rains of stones, dirt and other small objects; throwing or moving of objects, including large pieces of furniture; evil smells, loud noises and shrieks. Poltergeists are said to have caused interference in telephones and electronic equipment, and turned lights and appliances on and off. Some poltergeists are said to pinch, bite, hit and sexually attack the living.

Poltergeists are said to be usually mischievous and occasionally malevolent, manifesting their presence by making noises, moving objects, and assaulting people and animals. This author has had experience of sharing houses with squirrels, bats, birds and mice and feels that many experiences can be attributed to the noises that such animals make. Generally activity starts and stops abruptly, and is often associated with one individual. It may extend over several hours to several months, but some cases have lasted several years. They almost always occur at night when an individual is present. This person seems to act as an agent or magnet for activity, is usually female and often under the age of 20. In the late 1970s, a computer analysis was carried out of cases collected since 1800. Around 64 per cent involved the movement of small objects; 58 per cent were most active at night; 48 per cent featured rapping; 36 per cent involved movement of large objects; 24 per cent lasted longer than one year; 16 per cent featured communication between the poltergeist and the agent; and 12 per cent involved the opening and shutting of doors and windows. One of the first recorded instances of poltergeist activity was in 1682. Richard Chamberlain, Secretary to the Colony of New Hampshire, was staying in the tavern of George and Alice Walton in New Castle (then known as Great Island). He witnessed the attack of the *'Lithobolia'*, the *'Stone-Throwing Devil'*. Chamberlain wrote a pamphlet in 1698 describing the *'throwing about (by an Invisible hand) of Stones, Bricks, and Brick-Bats of all sizes, with several other things, as Hammers, Mauls, Iron-Crows, Spits, and other Utensils, as came into their Hellish minds, and this for space of a quarter of a year.'* The Epworth Poltergeist case is one of the best documented examples of poltergeist activity, which happened in December 1716 at Epworth Parsonage, Lincolnshire. All members of the Wesley family heard loud rappings and noises over a period of two months. Sometimes the noises were of a specific character, according to the well-kept notes of Mrs Wesley. During one incident when she and her husband were descending the stairs, they heard a noise as if someone was emptying a large bag of coins at their feet. This was followed by the sound of glass bottles being '*dashed to a thousand pieces*'. Other sounds heard were running footsteps, groans and a door latch being lifted several times.

Dr Friedbert Karger was one of two physicists from the Max Planck Institute who helped to investigate the Rosenheim Poltergeist in Germany. The agent seemed to be Annemarie Schneider, a 19-year-old secretary in a law firm in Rosenheim in 1967. There was disruption of electricity and telephone lines, the rotation of a picture, swinging lamps which were captured on video (which was one of the first times any poltergeist activity has been captured on film), and strange sounds that seemed electrical in origin were recorded. Fraud was not proven despite intensive investigation by the physicists, journalists and the police. The effects moved with the young woman when she changed jobs until they finally faded out, and never recurred. Dr Karger said: '*These experiments were really a challenge to physics. What we saw in the Rosenheim case could be 100% shown not to be explainable by known physics.*' The phenomena were witnessed by parapsychologist Hans Bender, the police force, the CID, press reporters and the physicists.

PYTHON - THE EARTH-DRAGON OF DELPHI

This female serpent resided at the Delphic Oracle, the cult centre for her mother, Gaia. The Greeks considered the site to be the centre of the earth, represented by a magic stone, the navel (*omphalos*), which Python guarded. Python incurred the emnity of the god Apollo, who slew her and made her former home and oracle the most famous in Greece, but now dedicated to him.

THE RAINBOW SERPENT AND THE EXTINCT SPECIES

This is a common motif in Aboriginal art and mythology. It is named for the snake-like meandering of water across a flat landscape, and the colour spectrum caused when sunlight strikes water at an appropriate angle making the surface look like a rainbow. The serpent is seen as the inhabitant of waterholes and the controller of the most precious resource of life. It is sometimes unpredictable, in conflict with the ever-present Sun, but replenishes stores of water, forming gullies and deep channels as it slithers across the landscape. 'Dreamtime' relates how the great Spirits created life, in animal and human form, from the barren and featureless earth. The Rainbow Serpent came from beneath the ground and created huge ridges, mountains and gorges as it pushed upward. The immense serpent is known both as a benevolent protector of its people (the groups from the country around) and as a malevolent punisher of law breakers.

Wonambi naracoortensis is one of just two species of very large Australian snakes of an extinct genus. They were not pythons, like Australia's other large constrictors. It grew to 20 feet (6 m) in length according to the fossil record. It was given the name *Wonambi* from the Aboriginal description

of the serpent of the Dreamtime. The family of this species, Madtsoiidae, became extinct in other parts of the world around 55 million years ago, but new species continued to evolve in Australia. These two Australian species are the last known to have existed, becoming extinct within the last 50,000 years. *Wonambi naracoortensis* lived in natural sun-traps beside local waterholes, where they would ambush kangaroo, wallaby and other prey coming to the water to drink. For this reason, children were forbidden in Aboriginal culture to play at such places, and only allowed to visit when accompanied by an adult. Mapping such locations in Western Australia has been found to be closely associated with areas still regarded as sacred sites. It has been hypothesized that the snake became extinct because of fire-stick farming by the Aborigines when fire was regularly used to burn away vegetation.

SALAMANDER - THE KING OF FIRE
The spotted salamander was so impervious to fire that it lived in volcanoes, and its spittle was so poisonous that a man's hair would fall off his body at its touch. Pliny recorded: *'The salamander is a shaped like a lizard, but is covered with spots. A salamander is so cold that it puts out fire on contact. It vomits from its mouth a milky liquid; if this liquid touches any part of the human body it causes all the hair to fall off, and the skin to change colour and break out in a rash. Salamanders only appear when it rains and disappear in fine weather… It is fatal to drink water or wine when a salamander has died in it, as is drinking from a vessel from which the creature has drunk.'* St Augustine in the fifth century wrote: *'If the salamander lives in fire, as naturalists have recorded, this is a sufficiently convincing example that everything which burns is not consumed, as the souls in hell are not.'* Isidore tells us: *'The salamander alone of animals puts out fires; it can live in fire without pain and without being burned. Of all the venomous animals its strength is the greatest because it kills many at once. If it crawls into a tree it poisons all of the fruit, and anyone who eats the fruit will die; if it falls in a well it poisons the water so that any who drink it die.'*

The skin of the salamander, which was 'known' to resist the action of fire, was reputedly made into a fabric for wrapping up precious items. These 'fireproof cloths' appeared to later analysis to be composed of the mineral asbestos, which when spun into fine filaments is capable of being woven into a flexible cloth. Asbestos was named by the ancient Greeks (it means 'inextinguishable'), but the Greek geographer Strabo and the Roman naturalist Pliny the Elder both noted that the material damaged the lungs of slaves who wove it into cloth. The Holy Roman Emperor Charlemagne was said to have had a precious tablecloth made of asbestos. In Persia, the cloth was brought by wealthy nobles from the Hindu Kush, and they impressed guests by cleaning the cloth by exposing it to fire. Some Persians believed the fibre was fur from an animal called a *'samander'* which lived in fire and died when exposed to water. Marco Polo described encountering these miraculous garments in his travels. Some archaeologists believe that shrouds were made of asbestos, in

Mythical Part-Human Monsters

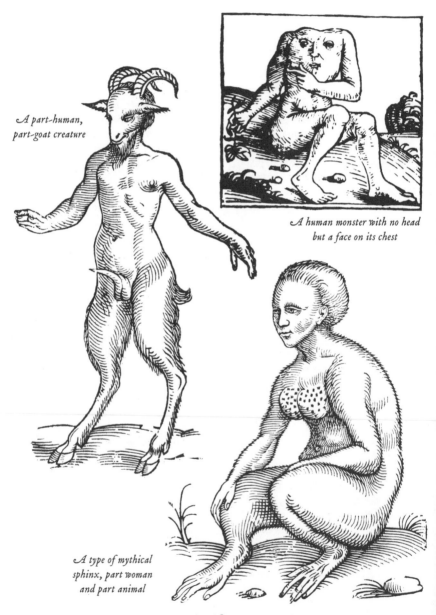

A part-human, part-goat creature

A human monster with no head but a face on its chest

A type of mythical sphinx, part woman and part animal

Pig-man

A monster with a
human face and five
cloven hooves

A legendary human
figure with the head
of a bear

which the bodies of kings were burned in order to preserve only their ashes, and not that of other materials in the funeral pyre. Others believe that asbestos was used to make perpetual wicks for sepulchral lamps. The foundation of the above fables is supposed to be the fact that the salamander secretes from the pores of its body a milky juice, which is produced in considerable quantity and would protect the body from fire. Symbolically, the salamander represents those who pass through the fires of passion and of this world without stain.

THE SATYROI NESIOI These satyrs lived on the remote string of islands off the African coast known as the Satyrides. In the second century CE, the geographer Pausanius recorded: *'Wishing to know better than most people who the Satyroi are I have inquired from many about this very point. Euphemos the Karian said that on a voyage to Italia he was driven out of his course by winds and was carried into the outer sea, beyond the course of seamen. He affirmed that there were many uninhabited islands, while in others lived wild men. The sailors did not wish to put in at the latter, because, having put in before, they had some experience of the inhabitants, but on this occasion they had no choice in the matter. The islands were called Satyrides by the sailors, and the inhabitants were red haired, and had upon their flanks tails not much smaller than those of horses. As soon as they caught sight of their visitors, they ran down to the ship without uttering a cry and assaulted the women in the ship. At last the sailors in fear cast a foreign woman on to the island. The Satyroi outraged her not only in the usual way, but also in a most shocking manner.'* They seem to be similar to the Libyan satyrs of the Atlas Mountains, and both were probably derived from travellers' tales of monkeys and apes. Satyrs are the minor gods of the woods and mountains. They are described as being half human and half beast, usually with a goat's tail, flanks and hooves. The upper part of the body is that of a human, but they also have the horns of a goat. They are the male companions of Pan and Dionysus, the god of wine, and they spend their time drinking, dancing, and chasing nymphs.

SCITALIS - THE BEAUTIFUL SNAKE

Isidore of Seville recorded: *'The scitalis has a skin that shines with such variety that by these marks it slows down any who see it. It creeps slowly and cannot pursue its prey, so it stupefies with its marvellous appearance. It is so hot that even in winter it sheds its skin.'*

SEPS - SMALL BUT DEADLY

Isidore relates of this small snake: *'The deadly seps devours a man quickly so that he liquefies in its mouth… The seps is a rare snake, the poison of which consumes the body and the bones.'*

THE SPHINX AND THE RIDDLE OF OEDIPUS

In Greek mythology, this was a female monster with the body of a lion, the breast and head of a woman, eagle's wings and sometimes a serpent-headed tail. Variously described as daughter of Typhon and Echidna, or Typhon and Chimaera, or Orthos and Chimaera, the Sphinx was sent by the gods to plague the town of Thebes. Pseudo-Apollodorus in the second-century CE wrote: *'While Kreon was king, a scourge held Thebes in suppression, for Hera set upon them the Sphinx, whose parents were Ekhidna and Typhon. She had a woman's face, the breast, feet, and tail of a lion, and bird wings. She had learned a riddle from the Mousai, and now sat on Mount Phikion where she kept challenging the Thebans with it. The riddle was: "What is it that has one voice, and is four-footed and two-footed and three-footed?" An oracle existed for the Thebans to the effect that they would be free of the Sphinx when they guessed her riddle, so they often convened to search for the meaning, but whenever they came up with the wrong answer, she would seize one of them, and eat him up. When many had died, including most recently Kreon's own son Haimon, Kreon announced publicly that he would give both the kingdom and the widow of Laios to the man who solved the riddle. Oedipus heard and solved it, stating that he answer to the Sphinx's question was man. As a baby he crawls on all fours, as an adult he is two-footed, and as he grows old he gains a third foot in the form of a cane.*

At this the Sphinx threw herself from the Acropolis.' Because of the Theban legend, sphinxes were popular as sculptural grave steles erected upon the tombs of men who died in youth. The Egyptian Sphinx is depicted as an unwinged lion lying down, with a human upper part of the body, and sculptures of it appear in avenues forming the approaches to temples. The greatest among the Egyptian Sphinxes is that of Ghizeh, which, with the exception of the paws, is made of one block of stone. The Egyptian Sphinxes are sometimes called *Androsphinges*, to distinguish them from those Sphinxes whose upper part was that of a sheep or ram.

STICK PEOPLE AND BIG FOOT

The Yakama Indians of Cascade Mountains in Washington State have a legend of the *Stick People* or little ones that live high in the hills. Some hills were sacred places for the Stick People and accessing them was discouraged, for fear of the Stick People doing the traveller harm. Stick People may also carry out unprovoked mischief, such as stealing your car keys. Robert Michael Pyle in *Where Bigfoot Walks: Crossing the Dark Divide* (1995) records: *'A vast body of lore pertains to Ste-ye-hah'mah, also called Stick-shower Man or Stick Man. The Yakama word means a spirit hiding under the cover of the woods. Some say the "stick" refers to this habit, others that these creatures poke sticks into lodges to extract or harass victims, or rain sticks down upon them. In a recent Quinault story, women put out shallow baskets of salmon and other food, and See'atco takes the provender in* exchange for firewood, which he places in the basket – another "stick" connection. Some Indians consider Stick Men to be spirits whose name should not even be mentioned; Don Smith – Lelooska – thinks the Stick Men have merely been conflated with Bigfoot.'

TALOS - THE FIRST ROBOT

Talos was a giant creature made of bronze by Hephaestus, the Greek god of fire and metalworking, who gave it to King Minos. In other accounts Talos was given by Zeus to Europa to guard the island of Crete. Hephaestus' robot guarded Crete by walking around the perimeter of the island three times a day and throwing rocks and other debris at ships so that they would not land. It was immensely strong but had one weak spot on its body, the vein in its ankle. The Argonauts encountered Talos on their way home from Libya. Medea convinced Talos that she would give it a secret potion that would make it immortal, if it would let her stop on the island. Talos agreed and drank the potion and fell asleep. Medea went to the sleeping Talos and pulled the plug from the vein in its ankle, whereupon Talos bled to death. Other stories say that when Medea tried to land on the island, Talos scraped its ankle on a rock while trying to repel her and bled to death. In an entirely different version, Talos was killed by an Argonaut Poeas, who shot it in the ankle with an arrow.

TYPHON - THE IMMORTAL STORM GIANT

Hesiod, in the seventh or eighth century BCE, writes: '*Now after Zeus had driven the Titanes out of heaven, gigantic Gaia [Earth], in love with Tartaros [the Pit], by means of golden Aphrodite, bore the youngest of her children,*

Typhoeus.' He was so huge that his head was said to touch the stars. He was man-shaped down to the thighs, with two coiled vipers in place of legs. Attached to his hands in place of fingers were 50 serpent heads per hand. He was winged, and had dirty matted hair and beard, pointed ears and eyes flashing fire. According to some sources, Typhon had 200 hands each with 50 serpents for fingers and 100 heads, one in human form with the rest being heads of bulls, boars, serpents, lions and leopards. As a volcano-daimon, Typhon threw red-hot rocks at the sky, and storms of fire erupted from his mouth. His offspring included the Hydra, the Harpies, Cerberus, the Chimera, the Caucasian Eagle, the Nemeian Lion, the Colchian Dragon, the Sphinx, the Gorgons, Scylla and the Trojan Dragons, amongst many other evil monsters. Typhon was defeated and imprisoned by Zeus for ever in the Pit of Tartarus, and was the source of devastating storm winds which issued from the underworld. Later poets envisage him trapped beneath the body of Mount Etna in Sicily.

WEREWOLVES

A werewolf is a man who is transformed, or who transforms himself, into a wolf under the influence of a full moon. Innocent people may become werewolves if they are cursed, or bitten by another werewolf. The werewolf is only active at night and during that period, he devours people and corpses. According to recent legend, werewolves can be killed by silver objects such as silver arrows or silver bullets. When a werewolf dies, he is returned to his human form. The word is a contraction of the old-Saxon words *wer* (man) and *wolf*. The term lycanthrope is sometimes used to describe werewolves, but it refers to someone who suffers from a mental disease and is deluded into thinking that he has changed into a wolf. The concept of werewolves is possibly based on the myth of Lycaon, king of Arcadia, who was notorious for his cruelty. He tried to buy the favour of Zeus by murdering his young son Nyctimus, and offering him on a plate to Zeus, but the outraged Zeus punished Lycaon and turned him into a wolf. In areas across the world where the wolf is not common, the figure of the werewolf is replaced by legends in which men can change themselves in tigers, lions, bears and the like. Church courts in the Middle Ages pressurized and tortured schizophrenics, epileptics and the mentally disabled to testify that they were werewolves in receipt of orders directly from Satan. After 1270 it was even considered heretical *not* to believe in the existence of werewolves. Not until the 17th century did the charge of being a werewolf disappear from European courts for lack of evidence. A possible explanation for the legend lies in the rare disease porphyria, which can cause unusual and excessive hair growth, sensitivity to light and darkness, and grotesque distortions in the fingers and teeth.

YALE (CENTICORE)

Pliny the Elder tells us: '*The yale is found in Ethiopia. It is a black or tawny colour, and has the tail of an elephant and the jaws of a boar. Its horns are more than a cubit in length and are moveable; in a fight the horns are used alternately, pointed forward or sloped backward, as needed.*' According to legend, its long and flexible horns can move independently in any direction. When it fights, it keeps one horn pointed backward, so that if the horn it is fighting with is damaged, it can bring the other to the front. The yale is the size of a horse. The basilisk is the enemy of the yale, and if a basilisk finds one asleep, it stings it between the eyes, causing its eyes to swell until they burst.

CHAPTER 3
Magical Places *of* Legend *and* Reality

AJANTA AND ELLORA CAVES

These were discovered in the 19th century by a group of British officers on a tiger hunt in Maharashtra state, India. Ajanta was established as a religious retreat for Buddhist monks over 2000 years ago. It is believed that itinerant monks sheltered in natural grottoes during monsoons, and began decorating them with religious images to help pass the rainy season. As the grottoes were expanded, they became permanent monasteries, housing around 200 monks and scholars in 29 ornate rock-cut rooms. The monks carved stairs, benches, screens, columns, sculptures and other decorations as they went, and these remain attached to the resulting floors, decorated ceilings and painted walls. The abandonment of the site in the seventh century came about because the Ajanta monks gradually relocated to nearby Ellora, closer to an important caravan route on which they could ask for alms. At Ellora, the excavation of handcrafted caves begins when the Ajanta caves ended. The Ellora cave complex is multicultural. The Buddhist caves came first, from about 200 BCE–600 CE followed by the Hindu 500–900 and Jain 800–1000. Of the 34 caves chiselled into the sloping side of the low hill at Ellora, 12 are Buddhist, 17 are Hindu, and five are Jain, with some caves being fashioned simultaneously. The Kailasa Temple (the Kailasanatha) is the masterpiece at Ellora, designed to recall Mount Kailasa in the Himalayas, the home of Lord Shiva, the God who destroys evil and sorrow. It looks like a freestanding, multi-storeyed temple complex, but it was carved out of one rock, and covers an area double the size of Parthenon in Athens. It is the largest monolithic structure in the world, carved top-down from a single rock. The temple contains the largest cantilevered rock ceiling in the world, and originally was covered with white plaster, increasing the similarity to snow-covered Mount Kailasa. The building of the temple entailed removing 200,000 tonnes of rock, and it is believed to have taken 7000 labourers 150 years to complete the project.

Unlike other caves at Ajanta and Ellora, Kailasa temple has a huge courtyard that is open to the sky, surrounded by a wall of galleries several storeys high.

Mount Kailasa – also known as Mount Kailash – is considered to be a holy place of eternal bliss in four religions: Buddhism, Hinduism, Jainism and Bön, and is located in Tibet. There have been no recorded attempts to climb the 21,778 feet (6638 m) mountain. It is considered off limits to climbers in deference to Buddhist and Hindu beliefs, and is the most significant peak in the world not to have been scaled. The word Kailasa means crystal in Sanskrit, and the Tibetan name for the mountain is Gang Rin-po-che, meaning 'precious jewel of snows'. Following the Chinese invasion of Tibet in 1950, pilgrimages to the legendary abode of Lord Shiva were stopped from 1954 to 1978. Since then, a limited number of Indian pilgrims have been allowed to visit the place, under strict supervision.

Travelling around the holy mountain has to be undertaken on foot, pony or yak, taking three days of trekking.

AREA 51 Area 51, also known as Groom Lake, is a secret military facility about 90 miles (145 km) north of Las Vegas (see also Roswell Incident). The number refers to a 60 square mile (155 km²) block of land, at the centre of which is an off-limits airbase. The site was selected in the mid-1950s for testing of the U-2 spyplane, and Groom Lake is America's traditional testing ground for 'black budget' secret aircraft before they are publicly acknowledged. The facility and surrounding areas are also associated with UFO and conspiracy stories. In 1989, Bob Lazar claimed on a Las Vegas television station that he had worked with alien spacecraft at Papoose Lake, south of Area 51. Since then, *Area 51* has become a popular symbol for the US Government UFO cover-ups. There have been hundreds of UFO sightings over the centuries, and Wikipedia has 'a list of UFO sightings' for interested parties to consult.

ARÈS UFO PORT The small seaside town of Arès (population 5500) in southwest France had a council meeting in 1976, enlivened by good food and drink (the French are the only people in the world who really know how to hold meetings). Amid laughter, the council approved a sum equivalent to approximately £600 to build the world's first UFO port. An American wrote to the council in the 1980s expressing his anger that President Reagan had failed to follow suit in America. The council, finding that the port attracts at least 20,000 visitors a year, in 2010 decided to extend it with new red and white high-visibility runway lights, and a large windsock so that aliens can judge landing conditions. During a party on the 'landing strip' in September 2010, oysters and white wine were on offer, and the highlight was the unveiling of metal artwork resembling a flying saucer on the landing strip, so 'aliens won't feel lonely when they land' according to Christian Esplandiu, chairman of the local tourist office.

ATLANTIS The first references to Atlantis are found in the dialogues of Plato (428–348 BCE), who referred to a lost land that was engulfed by the ocean as the result of an earthquake 9000 years before his own time, i.e. during the last Ice Age. Plato claimed it lay somewhere outside the Pillars of Hercules, now known as the Strait of Gibraltar: '*For it is related in our records how once upon a time your State stayed the course of a mighty host, which, starting from a distant point in the Atlantic ocean, was insolently advancing to attack the whole of Europe, and Asia to boot. For the ocean there was at that time navigable; for in front of the* *mouth which you Greeks call, as you say, 'the pillars of Heracles', there lay an island which was larger than Libya and Asia together; and it was possible for the travellers of that time to cross from it to the other islands, and from the islands to the whole of the continent over against them which encompasses that veritable ocean. For all that we have here, lying within the mouth of which we speak, is evidently a haven having a narrow entrance; but that yonder is a real ocean, and the land surrounding it may most rightly be called, in the fullest and truest sense, a continent. Now in this island of Atlantis there existed a confederation of kings, of great and marvellous power, which held sway over all the island, and over many other islands also and parts of the continent.'* According to Plato's uncle Critias (460–403 BCE), the Atlanteans had conquered the Mediterranean as far east as Egypt and the continent into Tyrrhenia (Etruria, now known as central Italy), and had subjected its people to slavery. The Athenians led an alliance of resistors against the Atlantean empire and, as the alliance disintegrated, they prevailed alone against the empire, liberating the occupied lands: *'But afterwards there occurred violent earthquakes and floods; and in a single day and night of misfortune all your warlike men in a body sank into the earth, and the island of Atlantis in like manner disappeared in the depths of the sea.'* There have been scores of locations proposed for Atlantis. Most of the them are in or near the Mediterranean Sea (islands such as Sardinia, Crete and Santorini), but some suggestions range as far afield as Antarctica, Indonesia and the Caribbean. Spartel is one candidate that would coincide with some elements of Plato's account. Spartel Bank (or Majuán Bank) is a submerged former island located in the Strait of Gibraltar near Cape Spartel, its highest point being around 150 feet (46 m) below the surface. It vanished around 12,000 years ago, owing to rising ocean levels from melting ice caps after the last Glacial Maximum, while Plato's land in the same area vanished around 11,500 years ago.

BAALBECK - THE CITY OF THE SUN

Baalbeck was a flourishing Phoenician city in eastern Lebanon, which the Greeks occupied in 331 BCE, when they renamed it Heliopolis (City of the Sun). They had identified the god of Baalbeck with the sun god. It became a Roman colony under Emperor Augustus in 16 BCE. On its acropolis, over the next 300 years, the Romans constructed a monumental ensemble of three temples, three courtyards and an enclosing wall built of some of the most gigantic stones ever crafted by man. At the southern entrance of Baalbeck lies a quarry where the stones were cut. A huge block, considered the largest hewn stone in the world, still sits where it was cut almost 2000 years ago. Called the *Stone of the Pregnant Woman*, it is 70 x 16 x 14 feet (21 x 5 x 4.25 m) in size and weighs an estimated 1000 tons. The site lay under rubble for centuries, but was restored from 1898. The Romans situated the present Great Court of the Temple of Jupiter over an existing temple and courtyard in the second century and began to build the Temple of Bacchus. When Christianity was declared an official religion of the Roman empire in 313 CE, the Byzantine Emperor Constantine officially closed the Baalbeck temples. After the Arab conquest in 636 the temples were transformed into a fortress, or qal'a. Baalbeck then fell successively to the Omayyad, Abbasid, Toulounid, Fatimid and Ayyoubid dynasties. Sacked by the Mongols in about 1260, Baalbeck later enjoyed a period of calm and prosperity under Mameluke rule. The podium of Jupiter's Temple is built with some of the largest stone blocks ever hewn. On the west side of the podium is the 'Trilithon', a famous group of three enormous stones weighing about 800 tons each. It was decided to furnish the temple with a monumental extension of the podium, which, according to Phoenician tradition, had to consist of no more than three layers of stone. The fact remains that this decision initiated the cutting, transporting and lifting of the largest and heaviest stones of all times. Not only had a wall of 40 feet (12 m) in height to be composed of only three ranges of stones, but in the interest of appearance the middle blocks were made four times as long as they were tall. Adding to this a depth equal to the height of the stones, their volume must have been up to 400 cubic yards (300 m³) per block, corresponding to a weight of almost 1000 tons. Technically, the builders of Baalbeck proved that they could do it, since three such blocks of the middle layer

are in place, but in terms of time they did not succeed – the podium remained incomplete. However, Baalbeck was known for a long time primarily as the site of the three stones, the Trilithon.

BABYLON AND THE TOWER OF BABEL

In Genesis, the Tower of Babel was described as a gigantic tower built in the plain of Shinar. Humanity had been united following the Great Flood, speaking a single language and migrating westward. They came to the land of Shinar (meaning two rivers, the land of Mesopotamia and Babylon), where they decided to build a city with a tower '*with its top in the heavens... less we be scattered abroad upon the face of the Earth*'. God observed what they did and said: '*They are one people and have one language, and nothing will be withheld from them which they purpose to do.*' Then God said, 'Come, let us go down and confound their speech.' And Yahweh scattered them across the face of the Earth, and confused their languages, and they left off building the city, which was called Babel '*because Yahweh there confounded the language of all the Earth.*' (Genesis 11:5-8). This confusion of tongues ('*confusio linguarum*') thus represents the initial fragmentation of human languages as a result of the construction of the Tower of Babel. Prior to the event, humanity spoke a single language, either identical to or derived from the language spoken by Adam and Eve in the *Garden of Eden*. In the confusion of tongues, this language was split into 70 or 72 dialects, depending on tradition.

Babel is composed of two words, '*bab*' meaning 'gate' and '*el*' meaning 'god', but in Hebrew, '*balal*' means confusion. The site of a square tower can be seen on Google Earth, in the centre of the site where Babylon stood, in Iraq. It was the Etemenanki Ziggurat, which may have been built as early as the 14th century BCE. The city of Babylon was destroyed in 689 BCE by Sennacherib, who claims to have destroyed the Etemenanki. The city was restored by Nabopolassar and his son Nebuchadnezzar II. It took 88 years to rebuild the city; its central features were

the temple of Marduk and the Etemenanki Ziggurat. The seven storeys of the ziggurat reached a height of 295 feet (90 m), according to a tablet from Uruk, and contained a temple shrine at the top. In Nebuchadnezzar II's own words recorded in around 610 BCE: '*A former king built the Temple of the Seven Lights of the Earth, but he did not complete its head. Since a remote time, people had abandoned it, without order expressing their words. Since that time earthquakes and lightning had dispersed its sun-dried clay; the bricks of the casing had split, and the earth of the*

The Scarlet Woman

The Israelites hated Babylon, as Nebuchadnezzar II had conquered Judea and Jerusalem, carrying off much of the population to Babylon. In the Book of Revelation we read: '*Then the angel carried me away in the Spirit into a desert. There I saw a woman sitting on a scarlet beast that was covered with blasphemous names and had seven heads and ten horns. The woman was dressed in purple and scarlet, and was glittering with gold, precious stones and pearls. She held a golden cup in her hand, full of abominable things and the filth of her adulteries. The title was written on her forehead. Mystery, Babylon the Great, The Mother of Prostitutes. And of the Abominations of the Earth.*' Thus the original 'scarlet woman' was represented by Babylon. However, it was here that the hour was first divided into 60 minutes, the months were named and movements

in the heavens were first observed in the western hemisphere. Babylonians calculated the times for the risings of zodiacal signs and their findings were the bases for later Greek scholarship, astronomy and mathematics.

interior had been scattered in heaps. Marduk, the great lord, excited my mind to repair this building. I did not change the site, nor did I take away the foundation stone as it had been in former times. So I founded it, I made it; as it had been in ancient days, I so exalted the summit.' Alexander the Great demolished it in 323 BCE, intending to rebuild the Tower of Babel, but died before work started. It is probable that the biblical story of the Tower of Babel was influenced by the building of Etemenanki that Hebrews would have heard of during the Babylonian captivity in the sixth century BCE.

THE BENNINGTON TRIANGLE
This is a part of southern Vermont from which people have vanished on a regular basis. Suspects have ranged from serial killers to 'Bigfoot' (q.v.). Native Americans have only used the area as a burial ground, as in their lore it is a spiritual place where the four winds meet.

THE BIMINI ROAD
In 1968 an underwater rock formation was found near North Bimini island in the Bahamas. It is considered by many to be a naturally made 'tessellated pavement' half a mile (800 m) in length. Concretions of shell and sand form hard sedimentary rock, which over time fractures into straight lines, and then again at ninety degree angles. They are quite common and are a tourist attraction on the island of Tasmania. However, because of the unusual arrangement of the stones, many believe them to be a part of the lost city of Atlantis. In 1938 Edgar Cayce made a prediction about Atlantis: *'A portion of the temples may yet be discovered under the slime of ages and sea water near Bimini… Expect it in '68 or '69 – not so far away.'*

In a more recent expedition, amateur archaeologist Dr Greg Little discovered another row of rocks in the same formation directly below the first, leading him to believe that the road is actually the top of a wall or water dock, the so-called Bimini Wall. There are two other linear features near the 'Wall' that appear to back up the claims of a dock, but geologists state that multiple rows of 'blocks' are seen elsewhere in the world, e.g. in Tasmania, and that systematic fracturing can cause multiple layers. Later explorers claim to have found an underwater pyramid off Bimini.

CAMELOT - THE COURT OF ARTHUR
Camelot is the most famous castle associated with King Arthur but it was absent from early Arthurian material. It did not appear until the 1170s and Chrétien de Troyes' poem on Lancelot,

where it was called Caerlion. Caerleon in Monmouthshire, Wales, with its huge Roman fort and amphitheatre, was always associated with Arthur's court and Round Table in Welsh stories, but Chrétien recorded this for the first time in his writings, as did Geoffrey of Monmouth in his *Historia Regum Britanniae*. Geoffrey's grand description of the magnificent ruins and bath-houses drew on the Welsh *Mabinogion* tale of *Culhwch and Olwen*, possibly first written down in the 11th century. It places one of Arthur's three principal courts at Celliwig in Cernyw. Cerniw (Cornwall) is not to be confused with this Cernyw, which was the name for the kingdom and subkingdoms that formed the early region of Glywyssing (Glamorgan, Monmouthshire and part of Gloucestershire). The name Cernyw had fallen out of use by the end of the sixth century, probably to avoid confusion with fellow-Britons in Cornwall. Later scholars unfortunately identified Camelot (Celliwig in Cernyw) with an unidentified place in Cornwall, but Celliwig (the forest grove) in Cernyw is placed on the Monmouthshire-Glamorgan border, a few miles from Caerleon. The sixth-century Bishop Bedwyn (Sir Baudwin in the legends) resided at Celliwig near Cardiff and was primate of Cernyw. He was associated with Arthur, who celebrated Christmas, Easter and Whitsun at Celliwig. Sir Baudwin was said to be one of Arthur's first knights, was made a constable of the realm and one of the governors of Britain (a comeregulus). He ended his life as a physician and a hermit. Whatever other theories there may be, Arthur's main court, whatever it was called, was within just a few miles of Newport in Monmouthshire.

THE CAPUCHIN CATACOMBS OF PALERMO

In 1599, a Sicilian monk died suddenly. Some months later other monks visited his crypt to find his body had been naturally mummified. After their deaths, fellow monks also chose to be deliberately mummified and placed in the catacombs. Later it became something of a status symbol and wealthy townspeople, dressed up in their best clothes, were also mummified or embalmed and stored in niches. Owing to lack of space, later corpses were hung on hooks, but they were grouped according to age, sex, occupation and social status. The practice was discontinued in the 1920s, but we can still see children in rocking chairs, lawyers at desks, soldiers in uniform, monks with ropes around their necks as penance and the like. The bodies were dehydrated in special cells for eight months, then washed in vinegar. People specified in their wills what clothes they wished to be dressed in, along with changes of clothes at specific times. Apart from the fascinating clothes whose styles and fashions span the last 400 years, some of the corpses still have well-preserved flesh, hair and eyeslashes.

COSTA RICA'S GIANT BALLS

Las Bolas Grandes were discovered in the Diquis Delta in Costa Rica in the 1930s when the United Fruit Company began clearances of the jungle to plant bananas. There are over 300 of these rock balls still in existence, nearly all moved from their original positions, and ranging in size from a few inches and weighing a few pounds to 8 feet (2.4 m) in diameter and weighing over 16 tons. Almost all of them are made of gabbro, a hard, igneous stone, and are monolithic sculptures made by human hands. There were thousands, but many were broken up in the hunt for treasure or moved into gardens as ornaments. In the 1940s Dr Samuel Lothrop of Harvard University learned of groups of up to 45 balls in different sites. Their origin lay in the mountains, many miles away, and they were carved into almost perfect spheres. Sometimes they were laid out in triangles, or in straight or curved long lines, and smaller ones were deposited in graves. Unfinished spheres were never found, and the finished ones had to be transported at least 50 miles (80 km) from their quarry. The balls were most likely made by reducing round boulders to a spherical shape through a combination of controlled fracture, pecking and grinding. The balls could have been roughly shaped and sheared at first through the application of heat (hot coals) and cold (chilled water). When they were close to spherical in shape, they were further reduced by pecking and hammering with stones made of the same hard material. Finally, they were ground and polished to a high lustre. This process is similar to that used for making polished stone axes and stone statues. Stone balls are known from archaeological sites and buried strata to belong to the Aguas Buenas culture of *c*.200 BCE–800 CE. One group of four balls was found to be arranged in a line oriented to magnetic north. Unfortunately, all but a few of these alignments were destroyed when the balls were moved from their original locations. Many of the balls, some of them in alignments, were found on top of low mounds. Balls sitting in agricultural fields have been damaged by periodic burning after crops have been harvested, which causes the once smooth surface of the balls to crack, split and erode, a process that has contributed to the destruction of the largest known stone ball.

CROP CIRCLES The earliest known formation was discovered in 1647 in England, the first crop circle in the USA was reported in 1964, but since the 1970s about 10,000 crop circles have been reported worldwide, almost everywhere except China and South Africa. Hoaxers have admitted to creating some circles, and electrical storms have been thought to have caused others, most of which are in fields of wheat or corn. The cause may be a vortex of gyrating air, suddenly whirling downwards into a crop before passing on. While many crop circles can be found in readily accessible fields, some are not, such as those found inside restricted areas, such as in military installations on the Salisbury Plain in Wiltshire. Also, several crop circles have been formed away from the farmer's tractor lines, making it almost impossible for circle fraudsters to hide evidence of their presence. Researchers have photographic evidence that the plants in genuine circles are woven together in a particular way when they are flattened. Hoaxers usually tread on a board or use a garden roller, which cannot achieve the same effect. One researcher noted that

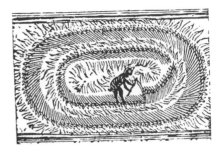

'*Crop circle formations often appear in canola* [oil seed rape] *fields. This plant has a consistency like celery. If the stalk is bent more than about 45-degrees, it snaps apart. Yet, in a "genuine" crop circle formation, the stalks are often bent flat at 90-degrees. No botanist or other scientist has been able to explain this, nor has it ever been duplicated by a human being.*' Another crop circle investigator has recorded electromagnetic (EM) measurements of 40–50 nano-Teslas at the centres of some formations, which he says is ten times the radiation level of a normal field. In 1991, two American nuclear physicists wrote a paper which was summarized thus: '*After subjecting a number of seed and soil samples to rigorous lab analysis, their main discovery was that the soil in genuine formations contained no less than four, short-lived radioactive isotopes – vanadium, europium, tellurium and ytterbium. Tests conducted on soil from the Beckhampton July 31 formation yielded alpha emissions 198% above control samples, beta emissions 48% above, both of which seemed "strikingly elevated", since they were two to three times as radioactive as soil from outside the formation.*' Some of the most common theories about their formation include whirlwind vortexes, plasma vortexes (balls of light sometimes seen when they were formed), Earth energies, extraterrestrials, underground archaeology, sound vibrations, heavenly or demonic forces, and military experiments including microwaves.

THE DELPHIC ORACLE

Delphi was inhabited since Mycenaean times (14th–11th century BCE) by small settlements which were dedicated to the Mother Earth deity. Then Greek mythology tells how the god Apollo

released his arrows one after the other until Python was killed. This dragon had guarded the hill of Gaia's sacred ground for hundreds of years. With his victory Apollo gained the right to call the slopes of Delphi his sanctuary. The worship of Apollo as the god of light, harmony and order was established between the 11th and ninth centuries, and the sanctuary grew in size and importance. Delphi was revered throughout the Greek world as the site of the *omphalos* stone, the 'centre of the universe'. During the eighth century BCE, Delphi became internationally known for the oracular powers of Pythia. The oracle predicted the future based on the lapping of water and the sounds of leaves rustling in the trees. She sat on the *Sibylline Rock*, or in a cauldron-shaped bowl on top of a tripod, breathing in vapours from the ground and uttering her strange predictions. In 2001 geologists traced the presence of ethylene in the rocks. If breathed in an enclosed space, it can have narcotic or hallucinogenic effects. Plutarch served as a priest at Delphi, and in his histories he tells us that Pythia entered the inner chamber of the temple (the *Adyton*), sat on a tripod and inhaled the (light hydrocarbon) gases that escaped from a chasm in the porous earth. After falling into a trance, she muttered words incomprehensible to mere mortals. The priests of the sanctuary then interpreted her oracles in a common language and delivered them to those who had requested them. Even so, the oracles were always open to interpretation and often ambiguous enough to support dual and opposing meanings.

The oracle exerted considerable influence in Greece, and was consulted before all major undertakings: wars, the founding of colonies, and so forth. The oracle is said to have taught Socrates of his own ignorance, and this claim is related to one of the most famous sayings: '*Know thyself*'. Another famous motto that came from Delphi is: '*Nothing in excess*'. King Croesus of Lydia in 532 BCE consulted the oracle as to whether he should attack the Persians. The oracle answered that if he crossed the River Halys and attacked the Persians, a great nation would be destroyed. He attacked, but unfortunately it was his own Lydian empire which was destroyed. When the Persians were poised to sack Athens, the Athenian general Themistocles asked the advice of the oracle. The oracle simply advised that 'wooden walls' would aid victory, and Themistocles interpreted this to refer to the wooden ships of the Athenian fleet. He won a resounding victory at the great sea battle of Salamis in 480 BCE. Greek and foreign dignitaries, heads of state and common folk all made the pilgrimage to the Delphi sanctuary, and paid great sums for Pythia's advice. Since the sanctuary only served the public for a few days over nine months out of the year, great sums were paid by the more affluent citizens in order to bypass the long line of waiting pilgrims. The sanctuary of Delphi fell into Roman hands in 191 BCE and was stripped of its treasures by General Sulla in 86 BCE in order to finance his siege of Athens. Just three years later Delphi was razed by the Thracians who are said to have extinguished the sacred fire, which had been burning uninterrupted for centuries. There are still extensive remains at Delphi.

THE DRIEST AND WETTEST PLACES ON EARTH

The Atacama Desert in northern Chile climbs to 10,670 feet (3252 m) altitude and extends over an area of 72,500 square miles (188,000 km²). It stretches like a rather narrow finger between the Pacific Ocean and the Andes mountains for a distance of 600 miles (1000 km), where a high pressure cell over the Pacific holds back moisture from the west. Mountains block clouds formed in the Amazon basin to the east. On the coast, the cold Peru Current from Antarctica chills the desert air, further inhibiting the formation of any rain clouds. The average annual rainfall is about one inch (2.5 cm) and, in some mid-desert spots, rain has never been recorded as long as humans have measured it. Not even cacti grow there. The air is so dry that metal objects never oxidize or rust, and meat left for long in the open air preserves for an unlimited time. Without moisture nothing rots. This is generally thought to be the driest place on Earth, but that title actually goes to an area of Antarctica known as the Dry Valleys. There is absolutely no precipitation in this 1900 square mile (4920 km²) region – an area that contains almost no water, ice or snow. Winds from the mountains are so full of water that gravity pulls them down and away from the Dry Valleys.

Mawsynram, in the Khasi Hills of northeast India with a yearly average rainfall of around 40 feet (12.2 m), and

Cherrapunji, 10 miles (16 km) away, are in competition for the title of wettest place on Earth. One weather station reported two years of daily rain there without a break. Periodically both towns suffer from severe water shortages. Because of deforestation, the soil has no absorption ability and the rainwater runs away to cause floods in Bangladesh.

EL DORADO - THE CITY OF GOLD

In the 16th century, Europeans thought there was a vast city called El Dorado hidden in the mountains of South America, with unimaginable mineral riches to be found. Spanish conquistadores made often deadly journeys to search for it. High in the Andes, in what is now Colombia, lived the geographically isolated Chibcha people. They mined gold and emeralds freely, and when they anointed a new priest-chief, they covered the man in balsam gum and then blew gold dust all over his body through cane straws until he looked like a statue of pure gold. 'El Dorado', literally 'the Golden One', then ceremonially bathed in the sacred Lake Guatavita. The custom ended around 1480 when they were subdued by another tribe. However, oral folklore spread across South and

Central America propagating the story of El Dorado, who ruled over a vast kingdom where nearly everything was made from gold, silver or precious stones. El Dorado came to represent his capital, the Golden City of incredible wealth. Francisco Pizarro conquered the Inca civilization in the 1530s in what is now Peru, and marvelled at their technically advanced and wealthy city of Cuzco. A messenger from an unknown Indian tribe appeared in Cuzco with a message for the Inca emperor, unaware that the Spanish now controlled the empire. Tortured by the Spanish, he told them that he came from the Zipa people in the Bogota region, but knew of another kingdom, high in the mountains to the east, where lived a tribe so wealthy that they covered their chief in gold. Spanish expeditions set off to find and plunder El Dorado but failed to locate it. A survivor of one of them, which explored around the Orinoco River, was assisted by friendly Indians. This man, Juan Martinez, said that they blindfolded him for days and led him to their kingdom, called Manoa, where everything in the royal palace was made of gold. Martinez said that riches had been given to him as a departing gift, but that they had been stolen by other Indians

on his way back. Sir Walter Raleigh heard the story in 1586 and set off to search for El Dorado, writing a book called: *The Discovery of the Large, Rich and Beautiful Empire of Guyana with a Relation to the Great and Golden City of Manoa.* He led another expedition which failed to find Manoa/El Dorado in 1618.

THE END OF THE WORLD

This prediction is based on a calendar produced by the ancient Mayan civilization, which flourished in the steamy rainforests of Central America for nearly 2000 years until its unexplained collapse around 900 CE. The lunar month (the period between successive new moons) lasts 29.5305 days, i.e. 2,551,435 seconds. The Mayans, without the help of telescopes or computers, calculated a figure only 34 seconds out from this count of over 2.5 million seconds. They also accurately forecasted the movements of planets including Jupiter and Mars, and the occurrence of both solar and lunar eclipses for many centuries to come. Given these extremely precise predictions, Doomsday theorists are alarmed that the Mayan 'Long Count' Calendar, appears to end abruptly on a date they recorded as 13.0.0.0.0. On the Gregorian calendar which we use today, this corresponds to 21 December 2012. The only clue as to what the Mayans thought might happen on that day comes from an ancient stone tablet, discovered during road works in Mexico in the 1960s. Carved upon it are hieroglyphics that refer to the year 2012 and an event that will involve *Bolon Yokte*, the Mayan god of war and creation. A crack in the stone has made the last part of the inscription illegible, but Mexican archaeologists have interpreted it as

saying: '*He will descend from the sky.*' This would be typical of this author's luck, as he would be expecting his first royalties from this book at around that time.

FATA MORGANA *Fata Morgana* comes from the Italian translation of Morgan le Fay, the shape-shifting half-sister of King Arthur, and refers to a very complex 'superior' mirage. It appears as an optical illusion with alternations of compressed and stretched zones, erect images and inverted images. A Fata Morgana is usually a fast-changing mirage, most common in polar regions. Its distortions and bending of the light can produce extremely strange effects. Ludovic Kennedy described an incident that took place below the Denmark Strait between Greenland and Iceland in May 1941, following the sinking of HMS *Hood*, in *Pursuit: The Chase and Sinking of the Bismarck.* The German battleship *Bismarck*, while being chased by the British cruisers *Norfolk* and *Suffolk*, passed out of sight into a sea mist. Within a matter of seconds, the ship seemed to reappear steaming towards the British ships at high speed. In alarm the cruisers separated, anticipating an imminent attack, and then observers from both ships watched in astonishment as the massive battleship fluttered, grew indistinct and faded away. Radar watch indicated that the *Bismarck* had in fact made no changes of course during this time.

GARDEN OF EDEN The Garden of Eden is described in the Book of Genesis as being the place where the first man and woman lived after they were created by God. Many religions believe in the past physical existence of the garden, with Genesis giving the geographical location

GARWAY - ST MICHAEL'S CHURCH Near Skenfrith on the borders of England and Wales, this church was formerly named Llangarewi, and was built near a Celtic Christian foundation in around 600 CE. The first stone-built church was established about 1180 by the Knights Templar, who were given the land by Henry II. This church was built with a very rare circular nave, the capped foundations of which were only found in 1927. It was one of only six Templar churches in England and Wales. The tower was built separately from the church in about 1200, and used as a place of refuge from Welsh attacks, and was only joined to the nave in the 15th century. The place was so important that it even received a visit from the Templars' last Grandmaster, Jacques de Molay, in 1294. The Knights Templar were dissolved by the king of France and the pope during the period 1307 to 1314, with de Molay being tortured and executed. Their land at Garway was passed to the Knights Hospitaller of nearby Dinmore, who replaced the circular nave with a conventional nave in the 15th century. It has become something of a cult visitor centre for those interested in Templar history and is a remarkable building with many strange and special features. Apart from the intriguing visit by the Templar Grandmaster from the continent, it was said that something very precious was taken there from the great library at nearby Raglan Castle before it was burned down in the Civil War. Some have postulated that it was the Holy Grail.

of Eden in relation to four major rivers. Most scholars locate the Garden somewhere in the Middle East, near Mesopotamia (modern Iraq). A genetic study in 2009 suggests that the origin of humanity lies in a shady, inhospitable region on the borders of Namibia and Angola. The area is populated by the Bushmen, or San people, who may be the closest thing to a Biblical Adam and Eve. Scientists suggest that the clicking sounds characteristic of San speech may be a remnant of original human speech. However, the San may have migrated from east to west Africa 50,000 years ago, so the geographical location may be misplaced. The same study calculates the point from which human beings – perhaps a single tribal band as small as 150 people – left about 50,000 years ago to populate the rest of the world. This exit point lies near the midpoint of the African coast bordering the Red Sea.

THE GLOZEL MYSTERY In 1924, Émile Fradin, a 17-year-old farmer's son from le Glozel, a small hamlet in Franc, stumbled upon one of the most contentious archaeological discoveries ever. On freeing the foot of a cow from a hole while he was ploughing, he and his father uncovered an oval brick-lined pit, containing a human skull and carved bones, carved pebbles, pots and clay tablets with mysterious symbols. Dr Antonin Morlet (1882–1965), an amateur archaeologist, began more extensive excavations and concluded that it was a unique Neolithic site. He immediately published his findings, but was called a charlatan, as the finds resembled no known Neolithic remains. The teenager Fradin was denounced as a forger, and there was a police raid on the family farm. Émile Fradin counter-attacked citing defamation of character, and he and his father set up a small museum in a farm outbuilding to display more than 2000 objects from le Champ des Morts (the Field of the Dead). Five decades later, scientists decided to test the ceramics from the site with the newly developed thermo-luminescence dating technique. The ceramics did not date from the 1920s, nor from Neolithic times, but from the Late Iron Age/Gallo-Roman periods (*c.*200 BCE to 400 CE). Over the next two decades it was discovered the oval pit seemed to be a 12th–13th century glass kiln, and there had also been early postmedieval activity involving human burial. Carbon-14 dating now showed that some carved bones were of medieval date, *c.*1100–1300. The finds which are firmly dated by thermo-luminescence

contain no single object typical of the well-documented cultures of that region and period. Were it not for the scientific dating undertaken in the mid-1970s onwards, many would have dismissed the site as a hoax.

HAKKA EARTH BUILDINGS
In the province of Fujian in south China are densely concentrated blocks of oddly shaped buildings, which American researchers once described as '*like something from another planet*'. The CIA spied on this '*suspicious Chinese nuclear base*' in the 1960s, which is now a World Heritage Site. The Fujian Hakka people came to Fujian from the Central Plains of China over a period of 1000 years ranging from the Qin Dynasty (221–207 BCE) to the Song Dynasty (960–1279). Calling themselves Hakka ('guest people'), these Han immigrants have retained much of their ancestors' lifestyle, religion and culture, including their unique earth buildings known as *tulou*. While the most common of these are round or square, others are rectangular, D-shaped, semi-circular or constructed in the shape of horseshoes, umbrellas, windmills or *Ba Gua* (an eight-sided diagram derived from the *I-Ching*, the ancient Chinese book of divination). The earth buildings are usually three to five storeys high, with a huge central courtyard onto which all the doors of the rooms and inner windows open. They are used for public activities, as ancestral temples and for homes. The buildings are made of earth, stone, bamboo and wood, and are well-lit, well-ventilated, windproof and earthquake-proof, and warm in winter and cool in

summer. As most Hakka traditionally lived in the mountains, these communal houses made of compacted earth were built to provide protection against bandits and wild animals – almost like small fortified castles. These buildings are exceptionally strong. The Huanji tulou was built in 1693, and in 1918 it withstood a severe earthquake measuring 6.2 on the Richter scale. In the Chinese civil war, the building was bombed by the Kuomintang, but water from its moat was used to extinguish the fire.

THE HOME OF THE MOTHER OF ALL APPLES The *Ur-apple* of Kazakhstan is the ancestor of all the 20,000 varieties of apple across the world. Technically, each apple that grows from a seed is unique. To keep a variety of the same apple, it must be grafted onto a rootstock to preserve its genetic qualities.

THE HOME OF THE RAREST APPLE Bardsey Island off northwest Wales is called in Welsh Ynys Enlli, Isle of the Currents, as it is so inaccessible. It is

The Heliades – The People of the Sun

In Greek mythology, this was a seven-island paradise of the far south, located beyond Ethiopia and India in the Great Ocean stream. A land of peace and plenty, there was no winter or war, and the isles were rich with forests of ever-fruiting trees. The inhabitants were beautiful and virtuous, tall and completely hairless except for their heads, chins and brows. The islanders had flexible, rubbery bones, large ears, and split tongues which allowed them to carry on two conversations at the same time. They could mimic the sounds of animals and birds, and dressed in rich purple linen robes. The People of the Sun, however, were required to undergo a form of euthanasia at the age of 150. They lay upon a magical plant which brought about a painless, sleep-like death. Their lives and bodies were otherwise untouched by death and disease, and accidentally severed limbs could be re-attached by means of a magical glue extracted from the blood of the *amphisbaena* (q.v.), the magical tortoises that lived on the isles. Each of the seven islands was ruled by a king, the oldest man on the island, who at the age of 150 was succeeded by the next eldest in line. The nation possessed no families, as the children were raised communally, in a way that prohibited all knowledge of parentage. At birth the infants were placed on the back of a magical bird to determine their spiritual disposition. Those who failed the test were rejected and left in the wilderness to die.

also known as the Island of 20,000 Saints because of the number of pilgrims buried there. Indeed, three trips to Bardsey were considered equal to a pilgrimage to Rome, and anybody buried on Bardsey was guaranteed eternal salvation. It has been a place of pilgrimage since the sixth century, and the remains of an abbey can be found there. Its oldest name was Afallach, Welsh for Isle of Apples, and it was reputedly the magical Isle of Avalon where Arthur was taken when mortally wounded after the fateful Battle of Camlan. However,

in recorded history, there are no references to apples on Bardsey. In 1998 two ornithologists found a gnarled apple tree, sheltered from the winds, growing up the side of one of the island's houses called Plas Bach. The fruit and the tree were free of disease, a very unusual occurrence in north Wales. At the National Fruit Collection at Brogdale in Kent, Dr Joan Morgan, Britain's leading fruit historian, declared that the fruit and the tree were unique. The media called it, *'The rarest tree in the world.'* The tree was dubbed 'Merlin's Apple' by locals. On the hillside above the house is a cave where King Arthur's sorcerer Merlin is reputedly buried in a glass coffin.

KING SOLOMON'S MINES

King Solomon was a king of Israel in the tenth century BCE. He accumulated enormous wealth, ruling the entire region west of the Euphrates. One of the most celebrated visits to Solomon was that made by the Queen of Sheba, who came from southern Arabia. Arabia was a country rich in gold, frankincense and myrrh. Solomon needed Sheba's

commodities and trade routes; the Queen of Sheba needed Solomon's cooperation in marketing her country's goods. The queen arrived with a large retinue of camels carrying spices, gold and precious stones. Recent research indicates that King David and his son Solomon controlled the copper industry in what is now southern Jordan. An international team of archaeologists has excavated an ancient copper-production centre at Khirbat en-Nahas, digging down to virgin soil through more than 20 feet (6 m) of industrial smelting debris, or slag. The 2006 dig has brought up new artefacts, and radiocarbon dating places the bulk of industrial-scale production in the tenth century BCE, in line with the Biblical narrative. Khirbat en-Nahas, which means 'ruins of copper' in Arabic, is in the lowlands of a desolate, arid region south of the Dead Sea in what was once Edom and is today Jordan's Faynan district. So Solomon's famed *'cargoes from Ophir'* appear to have been copper not gold. At the end of his reign it is calculated that he had amassed 500 tons of gold, making him worth £6 trillion in today's money, second only to Alexander the Great in ancient history's 'rich list'.

LEY LINES In 1921, Alfred Watkins discovered mysterious alignments connecting both natural features and ancient sites such as churches and tumuli. These are found all over the world. Watkins originally looked at fields named leas, and place-names ending in lay, lea or ley, which is where the term '*ley line*' comes from. The word *ley* derives from the Saxon word for a *cleared glade*. His theory was that ancient sites around Britain had actually been deliberately constructed to create alignments between and across the inhabited landscape of Britain. Thus stone circles, standing stones, long barrows, cairns, burial mounds and churches form straight alignments across the landscape. (Churches were generally built on the sites of older places of worship.) As ley lines can be '*dowsed*' (followed by the use of dowsing rods), they seem to denote some change in the Earth's magnetic field. Birds, whales, honeybees, fish and bacteria navigate using the Earth's magnetic field, using body tissue with magnetite in it. Magnetite enables them to sense magnetic changes, and it has now also been found in human brains. In magnetite-containing bacteria, magnetite crystals turn the bacteria into 'swimming needles' that orient themselves with respect to the Earth's magnetic fields. It seems that possibly at some time in the past man lost the ability to 'feel' the ley lines, and placed standing stones on their alignments to mark them. Burial mounds may have been so aligned so that someone on the top of a mound could see the next mound, and paths constructed between them and signals passed. The same principle holds true of Norman castles built across Wales. A message could be sent from the top of each castle by fire or signalling to the next castle if under attack, which explains the density of castles in the first areas to be conquered in Glamorgan and Monmouthshire.

THE 'LOST CITY OF APOLLO'

The idea of a 'lost city' comes from the Greek writer Diodorus Siculus (*c*.90–30 BCE), who produced his 40-volume *Historical Library* in around 36 BCE. In Book II Chapter 3 he describes the '*Far-Northerners*' (Hyperboreans), who worship Apollo and are favourably disposed towards the Greeks: '*And in the island* [of the Far-Northerners] *there exists a magnificent sacred precinct of Apollo and a noteworthy shrine, adorned with many offerings, ball-like in shape. And there exists a town sacred to the same god... The so-called Northerners – the descendants of Boreas – rule the same town and sacred precinct, the people deriving their leadership through descent.*' Diodoros says that the island is in the ocean by Gaul, and is as big as Sicily. Its citizens are said to be harp players who received Greek travellers in the past, who left inscriptions behind. The Moon is apparently larger in their country, as it is said to appear closer to the Earth. The climate there is so good that it is possible to raise two crops in a year. Stonehenge has been identified as the lost

city, and the harp players as druids. The Greeks and Phoenicians certainly traded with Britain hundreds of years before the Roman invasion.

THE LOST CITY OF Z

Colonel Percival Harrison Fawcett (1867 – c.1925) disappeared under unknown circumstances, along with his son, during an expedition to find 'Z', his name for an ancient lost city in Brazil. In 1906–7 he had mapped a jungle area between Brazil and Bolivia for the Royal Geographic Society. He claimed to have seen and shot a 62-feet (19-m) long giant anaconda, for which he was ridiculed by the scientific community. He claimed that he was travelling by canoe along the Rio Abuna, near to its confluence with the Rio Negro. Close to his canoe, several feet of broad, powerful, undulating, serpentine coils and a huge triangular head rose up above the surface of the river, and as he and his team watched in horror, a truly colossal anaconda began emerging onto the riverbank. Fawcett shot the snake dead, and then discovered that the portion of its body that had emerged from the water prior to being shot was 45 feet (13.7 m) long, and the portion remaining in the water was 17 feet (5.3 m) long. Fawcett and his team had no means of transporting an immensely heavy, rapidly decomposing 62-foot carcase back to civilization. There has never been a fully confirmed specimen of anaconda measuring over 30 feet (9 m) but there are four known species of aquatic boa inhabiting the swamps and rivers of tropical South America.

There have been unverified claims of enormous snakes alleged to be well over 50 feet (15 m). Fawcett reported other mysterious animals unknown to zoology at the time. He made seven expeditions between 1906 and 1924, collaborating with the native Indians. In 1908, Fawcett traced the source of the Rio Verde and in 1913 claimed to have seen dogs with two noses. (see page 330). After serving in the First World War, Fawcett returned to Brazil to search for a lost city that he believed existed somewhere in the Mato Grosso region, and which he named 'Z'. He left behind instructions stating that if the expedition did not return, no rescue expedition should be sent, lest the rescuers suffer his fate. With his son Jack and Jack's long-time friend Raleigh Rimell, he took two Brazilian labourers, two horses, eight mules and a pair of dogs. The last communication from the expedition was on 29 May 1925, when it was about to cross a tributary of the Amazon. Both Fawcett's son and friend were ill when last seen by Indians. An estimated 100 would-be-rescuers have died in the course of several expeditions sent to uncover Fawcett's fate and that of the lost city.

THE LOST WORLD This was a title of a 1912 adventure story by Sir Arthur Conan Doyle. It was set on a plateau in the Amazon, a place where dinosaurs still roamed the land. There are even now 'lost worlds' waiting to be found and species to yet be discovered. An expedition to the Foja Mountains in Papua, western New Guinea in 2007 uncovered two new mammals, a pygmy possum and a giant rat. A subsequent exploration a year later produced an even greater haul of new species, including several new mammals, a reptile, an amphibian, no fewer than 12 insects and the remarkable discovery of a new bird. They include a bizarre spike-nosed tree frog (nicknamed the Pinocchio Frog), an oversized, but notably tame, woolly vegetarian rat, a gargoyle-like gecko with yellow eyes, a tiny forest wallaby, the smallest member of the kangaroo family in the world, and a new species of imperial pigeon. Other discoveries included a new blossom bat, which feeds on rainforest nectar, a small new tree-mouse, a new flowering shrub, a new monitor lizard and a new black and white butterfly related to the monarch of North America. The tree frog, which was found on a bag of rice in the campsite, has a Pinocchio-like protuberance on its nose that points upwards when the male calls, but deflates and points downwards when he is less active. Rising to more than 7000 ft (2130 m), the Foja Mountains encompass an area of more than 1160 square miles (3000 km²) of undeveloped and undisturbed rainforest. It was called 'The Lost World' when news of the first expedition was released. A participant in the expedition, Dr Bruce Beehler, noted: *'While animals and plants are being wiped out across the globe at a pace never seen in millions of years, the discovery of these absolutely incredible forms of life is much needed positive news. Places like these represent a healthy future for all of us and show that it is not too late to stop the current species extinction crisis.'*

The Foja Mountains are a virtual island where species have evolved undisturbed for countless millennia.

In 2008 a team of conservationists from Kew Gardens returned from an expedition to an *'uncharted and unexplored Eden'* in the heart of Mozambique. The highly mountainous 27 square miles (70 km²) had been overlooked by wildlife experts and mapmakers because of its difficult landscape and its inaccessibility during decades of war. It came to light when British researchers spotted an unexpected patch of green forest on Google Earth. The expedition visited the untouched area surrounding Mount Mabu and discovered new species of wildlife including pygmy chameleons, Swynnerton's robin and butterflies such as the small striped swordtail and emperor swallowtail. There were three new species of butterfly, a previously undiscovered adder, a rarely seen orchid, giant snakes including the Gaboon viper and colonies of rare birds. More new species were expected to be discovered among the hundreds of plant specimens that were brought home.

MAGNETIC POLE REVERSAL

The strength of Earth's magnetic field, the force that protects us from deadly radiation from outer space, has been weakening dramatically over the last 100 years. Gauthier Hulot, of the Paris Geophysical Institute, has discovered that Earth's magnetic field seems to be declining most rapidly near the poles, an indication that a *'flip'* (reversal of the poles) may soon take place. *'Earth's*

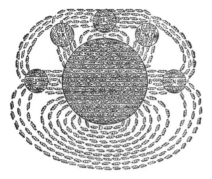

magnetic field has disappeared many times before – as a prelude to our magnetic poles flipping over, when north becomes south and vice versa. Reversals happen every 250,000 years or so, and as there has not been one for almost a million years, we are due one soon', according to Dr Alan Thomson of the British Geological Survey in Edinburgh. We do not know how long such a reversal could last. Records of past events, embedded in iron minerals in ancient lava beds, show some can last for thousands of years, during which time the planet will have been exposed to bombardment by solar radiation. On the other hand, some researchers say some flips may have lasted only a few weeks. The effects could be catastrophic. Powerful radiation bursts, which normally are diverted away from the atmosphere, would heat up its upper layers, triggering climatic disruption. Navigation and communication satellites would be destroyed and migrating animals left unable to navigate because they track the Earth's magnetic field. For humans, the greatest risk would come from intense solar radiation bursts. Normally these are contained by the planet's magnetic field that stretches into space, but if it disappears, particle storms will start to batter the atmosphere. Dr Paul Murdin,

of the Institute of Astronomy, Cambridge, tells us: *'These solar particles can have profound effects… On Mars, when its magnetic field failed permanently billions of years ago, it led to its atmosphere being boiled off. On Earth, it will heat up the upper atmosphere and send ripples round the world with enormous, unpredictable effects on the climate.'* One begins to wonder if the Mayan 'End of the World' scenario for 2012 (see page 108) might refer to this magnetic flip, which could wipe out life on Earth.

THE MARFA LIGHTS The Marfa lights are unexplained *'ghost lights'* that have been appearing on Mitchell Flat east of Marfa, Texas. The first published account of the lights was given in 1957, but Robert Reed Ellison (born 1880) reported them to his family and accounts of their appearances were circulating by word of mouth before the 1950s. The lights are the size of a basketball, floating in the air at around shoulder height. They are usually described as white, yellow, orange or red, but green and blue are sometimes reported. The lights sometimes appear in groups, and usually travel laterally but have been seen to move rapidly in various directions. The lights are possibly atmospheric reflections of the headlights of traffic passing on the nearby US Route 67, or they may be electric by-products of the predominantly quartz hills in the area. Because they usually appear above private property amidst terrain that is difficult to traverse, there are almost no reports of people being able to get close to the lights to inspect them at close range.

Megaliths

Megaliths are large stone structures or groups of standing stones that are found in Europe, Asia, Africa, Australia and North and South America. They are believed to have religious and/or astronomical significance. Many were built in the Neolithic and early Bronze Ages. Megaliths ('great stones') are classed in two general categories. *Dolmens* or chamber tombs or long tombs usually contain one or more chambers or rooms in which the dead were buried. Some dolmens also contain long stone chambers or halls which connect different rooms. Long chambers are also known as passage-graves. Tombs which are covered with earth to form mounds are called tumuli. Dolmens must have been used for other purposes besides burying the dead, because remains of bodies have not been found in all of them. Many have their openings aligned with the Sun at a particular solstice. The penetration of sunlight into the passage at the spring solstice can symbolize the fertilization of 'Mother Earth' by the god of the Sun, ensuring healthy crops and herds. *Menhirs* are large standing stones, or groups of standing stones, arranged in circles, or cromlechs. If a bank or ditch surrounds the stones, it is termed a henge. Menhir comes from the Welsh *maen* (stone) and *hir* (tall). These standing stones, especially those containing holes, were thought to have supernatural or magical powers to heal. Sick people would crawl through the holes hoping to restore their health. The greatest concentration of megaliths exists at Carnac, Brittany. Of the estimated original 11,000 stones, only 3000 still stand arranged in avenues, dolmens, mounds and cromlechs. One dolmen, covered with a tumulus, has been dated back to 4700 BCE.

Megalithic Stone Circles

Avebury stone circles, Wiltshire

The megalithic stone circle of Jersey

Druidical circle near Keswick in Cumbria

The Merry
Maidens
stone circle near
Penzance, Cornwall

Druidical stone circle
at Darab in Iran

Stonehenge on Salisbury
Plain, Wiltshire

MIRAGES In the desert near Ahwaz, Khuzestan, Iran, this writer once saw in the far distance, a fantastic city like the New York skyline, behind a shimmering lake, with its image reflected in the water. Upon closer inspection, it was simply a collection of mud huts, with no water within miles. It is almost impossible to explain the effects of this naturally occurring optical phenomenon. Light rays are bent to produce a displaced image of distant objects or the sky. A mirage can actually be captured on camera, since light rays are refracted to form the false image at the observer's location. Mirages can be categorized as 'inferior' (meaning lower), 'superior' (meaning higher) and *Fata Morgana* (see page 108) which consist of a series of unusually elaborate, vertically stacked images, which form one rapidly changing mirage. What the image appears to represent is determined by the interpretive faculties of the human mind, e.g. inferior images on land are very easily mistaken for the reflections from a small body of water.

THE MOON Because the Moon appears out of the darkness as a shining crescent-shaped sliver, then over the period of a month waxes and wanes, it has always been seen as a symbol of human birth, growth and death. One of the earliest Moon gods was Sin, worshipped in Ur, Mesopotamia 5000 years ago. Sin gave way to Thoth, the 'god of gods', who crossed the skies with his companion, Ra, the Sun god. Huge statues were erected to Thoth, who, the Ancient Egyptians believed, weighed your heart when you died. If you had angered him, Thoth would cut out your heart. The Greeks revered the Moon goddesses

Artemis, Selene and Hecate, whom the Romans turned into Diana, Luna and the unexpectedly named Trivia. The Moon is still worshipped in the modern occult movement of Wicca, whose covens meet 13 times a year under the full Moon. At this time of new beginnings, the high priestess tries to 'draw down the moon', channelling the energies of the Moon goddess to Earth. In the 18th century, Sir William Blackstone described a '*lunatic*' in his popular *Commentaries on the Laws of England*: '... *one who has had understanding, but by reason of disease or grief has lost his reason. A lunatic, is, indeed, one that has lucid intervals, sometimes enjoying his senses and sometimes not and that frequently depends on the change of the moon.*' This definition was used when framing the Lunacy Act of 1745, and there is indeed evidence that hospitals, police stations and fire stations are busiest during full Moons. Men were supposed to turn into werewolves at full Moon.

NANTEOS and the HOLY GRAIL
One of the *Thirteen Treasures* in Welsh mythology that Merlin had to guard was the '*Dysgl of Rhydderch*', the dish of Rhydderch, a sixth-century King of Strathclyde. It was a wide platter, on

which '*whatever food was wished for thereon was instantly obtained*'. This was also a description of the '*Drinking Horn of King Bran the Blessed*', in which one received '*all the drink and food that one desired*'. '*Ceridwen's Cauldron*' contains all knowledge, and she gave birth to Taliesin. The '*Cauldron of Diwrnach*' would give the best cut of meat to a hero, but none to a coward. Bran the Blessed also had a cauldron in which dead men could be revived. This recurring motif of a platter or cauldron in Celtic mythology seems to be a precursor of the Holy Grail, or Cup of the Last Supper. The cup used by Jesus Christ at the Last Supper was supposed to have been brought by Joseph of Arimathea to Glastonbury, and taken from there to Ystrad-Fflur (Strata Florida Abbey) for safety. When Henry VIII dissolved the monasteries between 1536 and 1541, the last seven monks are supposed to have taken the cup into the protection of the Powell family at nearby Nanteos Mansion. A tradition says that the remaining fragment of the wooden bowl inspired Wagner, when staying there, to write his opera *Parsifal*. Fiona Mirylees, the last Powell heiress, placed the treasured '*cwpan*' in a bank safe in Herefordshire, as the Powell family left Nanteos Mansion in the 1960s. The remaining ancient fragment is about 4 inches (10 cm) across and made of olive wood. So little is left, because supplicants used to wish to take a tiny splinter home with them. Nanteos Mansion has no fewer than three ghosts: an early Mrs Powell who appears as a grey lady with a candelabra when the head of the household is about to die; secondly

a lady who left her deathbed to hide her jewellery which has still not been found; and a ghostly horseman who appears on the gravel drive at midnight.

NAZCA LINES These lines in the Nazca Desert in Peru were unnoticed when the Pan-American Highway was built straight across them. The Nazca Lines are geoglyphs (drawings on the ground), spread over 168 square miles (435 km²), comprising 13,000 lines and pictures. The huge drawings include representations of a hummingbird, monkey, spider and lizard, to name just a few. One monkey has a huge spiral tail 100 yards (90 m) long, there is a pelican 320 yards (290 m) long and some straight lines run for miles. The lines can only be appreciated from the air, and they were made by removing iron-oxide-coated stones and gravel to reveal the lighter soil underneath them. They were created during the Nazca culture in the area, between 200 BCE and 600 CE. It has been suggested that the Nazca Lines presuppose some form of manned flight (in order to see them), and that a hot air balloon was the only possible available technology. The most famous theory was advanced by Erich von Däniken, who proposed that the lines were, in fact, landing strips for alien spacecraft. Another theory contends that the lines are the remains of 'walking temples', where a large group of worshippers walked along a preset pattern dedicated to a particular holy entity. They may have been praying for water, as sources began to dry up over a period of hundreds of years, so that the rain gods would pity them and grant rain.

OAK ISLAND MONEY PIT

The most intriguing of all the sites associated with buried pirate treasure, with links to Captain Henry Morgan and Captain Kidd, was first discovered in 1795. It is an island on the south shore of Nova Scotia, Canada. A few years later, digging through layers of logs and clay, a stone tablet was found, and it was decoded to read: '*Forty Feet Below Two million Pounds Are Buried*'. Over the years, booby traps and an artificial beach have been discovered, along with an extremely complicated drainage system. Four men died in 1965 excavating the site. There is no space here to describe this remarkable site in detail, but several books have been written about it, and the easiest accessible information is found on the terrific *Swashbuckler's Cove* website, '*The Money Pit of Oak Island*'.

ROANOKE COLONY In 1584, Sir Walter Raleigh dispatched an expedition to the east coast of North America as Queen Elizabeth I had given him permission to colonize Virginia. He returned from the trip with two American Indians and samples of indigenous animals and plants. Between 1585 and 1587, two groups of colonists were landed on Roanoke Island (part of present day North Carolina) to establish their settlement. Following fights with the local native tribes, the first colony ran low on food and men to defend the settlement, so when Sir Francis Drake visited after a raiding voyage in the Caribbean and offered to take them back to England, they accepted and departed. In 1857 121 new colonists arrived and found the local natives (the Croatans) to be friendly. The first English child born in the Americas was the daughter of one of these colonists. The group tried to befriend some of the other tribes with which the previous colonists had fought, but this resulted in the killing of George Howe. The remaining members of the group convinced its leader to return to England to get help. The leader (John White) sailed back to England leaving behind 90 men, 17 women and 11 children. When White returned in August 1590, the settlement was deserted. There were no signs of a struggle and no remains were found. The only clue was the word '*Croatoan*' carved into a post of the fort and '*Cro*' carved into a nearby tree. The settlement became known as the Lost Colony and none of its members were ever seen again. Some speculation exists today which suggests that the settlers left to live with some of the nearby tribes. This is supported by the fact that many years later some of the tribes were practising Christianity and understood English.

THE ROSWELL INCIDENT

The Roswell UFO incident in New Mexico involved the alleged recovery of extraterrestrial debris, including alien corpses, from an object which crashed near Roswell, New Mexico in June or July 1947. On 8 July 1947, Roswell Army Air Field (RAAF) issued a press release stating that personnel had recovered a crashed '*flying disc*' from a nearby ranch, arousing intense media interest. Another press release a couple of days later said that the debris of a 'radar-tracking' device had been found. The case was forgotten for more than 30 years until an interview was published with Major Jesse Marcel who was involved with the original recovery of the debris in 1947. Marcel expressed his belief that the military had covered up the recovery of an alien spacecraft, and his story spread through UFO circles, especially after he gave an interview to *The National Enquirer* in February 1980. Over the following years, more witnesses and reports emerged, adding significant new details, including claims of a huge operation to recover alien craft, and aliens themselves, from as many as 11 crash sites. Witnesses were said to have been threatened, and in 1989 a former mortician claimed that alien autopsies had been carried out at the military base at Roswell. A 1995 Government report stated that the recovered debris was from the secret Project Mogul, which used high-altitude balloons to detect sound waves caused by Soviet atomic bomb tests and ballistic missiles. Its second report, in 1997, stated that witnesses had innocently transformed their memories of the recovery of anthropomorphic dummies from tests, and memories of those who died in military accidents.

SANTORINI AND THE TEN PLAGUES

The magical Greek island of Santorini (also called Thera) is all that remains of an enormous volcanic explosion. This Minoan Eruption (or Thera Eruption) occurred 3600 years ago when the Minoan civilization of Crete was at its height. The eruption left a large caldera surrounded by volcanic ash deposits hundreds of feet deep and led indirectly to the collapse of the Minoan civilization on the island of Crete 68 miles (110 km) to the south, through the creation of a gigantic tsunami that struck the island and the long-term effects of the ash cloud upon agriculture. In the Book of Exodus, ten calamities were inflicted on the Egyptians for their treatment of the Israelites. It is possible that this story relates to this tremendous explosion. The plagues were total darkness, the Nile turning to blood, fiery hailstorms, a fatal cattle plague, plagues of boils, frogs, lice, flies, locusts and finally the death of all the first-born children.

In *The Moses Legacy*, Graham Phillips writes that these could all have been caused by the volcano's enormous ash cloud blocking the Sun over the Nile delta. When Mt St Helens exploded in Washington State in 1980, a cloud of ash obscured the Sun for an area of 500 miles (800 km). Hot volcanic debris fell like hailstones, flattening crops. Because of the acidic dust everywhere, hundreds of people suffered skin lesions and cattle died. Fish were found floating dead in rivers and lakes, and water had to be purified before it was potable. In the Bible: '... *the fish died, the river* [Nile] *stank and the Egyptians could not drink of* the river.' After the Mt St Helen's eruption, there was a plague of frogs across Washington State. So many were killed on the roads that driving became dangerous, as the roads were so slimy. Swarms of frogs infested houses and water pipes. The volcanic ash had killed off fish but not submerged frogspawn. Tadpoles hatched and turned into frogs, unharmed by any natural predators such as herons and other wildlife that had fled the area. Insect reproduction in vast numbers has also been noted after volcanic eruptions, as again their natural predators are either dead or have moved away. The insects search for food outside the ash-layer. After the Martinique eruption of 1901, survivors were attacked by swarms of hungry flying ants which acted like locusts, consuming anything that was still growing.

SHANGRI-LA Shangri-La was the name of a fictional place described in the 1933 novel *Lost Horizon* by British author James Hilton. Shangri-La has since entered into the language as a hidden, perfect place often associated with long life, health and happiness.

SODOM AND GOMORRAH

'*The Lord rained on Sodom and Gomorrah brimstone and fire out of the Heaven*' according to the Old Testament. In the 19th century the explorer Henry Layard found a clay tablet in the remains of the library in the royal palace at Nineveh. This was the capital of the Assyrian Empire, near Mosul in Iraq. Recently the tablet's symbols were decoded, and it turns out to be a 700 BCE copy of notes made by a Sumerian astronomer observing an asteroid. It seems to be an eye-witness account of this asteroid

destroying Sodom and Gomorrah, cities on what is now the Jordan-Israel border. Using computers to recreate the night sky, scientists have pinpointed his sighting to just before dawn on 29 June in 3123 BCE. Around this time there was an asteroid which smashed into the Austrian Alps at Köfels. As it travelled close to the ground it would have left a trail of destruction caused by supersonic shock waves and then slammed into the ground with a cataclysmic impact. Dr Mark Hempsall who cracked the code of the Layard tablet said that at least 20 ancient myths record devastation of the type and on the scale of the asteroid's impact, including the Old Testament tale of the destruction of Sodom and Gomorrah, and the ancient Greek myth of how Phaeton, son of Helios, fell into the River Eridanus after losing control of his father's Sun chariot. The findings of Dr Hempsall and Alan Bond are published in their 2008 book, *A Sumerian Observation of the Köfels Impact Event.*

THE SPHINX - THE OLDEST SCULPTURE IN THE WORLD?

This greatest monumental sculpture in the ancient world is carved out of a single ridge of stone 240 feet (73 m) long and 66 feet (20 m) high. The head, which has a different texture to the body, and consequently less severe erosion, is a naturally occurring outcrop of harder stone. To form the lower body of the Sphinx, enormous blocks of stone were quarried from the base rock. These blocks were then used in the core masonry of the temples directly in front and to the south of the Sphinx. It appears that the Sphinx was restored by the Pharaoh Chephren during his 4th Dynasty reign, and its date is unknown. The 'Inventory Stele' was uncovered on the Giza plateau in the 19th century and records that Cheops (also known as Khufu, reigned 2589–2556 BCE), Chephren's predecessor, ordered a temple built alongside the Sphinx. Recent geologists have confirmed that the extreme erosion on the body of the Sphinx could not be the result of wind and sand, as has been universally assumed, but rather the result of water. Wind erosion cannot take place when the body of the Sphinx is covered by sand, and the Sphinx has been in this condition for nearly all of the last 5000 years until the chest was uncovered in 1817. Geologists agree that in the distant past Egypt was subjected to severe flooding. Additional evidence for the great age of the Sphinx may perhaps be indicated by the astronomical significance of its shape, being that of a lion. Every 2160 years, because of the precession of the equinoxes, the Sun at the vernal equinox rises against the stellar background of a different constellation. For the past 2000 years that constellation has been Pisces the fish, symbol of the

Christian age. Prior to the Age of Pisces it was the age of Aries the ram, and before that it was the Age of Taurus the bull. During the 1st and 2nd millennia BCE, approximately the Age of Aries, ram-oriented iconography was common in Dynastic Egypt, while during the Age of Taurus the bull-cult arose in Minoan Crete. Geological findings indicate that the Sphinx seems to have been sculpted sometime before 10,000 BCE, and this period coincides with the Age of Leo the lion, which lasted from 10,970 to 8810 BCE. Computer programmes are able to generate precise pictures of any portion of the night sky, as seen from different places on Earth, at any time in the distant past or future. Graham Hancock stated in *Heaven's Mirror*: '*Computer simulations show that in 10,500 BCE the constellation of Leo housed the sun on the spring equinox – i.e. an hour before dawn in that epoch Leo would have reclined due east along the horizon in the place where the sun would soon rise. This means that the lion-bodied Sphinx, with its due-east orientation, would have gazed directly on that morning at the one constellation in the sky that might reasonably be regarded as its own celestial counterpart.*' It would be wonderful if the 10,000 BCE theory could be proved, but most experts believe the Sphinx to have been built by Cheops around 2560 BCE.

ST ELVIS CHURCH St Elvis Parish is the smallest in Great Britain, and the title Rector of St Elvis was superior to that of the vicar of nearby St Teilo's in Solva. The name St Elvis has appeared on maps

The Seven Wonders of the World

These are all found upon the Mediterranean rim, and seven were chosen because the Ancient Greeks believed it signified perfection and plenty. Our 'lucky' number seven stems from this belief. Both Herodotus (484–*c.*425 BCE) and Callimachus (*c.*305–240 BCE) made lists of '*thaumata*', 'things to be seen', which included:

1. **The Colossus of Rhodes** was a statue of the Greek god Helios, built between 292 and 280 BCE, and straddling the entrance to the harbour. Plated with brass, it stood over 107 feet (33 m) high on white marble blocks, themselves 50 feet (15 m) high.

2. **The Great Pyramid of Khufu at Giza** Erected around 2560 BCE as a tomb for the Pharaoh Khufu, Hemiunu, its architect, used 2,300,000 blocks of stone, each weighing more than a ton, and the site covered 13 acres (5 ha). It was the tallest building in the world for 4500 years, until the Eiffel Tower was built in 1889.

3. **The Hanging Gardens of Babylon** in Iraq were probably built by Nebuchadnezzar II around 600 BCE to please his wife and remind her of the fragrant plants of her homeland of Persia. A new theory proposes that they were built at Nineveh on the Tigris by Sennacherib, king of Assyria.

4. **The Ishtar Gate,** later replaced by the **The Lighthouse (Pharos) of Alexandria** The Ishtar Gate was in the earliest lists, and a reconstruction of one of the double gates is in Berlin's Pergamon Museum. It was the eighth gate to the Inner City of Babylon, made in 575 BCE for Nebuchadnezzar II and dedicated to the goddess Ishtar. It formed part of the walls of Babylon in Iraq, and most of its sculptures are now in Germany. The Lighthouse of Alexandria was built between 280 and 247 BCE on a small island off Alexandria, Egypt, and was between 390 and 460 feet (120 to 140 m) tall, an incredible achievement. Its ruins can be seen below the waters in the Eastern harbour.

5. The Mausoleum of Mausolus at Halicarnassus was built

around 350 BCE near Bodrum in Turkey to hold the bodies of Mausolus, a Persian *satrap* or ruler, and Artemisia, his wife and sister.

6. The Statue of Zeus at Olympia

The great Phidias sculpted the seated stature in about 432 BCE for the Temple of Zeus. In the 1950s Phidias's workshop was found here, with a cup bearing his name.

7. The Temple of Artemis at Ephesus was

constructed around 550 BCE in Turkey but hardly anything remains.

The above list was compiled in the Middle Ages, by which time all but the Great Pyramid had been destroyed. As a result, other lists were compiled of the 'Seven Wonders' e.g.:

The Catacombs of Kom el Shoqafa
The Colosseum
The Great Wall of China
Hagia Sophia
The Leaning Tower of Pisa
The Porcelain Tower of Nanjing
Stonehenge
Cairo Citadel
Cluny Abbey
Ely Cathedral
The Taj Mahal

In 2006 the newspaper *USA Today* in conjunction with the television programme *Good Morning America* revealed a list of 'New Seven Wonders' chosen by six judges. An eighth wonder, the Grand Canyon of Arizona, was chosen following viewer feedback. They were:

1. Potala Palace, Lhasa, Tibet
2. Jerusalem's Old City
3. Polar Ice Caps
4. Papahanaumokuakea Marine National Monument, Hawaii
5. The Internet
6. Maya Ruins of Yucatán Peninsula, Mexico
7. Great Migration of the Serengeti and Masai Mara, Tanzania and Kenya
8. Grand Canyon, Arizona

In 2007 a 'New Seven Wonders of the World' was announced, from a shortlist of 200 existing monuments. One wonders why Carnac in Brittany does not feature in any of these lists:

Chichen Itza, Mexico *c.*600 CE
Christ the Redeemer Statue, Brazil 1931
Colosseum, Rome *c.*80 CE
Great Pyramid of Giza c.2560 BCE
Great Wall of China Fifth century BCE −16th century CE
Machu Picchu, Peru *c.*1450
Taj Mahal *c.*1648 CE
Petra Jordan, *c.*150 BCE

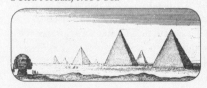

since at least the 16th century. On the site is the 5000-year-old St Elvis cromlech, a huge burial chamber with two tombs, and a few yards away the foundations of a square tower, possibly a lookout post or storage barn for the monks on this site. The remains of the church are large, and unusually aligned north-south. Nearby is St Elvis Holy Well, which was still pumping out 360 gallons (1636 lit) an hour during the great 1976 drought, and had to be used to water the cattle at that time. The well is near St Elvis Farm, where a barn was built in the early 20th century from the dressed stones of St Elvis Church. The last marriages took place in St Elvis Church in the 1860s and are recorded in the Haverfordwest Archives. The site, where the Preseli Hills sweep down to the sea, is just two fields inland, but would have been well hidden from Irish and Viking pirates. St Elvis Rocks, off the mouth of the picturesque Solva Harbour, are now known as Green Scar, Black Scar and The Mare. The name 'Elvis' as a place-name is only found here in all of Europe, and it seems to be a corruption of St Ailbe, so St Aelfyw's monastery became St Elvis' Church. Two very important ley lines are said to meet here, one going to Stonehenge, and the site is littered with graves. The farmer has said that often in building sheds etc., he has seen 'chalk-marks' in the soil, which when touched powder into dust, i.e. ancient bones. The holy well was not recorded by Francis Jones, but local tradition is that St David was baptised by his cousin St Elvis here, with water from the holy well, in the font at St Elvis Church. This font is now in St Teilo's in nearby Solva. St David's Cathedral is just a few miles away. A cross-marked sixth-century pillar, formerly a gatepost, was taken to St Teilo's Church, but its partner post was 'lost' in 1959. Even more intriguing, and of massive historical importance, is a square stone, with the simple face of a man carved into it. It is thought that National Trust employees used it to repair a field-bank. There are extremely few Dark Age facial representations among the ancient stones of Wales, and a non-intrusive survey may well find it. It was formerly in the centre of the ruined church and had holes bored into its top and bottom as sockets to allow it to act as a door, perhaps to a relic, which may make it unique. There is no record of this stone except in the memory of the farmer and his son who own the land, which is why it is being recorded here. This author noted in a previous book the name Elvis from near the Preseli Mountains, and his twin brother, father and mother all having Welsh names (Jesse Garon, Vernon and Gladys). The first recorded Presley in America was David Presley, another Welsh saint's name. There was international publicity on a 'Was Elvis Welsh?' theme in media after this comment was published. Perhaps the St Elvis holy well water should be bottled and exported to the USA for drinkers to order a 'bourbon and Elvis'.

THE TAOS HUM This is a low-pitched sound heard in numerous places worldwide, especially in the United States, Great Britain and northern Europe. It is usually heard only in quiet environments, and is often described as sounding like a distant diesel engine. As it has proven undetectable by microphones or VLF antennae, its source and nature is a mystery. In 1997 the US Congress directed scientists and observers from research institutes to look into a strange low frequency noise, a 'hum', heard by residents in and around the small town of Taos, New Mexico. It has given its name to this unexplained phenomena.

TEOTIHUACAN, THE CITY OF GODS

This was a great city, 25 miles (40 km) northeast of the ancient lake of Texcoco, which is the present-day site of Mexico City. It is Mexico's greatest archaeological visitor attraction. It was the largest city in the pre-Columbian Americas covering some 14–16 square miles (5.40 km²), with a population of between 100,000 to 250,000. It was inhabited from *c.*500 BCE until its violent end in 750 CE when much of the city was burned down. The site was later excavated by the Aztecs who gave it the name of Teotihuacan, *'the place of those who have the road of the gods.'* The pyramids of the Sun and the Moon dominate the site, along with the Temple of Quetzalcoatl, in a vast complex called the Ciudadela (Citadel) which covers 133,000 square yards (111,000 m²). These are located with other major constructions on a 2½ mile (4 km) causeway (remembered as *'the road of the gods'*) called the 'Avenue of the Dead'. Only recently has a cave and tunnel system under the Pyramid of the Sun been excavated. Enormous, thick sheets of mica were found by archaeologists on the fifth level of the Sun Pyramid. Later, around 400 yards (365 m) from the Sun Pyramid, another two mica slabs were found, 92 feet (8.5 m²) square, near the Avenue of the Dead. The sheets form two layers, one laid directly on top of

the other. Mica is a substance containing different metals, depending on the kind of rock formation in which it is found. As it sits underneath a stone floor, its use was obviously not decorative, but functional. These huge glittering sheets were identified as a type of mica that is found in Brazil, and nowhere else. How and why was this particular type of mica removed and transported some 2000 miles (3200 km) to be incorporated into the buildings? How could something this large be excavated, processed and transported in a 'Stone Age' period of history and still remain intact? We do not know the people who built the city. Similar finds of South American mica were discovered in certain Olmec sites.

THE TERRACOTTA ARMY AND THE ELIXIR OF LIFE

Emperor Qin Shi Huang (259–210 BCE), was king of the Chinese state of Qin during the *'Warring States Period'*, and became the first emperor of a unified China in 221. This first emperor of the Qin Dynasty then built a massive road system and the first Great Wall of China. He burned and outlawed many books to ensure stability, and built himself a city-sized mausoleum protected by 'The Terracotta Army'. As emperor, he searched feverishly for the *'elixir of life'* and visited Zhifu Island in the Bohai Sea three times looking for an elixir to try and achieve immortality. On the island there was a legend of a *'Mountain of Immortality'*, and he left the following inscriptions: *'Arrived at Fu, and carved the stone'* (218 BCE); and *'Came to Fu, saw enormous stone, and shot one fish'* (210 BCE). He sent a Zhifu islander with ships carrying hundreds of young men and women in search of the mystical Penglai Mountain where eight Immortals reputedly lived. They were sent to find Anqi Sheng, a 1000-year-old magician whom the emperor had supposedly met in his travels. These people never returned, because they knew that if they came back without the promised elixir, they would be executed. Legends claim that they reached Japan and colonized it. In 211 BCE a large meteor is said to have fallen near the lower reaches of the Yellow River. On it an unknown person inscribed the words *'The First Emperor will die and his land will be divided'*. No one would confess to the deed, so all the people living nearby were put to death. The stone was then burned and pulverized. Emperor Qin died touring eastern China, about two months away by road from his capital Xianyang. It was said that he succumbed after swallowing mercury pills, meant to make him immortal, but containing a fatal dose of the metal. After his death, his prime minister, who was accompanying him, began to fear that the news of his death could trigger an uprising or power struggle. It would take two months for him and his government officials to return to the capital, and it would not be possible to prevent a war, so he decided to conceal the death of the emperor while he journeyed back to Xianyang. Most of the imperial entourage accompanying the emperor was left ignorant of his death. The prime minister ordered that two carts containing rotten fish should be carried immediately before and after the wagon of the emperor. Trusted eunuchs also pulled down the shades so that no one could see his face, changed his clothes daily, and brought food. All conversations with the emperor had to be held via the prime minister. This was to prevent people from noticing the foul smell emanating from the wagon of the emperor, where his body was starting to decompose severely in the hot summer.

Qin Shi Huang's tomb was one of the first projects undertaken in his time as emperor of China. In 215 BCE, he ordered 300,000 men to begin construction. Other Chinese sources state that he ordered 720,000 non-paid labourers to build it to his specifications, but it is now thought that only 16,000 men were involved. The main tomb containing the emperor has yet to be opened and there is evidence suggesting that it remains relatively intact – he is said to be suspended in a pool of mercury. A description of the tomb refers to replicas of palaces and scenic towers, 100 rivers made of mercury, representations of the heavenly bodies and crossbows rigged to shoot anyone who tried to break in. The tomb was built on Li Mountain, 25 miles (45 km) from Xi'an. Archaeologists have inserted probes deep into the tomb, which reveal abnormally high levels of mercury, 100 times the naturally occurring rate. Most of the workmen who built the tomb were killed. The tomb lies under an earthen pyramid 250 feet (76 m) high and around 3770 square feet (350 m²) in area.

Only a portion of the site is presently excavated. The Terracotta Army statues were discovered by a group of farmers digging wells in 1974. The soldiers were created with a series of mix-and-match clay moulds, and then further individualized, so that each statue was unique. The figures vary in height from 6 feet (1.8 m) to 6 feet 4 inches (1.93 m), according to their roles, with the tallest being the generals. The statues include warriors, chariots, horses, state officials, acrobats, strongmen and musicians. Current estimates are that in the three pits containing the Terracotta Army there are over 8000 soldiers, 130 chariots with 520 horses and 150 cavalry horses, the majority of which are still buried. Each soldier's face is different, and they were all once painted.

TIAHUANACO GIANT BLOCKS

Near the southern shores of Lake Titicaca in Bolivia, Tiahuanaco was a major sacred ceremonial centre and focal point of a culture that spread across much of the region. It is a mystery because some researchers estimate that it is 17,000 years old, and because of its peculiar stone technology. There is a stone pyramid still there, but many beautifully carved stones were stripped from the site to build the cathedral in La Paz, Bolivia and other great buildings. The central and most conspicuous portion of the ruins, which cover almost a square mile (2.6 km²), consists of a great, rectangular mound of earth, originally terraced, each terrace supported by a massive wall of cut stones, and the whole surmounted by structures built of stone, parts of the foundations of which are still distinct. This structure is called the 'Fortress' and there are temples nearby. The most remarkable monument is the great monolithic gateway, too massive to be transported away. Just 12 miles (19 km) from the coast of sacred Lake Titicaca, Tiahuanaco seems the source of the creation myths, the social order and the extraordinary advances in astronomy that are a feature of South American cultures. The structure known as the *Puma Punka* seems to be the remains of a great wharf or pier (in the past Tiahuanaco was on Lake Titicaca's shores) and a massive, four-part, collapsed building. One of the construction blocks from which the pier was fashioned weighs an estimated 440 tons (447 tonnes), and several other blocks are between 100 and 150 tons (102 to 152 tonnes). The quarry for these giant blocks lay on the western shore of Titicaca, 10 miles (16 km) away. There is no known technology in the ancient Andean world that could have transported stones of such massive weight and size. The Andean people of 500 CE, with their simple reed boats, could not have moved them. Writers have suggested that these findings, and the astronomical alignments of the site, strongly point to the likelihood that the original Tiahuanaco civilization flourished thousands of years before the period assumed by conventional archaeologists. They believe that Tiahuanaco may be, along with Teotihuacan in Mexico, Baalbeck in Lebanon, the Sphinx and the Great Pyramid in Egypt, a surviving fragment of a long lost civilization.

The Puma Punku pyramid on the site was built with blocks weighing 200 tons (203 tonnes) and over, brought on to a plateau 13,000 feet (4000 m) high. There were no trees to act as rollers, as at Stonehenge, and the wheel had not yet been invented. Once the enormous stones were brought to the site, they were cut so precisely that they could be fitted together like puzzle pieces. Some of the stones have perfectly straight grooves in them that are only about a third of an inch (1 cm) deep, but the stones are made of diorite, the hardest granite in the world. Diorite needs diamond-tipped tools or water-blasting to work it today, but the builders placed these 200-ton stones together precisely. In the pyramid are red sandstone blocks, the largest of which are around 25 x 16 x 4 feet (7.6 x 5 x 1.2 m) and 25 x 8 x 6 feet (7.6 x 2.4 x 1.8 m), weighing 131 and 85 tons (133 and 96 tonnes) respectively. Archaeologists concluded that these and other red sandstone blocks were transported up a steep incline from a quarry near Lake Titicaca roughly 7 miles (11 km) away. Smaller andesite blocks that were used for stone facing and carvings came from quarries within the Copacabana peninsula and other places over 60 miles (96 km) away.

THE TOMB OF ALEXANDER THE GREAT

Alexander the Great died on the banks of the Euphrates River at Babylon in June 323 BCE. He wanted his body thrown into the river so that his corpse would disappear. Alexander reasoned that a myth would grow up that he had vanished into heaven to spend eternity at the side of the god Ammon (Amun) whom he claimed had fathered him. Alexander's generals,

however, planned a magnificent funeral. En route to its destination, probably in Macedonia, the funeral procession was met in Syria by Ptolemy, a Macedonian general in Alexander's army, who diverted the mummified body to Egypt where it was buried in a tomb at Memphis. In 305 BCE Ptolemy proclaimed himself king of Egypt as Ptolemy I, inaugurating the Ptolemaic Dynasty. Later, either in the reign of Ptolemy or his son Ptolemy II, the body was removed from Memphis and reburied in Alexandria. Ptolemy IV Philopator (222/21–205 BCE) later placed the bodies of his forebears, as well as that of Alexander, in a new communal mausoleum in Alexandria. Now there were three tombs for Alexander in Memphis and Alexandria. Neither the first or second tomb has been found. The third tomb was located at the crossroads of the major north-south and east-west arteries of Alexandria.

Octavian, the future Roman emperor Augustus, visited Alexandria shortly after the suicide of Cleopatra VII in 30 BCE. He is said to have viewed the body of Alexander, placing flowers on the tomb and a golden diadem upon Alexander's mummified head. Suetonius recorded: '*About this time Octavian had the sarcophagus and body of Alexander the Great brought forth from its inner sanctum, and, after gazing on it, showed his respect by placing upon it a golden crown and strewing it with flowers; and being then asked whether he wished to see the tomb of the Ptolemies as well, he replied, "My wish was to see a king, not corpses".*' Suetonius also noted that c.40 CE '*Caligula frequently wore the dress of a triumphing general, even before his campaign, and sometimes the breast-plate of Alexander the Great, which he had taken from his sarcophagus.'* Dio Cassius tells that in 200 CE: '[Emperor] *Severus inquired into everything, including things that were very carefully hidden; for he was the kind of person to leave nothing, either human or divine, uninvestigated. Accordingly, he took away from practically all the sanctuaries all the books that he could find containing any secret lore, and he sealed up the tomb of Alexander; this was in order that no one in future should either view his body or read what was mentioned in the aforesaid books.'* Herodian noted the last visit by a Roman Emperor, of Caracalla in 215 CE: '*As soon as Caracalla entered the city with his whole army he went up to the temple, where he made a large number of sacrifices and laid quantities of incense on the altars. Then he went to the tomb of Alexander where he took off and laid upon the grave the purple cloak he was wearing and the rings of precious stones and his belts and anything else of value he was carrying.'*

The tomb was probably damaged and perhaps even looted during the political disturbances that ravaged Alexandria during the reign of Aurelian shortly after 270 CE. By the fourth century, the tomb's location was no longer known, if one can trust the accounts of several of the early Church Fathers. John Chrysostom, *c.*400 CE wrote: '*For, tell me, where is the tomb of Alexander? Show it me and tell me the day on which he died… his tomb even his own people know not.'* After renewed excavations at the site of the so-called Oracle Temple in the Siwa Oasis in 1989,

it was claimed that Alexander was buried there because he wanted to be near his father Amun. Alexander visited Siwa in 331 BCE to consult a famous oracle of the god Amun. The oracle had supposedly proclaimed Alexander to be Amun's son. The location is 330 miles (530 km) west of Cairo near the Libyan border.

THE UNFINISHED OBELISK

This 3000-year-old obelisk in Egypt's Aswan quarry developed a flaw during quarrying and was never completed, but left to lie still attached to the rock. If it had been extracted and erected as originally conceived, the *Unfinished Obelisk* would have stood 137 feet (42 m) tall and weighed 1185 tons (1200 tonnes), dwarfing all others. The largest surviving obelisk, the *Lateran Obelisk* in Rome, rises 105 feet (32 m) and weighs 455 tons (462 tonnes).

Tombs, Standing Stones and Dolmens

Cromlech at Plas Newydd, Anglesey

Kit's Coty neolithic dolmen near Aylesford, Kent

Trevethy Stone, a dolmen or cromlech near Liskeard in Cornwall

*Constantine dolmen,
Cornwall*

*Harold's Stones, Trelech,
Monmouthshire*

*The Cheesewring,
Bodmin Moor,
Cornwall*

The Tower of the Winds

On Athens's Roman agora, overlooked by the Acropolis and the Parthenon, stands the octagonal marble building called the Horologion of Andronicos. It was erected by the Macedonian astronomer Andronicos around 50 BCE. Known as The Tower of the Winds, it was made of the same Pentelic marble as used by the greatest sculptors of Ancient Greece and from which the Elgin Marbles are made. The marble looks like shining glass, and the tower stands 40 feet (12 m) high. It was originally topped by a revolving bronze weather vane depicting the god Triton. To the ancients, the winds had divine powers and on the frieze of each of the eight sides below the conical rooftop there is a sculpted figure of the wind deity ruling the compass point to which it faces. The term *Horologion* also acknowledges the other features of the tower that Andronicos incorporated: sundials and a complicated internal water clock which was supplied from the Acropolis above.

Wind Direction	Wind Deity	Sculpted Character
North	Boreas	Man wearing a heavy cloak, blowing through a twisted shell
Northeast	Kaikias	Man carrying and emptying a shield of small round objects
East	Euros	Young man holding a cloak full of fruit and grain
Southeast	Apeliotes	Old man wrapped tightly in a cloak against the elements
South	Notos	Man emptying an urn and producing a shower of water
Southwest	Livas	Boy pushing the stern of a ship, promising a good sailing wind
West	Zephyros	Youth carrying flowers into the air
Northwest	Skiron	Bearded man with a bronze pot full of hot ashes and charcoal

THE UNIVERSE AND DARK
STUFF Visible matter, such as stars, gas, galaxies and dust, only makes up a tiny fraction of the mass of the universe, according to scientists. They give the term 'dark matter' or 'dark stuff' to the mass we cannot see through an astronomical telescope. It does not emit any light to be visually detectable, and its presence can only be deduced by its effects on visible matter through the action of gravity.

VALHALLA - HOME OF THE
GODS From the Old Norse *vair* (slain warrior) and *holl* (hall), in Norse mythology this was an enormous hall in Asgard, where those who died heroically in battle lived for eternity, feasting and drinking with Thor, and other gods and goddesses. Within the main hall of Valhalla exists Thor's hall Bilskimir, which contains 540 rooms. Of all the halls within Valhalla, the god Odin states that he thinks his son Thor's may be greatest. Odin rules the hall, and the warriors were selected by Odin's handmaidens, the *Valkyries*, who served ale and mead to the dead heroes in the skulls of their defeated enemies. It seems that some insanely brave warriors, the '*beserkers*', took magic mushrooms to reach a state of heightened awareness before going into battle.

VENUS - THE NIGHT STAR Not a
star, but a planet, it is the brightest object apart from the Moon in the sky at night. Its day is longer than its year, as it takes longer to spin on its axis (243 days) than it does to orbit the Sun (224.7 days).

One would think that Mercury, being the planet closest to the Sun, would be the hottest planet, with a temperature on its equator of 700 Kelvin (427° C or 800° F). Even at its poles, the temperature is 380 Kelvin (107° C or 225° F). At night, however, the temperatures drop down to just 100 Kelvin, or -173° C (-279° F). It is so hot in the day and cold at night because it has no atmosphere to trap the Sun's heat. However, Venus has the thickest atmosphere of all the planets, at 93 times the pressure we experience at sea level on Earth. The Venusian atmosphere is almost entirely composed of carbon dioxide, the 'greenhouse gas' which has the property of efficiently trapping heat from the Sun. Thus the average temperature on Venus is 735 Kelvin (462° C, or 864° F). Furthermore, it is the same temperature everywhere across Venus, whether day or night. Its thick atmosphere traps the heat from the Sun, and the weather distributes this temperature around the entire planet.

VITRIFIED FORTS These are crude stone enclosures found around Europe, often defensive hillforts, whose walls have been subjected to fire. They are generally situated on hills offering strong defensive positions. The walls vary in size, a few being upwards of 12 feet (3.6 m) high, and are so broad that they present the appearance of embankments. Weak parts of the defence are strengthened by double or triple walls, and occasionally vast lines of ramparts, composed of large blocks of unhewn and unvitrified stones, envelop the vitrified centre at some distance from it. No lime or cement has been found in any of these structures, and the walls seem to have been consolidated by the fusion of the rocks of which they are built. This fusion, caused by the application of intense heat, is not equally complete in the various forts. In some cases the stones are only partially melted and calcined. Elsewhere their adjoining edges are fused, so that they are firmly cemented together. Often pieces of rock are covered in a glassy enamel-like coating which binds them into a uniform whole. Sometimes the entire length of the wall presents one solid mass of vitreous substance. It is not clear why the walls were subjected to vitrification, as heating actually weakens the structure. Vitrification is a chemical process by which silicate-based rocks are turned into a glass-like amorphous solid. Calcination is the loss of moisture, reduction or oxidation in carbonate rocks. Battle damage is unlikely to be the cause, as the walls must have been subjected to carefully maintained fires to ensure they were consistently hot enough for vitrification to take place. About 50 examples have been discovered in Scotland, but around 100 others have been found in Ireland, Germany, Portugal,

Hungary and France. There are none in Wales, which has hundreds of hillforts, or in England. The burned forts range in age from the Neolithic to the Roman period. The heating was so extreme that some or all of the structures were vitrified or calcined. Granite, basalt, gneiss or other silicate rocks begin to crystallize at temperatures about 1200° F (658° C), and melt and vitrify when exposed to temperatures between 1920 and 2250° F (1050 and 1235° C). Carbonate rocks such as limestone and dolomite become calcined when exposed to temperatures of 1472° F (800° C). The reason for this remains a mystery.

THE WHITE PYRAMID

Scientists believed that there were pyramids in China, but popular stories about them really began to circulate after the Second World War. A US Air Force pilot named James Gaussman saw a white-topped pyramid during a flight between China and India in 1945: '*I banked to avoid a mountain and we came out over a level valley. Directly below was a gigantic white pyramid. It looked like something out of a fairy tale. It was encased in shimmering white. This could have been metal, or some sort of stone. It was pure white on all sides. The remarkable thing was the capstone, a huge piece of jewel-like material that could have been crystal. There was no way we could have landed, although we wanted to. We were struck by the immensity of the thing.*' The world's 'largest' pyramid was rumoured to be in Qin Lin county in a 'forbidden zone' of China. It was estimated at nearly 1000 feet (300 m) high and made of impounded earth and clay, and believed to hold vast tombs. (The Great

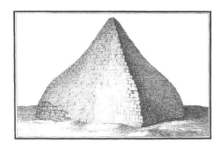

Pyramid of Giza is 450 feet/137 m). The Chinese government originally denied the existence of its pyramids, but the Maoling Mausoleum has been open since 1978 where are displayed the artefacts found at the 'White Pyramid'. Chinese pyramids are the ancient mausoleums and burial mounds of early Chinese emperors and their relatives. About 38 are located between 16–25 miles (26–40 km) northwest of Xi'an, in Shaanxi province. The most famous is the Mausoleum of the First Qin Emperor, a mile west of the Terracotta Warriors (see page 129) site. Chinese pyramids were also built during the Han, Tang, Song and Western Xia dynasties. They have flat tops, and thus are more similar in shape to the Mexican Teotihuacan pyramids (q.v.) rather than Egyptian pyramids. The tomb of Emperor Wu, (157–87 BCE), Maoling Mausoleum is about 25 miles (40 km) from Xian City. This mausoleum is called '*the Chinese Pyramid*' since it is not only the largest, but it also held the richest burial contents of all the mausoleums of emperors constructed during the Western Han Dynasty (206 BCE–24 CE). It took 53 years to build, with the emperor devoting a third of his income each year to its construction. It is about 153 feet (47 m) high and measures about 700 feet (213 m) along each side at the bottom.

Around Maoling Mausoleum, more than 20 tombs now still accompany Emperor Wu. Most of them are the burial places of imperial wives, meritorious ministers and worthy nobles. The tomb chamber was reached through four tomb passages, each of which was wide enough to allow a cart drawn by six horses to pass through. Swords and crossbows were concealed behind the four inlets of the tomb chamber to guard against thieves and looters. The tomb pit contained six horse-drawn carts, figures of tigers, leopards, and other animals; gold, silver and other precious objects; silk, cloth and grain; and daily necessities. The dead emperor had a piece of jade placed in his mouth, and was wrapped in jade clothes sewn with gold thread. At the end of the Western Han Dynasty, the *Red Eyebrows Army* (their brows were painted red as a mark of identification) took away gold and silver and numerous other treasures from the tomb.

WHY IS THE EARTH PERFECT?

Earth's gravity holds a thin layer of nitrogen and oxygen gases around the planet, and it extends about 50 miles (80 km) above the surface. If the Earth was smaller, this atmosphere would be chemically unachievable, as is the case with Mercury. If Earth was larger, the atmosphere would contain free hydrogen, like Jupiter. Only our atmosphere gives us the correct mixture of gases to sustain life as we know it. The temperature swings on our planet are roughly from -30 degrees to +120° F (-34 to 49° C). The Earth also lies at the optimum distance from the Sun, as if it were closer or more distant, we could not survive the more extreme temperatures that we would experience.

The Earth orbits the Sun at almost 67,000 mph (108,000 kph). As the Earth rotates daily on its axis, the whole surface of the Earth is warmed and cooled every day. The Moon is the perfect size and distance from the Earth for its gravitational pull to create ocean tides and currents. Thus ocean waters do not stagnate nor flood uncontrollably across the continents. Plants, animals and human beings consist mostly of water (about two-thirds of the human body is water). The presence of water allows us to live in an environment of fluctuating temperature changes, while maintaining our bodies at a steady 98.6° F (37° C) degrees. Its solvent properties mean that thousands of chemicals, minerals and nutrients can be carried throughout our bodies and into the smallest blood vessels. Because it is chemically neutral, water enables food, medicines and minerals to be absorbed and used by the body. Water has a unique surface tension, so that in plants it can flow upwards against the pull of gravity, bringing life-giving nutrients to the top of the tallest trees. Water also freezes from the top down and floats, so fish can live underneath it in the winter. About 97 per cent of the Earth's water is in the oceans. Salt is removed from the water that is taken up into the atmosphere from the seas, and rainfall is distributed across the world, ensuring life. The perfection of this system is often used as an argument for God's existence providing evidence of his *'intelligent design'* of life on Earth.

ZIMBABWE - THE GREAT RUINS

The Great Zimbabwe Ruins are a huge World Heritage Site, featuring large towers and structures built out of millions of stones, balanced perfectly on top of one another without the aid of mortar. The Great Zimbabwe society is believed to have become increasingly influential during the 11th century, trading gold and ivory for Portuguese and Arab porcelain, cloth and glass. As the Great Zimbabwe people flourished, they built an empire whose huge stone buildings which would eventually spread over 200 square miles (500 km²). By the 15th century, Great Zimbabwe was in decline due to overpopulation, the effects of disease and political disagreements. Formed of huge, rectangular granite stones, the ruins form an amazing complex. The structures were built by indigenous African people between 1250 and 1450 CE. The Great Enclosure has walls 36 feet (11 m) high and 18 feet (5.5 m) thick, extending approximately 820 feet (250 m). The Great Enclosure is the largest single ancient structure south of the Sahara. Two high walls form a narrow parallel passage, 190 feet (58 m)

long, that allows direct access to the famous Conical Tower. The ruins were not rediscovered until 1867, and during these colonial times of 'white supremacy' when the country was Rhodesia, many believed that Great Zimbabwe could not possibly have been built by black Africans, but by Phoenicians or Arabs. Not until 1929 was it conclusively proved that the great stone buildings were built by black Africans.

CHAPTER 4
Flying Monsters, Mysteries, Odd Happenings, Strange Sightings *and* Legends

AIRSHIPS OF 1896-7 In the United States at the end of the 19th century, phantom airships were reported over too wide an area for them to be explained away as prototypes. The sightings began over Sacramento, California in November 1896, when hundreds of people witnessed a huge glowing oblong object with tapered ends, a searchlight and propellers. It was seen three nights later 80 miles (130 km) away in Oakland, near San Francisco. Four days later an airship of a different description was noted in Tacoma, Washington, 700 miles (1125 km) away. Eight days after this, an airship landed north of San Francisco. On the night of 1 April 1897, thousands of people saw a ship about 30 feet (9 m) long over Kansas City, Missouri, and the next evening it was seen 160 miles (260 km) northeast at Omaha, Nebraska. The following night it was seen at Topeka in Kansas, and then again at Omaha. On 7 April it was over Sioux City, Iowa, and on 10 April at Chicago, being again seen by thousands of people. Airships were then seen over Iowa, Missouri, Kansas, Kentucky, Texas, Tennessee, New York and West Virginia. The first known successful flight of an airship was around the Eiffel Tower in 1901, and in that year Zeppelin built his first airship, which achieved a stately 18 miles per hour (29 kph). The US airship sightings included reports of much higher speeds and even the presence of aliens. On 16 April 1897 the *Saginaw Courier and Herald* stated that on 14 April an airship landed at Howard City, Michigan. A naked alien emerged, who used musical notes to try and communicate. On 20 April 1897 the *Houston Daily Post* told of a small person climbing down a rope to cut a snagged rope free from an airship.

THE ALERION There is only one pair of alerion in the world according to the myth. The alerion is an eagle-like bird and is considered to be *'Lord of the Birds'*. *'It is larger than an eagle, with razor-sharp wings and is the colour of fire. When the female is sixty years old, she lays two eggs, which take sixty days to hatch. When the young are born, the parents, accompanied by a retinue of other birds, fly to the sea, plunge in, and drown. The other birds return to the nest to care for the young alerion until they are old enough to fly'* (the *Bestaire* of Pierre de Beauvais). The alerion in heraldry is the equivalent of an eagle.

ALIEN ABDUCTIONS Many people believe that they, or someone they know, have been abducted by aliens aboard UFOs. The first modern record is that of Antonio Villas Boas in 1957, who claims that he was abducted late at night when working on an Argentinean farm. In 1961, there was the celebrated case of Barney and Betty Hill who were driving home to New Hampshire after holidaying in Canada. They drove towards a light moving over the forests and stopped their car. Using binoculars, Barney saw a huge spaceship and walked towards it, where he saw over a dozen aliens looking at him. Panicking, he raced back to his car and drove off. The couple became drowsy and heard a 'beeping sound'. Arriving home, they found that their watches were not working, and later discovered that they had taken two hours longer to travel home than they expected. Betty Hill began to have flashbacks and vivid dreams of being subjected to medical examination by aliens. In 1964 she began to visit a Boston psychiatrist, Dr Benjamin Simon, who used regression hypnosis to take her back to the night she was 'abducted'. Betty Hill believes that she had a probe inserted via her navel, as did another 'abductee', Betty Andreasson. Another abductee, Kathie Davis, believes she was taken aboard a UFO several times, undergoing artificial inseminations, resulting in nine 'hybrid children'.

ANGELS 'Angel' comes from the Greek *angelos*, which is possibly a translation of the Hebrew word *mal'akh*, meaning messenger. We tend to associate angels with winged immortals in human form, carrying messages to and from Heaven.

The Earliest Winged Deities: There is a room called the 'vulture shrine' in the earliest known town of Çatal Hüyük, that is being excavated at Anatolia, Turkey. It dates back to 6500 BCE and the vulture image appears to represent a god-form, responsible for removing the head (perhaps the soul) of the dead. The inhabitants may have practised 'sky-burials' (where corpses are left to the birds to eat). There is some evidence to suggest that over time, as this culture developed, the bird image evolved into that of a *'vulture-goddess'*. One of the painted murals from Çatal Hüyük seems to show a human being dressed in a vulture skin. In the 1950s archaeologists excavated a cave site in Kurdistan. It had been used for burials by the Zawi Chemi people around 8870 BCE according to carbon-dating. They found a number of goat skulls placed next to the wing bones of large predatory birds, including the bearded vulture, the griffon vulture, the white-tailed sea eagle and the great bustard. It is suggested that the wings of certain very large birds were used as part of a ritualistic costume, worn either for personal decoration or for ceremonial purposes. The scientists reported that, *'The Zawi Chemi people must have endowed these great raptorial birds with special powers, and the faunal remains we have described for the site must represent special ritual paraphernalia. Certainly, the remains represent a concerted effort by a goodly number of people just to hunt down and capture such a large number of birds and goats… either the wings were saved to pluck out the feathers, or that wing fans were made, or that they were used as part of a costume for a ritual. One of the murals from a Çatal Huyuk shrine… depicts just such a ritual scene; i.e. a human figure dressed in a vulture skin.'*

Within living memory Kurdistan has been home to three indigenous angel cults, the most famous being the Yezidis of Iraqi Kurdistan. Their belief system centres on supreme angelic being named *Melek Taus*, the *'peacock angel'*. Melek Taus is often depicted in the form of a strange bird icon known as a *sanjaq*, although the oldest known sanjaqs are apparently not peacocks at all, but have bulbous avian bodies and hooked beaks. The sanjaq idols may be representations of predatory birds similar to those (apparently) venerated by the shamanic Zawi Chemi people. *'Shamanism is a system of belief common to the Turks of Central Asia. Both men and women could be shaman priests and among old Turkish groups they were called a "Kam". Kams dressed in elaborate garments to display their supernatural powers. Accompanied by the beating of drums in their rituals, they believed they could fly with the aid of their own guardian animal. During such flights they reached various levels of Heaven or the Underworld. Upon returning to this world, they used the information they had learned during their journey for the benefit of their followers.'*

The Sumerian Connection: From *c.*3000 BCE we first see the use of a winged human motif in stone carvings and statues. The wings may signify an ability to travel to places that normal mortals cannot reach. They may also imply an ability to 'mediate' between the human world and some other 'higher' state or states. The region between the Tigris and Euphrates was the cradle of civilization, and is now in Iraq. Sumerians believed in a wide range of spirits and gods, including a belief in *'messengers of the gods'*, who ran errands between the gods and humans. They also believed, like many people today, that each person had a 'ghost' or *guardian angel* who was a constant companion for life. Altars that appear to be dedicated to guardian angels have been found in excavations of Sumerian houses. Sumerian domination of the Middle East came to an end around 2000 BCE, when Sumer was defeated and overlapping Assyrian and Babylonian cultures took over. Winged humans continued to be depicted in reliefs and statues. These Semitic tribes adapted the concept into hierarchies of angels answerable to each of their many gods. This idea was adopted by Zoroastrianism, monotheistic Judaism and Christianity.

Egyptian Idols: Most Egyptian gods can be traced back to around 2500 BCE and there seem to be cross-cultural links with Sumeria. Many Egyptian gods took the shape of an animal, which was regarded as the soul of the god. For instance, *Horus* (god of the sky) was represented as a falcon, and *Thoth* (god of the Moon and patron of writing, learning and the sciences) was depicted as a man with the head of an ibis. *Isis*, queen of all the Egyptian goddesses, is often represented as a woman with wings. There are around 500 deities in *The Egyptian Book of the Dead*, and another 1250 gods and goddesses were added in later centuries. Some were more like angels than gods, e.g. the *Hunmannit*, immortals depicted as rays of the Sun, invoked to look after the Sun, and to receive from and give messages to the Sun. They were also indirectly responsible for looking after mankind, so were a form of 'guardian angel' (and similar to seraphims of later religions). It is not known whether the winged human motif was imported into Egypt from Sumeria, or vice versa, or whether it arose independently possibly in what is now Turkey in eastern Europe.

Indo-European Migration: At the end of the fourth millennium BCE, there was a movement of people, whose ethnicity we have come to call 'Indo-European', from eastern Europe to western Europe, Central Asia, North India and North Africa. Thus there are similarities between Ancient Greek and Ancient Sanskrit. The god *Mithras* appears in Greece and Central Asia and his counterpart *Mitra* is mentioned 200 times in the ancient Hindu text, the *Rig-Veda*, which in spoken form goes back to around 3000 BCE. Mithras was a 'light-bringer' god, with a flourishing cult between 1500 BCE and around 300 CE, in lands as far apart as India and Great Britain, with a centre in what was then known as Persia. Mithraism was the most prevalent religion in Persia when Zoroaster was alive, and in Zoroastrianism Mithras is an angel who mediates between heaven and earth, later becoming judge and preserver of the created world. Mithras was worshipped, both as a distant sun-god and also as a close personal source of love and support, like a guardian angel. The images of Mithras often depict Mithras fighting the sacred bull, with his cloak billowing out behind him in a way that seems meant to suggest wings. In the *Rig-Veda*, Mitra appears often to be more of an angel than a god.

Zoroastrian Guardian Angels:
Zoroaster lived in Persia around 650 BCE. After receiving angelic communications, he spread a monotheistic message that subsequently became the religion of the Persian empire, and later influenced Muslim, Judaic and Christian thought. Zoroastrianism developed the idea of six main archangels: the Archangels of Immortality, Good Thoughts, Right,

Dominion, Prosperity and Piety. There were at least 40 lesser angels called the *'Adorable Ones'*. Some lesser angels were male, some female, and all were associated with a particular attribute. On the next level, the third rank of angels were the *'Guardian Angels'*, each one assigned as guide, conscience, protector and helpmate throughout the life of one single human being. All of the various hierarchies of angels were considered to be manifestations of the one *'Lord of Light'*. There was also a *'Lord of Darkness'*, with complementary demons and evil spirits. In the continual battle between light and darkness, it was believed that the forces of light would eventually triumph.

Judaism and Angels and the Arch Demon: Early Semitic peoples of the Middle East believed in nature spirits. This animistic belief, whereby intelligence is attributed to inanimate objects and natural phenomena, was later affected by

Zoroastrianism. The winged spirits of wind and of fire were especially significant, and appear to have been the basis for what we now know as *cherubim* and *seraphim*. Around the time of Moses, *c.*1300 BCE, polytheism evolved into monotheism (from many gods to one God), while retaining some earlier beliefs such as that in winged immortals. With the influence of Zoroastrianism spreading in the few hundred years before Christ, more and more angels acting as messengers of God appeared in the Jewish scriptures. After the Jews returned from captivity in Babylon around 450 BCE, angels became an integral part of Judaic monotheistic religion. Two archangels appear in the canonical Old Testament: Michael, the warrior leader of the heavenly hosts, and Gabriel, the heavenly messenger. Two more are mentioned in the apocryphal Old Testament: Raphael, (God's healer or helper), and Uriel (Fire of God), the watcher over the world and the lowest part of hell. The leader of the forces of evil was called Satan (the antagonist), or Belial (the spirit of perversion, darkness, and destruction) or Mastema (enmity or opposition), etc. The development of Satan as an *Arch Demon* in Judaism and then Christianity was probably due to the influence of Zoroastrianism. In the Book of Job the Judaic Satan was a prosecutor of men in the court of God's justice. However, later Christian writings altered and elevated Satan to the chief antagonist of Christ and humankind. Demons besides Satan are mentioned in the Judaic Old Testament (i.e. the Pentateuch, the first five books of the Christian Old Testament also known as the Torah). These include Lilith (a female demon of the night), Azazel (the demon of the wilderness), Leviathan and Rahab (demons of chaos) etc.

Graeco-Roman Influences: The Greek word '*daemon*' meant a guardian divinity or inspiring spirit. A number of their gods could fly, such as Hermes (Mercury) who had wings on his feet and was considered to be 'the messenger of the gods'. The English word *hermeneutics* derives from his name, which traditionally means '*interpreting the messages in holy texts*'. In Greek mythology we read of Icarus and Daedalus flying too close to the Sun. In Greek art the Sun-god Helios was often depicted with a halo, that is, a radiant circle or disc surrounding his head in an attempt to represent spiritual purity through the symbolism of light. In Roman times emperors were sometimes also depicted with halos. Because of its 'pagan' origin, however, this convention was avoided in early Christian art. Throughout the Middle Ages, however, angels were frequently depicted with haloes, circles of golden light surrounding their heads.

Christian Developments: In the New Testament in the book entitled the Revelation of St John the Divine, divine truths are reputed to have been revealed to John of Patmos by an angel. In the Gospels the angel Gabriel informs Mary of her forthcoming pregnancy. An angel informs Zachariah that he will have a son, John the Baptist, despite his old age. In the Gospel of Matthew an angel speaks at the empty tomb of Christ, following the Resurrection and the rolling back of the stone by angels. The earliest known Christian image of an angel, in the Catacomb of Priscilla in Rome, dates from the middle of the third century CE, but is without wings. The earliest known representation of angels with wings is on what is called the Prince's Sarcophagus, discovered near Istanbul, in the 1930s, and attributed to the time of Theodosius I (379–395). Clement of Alexandria, one of the early church fathers of Christianity, stated that angels functioned as the movers of the stars and controlled the four elements of earth, air, fire and water. In Christianity 'fallen' angels have traditionally been referred to as 'demons', and in the Middle Ages and the Reformation period in Europe, various hierarchies of demons were developed, such as that associated with the **seven deadly sins**: Satan (anger), Lucifer (pride), Mammon (avarice), Beelzebub (gluttony), Leviathan (envy), Asmodeus (lechery) and Belphegor (sloth). In 1259 St Thomas Aquinas gave a series of lectures on angels at the University of Paris, and the views that were expounded then continued to influence Christian thought for several centuries. In the New Testament we find

angels grouped into seven ranks: angels, archangels, principalities, powers, virtues, dominions and thrones. In addition to these were also added the Old Testament figures of cherubim and seraphim, which, with the seven other ranks, comprised the nine choirs of angels referred to in later Christian mystical theology.

Islamic Angels: The religion that Muhammad founded c.630 CE spread rapidly across the Middle East and central Asia. The archangel Gabriel communicated to Muhammad the basis of what subsequently became the Muslim faith. Angels can take on different forms. Muhammad, speaking of the magnitude of the angel Gabriel, said that his wings spanned from the eastern to the western horizon. Also, in Islamic tradition, angels used to take on human form. The Islamic hierarchy of demons is headed by Iblis (the devil), who also is called Shaytan (Satan). Lesser benign angels, malevolent demons and 'genies' (or 'djinn') are also frequently referred to in the Koran. For instance one of the five cardinal beliefs of Muslims is the idea of the *Day of Judgment*, when individuals are questioned about their faith by the two angels Munkar and Nakir after death. Other well-known examples are Jibril (Gabriel), the angel of revelation, Mikal (Michael), the angel of nature, who gives man both food and knowledge, Izrail, angel of death, and Israfil, the angel who sounds the trumpet on the day of the Last Judgment. Muslim scholars state that Allah has 3000 names, of which 1000 are only known to angels. Three hundred are found in the New Testament, 300 in the Psalms of David (Zabur), 300 in the Torah. 99 are in the Koran. The remaining 3000th name has been hidden by Allah, and is known as *'the Greatest Name of Allah'* or *'Ism Allah al-a'zam'*.

Modern Beliefs in Angels: Pope John Paul II emphasized the role of angels in Catholic teachings in his 1986 address titled *'Angels Participate in the History Of Salvation'*. He suggested that the modern world should come to see the importance of angels. A 2002 study based on interviews with 350 people who said they have had an experience of an angel, mainly in the UK, describes several types of such experiences: visions, sometimes with multiple witnesses present; auditions, e.g. to convey a warning; a sense of being touched, pushed, or lifted, typically to avert a dangerous situation; and pleasant fragrance, generally in the context of somebody's death. In the visual experiences, the angels described appear in various forms, either the 'classical' one (human countenance with wings), in the form of extraordinarily beautiful or radiant human beings, or as beings of light. In Canada, a 2008 survey of over 1000 Canadians found that 67 per cent believe in angels. An August 2007 Pew poll found that 68 per cent of Americans believe that 'angels and demons are active in the world'. Also in the USA, a 2008 survey of 1700 respondents published by *TIME Magazine*, found that 55 per cent of Americans, including one in five of those who say they are not religious, believe that they have been protected by a guardian angel during their lifetime. According to four

different polls conducted in 2009, a greater percentage of Americans believe in angels (55 per cent) than those who believe in global warming (36 per cent). According to a Gallup Youth Survey, in a 'Teen Belief in the Supernatural' poll in 1994, 76 per cent of 508 teenagers (aged 13–17) believe in angels, a greater percentage than those who believed in astrology, ESP, ghosts, witchcraft, clairvoyance, bigfoot and vampires. In 1978, 64 per cent of American young people believed in angels; in 1984, 69 per cent of teenagers believed in angels; by 1994, that number had grown to 76 per cent, while belief in other unexplained concepts, such as the Loch Ness Monster and ESP, have declined. In 1992, 80 per cent of 502 surveyed teenage girls believed in angels, and 81 per cent of Catholic teens and 82 per cent of regular church attendees harboured beliefs in angels.

THE ANGEL OF MONS

Arthur Jones-Machen (1863–1947), from Caerleon in Wales (pen name Arthur Machen), was hailed by Sir Arthur Conan Doyle as a *'genius'*, and John Betjeman stated that Machen's work changed his life. By 1894 he had translated the *Memoirs of Jacques Casanova* into 12 volumes comprising 5000 pages, and the translation has been reprinted 17 times. Oscar Wilde had encouraged him to move into fiction, and his first major work, *The Great God Pan* scandalized Victorian society. It was published by John Lane at the Bodley Head, also in 1894. Oscar Wilde congratulated him on *'un grand succes'*, and the book, a sensational Gothic novel that mixed sex, the supernatural and horror was quickly reprinted. His next major novel, his masterpiece, was set in Caerleon and London and traced a boy's search for beauty through literature and visions, finally ending in a drug-induced depraved tragedy. *The Hill of Dreams* was called '*the most beautiful book in the world*' by the American aesthete Carl Van Vechten in 1922, and was named as '*the most decadent book in all of English literature*' by the French critic Madeleine Cazamian in 1935. It was said to be a work '*worthy to stand upon the shelf beside Poe and De Quincey.*' He also made a scholarly case for the search for the Holy Grail being a remembrance of the lost liturgy of the Celtic church. His influence was massive. A *Spectator* article (29 October 1988) traced lines of descent from his ideas through Alistair Crowley and the 'Golden Dawn' movement to L. Ron Hubbard and Scientology, on to the Hippy movement and the revival of interest in ley lines and magical stones, to the Neo-Romantic art of Ceri Richards and Graham Sutherland. Many authors, including masters of the modern horror genre like Stephen King and Clive Barker, acknowledge their debt to Machen, and he earned the respect and praise of such major literary figures as T.S. Eliot, D.H. Lawrence, Henry Miller, Jorge Luis Borges, H.G Wells, Oscar Wilde, W.B. Yeats, Siegfried Sassoon, George Moore and John Betjeman. An interesting aside on the career of this forgotten genius is that he tried to boost morale and spread his supernatural beliefs by propagating the '*Angel of Mons*' story in the *London Evening News* in August 1914. British soldiers had seen weird figures in the sky during their retreat from Mons in the First World War. Machen suggested that it was St George leading Henry V's archers from Agincourt. His bowmen were 'replaced' in popular retelling and modern mythology by an angel, or a flock of angels.

THE BEE IS A BIRD For around 2000 years the bee was thought to be the smallest bird, born from the rotting bodies of oxen or calves, with a 'king bee' rather than a queen ruling the colony. Pliny the Elder wrote: '*Of all insects, bees alone were created for the sake of man. They collect honey, make wax, build structures, work hard, and have a government and leaders. They retire for the winter, since they cannot endure cold. They build their hives of many materials gathered from various plants. They gather honey from flowers close to the hive, and send out scouts to farther pastures when the nearby flowers are exhausted; if the scouts cannot return before nightfall, they make camp and lie on their backs to protect their wings from dew. They post a guard at the gates of the*

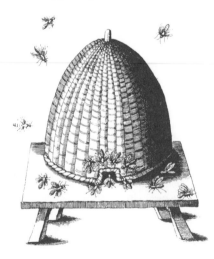

The World of the Quantum Honey Bee

Recent research postulates that bees can 'see' quark particles spinning in and out of existence in the world of quantum physics and see electrons in their orbits, as they inhabit six dimensions. A mathematician, Barbara Shipman, postulates that honey bees can not only perceive the energies of the subatomic quantum world directly, but they also use six-dimensional space to communicate with each other. Shipman is a mathematician at the University of Rochester in New York state, but her father was a bee researcher for the US Dept. of Agriculture. One aspect of bee behaviour which has baffled scientists for more than 70 years is the mysterious dance they perform when they return to their hives. The dance communicates to other bees where new sources of food can be found. By watching the dance of a scout bee, other bees, called 'recruits', get an exact idea of the direction and distance to where new food can be found. Shipman's work in mathematical theory led her to studying an area called 'manifolds', geometric shapes described by certain complex maths equations. There are an infinite variety of manifold configurations. They can describe shapes of many dimensions. Shipman was working with a six-dimensional structure called a 'flag manifold', when suddenly she realized that it very closely resembled the pattern of the honey bee 'waggle dance'. Because the flag manifold is a six-dimensional object, it cannot be perceived in our three-dimensional world. We can visualize only an approximation of what it looks like by projecting its 'shadow' into two-dimensional space. The shadow of an ordinary sphere, for example, projects onto two dimensions as a flat circle. When one projects a sixth-dimensional flag manifold onto two dimensions, it matches exactly the patterns dancing bees make. However, two-dimensional bee-dance patterns are not enough to explain how bees interpret these patterns to locate distant sources of food. An explanation may be that the bees actually perceive all six dimensions. Yet to do that, the eye or senses of the bee would need to be able to see subatomic activity directly. When a human scientist tries to detect a quark, by bombarding it with another particle in a high-energy accelerator, the flag manifold geometry is lost. If bees are using quarks as a script for their dance, they must be able to observe the quarks in their natural states. Scientists speculated that bees understand their flight directions in the same way as birds follow migration routes.

hive, and after sleeping until dawn they are woken by one of their number and all fly out together, if the weather is fine. They can forecast wind and rain so they know when not to go out. The young bees go out to collect materials while the old work indoors. Honey comes out of the air; in falling from a great height it accumulates dirt and is stained with the vapour of the earth; it becomes purified after the bees collect it and allow it to ferment in the hive. Smoke is used to drive away the bees so their honey can be collected, though too much smoke kills them. Out of several possible candidates, bees select the best to be king, and kill the others to avoid division; the king is twice as large as other bees, is brilliantly coloured, and has a white spot on his brow. The common bees obey and protect the king, as they are unable to be without him. Bees like the sound of clanging bronze, which summons them together. Dead bees can be revived if they are covered with mud and the body of an ox or bull.' In the fifth century, St Augustine wrote that bees had no sex, therefore there was no 'king bee', and that they were born out of corruption (from worms in rotting flesh). In the seventh century, Isidore of Seville recorded: '*Bees are formed by the transformation through decay of the putrid flesh of calves... Bees (apes) have their name either because they bind themselves together with their feet (pes), or because they are born without feet (a-pes), only later growing feet and wings. They live in fixed places, are diligent in producing honey, build their houses with great skill, gather honey from various*

flowers, weave wax to fill their homes with many offspring, have kings and armies with which they wage war, flee from smoke, and are irritated by noise. Witnesses say that they are born out of the corpses of oxen because they are created by beating the flesh of slaughtered calves; this causes worms to form which later become bees. It is correct to say that bees are born from oxen, just as hornets come from horses, drone-bees from mules, and wasps from asses. The Greek call the larger bees found in the farthest part of the hive oestri some say these are the kings, because they pitch camps (castra).'

BEELZEBUB, LORD OF THE FLIES The name *Ba'al Zebûb* literally means 'Lord of the Flies' and he was a Semitic deity worshipped by the Philistines in the city of Ekron (25 miles/40 km west of Jerusalem). Later, in the Bible he is identified as one of the 'Seven Princes of Hell'. The prophet Elijah condemned King Ahaziah of Israel to die by Yahweh's words, because the king sent a messenger to Beelzebub to see if he would recover from injuries caused by a fall. The Pharisees accused Jesus of driving out demons by the power of 'Beelzeboul', Prince of Demons. In the Testament of Solomon, Beelzebub is a former leading angel or cherubim associated with Venus, the evening star, who is identified with Satan or Lucifer. In medieval times he becomes the chief lieutenant of Lucifer. Some place him as one of the three most prominent fallen angels, the others being Lucifer and Leviathan, and associate him with the sons of pride and gluttony. Beelzebub was often accused of being the object of supplication in trials of witches, for example in the terrible Loudon 'possessions' of 1634 and the Salem Witch Trials. Lucifer, meaning *Light-Bearer*, was a name originally applied to Jesus as well as Venus, but St Jerome and others began identifying Lucifer with the fallen angel Satan, driven out of Heaven for his pride. Thus Lucifer over time has been regarded both as Jesus and Satan. Satan, in Aramaic, means adversary or enemy.

CALADRIUS - THE HEALING SNOWBIRD

In the second century CE Greek *Physiologus*, (a collection of beast tales that illustrate morals) and the 12th century *Aberdeen Bestiary* a caladrius is a snow-white bird, living in the palaces of kings. If the caladrius looks into the face of a sick man, he will live, but if the caladrius looks away, the person will die. If it wishes to cure the ill man, the caladrius looks at him, drawing the sickness out and flies away, dispersing the sickness and healing both itself and the sick man. The bird has come to be an allegory of Christ, pure white without any trace of the blackness of sin. Early Christian doctrine was that Christ turned his face away from the Jewish non-believers, and towards the Gentiles, taking away and carrying their sins to the Crucifixion. Christ will always turn away from the unrepentant and cast them off. However, he will accept the repentant, turn his face towards them, and make them whole again. White doves, herons or storks may be the origin of the figure, as doves would be kept in the king's houses and storks would nest on their roofs. *The bird called caladrius, as Physiologus tells us, is white*

all over; it has no black parts. Its excrement cures cataract in the eyes. It is to be found in royal residences. If anyone is sick, he will learn from the caladrius if he is to live or die. If, therefore, a man's illness is fatal, the caladrius will turn its head away from the sick man as soon as it sees him, and everyone knows that the man is going to die. But if the man's sickness is one from which he will recover, the bird looks him in the face and takes the entire illness upon itself; it flies up into the air, towards the sun, burns off the sickness and scatters it, and the sick man is cured. The caladrius represents our Saviour. Our Lord is pure white without a trace of black, 'who did no sin, neither was guile found in his mouth'. The Lord, moreover, coming from on high, turned his face from the Jews, because they did not believe, and turned to us, Gentiles, taking away our weakness and carrying our sins; raised up on the wood of the cross and ascending on high, "he led captivity captive and gave gifts unto men". Each day Christ, like the caladrius, attends us in our sickness, examines our mind when we confess, and heals those to whom he shows the grace of repentance. But he turns his face away from those whose heart he knows to be unrepentant. These he casts off; but those to whom he turns his face, he makes whole again. But, you say, because the caladrius is unclean according to the law, it ought not to be likened to Christ. Yet John says of God: "And as Moses lifted up the serpent in the wilderness, even so must the Son of man be lifted up"; and according to the law, "the serpent was more subtle than any beast of the field". (The Aberdeen Bestiary c.1200). Plutarch and Aelian stated that the caladrius cured jaundice, and in the 12th century Philippe de Thaon wrote that the marrow from a bone in its thigh would cure blindness. Most medieval accounts identify the caladrius as a maritime bird.

CAMPE (KAMPE) This she-dragon, or drakaina, was ordered by the Titan Kronos to guard the Hekatoneires (the three giant gods of storms) and Cyclopes (the three one-eyed giants) when he locked them in the Pit of Tartarus. Campe was a monstrous Centaurine creature who, from the waist up, had the body of a serpent-haired woman. Below that she had the body of a scaly dragon with a thousand vipers for feet. Sprouting from her waist were the heads of 50 fearsome beasts including

The Death of Campe

The Greek poet Nonnus, in the fifth-century *Dionysiaca*, an epic tale of the god Dionysus, tells us: '*Zeus ruling in the heights destroyed high-headed Campe with a thunderbolt, for all the many crooked shapes of her whole body. A thousand crawlers from her viperish feet, spitting poison afar, were fanning Enyo* [the war-goddess] *to a flame, a mass of misshapen coils. Round her neck flowered fifty various heads of wild beasts: some roared with lion's heads like the grim face of the riddling Sphinx; others were spluttering foam from the tusks of wild boars; her countenance was the very image of Scylla with a marshalled regiment of thronging dog's heads. Double-shaped, she appeared a woman to the middle of her body, with clusters of poison-spitting serpents for* hair. *Her giant form, from the chest to the parting-point of the thighs, was covered all over with a bastard shape of hard sea-monsters' scales. The claws of her wide-scattering hands were curved like a crooktalon sickle. From her neck over her terrible shoulders, with tail raised high over her throat, a scorpion with an icy sting sharp-whetted crawled and coiled upon itself. Such was manifold-shaped Campe as she rose writhing, and flew roaming about earth and air and briny deep, and flapping a couple of dusky wings, rousing tempests and arming gales, that black-winged Nymph of Tartaros: from her eyelids a flickering flame belched out far-travelling sparks. Yet heavenly Zeus… killed that great monster, and conquered the snaky Enyo of Kronos.*'

lions and boars. Dark wings rose from her shoulders and above her head she lifted a furious scorpion's tail. After ten years of war fighting the Titans, Zeus was told that he would never win unless he rescued the giants from Tartaros, so he slew Campe and freed the giants from their prison to help him.

THE CAUCASIAN EAGLE

The immortal Titan Prometheus was the son of Typhon and Echidna, and was chained to the peak of Mount Kaukasos by Zeus as punishment for stealing fire from the gods to give to mortals. Zeus further punished him for his crime by having a gigantic eagle eat his liver every day, only to have it grow back overnight to be eaten again the next day. (Some sources state that the eagle was a bronze automaton made by the god Hephaestos.) However, Prometheus had foretold to the Argive priestess and heroine Io that he would be freed from his torture by one of her descendants, Hercules, the greatest hero in the world. Years later, Hercules set out to release Prometheus, shooting

> # Greek Medical Knowledge
>
> The myth that Prometheus's liver was eaten every day by the eagle only to 'regenerate' in the night probably indicates that ancient Greeks knew that the liver has the ability to regenerate if surgically removed or injured. The Greek word for the liver – *hêpar* – derives from the verb *hêpaomai* which means to mend or repair. Hêpar roughly translates as 'repairable'.

down the Caucasian eagle with a volley of arrows. He then broke the chain binding the Titan. The Eagle, the Titan and the Arrow were all placed amongst the stars in the form of the constellations Aquila, the Kneeler and Sagittarius.

CINNAMALOGUS – THE CINNAMON NEST BIRD

The cinnamalogus was an Arabian bird, building its nest using the branches of the cinnamon tree, which men valued greatly for its spice. Those wanting cinnamon could not climb the tree to reach the nest, because the nest was too high and the tree branches too delicate, so they threw lead balls or shot lead arrows to knock down the cinnamon. Cinnamon obtained from the nest of the cinnamalogus was accounted the most valuable of all. In the fifth century BCE Herodotus wrote: '*Still more wonderful is the mode in which they collect the cinnamon. Where the wood grows, and what country produces it, they cannot*

Some Mythical Flying Monsters

Draco, a type of mythical dragon

Cockatrice

Phoenix

Griffin

Marchosias, a legendary she-wolf with griffin's wings and a serpent's tail

tell – only some, following probability, relate that it comes from the country in which Bacchus was brought up. Great birds, they say, bring the sticks which we Greeks, taking the word from the Phoenicians, call cinnamon, and carry them up into the air to make their nests. These are fastened with a sort of mud to a sheer face of rock, where no foot of man is able to climb. So the Arabians, to get the cinnamon, use the following artifice. They cut all the oxen and asses and beasts of burthen that die in their land into large pieces, which they carry with them into those regions, and place near the nests: then they withdraw to a distance, and the old birds, swooping down, seize the pieces of meat and fly with them up to their nests; which, not being able to support the weight, break off and fall to the ground. Hereupon the Arabians return and collect the cinnamon, which is afterwards carried from Arabia into other countries.'

COCKERELS ARE ASTRONOMERS

The rooster was thought to have the innate intelligence that it could tell the time and so knew when to crow. Some stories related how lions are frightened of a white cockerel. Pliny the Elder, in the first century CE, wrote: '*The cock was designed by nature to announce the dawn; by singing they awaken men. They are skilled astronomers; sing at the start of every three hour period, go to bed with the sun, and at the fourth hour of the night awaken us with their song. They duel with each other to determine who will rule, with the winner strutting proudly and the loser forced to serve; a conquered cock does not crow. Some cocks are bred only to fight. Cocks carry themselves so proudly that even the noble lion is afraid of them. Omens and auspices can be read in the behaviour of cocks.*'

CROWS AS GUIDES

Crows are monogamous, long-lived and are possibly the most intelligent members of the bird family. The ancients noted that they took responsibility for feeding their chicks, and escorted their young in flight. The crow's voice predicted rain, and the crow was said to be able reveal ambushes and foretell the future. Crows led flocks of storks crossing cross the sea to Asia. Pliny the Elder referred to the intelligent habits of these birds: '*If a nut is too hard for a crow to crack with its beak, it will carry the nut into the air and drop it on rocks or roofs until it breaks. The croaking sound of a crow is thought to be unlucky, particularly during its breeding season. Unlike other birds, crows continue to feed their young even after they can fly.*' In the seventh century, Isidore of Seville wrote: '*The crow is an old bird. Seers say that it increases anxiety by the indications it gives, reveals ambushes, predicts rain, and foretells the future. But it is a great wickedness to believe that God gives his counsel to crows.*' In the 13th century Bartholomaeus Anglicus wrote:

'The crow is a bird of long life, and diviners tell that she takes heed of spyings and awaitings, and teaches and shows ways, and warns what shall fall. But it is full unlawful to believe, that God shows His privy counsel to crows. It is said that crows rule and lead storks, and come about them as it were in routs, and fly about the storks and defend them, and fight against other birds and fowls that hate storks. And take upon them the battle of other birds, upon their own peril. And an open proof thereof is: for in that time that the storks pass out of the country, crows are not seen in places there they were usually seen. And also for they come again with sore wounds, and with voice of blood, that is well known, and with other signs and tokens and show that they have been in strong fighting. Also there it is said, that the mildness of the bird is wonderful. For when father and mother in age are both naked and bare of covering of feathers, then the young crows hide and cover and cover them with their feathers, and gather meat and feed them.'

CUCKOO FLIGHT AND CLOCKS

Isidore of Seville tells us: *'Cuckoos arrive at a fixed time, riding in the shoulders of kites, because their flight is short and weak; in this way they do not grow tired in the long spaces of the air. Their saliva generates cicadas [grasshoppers].'* In the 1949 film *The Third Man*, Orson Welles improvised on Graham Greene's script, saying: *'In Italy, for 30 years under the Borgias, they had warfare, terror, murder and bloodshed, but they produced Michelangelo, Leonardo da Vinci and the Renaissance. In Switzerland, they had brotherly lover, 500 years of democracy and peace – and what did they produce? The cuckoo clock.'*

Since antiquity there have been timepieces featuring an automaton bird, first one being credited to the Greek mathematician, Ctesibius of Alexandria (*c.*285–222 BCE), who used water to sound a whistle and make a model owl move. In 797 or 801, the Caliph of Baghdad, Harun al-Rashid, gave the Emperor Charlemagne an Asian elephant and a mechanical clock, out of which came a mechanical bird to announce the hours. Austria and Germany pioneered the cuckoo clocks which we know today, and not the Swiss as one might have believed.

DEMONS, DEVILS AND JINN

A demon is thought to be a malevolent, supernatural spirit. However, the original Greek word *'daimon'* simply meant a spirit or divine power, without the negative and 'unclean' connotations that later attached to it in Christian religion. It is thought that some demons are 'fallen angels' and others were forged in hell itself. Freud believed that the concept of demons was derived from our relation to the recently deceased: *'The fact that demons are always regarded as the spirits of those who have died recently shows better than anything the influence of mourning on the origin of the belief in demons.'* In Babylon and Chaldea, there were seven evil deities, the *'storm-demons'*, represented as winged bulls. In Hebrew mythology, *'the destroyer'* or *'destroying angel'* was a

malignant demon, whose presence was warded off by blood sacrifices sprinkled on lintels and doorposts. A 'destroying angel' could bring pestilence and plague as a messenger of the Lord, however. Other Hebrew demons were independent of heaven, coming from hell, and brought diseases of the brain, nightmares, epilepsy, catalepsy and headaches. The demon of blindness, '*Shabriri*' ('dazzling glare'), rested on uncovered water at night and brought blindness to those who drank the water. These demons entered the body and caused the disease while overwhelming or 'seizing' the victim (hence the term 'seizure'). To cure such diseases, it was necessary to draw out the evil demons by certain incantations and talismanic performances. In today's Christianity, demons are generally considered to be angels who fell from grace by rebelling against God. However, some schools of thought in Christianity or Judaism teach that demons, or evil spirits, are the result of the sexual relationships between fallen angels and human women. Pre-Islamic mythology does not discriminate between gods and demons. The '*jinn*' are divinities of inferior rank, having many human attributes: they eat, drink and procreate sometimes in conjunction with human beings. The jinn smell and lick things, and have a liking for food leftovers. In eating they use the left hand. They haunted waste and deserted places, especially the wildnesses where wild beasts gathered. Cemeteries and dirty places were also popular abodes. When appearing to man, jinn sometimes assumed the forms of beasts and sometimes those of men. Generally, jinn are peaceable and well disposed toward men, but there are also evil jinn, who contrive to injure men. In Islam, jinn are not all evil, as demons are described in Christianity, but are regarded as creatures that co-exist with humans. Evil jinn are referred to as the *shayatin* (devils), and Iblis (Satan) is their chief. Iblis was the first jinni who disobeyed Allah. The jinn are made from the fire, but angels are made from light while mankind is made from altered clay. According to the Koran, Iblis was once a servant of Allah, but when Allah created Adam from clay, Iblis became jealous and arrogant, and disobeyed Allah. Adam was the first man, and man was the greatest creation of Allah. Iblis could not stand this, and refused to acknowledge a creature made of 'dirt', so Allah condemned Iblis to be punished after death eternally in hellfire.

DOVES - COLOUR AND MEANING All pigeons used to be known as doves. It was thought that the 'red' dove ruled over all the others and brought other doves into the dovecot. Red was regarded as the predominant colour because Christ redeemed man with his blood. Speckled doves displayed the diversity of the 12 prophets. Gold doves symbolized the three boys who refused to worship the golden image. 'Air-coloured' (blue) doves represented the prophet Elisha, who was taken up into the sky. Black doves were obscure sermons, and 'ash-coloured' (grey) birds reminded Christians of Jonah, who preached wearing a hair shirt and covering himself with ashes. Stephanite doves symbolized Stephen, the first martyr. White doves represented John the Baptist and the cleansing ritual of baptism. The dove was associated with Christ and the Holy Spirit, as God had sent his spirit in the form of a dove to gather mankind into his church. Just as there were many colours of doves, there were many ways of speaking through the religious laws and the holy prophets. These messengers of God, however, were bred in dovecots as meat for rich men's tables. In the seventh century, Isidore of Seville related: '*Doves (columbae) are tame birds that live in company with men; their necks change into different colors, they have no gall, they are often in the nests and make love with a kiss. Ring doves (palumbes) are chaste birds; if it loses its mate it lives alone and never takes another.*' Medieval bestiaries tell us that their song is mournful, that they fly in flocks and continually kiss, and have twin young. They sat on small pools of shallow water so that they could see the reflection of the hawk, and so escape. When menaced by a dragon, doves would fly to the fabled peridexion tree for safety.

DRAGONS - THE ELEPHANT KILLERS

In the first century CE, Pliny the Elder related that India produced the largest elephants as well as the largest dragons, which were perpetually at war with the elephants. The dragon was so enormous that it could easily envelop the elephant in its coils. The dragon watched from a neighbouring tree the route which the elephants took when going to feed, and then darted down upon them. The elephant when attacked, being unable to disengage itself from the serpent's coils, sought a tree or rock on which to rub itself, in order to kill the dragon. To prevent this, the dragon wrapped itself around the elephant's legs, and attacked its nostrils and other tender parts, especially its eyes. This was the reason why elephants were often found blind and worn to a skeleton with hunger and misery. He mentions the dragon as having no venom. Pliny says that the blood of the elephant is remarkably cold, for which reason in the parching heats of summer it is sought by the dragon. The dragon also lay coiled in the rivers, and when the

elephant came to drink, fastened itself round its trunk and fixed its teeth behind the elephant's ear, which was the only place which the elephant could not protect with its mighty trunk: '*The dragons, it is said, are of such vast size that they can swallow the whole of the elephant's blood; consequently the latter, being thus drained, falls to the earth exhausted, while the dragon, intoxicated with the draught, is crushed beneath it and so shares its fate.*' Pliny related how cinnabar, or 'dragon's blood', was held in the highest esteem and that it is the name given to the thick matter which issues from the dragon when crushed by the dying elephant, mixed with the blood of either of them. He said that it was the only colour that in painting that gave a proper representation of blood. Isidore of Seville wrote: '*The dragon is the largest serpent, and in fact the largest animal on earth. Its name in Latin is* draco, *derived from the Greek name* drakon. *When it comes out of its cave, it disturbs the air. It has a crest, a small mouth, and a narrow throat. Its strength is in its tail rather than its teeth; it does harm by beating, not by biting. It has no poison and needs none to kill, because it kills by entangling. Not even the elephant is safe from the dragon; hiding where elephants travel, the dragon tangles their feet with its tail and kills the elephant by suffocating it. Dragons live in the burning heat of India and Ethiopia… Dracontites is a stone that is forcibly taken from the brain of a dragon,*

and unless it is torn from the living creature it has not the quality of a gem; whence magi cut it out of dragons while they are sleeping. For bold men explore the cave of the dragons, and scatter there medicated grains to hasten their sleep, and thus cut off their heads while they are sunk in sleep, and take out the gems.'

The French cleric Hugo de Folieto (*c*.1110–72) tells us that the dragon is venomous, seems to fly, and also attacks ships at sea: '*The scripture teaches us that the greatest of the serpents is the dragon and that it deals death by its poisonous breath and by the blow of its tail. This creature is lifted by the strength of its venom into the air as if it were flying, and the air is set in motion by it. It lies in wait for the elephant, the most chaste of animals, and encircling its feet with its tail it tries to suffocate it with its breath, but is crushed by the elephant as it falls dead. But a valuable pigment is obtained from earth which has been soaked with its blood. The reason of their hostility is this. The poison of the dragon boils with exceeding great heat, but the blood of the elephant is exceedingly cold. The dragon therefore wishes to cool its own heat with the blood of the elephant. The Jews say that God made the great dragon which is called Leviathan, which is in the sea; and when folk say that the sea is ebbing it is the dragon going back. Some say that it is the first fish created by God and that it still* lives. *And this beast, at one time called a dragon and at another Leviathan, is used in the Scripture symbolically. The dragon, the greatest of all serpents, is the devil, the king of all evil. As it deals death with its poisonous breath and blow of its tail, so the devil destroys men's souls by thought, word and deed. He kills their thoughts by the breath of pride; he poisons their words with malice; he strangles them by the performance of evil deeds, as it were with his tail. By the dragon the air is set in motion, and so is the peace of spiritually minded people often disturbed in that way. It lays wait for a chaste animal; so he persecuted to the death Christ the guardian of chastity, being born of a chaste virgin; but he was overcome, having been crushed by him in his death. As for the precious colour which is got from the ground, that is the Church of Christ adorned by his precious blood. The dragon is the enemy of a pure animal; likewise is the devil the enemy of the Virgin's Son.'*

THE DRAKONES OF MEDEA

This pair of winged serpentine dragons were born from the blood of the Titans and drew the flying chariot of the witch Medea. Her grandfather Helios, the sun god, gave them to her. She summoned them to escape from Korinthos following her murder of King Kreon, his daughter Kreousa and her own sons by Jason. Ovid, in his *Metamorphoses*, called them Titan Drakones and related '*Had she* [Medea] *not soared away with her winged Serpentes* [from Thessalia following the murder of King Pelias], *she surely must have paid the price. Aloft, over the peak of shady Pelion… she fled, and over Othrys…* [Until] *at last,*

borne on her Vipereae's [Drakones'] *wings, she* [Medea] *reached Ephyra* [Korinthos], *Pirene's town… But when her witch's poison had consumed the new wife* [Jason's new wife Glauke], *and the sea on either side had seen the royal palace all in flames, her wicked sword was drenched in her son's blood; and, winning thus a mother's vile revenge, she fled from Jason's sword. Her Dracon team, the Dracones Titaniaci* [Titan-Drakones], *carried her away to Palladiae* [the city of Athens].'

THE EAGLE AND REBIRTH

The eagle has always been associated with belief in renewal or rebirth. In Babylon, King Erana was taken to the heavens on the wings of an eagle. In many ancient cultures eagles were released at the funeral of a ruler. The soaring flight of the eagle, as the body was cremated, symbolized the departure of the soul to live in the heavens among the gods. In Palmyra in Syria, the eagle was associated with the Sun-god, and could rejuvenate like the phoenix (see page 179). As the eagle killed serpents and dragons, the king of birds symbolized the victory of light over dark. In Christian iconography, the eagle symbolized Adam, the first man, in medieval bestiaries. Adam originally dwelt close to heaven, but lost his glory when sighting the forbidden fruit. Similarly, the eagle interrupts his elegant flight to swoop down on his prey to satisfy his carnal needs. The eagle also variously symbolizes John the Evangelist, the ascension of the prophet Elijah and the ascension of Jesus Christ. Its ability to fly high is why it symbolizes Christ's ascension, and the eagle is frequently depicted on baptismal fonts.

Birds Associated With Legends

Magpie

Ostrich

Owl

Partridge

Peacock

Raven

The Eagle of Zeus

In some accounts this gigantic golden eagle was a creation of the primordial goddess Gaia, the Mother Goddess representing Earth. At the beginning of the great Battle of the Titans, it appeared before Zeus. Zeus thought this a good omen of victory, so used the emblem of a golden eagle on his war standard. In Fulgentius's *Mythologies* we read: *'For so happy an omen, especially since victory did ensue, he made a golden eagle for his war standards and consecrated it to the might of his protection, whereby also among the Romans, standards of this kind are carried.'* In another account, the eagle was once Periphas, a priest of Apollo who became a king in Attica. However, Zeus became jealous because King Periphas was now revered to the same extent as he was and so wished to destroy him. In his anger, Zeus was about to kill Periphas with a thunderbolt, but Apollo intervened on behalf of his former priest. Zeus relented and transformed both King Periphas and his wife Phene into an eagle and a vulture respectively.

The heavenly vulture became known as Lyra, one of the 48 constellations noted by Ptolemy. (In some sources, Queen Phene becomes an osprey). It may be that Periphas represents the constellation of Aquila (eagle) rather than the Caucasian eagle which fed on Prometheus's liver. The eagle of Zeus had the privilege of being able to approach the throne of Zeus, and was the protector of Zeus's sacred sceptre, while his wife (now known as Lyra) was a sign of good omens. The eagle was later sent by Zeus to carry the handsome youth Ganymede up to heaven to become the cupbearer of the gods.

FLYING (MAGIC) CARPET

In *One Thousand and One Nights*, the tales of the magic carpet of Tangu, also called '*Prince Housain's carpet*' came to the attention of the Western world. The literary traditions of several other cultures also feature magical carpets. In Hebraic tradition, Solomon's carpet was made of green silk with a golden weft, 60 miles long and 60 miles wide: '*when Solomon sat upon the carpet he was caught up by the wind, and sailed through the air so quickly that he breakfasted at Damascus and supped in Media*' [the land of the Medes]. The wind followed Solomon's commands, and ensured the carpet would go to its destination. Because Solomon became proud of his many accomplishments, the wind shook the carpet and 40,000 people plunged to their deaths. His carpet was shielded from the sun by a canopy of birds. A supplemental note to Sir Richard Burton's translation of the *Thousand Nights and a Night* (1001 Nights) reveals: 'The great prototype of the Flying Carpet is that of Sulayman bin Daud [i.e. King Solomon], *a fable which the Koran (chap. xxi. 81) borrowed from the Talmud, not from "Indian fictions." It was of green sendal* [a thin light silk used in the Middle Ages for fine garments such as church vestments, and banners], *embroidered with gold and silver and studded with precious stones, and its length and breadth were such that all the Wise King's host could stand upon it, the men to the left and the Jinns to the right of the throne; and when all were ordered, the Wind at royal command, raised it and wafted it whither the Prophet would, while an army of birds flying overhead canopied the host from the sun. In the Middle Ages the legend assumed another form. Duke Richard, surnamed "Richard sans peur", walking with his courtiers one evening in the forest of Moulineaux, near one of his castles on the banks of the Seine, hearing of a prodigious noise coming towards him, sent one of his esquires to know what was the matter, who brought him word that it was a company of people under a leader or King. Richard, with five hundred of his bravest Normans, went out to see a sight which the peasants were so accustomed to, that they viewed it two or three times a week without fee. The sight was of the troop, preceded by two men, who spread a cloth on the ground, made all the Normans run away, and leave the Duke alone. He saw the strangers form themselves into a circle on the cloth, and on asking who they were, was told that they were the spirits of Charles V, King of France, and his servants, condemned to expiate their sins by fighting all night against* the wicked and the damned. Richard desired to be of their party, and receiving a strict charge not to quit the cloth, was conveyed with them to Mount Sinai, where, leaving them without quitting the cloth, he said his prayers in the Church of St. Catherine's Abbey there, while they were fighting, and returned with them. In proof of the truth of this story, he brought back half the wedding ring of a knight in that convent, whose wife, after six years, concluded him dead, and was going to take a second husband.'

THE FURIES OR THE VENGEFUL ONES

The Greeks termed these female personifications of vengeance the *Erinyes* or *Eumenides*, and the Romans called them the Furies. They were also known as the Semnai (the venerable ones), the Potniae (the awful ones), the Maniae (the madnesses) and the Praxidikae (the vengeful ones). They were hideous in appearance, something like the Keres, and dressed in black with long claws and red hair full of serpents. Often they had the wings of a bat or bird, and sometimes the body of a dog. Carrying whips and torches, they are depicted chasing their victims. They are sometimes also represented as flies which harass their victims as remorse. They were

born from the drops of blood that fell from Ouranos after he had been castrated by his son Kronus. Other legends identify them as the daughters of Mother Earth and Darkness, or of Kronus and Eurynome, or Kronus and Night. Their number is unknown, but Virgil noted three: Tisiphone (the avenger), Megaira (the jealous), and Aleto (the unresting). Initially the task of the Furies was to guard the entrance to the underworld of Tartarus, to ensure that those who entered had atoned for their sins. Those who had not atoned were rejected and had to wander as ghosts. The Furies' function then seemed to grow so that they tormented those who had committed any sin. They would relentlessly harass and injure victims but not kill them, often driving them to suicide. They would extend their torments into the underworld, cruelly lashing the offenders.

GORGONS - THE WINGED DEMONS

The Gorgons were three powerful, winged demons named Medusa, Stheno and Euryale. They were depicted in ancient Greek vase painting and sculpture as winged women with broad round heads, serpentine locks of hair, large staring eyes, wide mouths, the tusks of swine, lolling tongues, flared nostrils, and sometimes short coarse beards. Pliny thought that they were a race of savage, swift and hair-covered women. Diodorus depicted them as a race of women inhabiting the western parts of Libya, who were exterminated by Hercules. Gorgons sometimes are depicted as having golden wings, sharp claws, boars' tusks, but most often with the fangs and the skin of a snake. In mosaic art Medusa's face was wreathed around with coiling snakes and adorned with a pair of small wings sprouting from her brow. Medusa, who

Geryon- The Three-Bodied, Four-Winged Giant

Geryon possessed a fabulous herd of oxen whose coats were tinged red by the light of sunset. Hercules was sent to fetch these as one of his '12 labours', sailing to the western island in a golden cup-boat borrowed from the Sun-god Helios. There he killed the cattle-herder Eurytion, the two-headed guard dog Orthros, and finally the three-headed Geryon himself with a poisoned arrow.

Gorgons in Architecture

Because of their legendary gaze, images of the Gorgons were depicted on objects and buildings for protection. The oldest stone pediment in Greece featuring a gorgon is in Corfu and is dated to *c.*600 BCE. The oldest oracles were said to be protected by serpents and a Gorgon image often was associated with those temples. A 'Gorgoneion' became a major symbol in Greek architecture, placed on doors, walls, floors, coins, shields, breastplates and tombstones to ward off evil. It was a stone head, engraving or drawing of a

Gorgon face, often with snakes protruding wildly and the tongue sticking out between her fangs.

alone of her sisters was mortal, was at first a beautiful maiden, but her hair was changed into serpents by Athena, as Medusa had been impregnated by Poseidon in one of Athena's temples. Medusa's head was now so terrible that anyone who looked at it was changed into stone. As Medusa was mortal, King Polydectes commanded the hero Perseus to fetch her head. Perseus accomplished this with the help of the gods who gave him a reflective shield, a curved shiny sword, winged boots and the helm of invisibility. When he decapitated Medusa, two creatures sprang forth from the wound – the children of Poseidon, the winged horse Pegasus and the giant Chrysaor. Perseus fled with Medusa's head in a sack, and her two angry sisters

following close behind him. According to some accounts, either Perseus or Athena used the head of Medusa to freeze Atlas into stone, transforming him into the Atlas Mountains that held up both heaven and earth. Perseus used it against King Polydectes, who had sent him to kill Medusa in the hopes of Perseus being killed, while the king pursued Perseus's mother, Danaë. Perseus returned to the court of King Polydectes, who sat at his throne with Danaë . The king asked if Perseus had the head of Medusa. Perseus replied *'Here it is'* and held it aloft, turning the whole court to stone. The poet Hesiod seems to have imagined the Gorgons as reef-creating sea-daemones, personifying deadly submerged reefs to ancient mariners.

GRYPHON THE LION-EAGLE

The gryphon (also known as griffin or griffon) had the head, wings and front talons of an eagle, and the body of a lion with its back covered in feathers. Sometimes it had the tail of a serpent, and it was big enough to block out the Sun. They lived in the mountains, and made nests of gold, called eyries. The Arimaspians, the one-eyed tribe of Scythia, often attempted to steal the gryphon's gold, so the gryphons guarded their eyries carefully. In some myths, the gryphons laid an egg of agate in these nests, making them doubly valuable. Gryphons knew where buried treasure was, and guarded it from plunderers. They preyed on dead men and devoured horses. The gryphon myth originates in the Near or Middle East, and the fabulous beast is depicted in ancient Babylonian, Assyrian and Persian sculptures. In around 3000 BCE, gryphons became the pharaoh's companions in Egypt, and later they became sacred guardians in Minoa. India was thought to be its native country, and the people were reputed to make its huge talons into drinking cups, as they were said to be able to detect poison. In Greece, they were the pets of the gods. The gryphon was sacred to Apollo, as depicting the gold of the Sun, and in hieroglyphics the gryphon represents heat and summer. It was also sacred to Athene as having the wisdom to find treasure, and to Nemesis as retribution for anyone stealing treasure. In his 14th century *Travels*, Sir John Mandeville assures us: '*In that country* [Bacharia, somewhere near China] *are many griffins, more plenty than in any other country. Some men say that they have the body upward as an eagle and beneath as a*

Gryphon Eggs

One possible origin of the gryphon myth is the sight of cats trapping birds. A more recent theory is that Scythian nomads talked to Greeks of mining gold deposits in the mountains in Mongolia and China. In this rugged area are thousands of well-preserved *Protoceratops* dinosaur fossils and their fossilized eggs in nests. The lion-sized dinosaurs had beaked faces and large claws and so may be the model for the gryphon.

lion; and truly they say sooth, that they are of that shape. But one griffin hath the body more great and is more strong than eight lions, of such lions as be on this half, and more great and stronger than an hundred eagles such as we have amongst us. For one griffin there will bear, flying to his nest, a great horse, if he may find him at the point, or two oxen yoked together as they go at the plough. For he hath his talons so long and so large and great upon his feet, as though they were horns of great oxen or of bugles or of kine, so that men make cups of them to drink of. And of their ribs and of the pens of their wings, men make bows, full strong, to shoot with arrows and quarrels [crossbow bolts].' Bugles are young wild oxen, or can be buffaloes. The musical instrument called a bugle was originally made from its horn. Kine is the ancient name for cattle or steers. In British heraldry, the 'male griffin' is shown without wings, its body covered with tufts of formidable spikes. Confusingly, the 'griffin' is depicted as having male sex organs.

Hippogriffin - the Horse Eagle

Hippogriffins had the wings, head, plumage and front talons of a gryphon, and the lower quarters of a horse instead of a lion. It was the uncontrollable horse

of the wizard Atlantis, in Ariosto's poem *Orlando Furioso* of 1532. The idea of the hippogriffin came from Virgil's metaphor '*to cross gryphons with horses*', meaning to attempt the impossible.

Lupogriffin - the Dog Eagle

Lupogriffins have canine parts instead of feline parts. Early accounts of the Persian bird Simurgh depicted it as half-dog and half-bird. Simurgh represented the union between the earth and the sky. It roosted in the Tree of Life, and lived in the land of the sacred Haoma plant, whose seeds could cure all evil. Simurgh had an enmity towards snakes, and was said to live for 1700 years, before plunging itself into flames, as the Phoenix does.

HARPIES - THE HOUNDS OF ZEUS
In Graeco-Roman mythology, the Harpies were the storm-spirits, depicted as two- or three-winged women, with the lower bodies of birds and long, sharp claws. In Homer's *Odyssey* they were winds that carried people away, but they later came to have faces, pale with hunger, and surpassing all winds and birds in the speed of  their flight. The Harpies were despatched by Zeus to snatch away people and things from the earth, so mysterious disappearances were attributed to them. People thought that they stole small children, and that they also carried away the weak and the wounded. In this form they were the agents of the punishment of Zeus, abducting and torturing victims on their way to Tartarus, the dungeon of torment beneath the underworld. They were vicious, cruel and violent, only obeying Zeus. In sculpture, the Harpies

Harpies Sent As Punishment

The Harpies were sent by Zeus to plague the blind King Phineas, the Phoenician king of Thrace, as punishment for revealing the secrets of the gods. Whenever a plate of food was set before him, the Harpies would swoop down and snatch it away, fouling any scraps left behind. When Jason and the Argonauts stopped there, the king promised to tell them which course to take, in return for deliverance from the monsters. The Harpies were chased away by two winged Argonauts, who were sons of the North Wind, to the Strophades Islands. Here, Iris, goddess of the rainbow, commanded the Argonauts to turn back and leave the storm-spirits unharmed. Thus the two small Strophades Islands (in the Ionian group), meaning '*Islands of Turning*', became the dwelling-place of the Harpies, and they drove the Trojans from the isles.

were represented as demons of death, carrying away the souls of the deceased, but their presence as tomb figures makes it possible that they were also seen as ghosts. In the Middle Ages, the harpy, often called the 'virgin eagle', became a popular device in heraldry.

HERCINIA - THE GLOWING BIRD
The hercinia is a bird born in the Hercynian forest in Germany, which acts as a beacon for travellers because its feathers glow so brightly in the dark that they light the path. It was recorded by both Pliny the Elder and Isidore of Seville. Some illustrations of the hercinia show the bird covered in gold or silver leaf to indicate its bright glow. The Hercynian Forest was a vast ancient woodland that stretched eastward from the Rhine across southern Germany. The Black Forest is a western remnant.

HERON - THE WISEST BIRD
Isidore of Seville tells us that: '*The heron (ardea) is named as if it were ardua, in flight for others. It is afraid of lightning and so flies above the clouds to avoid the gusts; when it flies high it signifies a storm.*' The heron was thought to be wiser

than all other birds, because it does not have many resting places, but lives near its food supply, nesting in high trees above water. It was admired because it never ate carrion, and used its beak to defend the young in its nest from other birds.

HOOPOE - THE CARING BIRD

'When the bird called the hoopoe sees that its parents have grown old and that their eyes are dim, it plucks out their old plumage and licks their eyes and keeps them warm, and its parents' life is renewed. It as if the hoopoe said to them: "Just as you took pains in feeding me, I will do likewise for you."... Let man, who is endowed with reason, learn his duty to his mother and father, from the way in which this creature, which lacks reason, provides (as we have already shown) for its parents' needs when they are old.' (The Aberdeen Bestiary c.1200). However, the Greeks thought that it roosted in human faeces and burial places, feeding on excrement. The hoopoe was said to take pleasure in grief, and if the blood of the hoopoe is rubbed on a sleeping man, he would have nightmares about demons suffocating him.

THE HUS KLAZOMENAIOS

This mythical beast, a gigantic winged sow terrorized the ancient Greek town of Klazomenai, on an island west of Smyrna. Aelian wrote in the second century CE: *'I have heard that on Klazomenai there was a Sow with wings, and it ravaged the territory of Klazomenai. And Artemon records this in his "Annals of Klazomenai". That is why there is a spot named and celebrated as "The Place of the Winged Sow", and it is famous. But if anyone regards this as myth, let him do so.'*

IBIS - THE SACRED BIRD OF EGYPT

The Greek historian Herodotus told how every spring winged snakes came flying from Arabia towards Egypt, but they were met in a gorge by ibises, who destroyed them all. Thus the Egyptians held the ibis in reverence. Pliny later wrote: *'The ibis is a bird from Egypt. It uses its curved beak to purge itself ... through the part by which it is most conducive to health for the heavy residue of foodstuffs to be excreted... The people of Egypt invoke the ibis to guard against the arrival of snakes... The ibis is born black at Pelesium, but is white everywhere else.'* Isidore of Seville noted: *'The ibis is a bird of the river Nile. It eats the eggs of snakes, and purges itself by pouring water into its anus with its beak.'* Aelian noted: *'The Black Ibis does not permit the Ophies Pterotos [Winged Serpents] from Arabia to cross into Aigyptos but fights to protect the land it loves.'*

MAGPIE EGG MOVEMENT

Pliny the Elder wrote: *'If magpies see someone watching their nest, they move the eggs to another location. Since the claws of these birds are not suited to carry eggs, they use a clever method: they place a twig across two of the eggs and attach it with glue from their stomach, then put their neck under the twig, and balancing the eggs on either side, carry them away... There is a certain kind of magpie that can learn words; they become fond of some words, and not only repeat them but can be seen to ponder them. To learn a word they must hear it said often, and if a word is too difficult for them to learn they may die. When they forget a word they cheer up greatly when they hear it spoken.'*

NIGHTINGALES COMPETE TO THE DEATH

The nightingale sings to relieve the tedium as it sits on the nest through the night, and at dawn it sings so enthusiastically that it almost dies. Pliny the Elder recorded: '*Nightingales sing continuously for fifteen days and nights when leaves first appear in the spring. This bird has a remarkable knowledge of music, and uses all of the arts that human science has developed in the mechanism of the flute. Each bird knows several songs, with the songs differing beween birds. There is great competition and rivalry between them; the one who loses the competition often dies, her breath giving out before her song. Young nightingales are taught music by their elders; they are given verses to practise, and improve their singing under the criticism of the instructor.*'

OPHIES PTERETOS

These feathered winged serpents guarded the frankincense of Arabia, and were sometimes called *Ophies Amphipterotoi*, or 'Serpents with Two Pairs of Wings'. Herodotus recorded: '*Arabia is the most distant to the south of all inhabited countries: and this is the only country which produces frankincense and myrrh and cassia and cinnamon and gum-mastic. All these except myrrh are difficult for the Arabians to get. They gather frankincense by burning that storax which Phoenicians carry to Hellas [Greece]; they burn this and so get the frankincense; for the spice-bearing trees are guarded by small Winged Snakes of varied colour, many around each tree; these are the snakes that attack Egypt. Nothing except the smoke of storax will drive them away from the trees...*

So too if the vipers and the Winged Serpents of Arabia were born in the natural manner of serpents, life would be impossible for men; but as it is, when they copulate, while the male is in the act of procreation and as soon as he has ejaculated his seed, the female seizes him by the neck, and does not let go until she has bitten through. The male dies in the way described, but the female suffers in return for the male the following punishment: avenging their father, the young while they are still within the womb gnaw at their mother and eating through her bowels thus make their way out. Other snakes, that do no harm to men, lay eggs and hatch out a vast number of young. The Arabian Winged Serpents do indeed seem to be numerous; but that is because (although there are vipers in every land) these are all in Arabia and are found nowhere else.' Aelian relates: '*Megasthenes states that in India there are... snakes (ophies) with wings, and that their visitations occur not during the daytime but by night, and that they emit urine which at once produces a festering wound on any body on which it may happen to drop.*'

ORPHAN BIRD

This lives in India in a sea called '*la mer darenoise*', according to Pierre de Beauvais' 13th-century *Bestiaire*. It has a crest, a neck and chest like those of a peacock, the beak of an eagle, the feet of a swan, and the body of a crane. Its wings are red, white and black. It lays its eggs on the surface of the water. The mother can tell which eggs hold the best chicks: the good eggs float a little below the mother, while the bad ones sink to the sand at the bottom of the sea.

OSTRICH - THE ROCK THROWER

The ancients believed that it could digest anything, even iron, and only laid its eggs when it saw the star Virgilia (the Pleiades) rising. Pliny the Elder wrote: *'The ostrich, found in Ethiopia and Africa, is the largest of birds, being taller and faster than a mounted horseman. It cannot fly. Its wings are used only to assist it in running. Its feet, which it uses as weapons, resemble the hooves of stags, being cloven in two. When it runs from pursuers it picks up rocks with its feet and throws them back at the enemy. It has a remarkable ability to digest anything it swallows. Its stupidity is shown when it hides its head in a bush and thinks it is invisible, even though its large body is not hidden.'*

OWL - THE FUNEREAL BIRD

Bestiaries divide the species into *noctua*, the night-owl, which lives in the walls of ruined houses and hates the light; *nictocorax*, the night-raven; and the *bubo*, the common owl, a dirty bird that pollutes its nest. In The Bible (Leviticus), Hebraic law states that a variety of owls are included in *'the birds you are to detest and not eat because they are detestible'*. Christians have regarded the owl as representing the Jews, who preferred darkness to light when they rejected Christ. Its long hooked beak was emphasized in religious illustrations to further identify it with Jews. Pliny the Elder wrote that: *'The eagle-owl is thought to be a very bad omen, being as it is a funereal bird. It lives in deserts and in terrifying, empty and inaccessible places. Its cry is a scream. If it is seen in a city, or during the day, it is a*

direful portent, and several cases are known of an eagle-owl perching on private houses without fatal consequences... The owl never flies directly to where it wants to go, but always travels slantwise from its course... Night-owls are crafty in battles with other birds; when surrounded and outnumbered they lie on their backs and fight with their feet, bunching themselves up so they are protected by beak and claws. The have an alliance with the hawk which comes and aids them in the war. Nigidius says that night-owls hibernate for 60 days in the winter.' Isidore of Seville noted: *'Another kind of screech owl (strix) has its name from its strident (stridet) call. It is also called by the Greek word amma (nurse) because it loves (amando) infants and is said to offer milk to the newborn.'*

PARTRIDGE - THE HOMOSEXUAL WIND-BREAKER

Pliny the Elder tells us: *'Partridges protect their nests with thorns and twigs so that they are safe from animals. After the eggs are laid the partridge moves them somewhere else, so that the laying place does not become known, and covers them with soft dust. The hens hide their eggs even from their mates, because the males break the eggs so that the females remain available to them. The cocks fight duels with each other over their desire for the hens; it is said that the loser in the fight has to submit sexually to the winner. The hens can become pregnant by merely standing facing the cock, and if they open their beak and put out their tongue at that time, they are sexually excited. Even the air blown from a cock partridge flying overhead, or the sound of a cock crowing, is enough to cause pregnancy. If a fowler approaches the* nest, the hen will lure him away by running away while pretending to be injured. If the hen has no eggs to protect, she does not run but lies on her back in a furrow and holds a clod of earth in her claws to cover herself.' Isidore of Seville elaborates: 'The partridge [perdix] gets its name from perdesthai [to break wind]. It is an impure bird because through lust males have sex with males. It is a deceitful bird that steals and hatches the eggs of other birds, but it gets no benefit from this, because when the chicks hear the voice

of their true mother they leave the one who hatched them and return to their mother.'

PEACOCK - THE VOICE OF A FIEND Again Pliny's *Natural History* has a characteristically intriguing description. 'The peacock is conscious of its own beauty and takes pride in it. When praised, it spreads out its feathers to face the sun, so they shine more brilliantly, and curves its tail to throw shadows on its body, because the colours there shine more brightly

Pegasus – the Winged Horse

In Greek mythology, Pegasus was sired by Poseidon on the Gorgon Medusa, after Poseidon violated her in Athena's shrine. When Medusa's head was cut off by the Greek hero Perseus, Pegasus flew from her pregnant body, or from her blood when it touched the earth. Athena caught and tamed Pegasus and presented him to the Muses on Mt Helicon, where, having struck the ground with his hoof, a spring began to flow, which became sacred to the Muses as the fountain Hippocrene. While Pegasus was drinking from the well, the Corinthian King Bellerophon was able to capture him by using a golden bridle, a gift from Athena. With the help of Pegasus, Bellephoron was then able to destroy the three-headed monster Chimaera. Unfortunately,

however, proud Bellerophon then attempted to fly on Pegasus to join the gods on Mt Olympus. Zeus was angry, and sent an insect to sting Pegasus, causing the horse to throw Bellerophon from his back. Bellophoron did not die from his fall but remained lame and blind as a consequence. Pegasus was then installed in the Olympian stables where he was entrusted to bring Zeus his lightning and thunderbolts. The horse was also placed amongst the stars as a constellation, the rising of which marked the arrival of the warmer weather of spring and seasonal rainstorms. (Pegasos means 'springing forth'.) Pegasus's story became a favourite theme in Greek art and literature, and Pegasus's soaring flight was interpreted as an allegory of the soul's immortality.

in the dark. It is pleased when others look at the eyes on its tail feathers; it pulls them all together in a cluster for this purpose. When the peacock's tail feathers drop out during the Autumn moult, it is ashamed and hides itself until new feathers grow in. Peacocks live for 25 years, but their colours begin to fade at the age of three. Some say that this bird is spiteful as well as ostentatious. The orator Hotensius was the first person to kill a peacock for use as food; later Lurco made great profits in the fattening and sale of peacocks for the table.' St Augustine wondered why its flesh had an '*antiseptic property*', as, when cooked, it did not decay over the period of a year. Isidore of Seville also remarked on the fact: '*The peacock [pavo] takes its name from the sound of its voice. Its flesh is so hard that it barely decays and is difficult to cook.*' Bartholomaeus Anglicus, a 13th-century English monk who wrote an encyclopedia called *De proprictatibus rerum* (On the nature of kings), wrote: '*The peacock has an unsteadfast and evil-shapen head, as it were the head of a serpent, and with a crest. And he has a simple pace, and small neck and area red, and a blue breast, and a tail full of eyes distinguished and high with wonderful fairness, and he has foul feet… And he wonders at the fairness of his feathers, and rears them up as it were a*

circle about his head, and then he looks to his feet, and sees the foulness of his feet, and as if he were ashamed he lets his feathers fall suddenly, and all the tail downward, as though he took no heed of the fairness of his feathers. And as one says, he has the voice of a fiend, head of a serpent, pace of a thief. For he hath an horrible voice.'

THE PEGASOI AITHIOPES

This tribe of winged, horned horses was native to Ethiopia (subSaharan Africa). Pegasus himself was said to have been born near Ethiopia, on the Red Sea island of Erytheia. Pliny the Elder noted: '*Aethiopia produces… many monstrosities… [including] winged horses armed with horns, called Pegasoi.*'

THE PELICAN IN HER PIETY

Pliny the Elder thought that: '*Pelicans have a second stomach in their throats, in which the insatiable creatures place food, increasing their capacity; later they take the food from that stomach and pass it to the true stomach.*' Isidore of Seville related: '*The pelican is an Egyptian bird that lives in the solitude of the river Nile. Its is said that she kills her offspring and grieves for*

them for three days, then wounds herself and sheds her blood to revive her sons. It has a Greek name (onocrotalos) from its long beak; there are two kinds, aquatic and solitary.' In Guillaume le Clerc's 13th-century *Bestaire* we read: 'The pelican is a wonderful bird which dwells in the region about the river Nile. The written history tells us that there are two kinds, those which dwell in the river and eat nothing but fish, and those which dwell in the desert and eat only insects and worms. There is a wonderful thing about the pelican, for never did mother-sheep love her lamb as the pelican loves its young. When the young are born, the parent bird devotes all his care and thought to nourishing them. But the young birds are ungrateful, and when they have grown strong and self-reliant they peck at their father's face, and he, enraged at their wickedness, kills them all. On the third day the father comes to them, deeply moved with pity and sorrow. With his beak he pierces his own side, until the blood flows forth. With the blood he brings back life into the body of his young.' Bartholomaeus Anglicus believed that the mother, not the father, pelican brought the young back to life, and 'The Pelican in Her Piety' is an illustration of the event found in many manuscripts, sculptures, and church carvings such as misericords. There is even an old pub known to this author, called 'The Pelican in Her Piety' on the River Ogmore near Ewenni, Glamorgan.

PERYTON - THE WINGED DEER

This is a hardly recorded legendary creature, a combination of a stag and a bird, said to hail from the lost continent of Atlantis, and which played a part in the fall of Rome. It possessed the head, neck, forelegs and antlers of a

stag, along with the plumage, wings and hindquarters of a large bird. It developed large incisors with a ravenous taste for human flesh. The Sibyl of Erythraea is said to have foretold that the city of Rome would finally be destroyed by perytons. In 642 CE most of the records of the Sibyl's prophecies were burnt in Omar's destruction of Alexandria's Library, however. In the 16th century a rabbi from Fez, probably Jakob Ben Chaim, left a work in which he quoted a Greek source: 'The Perytons had their original dwelling in Atlantis and are half deer, half bird. They have the deer's head and legs. As for its body, it is perfectly avian, with corresponding wings and plumage... Its strangest trait is that, when the sun strikes it, instead of casting a shadow of its own body, it casts the shadow of a man. From this, some conclude that the Perytons are the spirits of wayfarers who have died far from their homes and from the care of their gods... and have been surprised eating dry earth... flying in flocks and have been seen at a dizzying height above the Columns of Hercules... they [Perytons] are mortal foes of the human race; when they succeed in killing a man, their shadow is that of their own body and they win back the favour of their gods... and those who crossed the seas with [Publius Cornelius] Scipio [237–183 BCE] to conquer Carthage came close to failure, for during the passage a formation of Perytons swooped down on the ships, killing and mangling many... Although our weapons have no effect against it, the animal if such it be can kill no more than a single man... wallowing in the gore of its victims and then fleeing upward on its powerful wings... in Ravenna, where they were last seen, telling of their plumage which they described as light blue in colour, which greatly surprised me for all that is known of their dark green feathers.' The rabbi's treatise was last known to be in Dresden's university library, and it is not known whether it was burnt by the Nazis, or destroyed in the bombing of Dresden.

PHOENIX - THE FIREBIRD

There are two versions of the legend of the phoenix. In the first, it is an Indian bird which lives to 500 years of age, when it flies to a frankincense tree and fills its wings with spices. In early spring a priest at Heliopolis covers an altar with twigs. The phoenix comes to the city, sees the altar, lights a fire there and is consumed by it. The next day a small, sweet-smelling worm is found in the ashes. On the second day the worm has transformed into a small bird, and on the third has the form of the phoenix again. The bird then returns to its place of origin in India. The other version says that the phoenix is a purple or red bird that lives in Arabia. There is only one living phoenix in the world at any time. When it is old, it builds a pyre of wood and spices and climbs on to it. It faces the sun and the fire ignites, and the phoenix fans the fire with its wings until it is completely consumed. A new phoenix rises from the ash of the old. Some tales mix the two stories. Lapis Excilis was the name given to the fabulous precious stone which caused the phoenix to renew her youth, and Wolfram von Eschenbach equated it with the Holy Grail. In the fifth century BCE, Herodotus wrote: '*They have also another sacred bird called the phoenix which I myself have never*

seen, except in pictures. Indeed it is a great rarity, even in Egypt, only coming there (according to the accounts of the people of Heliopolis) once in five hundred years, when the old phoenix dies. Its size and appearance, if it is like the pictures, are as follows:- The plumage is partly red, partly golden, while the general make and size are almost exactly that of the eagle. They tell a story of what this bird does, which does not seem to me to be credible: that he comes all the way from Arabia, and brings the parent bird, all plastered over with myrrh, to the temple of the Sun, and there buries the body. In order to bring him, they say, he first forms a ball of myrrh as big as he finds that he can carry; then he hollows out the ball, and puts his parent inside, after which he covers over the opening with fresh myrrh, and the ball is then of exactly the same weight as at first; so he brings it to Egypt, plastered over as I have said, and deposits it in the temple of the Sun. Such is the story they tell of the doings of this bird.'

Pliny the Elder believed: '*The phoenix, of which there is only one in the world, is the size of an eagle. It is gold around the neck, its body is purple, and its tail is blue with some rose-coloured feathers. It has a feathered crest on its head. No one has ever seen the Phoenix feeding. In Arabia it is sacred to the sun god. It lives 540 years; when it is old it builds a nest from wild cinnamon and frankincense, fills the nest with scents, and lies down on it until it dies. From the bones and marrow of the dead phoenix there grows a sort of maggot, which grows into a bird the size of a chicken. This bird performs* funeral rites for its predecessor, then carries the whole nest to the City of the Sun near Panchaia and places it on an altar there.'

There are firebird traditions across the world, in Phoenicia, Greece, Arabia, Russia, China and Egypt among other regions. The phoenix is associated with resurrection, immortality, triumph over adversity, and that which rises out of the ashes, so became a favourite symbol on early Christian tombstones. Romans placed the phoenix on coins and medals as an emblem of their desire for the Roman empire to last forever. The Egyptians identified the phoenix with a stork-like bird called a bennu, identified in

their funerary text *The Book of the Dead* as one of the sacred symbols of worship in Heliopolis, associated with the rising Sun and the Sun-god Ra. From this description, some people believe that the phoenix is actually the pink flamingo. The flamingo nests on salt flats in Africa which are too hot for its eggs to be viable. Thus they build mounds to support and slightly cool the eggs, and the convection currents surrounding the nests suggest the turbulence of flames. This author has seen mirages and the hot, shimmering air seems like a fire haze. Flamingos are part of the Phoenicopteridae family, meaning 'phoenix-winged', and the oldest living bird is over 75 years old.

Phoenix Rising

In Ovid's first-century *Metamorphoses*, Book 15, we read: '*…there is one, a bird, which renews itself, and reproduces from itself. The Assyrians call it the Phoenix. It does not live on seeds and herbs, but on drops of incense, and the sap of the cardamom plant. When it has lived for five centuries, it then builds a nest for itself in the topmost branches of a swaying palm tree, using only its beak and talons. As soon as it has lined it with cassia bark, and smooth spikes of nard [lavender], cinnamon fragments and yellow myrrh, it settles on top, and ends its life among the perfumes. They say that, from the parent's body, a young phoenix is reborn, destined to live the same number of years. When age has given it strength, and it can carry burdens, it lightens the branches of the* tall palm of the heavy nest, and piously carries its own cradle, that was its father's tomb, and, reaching the city of Hyperion, the sun-god [Heliopolis in Egypt], through the clear air, lays it down in front of the sacred doors of Hyperion's Temple of the Sun.'

QUETZALCOATL - THE PLUMED SERPENT GOD

Quetzalcoatl ('feathered serpent' or 'plumed serpent') is the Nahuatl name for the winged serpent-god of ancient Mesoamerican Olmec, Mixtec, Toltec and Aztec civilizations who may have adopted it from the people of Teotihuacan, and the Maya. It was also the name given to some Toltec rulers. It was worshipped for almost 2000 years, until the Spanish Conquest. The snake represents the earth and vegetation, but it was in Teotihuacan (around 150 BCE) that the snake acquired the precious feathers of the quetzal bird, as seen in murals in the city. The most elaborate representations come from the ancient Quetzalcoatl Temple built around 200 BCE, which show a rattlesnake with the long green feathers of the quetzal. In time Quetzalcoatl was mixed with other gods, and acquired some of their attributes. Eventually Quetzalcoatl was transformed into one of the gods of the creation. The Aztec Emperor Moctezuma II initially believed that the landing of conquistador Hernán Cortés in 1519 signified Quetzalcoatl's return. As a gift, Moctezuma specifically sent Cortés treasures depicting Quetzalcoatl. It is believed by many Mormons that Quetzalcoatl was a name given to Jesus Christ when he visited the Nephites (or group of Native Americans) on the American continent shortly after his Resurrection, as is depicted in *The Book of Mormon*.

THE ROC - THE ELEPHANT-CARRYING BIRD

A roc (from the Persian *rokh*) is a huge mythical bird, usually white, that is reputed to have been able to carry off and eat elephants. It was popularized by Marco Polo's *Book of Travels* and the *1001 Nights* tales of Abd al-Rahman and Sinbad the Sailor. According to Marco Polo, the wingspan of the roc was 16 yards (15 m) and the feathers 8 yards, and its feathers were as big as palm leaves. The roc could carry an elephant in its claws and it would kill it by flying to a great height then dropping the unfortunate creature to crash to its death on the rocks below. According to Arabic tradition, the roc never lands on earth, only on the mountain Qaf, the centre of the world. The home of the bird was thought to be in Madagascar, from where gigantic fronds of the raffia palm, very like feather quills in form, appear to have been taken to the Great Khan under the name of 'roc's feathers'. In fact Madagascar was the home of the gigantic bird the *Aepyornis maximus* or '*elephant bird*'. Although unable to fly, the bird may not have gone extinct until the 16th century.

ROPEN - THE INDONESIAN PTEROSAUR

The ropen is a fabulous creature and a cryptid (an undiscovered creature, like Bigfoot or the Loch Ness Monster) in the Umboi and Manus islands near Papua New Guinea. It is said to possess two leathery wings like a bat, a long tail with a flange on the end, a beak filled with teeth and razor-sharp claws. According to Jonathan Whitcomb's book *Searching for Ropens*, it is '*any featherless creature that flies in the Southwest Pacific, and has a tail-length more than 25% of its wingspan.*' The ropen is believed to be nocturnal and to exhibit bioluminescence, which the natives call '*indava*'. It lives on a diet of fish, although there have been reports of the creature feasting on human carrion after a grave robbery. A pilot, Duane Hodgkinson, was stationed in Papua New Guinea in 1944. Once he was startled by a crashing in the brush and a large bird-like creature slowly rose from the ground, circled and flew away. Hodgkinson estimated the wingspan to be about 20 feet (6 m), and said that it was dark grey, with a long serpentine neck and distinctive head crest. In 1987, Tyson Hughes, an English missionary, began an 18-month contract to assist the Moluccan tribespeople of Ceram Island, Indonesia to develop efficient farms. He heard stories about a terrifying creature called the *Orang-bati* ('men with wings') with enormous leathery wings like a bat and which lived in the caves of Mount Kairatu, an extinct volcano situated in the centre of the island. There was a sighting in 1994 of a ropen with a 20-foot (6-m) wingspan, and a mouth like that of a crocodile. There are many reports of the beast, often with different names, being spotted by remote tribes. It may be simply a misidentification of a frigate bird or flying fox fruit bat, but some western investigators believe it may be a surviving long-tailed pterosaur (a flying reptile that lived at the same time as the dinosaurs), that has somehow remained living in caves in the Bismarck Archipelago.

SERAPHIM AND OTHER ANGELS

The First Sphere of Angels:

There are many different rankings of angels (see also pages 144–149), with the writings of Clement of Rome, St Ambrose, St Jerome, St Gregory, St Isidore and St Thomas Aquinas all offering differing accounts. However, in the generally accepted hierarchy of celestial beings, seraphim, cherubim and ophanim are in the top rank, or 'first sphere'.

Seraphim - The Burning Ones are

mentioned in Isaiah and act as the caretakers of God's throne, continuously proclaiming: '*Holy, holy, holy is the Lord of hosts. All the earth is filled with His Glory.*' The seraphim have six wings; two covering their faces, two covering their bodies and two with which they fly. The seraph known as *Seraphiel* is said to have the head of an eagle. Such a radiant light emanates from them that nothing, not

even other angelic beings, can look upon them. Four seraphim surround God's throne, where they burn eternally from love and zeal for God.

Cherubim have four faces: one each of an ox, lion, eagle and man. The ox-face is considered the 'true face' as in the Book of Ezekiel the ox's face is called a cherub's face. Cherubim have four conjoined wings covered with eyes, and they have the feet of an ox. They are the elect beings for the purpose of protection, guarding the throne of God and the way to the Tree of Life in the Garden of Eden. For some reason we now confuse the 'putti', the winged human baby-like beings used in figurative art, as cherubs.

Ophanim or Thrones or Erelim or Elders or Wheels Mentioned by Paul of Tarsus, they are living symbols of God's justice and authority, and have as one of their symbols the throne. In the vision of Daniel, they appear as a beryl-coloured wheel inside another wheel, their rims covered with hundreds of eyes. In Ezekiel, they are associated with the cherubim: '*When they moved, the others moved; when they stopped, the others stopped; and when they rose from the earth, the wheels rose along with them; for the spirit of the living creatures* [cherubim] *was in the wheels.*'

The Second Sphere of Angels:
Angels of the Second Sphere work as heavenly governors:

Dominions or Lordships or Hashmallim These regulate the duties of lower angels, and it is extremely rare for these lordships to make themselves known to humans. They are also the angels who preside over nations. Dominions are supposed to look like divinely beautiful humans with a pair of feathered wings, much like the common representation of angels, but are distinguished from celestial beings by wielding orbs of light fastened to the heads of their sceptres or on the pommels of their swords.

Virtues or Strongholds They lie beyond the ophanim, supervising the movements of the heavenly bodies in order to ensure that the cosmos remains in order. They are presented in religious paintings as the Celestial Choir.

Powers or Authorities Their duty is to oversee the distribution of power among humankind, hence their name, and they collaborate, in power and authority, with the principalities. They are the bearers of conscience and the keepers of history. They are also the warrior angels created to be completely loyal to God. Some believe that no power has ever fallen from grace, but another theory states that Satan was the chief of the powers before he fell.

The Third Sphere of Angels:
Angels who act as heavenly messengers and soldiers.

Principalities or Princedoms or Rulers
These celestial beings appear to collaborate in power and authority with the powers. The principalities are depicted wearing a crown and carrying a sceptre. They carry out the orders given to them by the dominions and bequeath blessings to the material world. Their task is to oversee groups of people. They are the educators and guardians of the realm of Earth. Like beings related to the world of the germinal ideas, they are said to inspire living things to create art and to pursue scientific enquiry.

Archangels or Chief Angels Only Michael (the chief archangel) and Gabriel are mentioned in the *New Testament*. Raphael is mentioned in some sources as an archangel, as is Uriel (Fire of God). There may be as many as seven archangels, possibly representing the seven spirits of God that stand before the throne described in the books of Revelation and Enoch. They are also said to be the guardian angels of nations and

countries, and are concerned with the issues and events surrounding them, including politics, military matters, commerce and trade.

Angels or Malakhim or Messengers
The lowest order of the angels, and the most recognized. They are the ones most concerned with the affairs of living things. The angels are sent from heaven as messengers to mankind.

SIMURGH - THE PERSIAN DOG-BIRD Also known as *Angha*, this is the Persian name for a mythical, benevolent flying creature. It is depicted as a winged creature in the shape of a bird, gigantic enough to carry off an elephant or a whale. It appears as a kind of peacock with the head of a dog and the claws of a lion, but sometimes has a human face. The simurgh is female, and inherently benevolent. Its feathers are copper-coloured, and she was originally described as being a 'Dog-Bird', but was

shown with either the head of a human or a dog. Persian legends consider the bird so old that it had seen the destruction of the world three times over and had learned so much by living so long that it possessed the knowledge of all the ages. In one tale, the simurgh lived for 1700 years before plunging itself into flames, like the phoenix. It purified the land and waters and hence bestowed fertility. The creature represented the union between the earth and the sky, serving as mediator and messenger between the two, much like an angel. It roosted in the Tree of Life, which stood in the middle of the world sea. When the simurgh took flight, the leaves of the Tree of Life shook, making all the seeds of every plant in the world to fall out. These seeds floated around the world, taking root to become every type of plant that ever lived, and able to cure all the illnesses of mankind.

WYVERN A wyvern or wivern is a legendary winged reptile with the head of a dragon, the hindquarters of a snake or lizard with either two legs or none, and a barbed tail. The wyvern is often found in medieval heraldry and its name is derived from Middle English wyvere, from Old North French wivre meaning 'viper'. Wyverns are mentioned in Dante's *Inferno* (Canto XVII) as the body for one of his creatures in hell. The wyvern is frequently used as a mascot, especially in Wales and Wessex, but also farther afield in the counties of Herefordshire and Worcestershire, where the rivers Wye and Severn run through the county towns of Hereford and Worcester respectively. Some cryptozoologists have interpreted wyverns as surviving pterosaurs, which went extinct around 65 million years ago. There are alleged sightings of pterosaur-like creatures in remote areas of the world, such as the Kongamato in Africa.

CHAPTER 5
Mysteries *of* *the* Deep

ARGO AND THE GOLDEN FLEECE

In Greek mythology, Jason and the Argonauts sailed in a ship called the *Argo* to find the Golden Fleece, the skin of a fabulous winged ram. She was built by Argus, helped by the goddess Athena, and the goddess Hera protected her crew. After her successful voyage, she was consecrated to the sea god Poseidon at Corinth, and then turned into the constellation of Argo Navis. The Argonauts seem to be symbols of the first Greek mariners who discovered that the Black Sea was not an open sea. The voyage has been traced to Lemnos, Samothrace, through the Hellespont to Kyzikos and Colchis on the Black Sea, then along the Rivers Danube, Po and Rhône and across the Mediterranean Sea, to Libya and Crete etc. A 'replica' of the *Argo*, a 50-oar galley carrying a crew from all 27 EU member states, sailed from the Corinth Canal in 2008. The intention was to sail and row from Iolkos (near Volos) to the ancient Black Sea kingdom of Colchis in modern

Georgia. However, Turkish authorities could not guarantee a safe passage, so the *Argo* travelled 1200 nautical miles (2200 km) from Volos to Venice.

ATLANTIS and LEMURIA

During the most recent Ice Age the world's sea level stood about 330 feet (100 m) lower than it is today. Sea water had evaporated and been deposited as ice and snow in glaciers. Most of these glaciers had melted by about 10,000 years ago, and the thawing of the remaining glaciers has caused rising sea levels ever since – global warming is not a new phenomenon. These sea level rises have probably helped to generate folk-tales of the lost lands of Atlantis and similar legends all around the world. Many creation myths involve a great flood. Factual details are confusing because of the abundance of variables, but we may currently be experiencing acceleration in rising seas. The sea level has risen an average of 4–10 inches (10–25 cm) in the last century, and the rate is increasing. Because the oceans react very slowly to change, levels will continue to rise even if the global climate is stabilized soon. Loss of ice on Antarctica has the potential to be the biggest cause of rising sea levels in coming decades. If all the ice melted, which scientists consider highly unlikely by 2100, it is estimated that the sea level would rise by around 200 feet (61 m), compared with 22 feet (7 m) if all of Greenland's glaciers were to melt. The fabled land of Atlantis seems to be a folk memory of days before the oceans rose and inundated fertile lowlands, and also perhaps of natural catastrophes which wiped out parts of the land. Places with a claim to be 'Atlantis' include an area

Lemurians were both highly evolved and very spiritual, and survivors are said still to live in tunnels in Mt Shasta in northern California. However, scientists say that the concept of Lemuria has been rendered superfluous by the modern understanding of plate tectonics.

THE BARHAM AND THE

WITCH The British battleship HMS *Barham* had an interesting history. She was hit five times at the Battle of Jutland in 1916, and in 1939 was damaged by a German U-boat in the North Sea. In 1940 she was again badly damaged by shells from the French battleship *Richelieu* and a torpedo from a French submarine *Beziers*, while attempting to land Free French troops at Senegal. In 1941 she sustained bomb damage off Crete. The battleship was later torpedoed on 25 November 1941, with the loss of 861 lives, but the Admiralty did not announce the disaster for fear of harming morale. The Germans did not know that their submarine *U-331*

off Bimini in the Bahamas, the west coast of Wales (with the bells of Aberdyfi still ringing under the waves), the coast of Ireland, the Peloponnese, Nigeria, Heligoland, the Black Sea, Tunisia, the Aegean, Santorini, America, Spain, Germany and Madeira. Fossilized trees are found at low water marks in some of these places, for instance in Wales. One simple illustration of global warming is provided by the fact that there was a stagecoach from London to Holyhead in Anglesey for people to take a ship to Ireland in the 17th century. The coach used to leave mainland Wales for the island of Anglesey at low tide. At low tide now, about 300 years later, there is at least ten feet (3 m) in the way. It has long been postulated that a 'lost' civilization existed prior to, and during, the time when Atlantis flourished. Some believe that these people lived in *Lemuria*. This was thought to lie largely in the Southern Pacific, between North America and Asia/Australia. Lemuria is also sometimes referred to as *Mu*, or the *Motherland*. The

had sunk the *Barham*, so the Admiralty kept the news secret to mislead them. Helen Duncan was one of Britain's best-known mediums at the time, and she lived in Portsmouth. At a séance a day or so after the sinking she saw a sailor with the hatband HMS *Barham* who told her '*My ship has sunk*'. The Admiralty later informed the relatives of the crew and asked them to keep the sinking secret. The Admiralty placed Helen Duncan under observation, and she was arrested in January 1944, over two years after the event. At her ten-day trial in March 1944, the prosecution could not prove that she was a traitor, so had her convicted under the 1735 Witchcraft Act. She was the last person jailed as a witch in Great Britain, and served nine months in Holloway Prison. Helen Duncan, a mother of six and a grandmother, was arrested again in 1956 after a police raid on a séance and died soon afterwards. Her grandchildren are trying to win a posthumous pardon for the medium.

BERMUDA TRIANGLE (DEVIL'S TRIANGLE)

The 500,000 square miles (1.3 million km²) of sea between Bermuda, San Juan in Puerto Rico and Miami is where we find *'hurricane alley'*. Millions of pounds of treasure lie in sunken Spanish and Portuguese galleons in this area. The term 'Bermuda Triangle' comes from a magazine article written in 1964 about the disappearance of *Flight 19* (see page 195) The currents in this area are strongly affected by the Gulf Stream, which flows northeasterly from the tip of Florida. Seamen unfamiliar with the area can easily be pushed off-course either to the north or northeast by the Triangle's swift currents. Navigational errors, compounded by sudden freak storms, make this a dangerous area for shipping. Huge amounts of warm water press through the Florida Straits into the Gulf Stream. Because of evaporation, they are extremely saline, and the dynamics of this heavier water sinking, while lighter water rises, causes whirlpools and heavy turbulence in the sea. The sharp and deep drop from the continental shelf also causes strange maritime conditions. Another problem may be that earth tremors release vast pockets of methane gas from the ocean floor, which can cause

sea conditions in which a ship will quickly founder. As recently as 1963, the *Marine Sulphur West*, an 11,000-ton tanker with a crew of 39, simply disappeared without trace 200 miles (320 km) off Key West in Florida.

BISHOP-FISH - THE CHRISTIAN SEA-MONSTER

The bishop-fish is a type of European sea-monster. It has the shaved head of a Catholic monk and the body of a huge fish. Its existence was documented as early as the 13th century when one was caught swimming in the Baltic Sea. It was then taken to the king of Poland, who wished to keep it. It was also shown to some Catholic bishops, to whom the bishop-fish gestured, appealing to be released. They granted its wish, at which point it made the sign of the cross and disappeared into the sea. Another was captured in the ocean near Germany in 1531. It refused to eat and died after three days.

THE BLOOP

This is the name given to an ultra-low frequency underwater sound detected by the US National Oceanic and Atmospheric Administration several times during 1997. The source of the sound remains unknown, but it was detected repeatedly by the Equatorial Pacific Ocean autonomous hydrophone array, equipment originally designed to detect Russian submarines. According to the USNOAA description, it *'rises rapidly in frequency over about one minute and was of sufficient amplitude to be heard on multiple sensors, at a range of over 5000 km.'* While it bears the varying frequency hallmark of marine animals, it is far more powerful than the calls made by any creature known on Earth, the *New Scientist* recorded. The largest dead squid on record measured about 60 feet (18 m) in length including tentacles, but no one knows how big the creatures might grow. However, these cephalopods have no gas-filled sac, so it seems that they cannot make that type of noise. The listening stations lie hundreds of yards below the ocean surface, at a depth where sound waves become trapped in a layer of water known as the *'deep sound channel'*. Here temperature and pressure cause sound waves to keep travelling without being scattered by the ocean surface or the bottom of the sea. Most of the sounds detected obviously emanate from whales, ships or submarine earthquakes, but some very low frequency noises have proved baffling to scientists.

CHESSIE The creature has been sighted in the Chesapeake Bay area off the northeast coast of the United States since the 19th century. It is described as being a

long, dark, serpent-like creature. In 1982, Robert Frew filmed it from a house on Kent Island which overlooked the bay The creature is about 30–35 feet (9–10 m) long, dark brown with a humped back. The photographs and film that exist of *Chessie* were studied by Smithsonian officials and they concluded that it was a living animal that was pictured, but they could not identify it. Sightings of Chessie occur more frequently from May through September, and its appearance has been correlated to the appearance of shoals of bluefin tuna in the area, suggesting that they are a food source. In 1980 four charter boats carrying 25 people observed what seemed to be a version of the creature. In the 1800s animals very similar to Chessie were reported to be living off the coast of New England, and particularly the port of Gloucester. The descriptions of the creatures are so similar that some have speculated that the New England creatures migrated south to the Chesapeake Bay around 1900.

COLOSSAL SQUID - THE ORIGIN OF THE SEA SERPENT?

The giant squid is probably only exceeded in size by the colossal squid, *Mesonychoteuthis hamiltoni*. The colossal squid is sometimes called the Antarctic or giant cranch squid, and is the only member of its genus. Current estimates put its maximum size at 39–46 feet (12–14 m) long, based on analysis of smaller and immature specimens. Its eyes are the size of beachballs. Unlike the giant squid, whose tentacles are equipped with suckers lined with small teeth, the suckers at the tips of the colossal squid's tentacles have sharp swivelling hooks. Its body is wider and stouter, and therefore

squid. The species was first discovered in 1925 in the shape of two tentacles found in the stomach of a sperm whale. In 2007 the largest ever specimen, measuring 33 feet (10 m) in length, was captured by a New Zealand fishing boat. It weighed 1091 pounds (495 kg). It was brought to the surface as it was feeding on a Patagonian toothfish that had been caught on a longline. Not a lot of people know that squid have three hearts (and whales have three stomachs).

DAVY (DAVEY) JONES'S LOCKER

The first clear reference comes in Tobias Smollet's novel *The Adventures of Peregrine Pickle* in 1751: '*By the Lord, Jack, you may say what you will; but I'll be damned if it was not Davey Jones himself. I know him by his saucer eyes, his three rows of teeth, and tail, and the blue smoke that came out of his nostrils. This same Davy Jones, according to the mythology of sailors, is the fiend that presides over all the evil spirits of the deep, and is often seen in various shapes, perching among the rigging on the eve of hurricanes, ship-wrecks, and other disasters to which sea-faring life is exposed, warning the devoted wretch of death and woe.*' Davy Jones was a spirit, or sea-devil, who lived on the ocean floor. Sending someone to *Davy Jones's locker* meant despatching them to the ocean's depths. The '*locker*' was the bottom of the sea, the last resting place for sunken ships and human bones. How this Welsh name became attached to a sea-devil is not made clear in dictionaries, but the author believes that it probably refers to a Welsh pirate in the Indian Ocean called David Jones. Serving under Captain William Cobb, then under Captain William Ayres, Jones was

heavier, than that of the giant squid. Colossal squid are believed to have a much longer mantle than giant squid, although their tentacles are shorter. The squid is primarily an inhabitant of the circumantarctic Southern Ocean, and it is believed to hunt large fish like the Patagonian toothfish and also other squid, using bioluminescence in the deep ocean. The adult squid ranges at least to a depth of 7000 feet (2200 m). Colossal squid are a major prey item for bull sperm whales, and 14 per cent of the squid beaks found in the stomachs of these sperm whales are those of the colossal squid, which indicates that these creatures make up around 77 per cent of the biomass consumed by these whales. Many sperm whales carry scars on their backs believed to be caused by the hooks of colossal in charge of a lightly manned, recently taken prize ship filled with loot. He was accompanying Ayres in the *Roebuck*. The East India Company ship *Swan* under Captain John Proud took Ayres's ship in 1636 off the Comoros Islands. Jones knew he could not escape with his heavily laden ship, so he scuttled it with all its incriminating evidence. 'Old Davy' was also another name for the devil in the 18th century. Another source tells us that David Jones ran a London tavern. He ran his own press gang and drugged his unwary patrons, storing them in the ale lockers at the back of the inn until they could be taken aboard some departing ship. Phrases from these times include the following: '*I'll see you in Davy Jones's*' (a threat to kill someone); '*He's in Davy's grip*' (he is scared, or close to death); and '*he has the Davys*' or '*he has the Joneseys*' (he is frightened).

DOLPHINS AS CROCODILE-KILLERS In the first century, Pliny the Elder relates in his *Natural History*: '*Dolphins enter the mouth of the Nile river, but are driven away by crocodiles that claim the river as their own. Crocodiles are much stronger than dolphins, so the dolphins must use strategy rather than strength. To defeat the crocodiles, dolphins dive below them and cut open their soft bellies with the sharp fin the dolphin has on its back... Dolphins are the swiftest of all animals found in the sea or on land. Because their mouths are much below their snouts, they must turn on their*

back in order to seize fish. They breathe air from their backs. While pursuing fish to great depths, and so having held their breath too long, dolphins shoot up to the surface with such force that they fly into the air, sometimes flying over a ship's sails. Dolphins usually travel in mated pairs. Their voice is like a human moan. Their snouts are turned up, so they all answer to the name 'Simonis' [Snubnose] and prefer that name to any other. Dolphins love music, and can be charmed by songs sung in harmony or by the sound of the water-organ. Dolphins are friendly to mankind; they often play around ships and race with them.' Isidore of Seville also made reference to the killing of crocodiles in the seventh century: '*Delphini [dolphins] have their name because they follow human voices or because they join together to sing. They are the fastest beasts in the sea; they can jump over most ships that attack them. When they play in strong waves they appear to forecast a storm. The dolphins of the Nile have a saw-shaped back; with this they kill crocodiles by cutting the soft parts of their bellies.*' The name delphini comes from the Greek *delphus*, womb, and refers to the fact that dolphins are mammals giving birth to live young.

DRAGON'S TRIANGLE – THE DEVIL'S SEA Stretching south of Tokyo towards Guam, hundreds of ships and aircraft, including 13 Russian submarines, have vanished here without warning. Two of the sides are deep sea trenches, 5 miles (8 km) and 8 miles (13 km) deep respectively, and there are reports of three-sided '*triangular*' waves occurring in the region. It is designated a 'danger zone' by the Japanese government, and the Japanese name for it is Ma-no Umi, '*the Sea of the Devil*'.

The Demon Dolphin

Killer whales were so named by Spanish sailors who observed them killing grey whales. Killer whales also often attack seals when they are beached and pull them back into the sea to devour them. The killer whale, *Orcinus orca*, is in fact a type of dolphin, formerly classified as *Delphinus orca*. Orca comes from the Latin *Orcus*, or Underworld, so the mammal was known as literally the Demon Dolphin by the ancients. The animal's French name of *orque gladiateur* and Dutch name *swaardvis* both refer to the large sword-like dorsal fin, over 6 feet (2 m) long on males. This is presumably what Herodotus, Pliny and other writers referred to when describing how Nile crocodiles were killed. Killer whales can be found off all African coasts, with males growing to 25 feet (7.6 m) in length. They were probably more prevalent in ancient days as there was more food available in the Mediterranean. The killer whale is now only regarded as a 'visitor' species in the Mediterranean, but there is a resident population in the Straits of Gibraltar. Pliny the Elder refers to a killer whale which was apparently stranded in the Roman harbour of Ostia *'after gorging on skins from a sunken ship'* and was killed by the Emperor Claudius (reigned 41–54 CE) and his guard. In summer and autumn 1985 a killer whale was sighted repeatedly in the Ligurian Sea over a period of almost two months. Two days later the sighting of two killer whales was reported 20 miles (32 km) south of San Remo. The larger of the two had an extremely tall dorsal fin. Another sighting in October 1985 was of a killer whale south of Finale Ligure on the Italian Riviera coast. It was feeding on the floating disembowelled carcass of a freshly-killed 20-foot (6m)-long Cuvier's beaked whale.

THE DUTY OF NOT SAVING A DROWNING MAN In the late 19th century, fishermen in Bohemia refused to rescue a drowning man from the waters, as ill luck would follow. Sir Walter Scott in *The Pirate* recounts how Bryce, the pedlar, refuses to save the shipwrecked sailor from drowning, and remonstrates with him on his actions. *'Are you mad?'* responded the pedlar, *'you that have lived*

so long in Zetland to risk the saving of a drowning man? Wot ye not, if you bring him to life again he will be sure to do you some capital injury.' The same superstition was found among the St Kilda islanders, Danube boatmen and some French and English sailors. The idea seems to be that when a man is drowning it is the intention of the gods that he should be drowned. Thus the rescuer, if successful in rescuing him, must be the substitute and be drowned in his place at a later date.

EELS AND THE RAISING OF THE DEAD

The eel is claimed to possess many marvellous virtues. If it is left to die out of water, its body steeped in strong vinegar and the blood of a vulture, and the whole placed under a dunghill, the composition will raise from the dead anything brought to it, and will give it life as before. It is further said that he who eats the warm heart of an eel will be seized with the spirit of prophecy, and will predict things to come. The Egyptians worshipped the eel, which their priests alone had the right to eat. 'Magic eels' were made in the 18th century of flour and the juices of mutton. The 12th-century English historian William of Malmesbury wrote that a dean of the church of Elgin, in the county of Moray in Scotland, having refused to cede his church to some pious monks, was changed with all of his canons into eels, which the brothers cooked and made into a stew. The 19th-century Welsh scholar John Rhys made these observations in his book *Celtic Folklore* (1900), '*Mrs. Williams-Ellis, of Glasfryn Uchaf, who tells me that one day not long ago, she met at Llangybi a native who had not visited the place since his boyhood: he had been away as an engineer in South Wales nearly all his life, but had returned to see an aged relative. So the reminiscences of the place filled his mind, and, among other things, he said that he remembered very well what concern there was one day in the village at a mischievous person having taken a very large eel out of the well. Many of the old people, he said, felt that much of the virtue of the well was probably taken away with the eel. To see it coiling about their limbs when they went into the water was a good sign: so he gave one to understand. As a sort of parallel I may mention that I have seen the fish living in Ffynnon Beris, not far from the parish church of Llanberis. It is jealously guarded by the inhabitants, and when it was once or twice taken out by a mischievous stranger he was forced to put it back again. However, I never could get the history of this sacred fish, but I found that it was regarded as very old. I may add that it appears the well called Ffynnon Fair (Mary's Well), at Llanddwyn, in Anglesey, used formerly to have inhabiting it a sacred fish, whose movements indicated the fortunes of the lovesick men and maidens who visited there the shrine of St. Dwynwen.'*

THE EVIL OF THE BANANA

Despite being the world's most popular fruit, bananas have been demonized at sea for centuries. It was widely believed that having a banana on board was an omen of disaster. In the early 1700s, when Spain's South Atlantic and Caribbean trading empire was at its height, it was observed that nearly every ship that disappeared at sea was carrying a cargo of bananas. Later, the fastest sailing ships were used to carry bananas from the tropics to US ports along the east coast, to land the bananas before they could spoil. The banana boats were so fast that sailors never caught anything while fishing from them, and this may have added to the 'unlucky' superstition. Another theory is that bananas carried aboard slave ships fermented and gave off methane gas, which would be trapped below deck. The slaves in the hold would succumb to the poisoned air, and anyone trying to climb down into the hold to help them would also die. Also, if crewmen suddenly died of spider bites after bananas were brought aboard they would be considered a bad omen, possibly resulting in the cargo being tossed into the sea. Some captains have gone so far as to ban banana bread and the use of *Banana Boat* brand suntan lotion, or other banana-named items on their vessels.

FLIGHT 19 AND THE BERMUDA TRIANGLE

Flight 19 was the designation of five US Navy Avenger torpedo bombers that disappeared on 5 December 1945. They were on an overwater navigation training flight from Fort Lauderdale, Florida. All nine airmen on the flight were lost, as were all 12 crew members of a Mariner flying boat which was assumed to have exploded in mid-air while searching for the flight. Navy investigators could not determine the cause for the loss of Flight 19 but said the pilots may have become disoriented and ditched in rough seas when the aircraft ran out of fuel. In 1986, the wreckage of

an Avenger was found off the Florida coast during the search for the wreckage of the Space Shuttle *Challenger* that plunged into the sea after exploding shortly after take-off. It was raised from the sea bed in 1990 but no positive identification could be made. Records showed training accidents between 1942 and 1946 accounted for the loss of 94 aviation personnel from the US Navy airbase at Fort Lauderdale (including Flight 19). In 1992, another expedition located scattered debris on the ocean floor, but nothing could be identified. In the last decade, searchers have been widening the net to include areas farther east stretching out into the Atlantic Ocean. No trace of the wreckage or dead of the Mariner flying boat was found either. The loss of Flight 19 began the modern legend of the Bermuda Triangle.

THE FLYING DUTCHMAN

For more than 300 years this has been the most famous maritime ghost story. Captain Cornelius Vanderdecken (or Vanderbilt) gambled his salvation to round Cape of Good Hope in a storm, when he was homeward bound from Batavia (now Jakarta, Indonesia). The captain battled against headwinds for

nine weeks but could not make progress. He swore at God and said that he would round the Cape if it took him to the Day of Judgment. He was doomed from that moment on. The accursed ship has ever since sailed backwards and forwards on its endless voyage, manned by a ghostly crew crying for help as they work the rigging. The superstition is that any mariner who sees this ghost ship will die within the day. The real *Flying Dutchman* appears to have set sail in 1660. The second legend is that Captain Bernard Fokke, in the second half of the 17th century, swore that his would be the fastest ship afloat. He cased his masts in iron to enable them to carry more sail than any other ship of the time, and sailed from Rotterdam to the East Indies in the miraculous time of 90 days. To beat his record, he sold his soul to the devil, and on Fokke's death his body and his ship vanished. He is forever sailing the

Recent Sightings of the Flying Dutchman

The ensign on watch on the iron-clad screw frigate HMS *Inconstant* made an entry in the ship's log on the night of 11 July 1881, of a sighting in the south Atlantic: '*At 4.00 A.M. "The Flying Dutchman" crossed our bows. She emitted a strange phosphorescent light as of a phantom ship all aglow, in the midst of which light the masts, spars and sails of a brig 200 yards distant stood out in strong relief as she came up on the port bow where also the officer of the watch saw her, as did also the quarterdeck midshipman, who was sent forward at once to the forecastle, but on arriving there was no vestige nor any sign whatever of any material ship to be seen either near or right away to the horizon, the night being clear and the sea calm.*' That writer later became King George V. She was also seen that night by the warships *Tourmaline* and *Cleopatra*. There have been dozens of sightings in the 20th century alone. Toward the end of the Second World War, Admiral Doenitz, the commander of Germany's U-Boat fleet, complained about the superstitious fright of his submariners after their encounters with the Dutchman: '*They said on their return to base they much preferred facing allied depth charges than know the terror of a second meeting with the phantom vessel.*' US Navy ships had the same problem. In 1942 the destroyer USS *Kennison* twice spotted the apparition at close range and though neither time was it picked up by radar, it was visible to the entire frightened crew. A typical Second World War sighting by the British Navy occurred near Cape Town, South Africa. HMS *Jubilee* had to rapidly change course to avoid hitting the phantom ship and the captain reported the Flying Dutchman was last seen '*moving quickly away under full sail though there was absolutely no wind!*'

route, with only his boatswain, cook and pilot as crew, condemned forever to sail into heavy gales and never progressing.

GIANT SQUID – THE MYSTERY

Architeuthis dux is also known as the Atlantic giant squid, and it is debatable whether the giant squid or colossal squid is the biggest invertebrate, because the giant squid has longer tentacles but the colossal squid has a bigger mantle (torso). Specimens of the giant squid have measured up to 59 feet (18 m) in length and 1989 pounds (900 kg) in weight. The Atlantic giant squid (or possibly the colossal squid) has larger eyes than any other animal. A specimen found washed up in Canada in 1878 had eyes with an estimated diameter of 20 inches (51 cm). Less than 50 giant squid have been found in the last 100 years, and it is believed that they live isolated lives. The only enemy of the giant squid seems to be the sperm whale (and possibly the sleeper shark). These whales seek out giant squid, and dive to great depths to find them. Dead whales have been found washed up on beaches with large sucker marks on their bodies, apparently from squid trying to defend themselves. Scientists are even unsure if there are eight species of this genus *Architeuthis*, or just one. There have been claims reported of specimens of up to 66 feet in length, but no animals of such size have been scientifically documented. In 2004, researchers from the National Science Museum of Japan took the first images of a live giant squid in its natural habitat. Like all squid, a giant squid has a mantle, eight arms and two longer tentacles. The arms and tentacles account for much of the squid's great length, so giant squid are much lighter than their chief predators, sperm whales. Their large eyes can better detect light (including bioluminescent light) which is scarce in deep water. They catch prey using the two tentacles, gripping it with serrated sucker rings on the ends. Then they bring it towards the powerful beak, and shred it with the radula (a tongue with small, file-like teeth) before it reaches the oesophagus. They are believed to be solitary hunters, as only individual giant squid have ever been caught in fishing nets. The colossal and giant squid are among the largest creatures on out planet, but very little is known about them.

THE GREAT FLOOD

In 2008, a Danish NordGrip ice-drilling project in Greenland conclusively determined the exact date of the end of the last Ice Age. The extensive scientific study shows that the last Ice Age ended precisely 11,711 years ago. Ice core researcher Jørgen Peder Steffensen at the Centre for Ice and Climate at the Niels Bohr Institute of at the University of Copenhagen stated: '*Our new, extremely detailed data from the examination of the ice cores shows that in the transition from the ice age to our current warm, interglacial period the climate shift is so sudden that it is as if a button was pressed.*' Hundreds of cultures refer to a myth of a great flood sent by a god or gods to destroy civilization as an act of divine retribution. Among the best-known stories today are those of Noah's Ark in the Bible and *Qur'an* (the Koran), the Hindu Puranic story of *Manu* saving mankind from the flood, Utnapishtim in the *Epic of Gilgamesh* and the *Deucalion* in Greek mythology. Sometimes parallels are drawn with the primeval waters of the creation myths, as flood waters can cleanse humanity for rebirth into the 'true' faith. The historian Adrienne Mayor has hypothesized that flood stories were inspired by ancient observations of seashells and fish fossils found inland and even on the sides of mountains. Greeks, Egyptians, Romans and Chinese all wrote about finding such remains in these locations, and the Greeks hypothesized that Earth had been covered by water several times, noting seashells and fish fossils found on mountain tops as evidence. Some geologists believe that quite dramatic flooding of rivers in the distant past might have influenced various legends across the world. The Minoan (also called the Thera or Santorini) volcanic eruption of around 1600 BCE probably caused a tsunami that hit the civilizations of Crete, the South Aegean islands and probably even Egypt, although Athens, Thebes and other mainland Greek cities apparently were not affected. This could have inspired legends of the lost lands of Atlantis in the Mediterranean. Around 3000 BCE, a meteor or comet crashed into the Indian Ocean east of Madagascar, creating the huge undersea Burckle Crater, some 19 miles (30 km) across, which would have created a tsunami which flooded coastal areas. There was also probably a sudden rise in sea levels caused by the rapid draining of the glacial Lake Agassiz at the end of the last Ice Age, about 8400 years ago. This was in the centre of North America. It was fed by glacial run-off at the end of the last glacial period, and held more water than is contained by all the lakes in the world today.

The Ryan-Pitman Theory argues for a catastrophic deluge about 5600 BCE from the Mediterranean Sea into the Black Sea, via the Bosphorus. Before then, glacial meltwater had turned the Black and Caspian Seas into vast freshwater lakes, which drained into the Aegean Sea. With the retreat of glaciers, some of the rivers emptying into the Black Sea declined in volume and changed course to drain into the North Sea (causing the loss of lands there). The levels of the lakes also dropped through evaporation owing to the change in climate, while changes in worldwide hydrology caused sea levels to rise. The rising Mediterranean eventually spilled over a rocky sill of land at the Bosphorus, flooding 60,000 square miles (155,000 km²) of land. The Black Sea shoreline was significantly expanded to the north and west. At this time we witness the exodus of the agrarian Celts from the area of

Anatolia next to the Black Sea, spreading their civilization, building techniques and agrarian practices across Europe and North Africa. According to Ryan and Pitman, *'Ten cubic miles* [42 km³] *of water poured through each day, two hundred times what flows over Niagara Falls… The Bosporus flume roared and surged at full spate for at least three hundred days.'* A team of marine archaeologists led by Robert Ballard identified what appeared to be ancient shorelines, freshwater snail shells, drowned river valleys, tool-worked timbers, and man-made structures in roughly 300 feet (100 m) of water off the Black Sea coast of modern Turkey, and radio-carbon dating placed artefacts and shells at around 5600 BCE. This could well be the origin of the Noah's Ark story, and of many other European, Near Eastern and North African flood legends.

HADDOCK AND ST PETER THE FISHERMAN *Melanogrammus aeglefinus* is a fish found on both sides of the North Atlantic. Its most distinctive feature is a large, black, thumb-print-shaped spot below the lateral line, just behind the head on each side of the body. These spots have been variously described as *'Satan's (or the Devil's) thumb-marks'* or *'St Peter's marks'* (or *thumbprints*). A former French Canadian name for haddock was *'poisson de St Pierre'*. The spots are reputedly the marks of St Peter's finger and thumb when he drew one of the haddock's ancestors from the Lake of

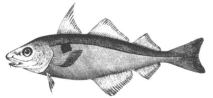

Genneserat. Haddock have never lived in those waters, so this could be regarded as a miracle. Haddock is good to eat and excellent smoked, when it used to be known as *'finnan haddie'*.

HALCYON DAYS In Greek mythology, the halcyon was a bird which nested on the sea and could quieten the waves to hatch its chicks. It is commonly associated with the kingfisher. The phrase 'halcyon days' is given to the period of calm weather usually experienced before and after the shortest day of the year, 21 December. *The Aberdeen Bestiary* (*c.*1200) tells us: *'The halcyon is a seabird which produces its young on the shore, depositing its eggs in the sand, around midwinter. It chooses as the time to hatch its young, the period when the sea is at its highest and the waves break more fiercely than usual on the shore; with the result that the grace with which this bird is endowed shines forth the more, with the dignity of an unexpected calm. For it is a fact that when the sea has been raging, once the halcyon's eggs have been laid, it suddenly becomes gentle, all the stormy winds subside, the strong breezes lighten, and as the wind drops, the sea lies calm, until the halcyon hatches its eggs. The eggs take seven days to hatch, at the end of which the halcyon brings forth its young and the hatching is at an end. The halcyon takes a further seven days to feed its chicks until they begin to grow into young birds. Such a short feeding-time is nothing to marvel at, since the completion when the hatching process takes so few days. This little bird is endowed by God with such grace that sailors know with confidence that these fourteen days will be days of fine weather and call them the halcyon days, in which there will be no period of stormy weather.'*

Some Mythical Sea Creatures

Boar whale, as described by
Olaus Magnus in his description
of the Northern Seas

A sea creature sighted
between Antibes and
Nice in 1562

A mythical dolphin-
like creature with a
saw blade projecting
from its head

Mermaid and merman

A group of sea monsters

A sea witch

HELEN OF TROY - THE SHIP-DESTROYER

The Greek tragedian Aeschylus (525–456 BCE) called Helen a 'ship-destroyer' in his play *Agamemnon*: *'Hell to ships, hell to men, hell to cities.'* On the other hand, the Elizabethan dramatist Christopher Marlowe (1564–93) described her in *Dr Faustus* somewhat differently:

'Was this the face that launched a thousand ships
And burnt the topless towers of Ilium?
Sweet Helen, make me immortal with a kiss.
    (kisses her)
Her lips suck forth my soul; see where it flies!
Come, Helen, come, give me my soul again.
Here I will dwell, for heaven be in these lips,
And all is dross that is not Helena.
I will be Paris, and for love of thee,
Instead of Troy, shall Wittenberg be sacked;
And I will combat with weak Menelaus,
And wear thy colours on my plumed crest;
Yea, I will wound Achilles in the heel,
And then return to Helen for a kiss.
Oh, thou art fairer than the evening air
Clad in the beauty of a thousand stars…'

HIPPOKAMPOI (HIPPOCAMPI)

These marine monsters were depicted as composite creatures, with the head and foreparts of a horse and the serpentine tail of a fish. *Hippos* in Greek means horse, and *kampos* means sea monster. The ancients thought that they were the adult-form of the creatiure we call the 'sea-horse', ridden by the Nereid nymphs and sea-gods, while Poseidon, god of the sea, drove a chariot drawn by two or four of them. There was a pantheon

of composite sea-monsters in ancient art including the *Leokampos* (fish-tailed lion), *Taurokampos* (fish-tailed bull), *Pardalokampos* (fish-tailed leopard) and *Aigikampos* (fish-tailed goat). The Greek geographer Pausanias, in the second century CE, described the temple of Poseidon in Korinthos (Corinth): *'The other offerings are images of Galene [Calm] and of Thalassa [Sea] and a horse like a whale [ketos] from the breast onwards [i.e. a hippokampos].'* The Roman poet Statius wrote: *'He [Poseidon] towers on high above the peaceful waves, urging his team [of hippokampoi] with his three-pronged spear: frontwise they run at furious speed amid showers of foam, behind they swim and blot out their footprints with their tails.'*

HYDRA LERNAIA - THE NINE-HEADED WATER SERPENT

This giantess daughter of Typhon and Echidna lived in the swamps of Lemae near Argos, and it was one of Hercules's 12 labours to destroy her. However, for each of her heads that he decapitated, two more sprang forth. With the help of Iolaos, he therefore applied burning brands to the severed stumps, cauterizing the wounds and preventing regeneration. The ninth head was immortal, however,

How To Live Forever

Try to become a sea anemone in your next incarnation. With their bright colours and daisy-like shape, sea anemones are the flowers of the sea. Despite their beauty, they are predatory animals, using their stinging tentacles to catch their prey. Sea anemones are grouped in the class Anthozoa, with corals. They form polyps and belong to the same phylum as the jellyfish. There are 6500 species. Sea anemones are anecdotally very long-lived, reaching 60–80 years and more. Like other cnidarians, they do not age, meaning they have the potential to live indefinitely. However, most fall foul to predators before old age is reached. Mayflies live for a few hours, bristlecone pines for thousands of years. Maximum human lifespan has remained at 100–120 years throughout human history: the verified world record for longevity being set by Frenchwoman, Jeanne Calment, who lived for 122 years, 164 days. But certain fish, reptiles and sea anemones show 'negligible senescence': meaning that they repair themselves continuously and don't usually die unless something kills them.

so he buried it under a huge rock. Having conquered the monster, he poisoned his arrows with its bile, so that the wounds inflicted by them became incurable. In the battle he also crushed a massive crab which had come to assist Hydra beneath his heel. The Hydra and the Crab were afterwards placed among the stars by Hera as the Hydra and Cancer constellations.

KRAKEN This mythical sea monster was feared by Northern European seamen for centuries. It would float on the waves. Passing ships would think it was a small island, but it would use its tentacles to pull the ship under water and devour its crew. It seems to be based on sightings of the giant or colossal squid. According to legend this huge, many armed creature could reach as high as the top of a sailing ship's main mast. A kraken would attack a ship by wrapping its limbs around the hull and capsizing it. The crew would drown or be eaten by the monster. The Greek legend of the Scylla, a monster with six heads that Odysseus must sail past during his travels, is an example of this tradition. In 1555 the Swedish ecclesiastic Olaus Magnus (1490–1557) wrote of a sea creature with '*sharp and long Horns round about, like a Tree root up by the Roots: They are ten or twelve cubits*

long, *very black, and with huge eyes...*'
The term *kraken* is first found in *Systema Naturae* (Carolus Linnaeus, 1735), and stories about this monster seem to date back to 12th-century Norway. In 1752, when the Bishop of Bergen wrote his *The Natural History of Norway*, he described the kraken as *'incontestably the largest Sea monster in the world... It seems these are the creature's arms, and, it is said, if they were to lay hold of the largest man-of-war, they would pull it down to the bottom.'* On at least three occasions in the 1930s giant squid reportedly attacked a ship. Their natural predators are whales, and perhaps they mistook the hull of a ship for an oncoming whale.

LAUNCHING A SHIP WITH A BOTTLE
The oldest reference to the custom of a ship launching is found on an Assyrian tablet from 2100 BCE, which tells of the building of an ark in the Great Flood, at the launching of which oxen were sacrificed. The Fiji islanders and Samoans made human sacrifice to the sharks, which to them were gods, when a boat was launched, washing down their new canoes in the victims' blood. Viking legends say that young men were crushed in sacrifice under the keels of ships being launched. Around the 14th

century, the custom of toasting the new vessel from silver wine goblets began. The goblets were thrown into the sea to prevent further toasts, which might have brought bad luck. For reasons of economy a wine bottle was substituted in 1690. It was usual for a prince or other male member of royalty to smash the bottle against the bow, but after 1811 the honour was given to prominent ladies. Scores of passengers on board the £300 million ocean liner, launched by Camilla, Duchess of Cornwall, were struck down by a highly contagious stomach bug only three weeks after the naming ceremony. The champagne bottle swung against the hull of the *Queen Victoria* failed to break. On its second voyage, the 90,000-ton vessel was hit by an outbreak of norovirus, the 'winter sickness bug' that causes vomiting and diarrhoea. Seventy-eight of the 3000 passengers and crew on board the *Queen Victoria* were hit by the bug and treated in their cabins. All of Cunard's previous 'Queen' ships – the *Queen Mary*, *Queen Elizabeth*, *QE2* and the *Queen Mary 2* – were named by a British queen. When *Queen Victoria* returned to port, she moored near the *Aurora*, the P&O cruiser named by Princess Anne in 2000 at another ceremony where the bottle did not break. The *Aurora* then broke down on her maiden voyage. Three years later its passengers were plagued by a virus, and in 2005 its engines failed.

LUSCA - THE BAHAMAS SEA-MONSTER
Lusca is variously described as half-shark, half-octopus or half-dragon, half-octopus, and lurks deep among the waters of the blue holes and inland caverns that are found around Andros, the largest island in the Bahamas. Along with

mermaids and other legendary creatures, Lusca feeds on marine debris containing plankton and other small creatures that are brought in with the tidal currents. Local legend holds that the tidal currents of the inland blue holes are none other than the '*breath of Lusca*'. As it breathes in, water pours in strongly enough in some caverns to form a whirlpool, and when it exhales, cold, clear water boils to the surface. It is said that any encounter with Lusca almost always results in the death of whoever was unfortunate enough to stray too close to its hiding places. This extends not only to intrepid divers who have dared to brave the labyrinthine depths of the blue holes, but also to those unwary enough to stand too close to the shoreline, as the Lusca has been known to use its tentacles to drag victims from the land itself to their watery graves. Onlookers have even described seeing fishermen's boats suddenly being yanked below the surface of the blue holes, only to watch in horror as the indigestible flotsam of these broken vessels slowly rises to the surface later on, the fishermen having vanished forever.

MARY CELESTE On 7 November 1872 Captain Benjamin Spoone Briggs, his wife and two-year-old daughter and a crew of two Americans, three Dutchmen, one German and one Dane sailed from New York to Genoa. The half-brig *Mary Celeste* was carrying 1700 barrels of industrial alcohol to fortify wine in Europe. On 5 December, she was spotted sailing erratically off the Azores by the *Dei Gratia*. Its captain, David Morehouse, was a friend of Briggs and he sent a crew to board the *Mary Celeste*. The lifeboat had gone but her cargo, food and water were still there. There were no signs of struggle on board, but all documents except the captain's log were missing. The last entry in the log-book was made on 25 November off the Azores. One theory was that the crew had eaten bread contaminated by the mould ergot, hallucinated as a result of ingesting this fungus, and jumped overboard. The likeliest explanation is that of Charles Edey Fay. He thought that Captain Briggs had taken advantage of calm conditions to ventilate the hold. Nine barrels of alcohol were shown to be leaking, and the crew may have feared an explosion. The crew perhaps took to the lifeboat, but kept the halyard, a thick robe cable, attached to the ship. Records of the time show that there was a violent storm after a flat calm on the night of the last log-book entry. The halyard was found frayed and hanging over the side of the ship, so it perhaps had broken and the captain and crew drifted away into the night. She had been an unlucky ship, launched in Nova Scotia in 1860 as *Amazon*. She was only 103 feet (31 m) overall, displacing 280 tons, and over the next ten years she was involved in several accidents at sea and passed through the hands of a number of owners. Eventually she turned up at a New York salvage auction where she was purchased for $3000. After extensive repairs she had been put under American registry and renamed *Mary Celeste*. It has always been a nautical superstition that it is unlucky to rename a ship.

Curious Creatures from the Deep

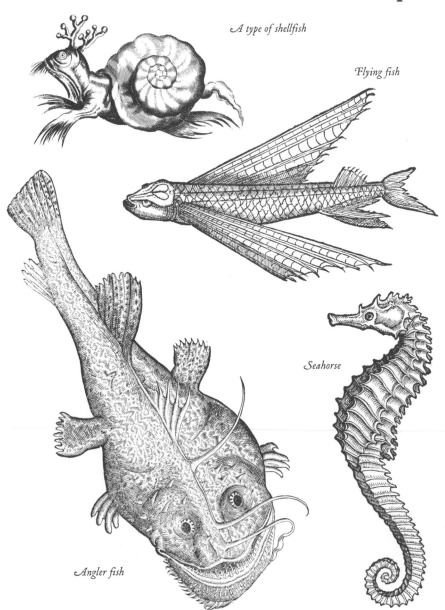

A type of shellfish

Flying fish

Seahorse

Angler fish

Walrus

Sea serpent

Marine turtle

MERMAIDS The mermaid has the body of a woman from head to waist, and that of a fish below. Vain, they are usually depicted holding a mirror and a comb, symbols of pride and luxury.

MERMAIDS AND MANATEES
One of the earliest recorded mermaids was Syria's Atargatis, loosely related to Astarte and Aphrodite, and perhaps also to Pisces. Sometimes this goddess is portrayed with the lower body of a fish, linking her to the cycles of the Moon and the tides. She is also shown with a sheaf of wheat arched over her head, relating to a plentiful harvest. Mermaids were reputed to be beautiful ladies with tails like a fish.

In 1608 Henry Hudson recorded that two of his men, Thomas Hilles and Robert Rayner, had sighted one: '*This morning*

Mermen and Neptune

Over 7000 years ago, the Babylonians honoured a merman called Ea, later named Oannes by the Greeks. As god of the sea, he had the upper body of a man and the lower body of a fish. He spoke to the people in their own language, and provided important knowledge about the arts and sciences. His later Greek and Roman counterparts were Poseidon and Neptune, but only their descendants appear in myth as mermen. In Roman mythology, Neptune is a god of water. Neptune is the son of the god, Saturn, and his legend draws heavily on that of the Greek god Poseidon. Poseidon, god of the sea, was the son of Kronos and the brother of Zeus and Hades. When the world was divided, Zeus took the sky, Hades took the underworld, and Poseidon took the seas. Although he is shown with a human body, Poseidon was able to live on land or under the sea. Neptune married the sea nymph Amphitrite and their son was Triton, half-man and half-fish, the most famous merman in history. Triton has the upper body of a man and lower body of a fish. In art, he is usually shown rising from the sea, blowing on a conch shell.

*one of our companie looking over boord
saw a mermaid, and calling up some of the
companie to see her, one more came up and
by that time shee was come close to the ships
side, looking earnestly on the men. A little
after the sea came and overturned her.
From the navill upward her backe
and breasts were like a womans,
as they say that saw her,
but her body as big as one
of us. Her skin very white,
and long haire hanging
downe behinde of colour
blacke. In her going doune
they saw her tayle, which
was like the tayle of a porposse,
and speckld like a macrell.'* One
possible explanation for this sighting, and
for the legends of mermaids generally,
is that the sailors actually saw a marine
mammal called a manatee, or sea cow.
Mermaids were believed to have the
power to lure sailors to their deaths. This
reputation was probably based on the
fact that manatees like shallow waters
near mangrove swamps, so a ship could
easily be grounded near them. The French
adventurer John Esquemeling (Alexandre
Exquemelin) describes manatees: *'Thence
we directed our course for a place called
Boca del Dragon, there to make provisions
of flesh, especially of a certain animal which
the Spaniards call manentines, and the
Dutch sea-cows, because the head, nose and
teeth of this beast are very much like those of
a cow… Nigh unto the neck they have two
wings, under which are seated two udders
or breasts, much like unto the breasts of a
woman'.* According to Tristan Jones in *The
Incredible Voyage*, because the manatee
suckles its young *'and moans in the night
like a woman'*, this is the origin of the
mermaid legend.

MOTHER CAREY'S CHICKENS

The storm petrel can run lightly over the
sea's surface. The bird's name comes from
'Petrello' (little Peter in Italian – St Peter
briefly walked on water). When seamen
saw them near a ship, they expected a
storm to be in the offing. Storm
petrels are called *'les oiseaux
de Notre Dame'* in French,
the birds of Our Lady. In
Latin, these *'Aves Sanctae
Mariae'* belonged to *'Mater
Cara'*, which the British
corrupted to Mother Carey.
Where *'chickens'* comes from
is beyond the author's skills
as a researcher or etymologist.
Another version of the legend is that
Mother Carey was the lady in charge
of the drowned seaman's resting place,
Fiddler's Green. She allowed her guests
now and then to visit the upper world in
the form of storm petrels, so no real sailor
would ever harm a storm petrel.

NAUTICAL COINCIDENCES

Thomas Paine (1737–1809) was born
Thomas Pain, and is sometimes called
'the Founder of the American Revolution'.
The Pain family's stay-making business
hardly made profits, so to afford her son's
education at grammar school, his mother
had to ask for money from her unmarried
sister. Possibly inspired by the recently
published adventures of *Robinson Crusoe*
and *Gulliver's Travels*, Tom Pain ran away
from home in 1756. Arriving in London,
he tried and failed to get various jobs as
a journeyman. However, a notice in the
Daily Advertiser caught his eye: *'To cruise
against the French, the Terrible Privateer,
Captain William Death. All Gentlemen
Sailors, and able-bodied Landmen, who*

are inclinable to try their Fortune, as well as serve their King and Country, are desired to repair on board the said Ship.' The *Terrible* had been refitted and equipped in Execution Docks on the Thames. Pain made his way to Execution Docks, and was waiting to sign on to the *Terrible*, when he heard someone calling his name. His father Joseph had tracked him down, and was able to convince Thomas to reconsider a career on the high seas, which almost certainly saved his life and possibly changed the course of history. Immediately after entering the English Channel, the *Terrible* was attacked by a French privateer. Only 16 crewmen survived of the 180-man crew, and Captain Death indeed died. However, Thomas refused to return home with his father, and in 1757 returned to the docks to become a crewman on the *King of Prussia*. This privateer took eight foreign ships in eight months, and Pain returned to London as a successful man, with £30 in wages, a fortune for those times. He could now affect the life of a gentleman – and his future life affected world history. Pain altered his name to Thomas Paine, and became a radical revolutionary, intellectual and pamphleteer.

To return to the fate of the 200-man, 26-gun *Terrible*, in 1757 she captured a large French ship, *Alexandre le Grande*. Captain William Death's brother John and 16 men were killed in the action, with others badly injured. However, a few days later the 360-men, 36-gun French warship *Vengeance* caught up with *Terrible* and her prize, which were making slow headway towards Plymouth because of the battle damage. The *Vengeance* first took the prize

ship and re-manned her. Together both French ships then attacked the *Terrible*, and in the first broadside her mainmast was shot away. She was virtually stationary and took a terrible pounding, but Captain Death would not strike her colours to signify capitulation. The captain of the *Vengeance* and his second-in-command were killed. On the *Terrible*, Captain Death died, along with his lieutenant and surgeon, by the name of Devil and Ghost respectively. The *Terrible* was at last boarded and the French found only 36 men left alive. Twenty-six of these had lost an arm or a leg and the other ten were badly injured. Only 16 appear to have survived. A contemporary naval ballad, said to have been written by a survivor, ends with the verses:

'At last the dread bullet came, wing'd with his fate,
Our brave captain dropped – and soon after his mate;
Each officer fell, and a carnage was seen,
That soon dyed the waves, to a crimson, from green:
And Neptune rose up, and he took off his wreath,
And gave it a Triton to crown Captain Death.

Thus fell the strong Terrible, bravely and bold;
But sixteen survivors the tale can unfold;
The French were the victors – though much to their cost,
For many brave French were with Englishmen lost.
And thus says Old Time, from good Queen Elizabeth,
I ne'er saw the fellow of good Captain Death.'

NERO and BOAT DESIGN

Emperor Nero of Rome has been much vilified over the years, and this excerpt from the *Lives of the Caesars* by Suetonius (*c.*69/75–*c.*130/135) gives a flavour of the man: '*This plan* [to make his mother Agrippina's bedroom ceiling fall in on top of her while she was in bed] *unfortunately got abroad so Nero was obliged to think of something else. This time, he invented a boat so constructed that, if it did not sink of itself, the cabin-roof could be made to fall in and kill her. He then pretended to be once again on the best of terms with her and wrote an affectionate letter inviting her to come to Baiae to celebrate the feast of Minerva with him. When he arrived, he told his sea-captains to wreck the galley which had brought her by 'accidentally' running it down, and then, when she asked, after a deliberately protracted meal, to sail back to Bauli, he offered her his own contraption instead of her damaged galley. She accepted perforce, and he escorted her on board in the best of spirits, kissing her breasts by way of goodbye. The remainder of the night was an anxious time for him; he could not sleep a wink, until he should know whether or not his plan had succeeded. Unfortunately, everything went wrong, and news came next morning that she had swum ashore in safety.*' The events are described in far more detail by Tacitus. Nero next hired assassins to successfully knife her to death.

NOAH'S ARK - THE MOST FAMOUS SHIP OF ALL TIME

The original version of the story seems to have come from Mesopotamia, where four gods planned a great flood. Another god, called Ea, told a mortal named Utnapishtim to build a boat to precise measurements, and provision it with gold, silver, wild animals and his own family. For seven days and nights there was a terrible storm which flooded the lands, and the boat came to rest on a mountain. Utnapishtim sent out a dove, then a swallow, and then a raven. The dove and swallow returned but the raven did not, so Utnapishtim deduced that the waters had subsided, and made a sacrifice to the gods for his salvation. There are many parallels with the tale of Noah, who also made a sacrifice to thank God. 'Ark' means box, not a boat, in Hebrew. In Genesis, God regrets creating wicked humans, except for the 600-year-old Noah and his family. God thus decides to drown the whole world in a flood. To save himself and animals, Noah is told to build a huge box which will save them from drowning. In Genesis 6:19–21, we read: '*And of every living thing of all flesh, two of every sort shalt thou bring into the ark, to keep them alive with thee; they shall be male and female. Of fowls after their kind, and of cattle after their kind, of every creeping thing of the earth after his kind, two of every sort shall come unto thee, to keep them alive. And take thou unto thee of all food that is eaten, and thou shalt gather it to thee; and it shall be for food for thee, and for them*'. However,

in Genesis 7:2–3, we read: '*Of every clean beast thou shalt take to thee by sevens, the male and his female: and of beasts that are not clean by two, the male and his female. Of fowls also of the air by sevens, the male and the female; to keep seed alive upon the face of all the earth*'. Thus Noah was to take two 'unclean' pigs or shrimps or rats, but seven pairs of 'clean' goats or chickens or cows.

It has been estimated that the Ark had a gross volume of about 1.5 million cubic feet (40,000 m³), a displacement a little less than half that of the *Titanic* at about 22,000 tons, and total floor space of around 100,000 square feet (9300 m²). The question of whether it could have carried two (or more) specimens of the various species (including those now extinct), plus food and fresh water, is a matter of much debate, even bitter dispute, between literalists and their opponents. Biblical scholars originally estimated that Noah needed to round up and save around 16,000 pairs of animals. Others now claim that the number of species involved would have reached up to five million to include insects such as fleas and mosquitoes. A major problem is that a universal flood would mix the seas with freshwater lakes, rivers and streams and kill the vast majority of fish species, so he would have to add various aquaria on board. Each aquarium would need plants and molluscs and other fish for fish to feed on, plus plankton for some whales. One

calculation was that the ark was 450 feet (137 m) long, 75 feet (23 m) wide and 45 (14 m) feet deep, which would scale up to around 2430 tons for the ship's weight, with about 1600 tons of cargo, including people, animals and food for all of them. A cow weighs around half a ton, so seven pairs of clean cattle would weigh 7 tons. Elephants weigh rather more, as do hippos. Plants would have to be taken on board to replant the Earth when the waters receded, and to provide food for herbivorous species. Other species would be needed to feed the carnivores. Another problem is fresh water – elephants need 200 gallons (900 lit) a day and the sea would be too saline to drink. In Genesis Chapter 7 we discover that all the animals lived on the Ark for six months before the floods receded (where did the water go?). Presumably Noah's three sons had full-time employment feeding and watering the animals, let alone clearing away their waste matter. If the Earth was covered with the seas for six months, there would be a single band of alluvial mud deposited across every country, but it seems to have miraculously vanished. A 'resting place' for the Ark is said to be Mt Ararat in Turkey. Presumably the pandas then travelled overland to China for bamboo on which to feed, and the koalas hitched a ride on tree trunks to Australia for eucalyptus. leaves The Komodo dragons went wherever they wanted. Truly God works in mysterious ways.

OARFISH - THE LONGEST BONY FISH The oarfish (*Regalecus glesne*) is the longest bony fish in the world. It has a snakelike body with a wonderful red fin along its 20–40 feet (6–12 m) length, a horselike face and blue gills. It accounts for many sea-serpent (see page 218) sightings. The oarfish weighs upwards of 400 pounds (181 kg), dwells at depths of around 700 feet (213 m), and only comes to the surface when it is sick or injured. It appears like a prehistoric eel, measuring 4 feet (1.2 m) in circumference.

THE RIME OF THE ANCIENT MARINER Coleridge's 1798 poem recalls a ship's crew dying after falling under a curse when one of their number kills an albatross. The privateer Simon Hatley shot a black albatross on Captain George Shelvocke's passage around Cape

Horn in 1719, and Coleridge's tale is based on that incident. When the frigate *Speedwell* was beset by storms near Cape Horn, Hatley shot a black albatross, fearing that it was a bird of ill omen and hoping that the ship would have better winds once the bird was gone. Hatley was captured off the Peru coast near Paita, taken slightly wounded to Lima in chains, where he remained for at least a year. On his return to England, Captain Shelvocke published an account *A Voyage Round The World by Way of the Great South Sea* (1726), and mentioned Hatley's act: '*We all observed, that we had not the sight of one fish of any kind, since we were come to the Southward of the straits of Le Mair, nor one sea-bird, except a disconsolate black Albatross, who accompanied us for several days (...), till Hattley, (my second Captain) observing, in one of his melancholy fits, that this bird was always hovering near us, imagin'd, from his colour, that it might be some ill omen. (...) He, after some fruitless attempts, at length, shot the Albatross, not doubting we should have a fair wind after it.*' Hatley's experiences after killing the bird meant that it became superstitiously regarded as ill-luck to kill an albatross.

THE SARGASSO SEA - THE DUNGEON OF LOST SOULS East of the Bahamas, an extremely strong eddy causes the Sargasso weed or sargassum (*Fucus natans*) to collect in vast quantities on the surface. Columbus mentioned the difficulty of sailing through the waters and the weeds fouling his ships. Northeast of Bermuda, the sea depth ranges from a mile to four miles (1600 to 6400 m). The 'sea' here is a large pool of very warm water, rotating clockwise very slowly. Both the Equatorial Current and the Gulf Stream push warm water past it, it rarely rains and the weather, like the water, remains very calm. It is also very humid and often extremely hot. It has been likened to a desert in the middle of the ocean. The lack of rainfall makes the water very saline. There are millions of clumps of sargassum, mainly accumulating towards the centre of the sea and, with little current and little wind, sailing ships could be trapped here for long periods Becalmed ships ran out of drinking water. Records show that the Spanish threw their war-horses over the side to conserve precious supplies. Hence the area became known as the '*Horse Latitudes*'. The ghosts of these horses and ships and sailors were thought to haunt the area. Other names for it were '*The Doldrums*', '*The Sea of Berries*', and '*The Dungeon of the Lost Souls*'. In 1492, Columbus was entangled in the 'weed', and he noted the strange effects of light on the water (due to its salinity) and the extreme compass variations that he experienced. His sailors implored him to return home. The phenomenon was magnetic variation.

SAWFISH - SHIP-SINKER
The sawfish was viewed in the past as a sea monster with enormous wings. When it saw a ship, it raised its wings so it could race away. The sawfish tired after 30 or 40 miles (50 or 65 km) and dived back into the water to devour fish. When it raised its wings, they held back

the wind from ships. Isidore of Seville wrote: '*The sawfish (serra) has its name from the saw-toothed crest on its back, with which it cuts a ship when swimming under it.*' Vincent de Beauvais related: '*The saw fish swimming hidden beneath the ship cuts through its bottom, so that as the water rushes in, it drowns the crew by its crafty device and gorges itself on their flesh.*' Critically endangered sawfishes (or carpenter sharks) are today recognized as a family of marine animals related to rays, with a long, toothy snout (or rostrum). Several species can attain massive sizes up to 23 feet (7 m) in length. They are members of the family Pristidae.

SCYLLA AND CHARYBDIS
Between Scylla and Charybdis is the origin of the phrase 'between the rock and the whirlpool' (referring to the rock upon which Scylla dwelt and the whirlpool of Charybdis) and may also be the origin of the phrase 'between a rock and a hard place'. In Greek myth the beautiful maiden Scylla was turned into a monster by a jealous goddess. Charybdis, born from Gaia and her son Poseidon, was originally a sea nymph who flooded land to enlarge her father's underwater kingdom, until Zeus turned her into a monster. Charybdis swallows huge amounts of water three times a day and then belches them back out again, destroying all the boats that sail near it. It takes on the form of a huge vortex that lives on one side of a narrow channel of water. On the other side of the strait lay Scylla, another sea-monster, with six arms, six heads with four eyes each and, at the lower part of her body, six hideous dogs with mouths

containing three rows of razor sharp teeth. With necks fully expanded, Scylla was 15 feet (4.5 m) tall; the necks were each 5 feet (1.5 m) long. Hidden in a cave at the bottom of a cliff, Scylla would rear up out of the chasm, grabbing dolphins or any human or animal that ventured nearby. The two sides of the strait lay within an arrow's range of each other, so close that sailors attempting to avoid Charybdis would pass too close to Scylla, and vice versa. The hero Odysseus chose to risk Scylla at the cost of some of his crew rather than lose the whole ship to Charybdis. Traditionally, the location of Charybdis has been associated with the Strait of Messina off the coast of Sicily, opposite a dangerous rock called Scylla. The whirlpool there is caused by the meeting of currents, but is seldom dangerous to shipping.

THE SEA OF MILK In a ship report dated 25 January 1995, a captain of a merchant ship noted that his vessel had sailed into a '*milky sea*', and then out of the other side six hours later. The positions reported matched precisely the edges of the feature seen by satellite. The event was detected by the satellite again on the nights of 26 and 27 January. The observation, off the Horn of Africa,

spanned more than 100 miles (160 km), covering an area of 6000 square miles (15,000 km^2) which is about the size of the Hawaiian islands. In Jules Verne's *Twenty Thousand Leagues Under the Sea* (1870), the submarine *Nautilus* spent some time travelling through a milky sea: '*At seven o'clock in the evening, the Nautilus, half-immersed, was sailing in a sea of milk. At first sight the ocean seemed lactified… "It is called a milk sea," I explained. "A large extent of white wavelets often to be seen on the coasts of Amboyna, and in these parts of the sea… the whiteness which surprises you is caused only by the presence of myriads of infusoria, a sort of luminous worm, gelatinous and without colour, of the thickness of a hair, and whose length is not more than seven-thousandths of an inch… you need not try to compute the number of these infusoria. You will not be able, for, if I am not mistaken, ships have floated on these milk seas for more than forty miles.*" Incredibly this fictional sighting was also dated 27 January. In the novel, it is said to be impossible to calculate the number of micro-organisms (*infusoria*) involved, but scientists conservatively estimated that 40 billion trillion bioluminescent bacteria must have been present. This vast number is equivalent to the number of grains of sand it would take to cover the whole Earth with a layer 4 inches (10 cm) thick. Milky seas are unusual phenomena which have been noticed by mariners for centuries, but which remain unexplained by scientists. These events occur when the surface of the ocean, often from horizon to horizon, glows with a continuous uniform milky light. Although the origins of this light are not well investigated, the most plausible explanation is that

Sea Changes and Mass Extinctions

So many species have vanished in a series of six cataclysmic mass extinctions over the course of time that it is estimated that 99.9 per cent of all species that have ever existed on Earth are extinct.

1. **The Ordovician-Silurian Extinction** *c.*439 million years ago
Glaciers melted and sea levels rose, and 25 per cent of marine families and 60 per cent of marine genera (the classification above species) were lost.

2. **The Late Devonian Extinction** *c.*364 million years ago
Warm water marine species were the most severely affected, so it is believed that global cooling may have lead to the Devonian extinction. There are glacial deposits of this age in northern Brazil. Apart from widespread lowering of the sea-level, meteorite impacts may have caused extinctions. Twenty-two per cent of marine families and 57 per cent of marine genera were lost.

3. **The Permian-Triassic Extinction** *c.*251 million years ago
Some scientists believe that a comet or asteroid impact led to this extinction. Others think that volcanic eruption, coating large stretches of land with lava from the Siberian Traps which are centred on the Siberian city of Tura, and related loss of oxygen in the seas were the cause of this mass extinction. Still

other scientists suspect that the impact of the comet or asteroid triggered the volcanism. It was Earth's worst mass extinction when 95 per cent of all species, 53 per cent of marine families, 84 per cent of marine genera, and around 70 per cent of land species, such as plants, insects and vertebrate animals, became extinct.

4. **The Triassic-Jurassic Extinction** *c.*205 million years ago
This was probably caused by massive floods of lava erupting from the central Atlantic magmatic province triggering the breakup of the continent of Pangaea and the opening of the Atlantic Ocean. The volcanism may have led to deadly global warming. Rocks from the eruptions now are found in the eastern United States, eastern Brazil, North Africa and Spain. Twenty-two per cent of marine families, 52 per cent of marine genera, and an unknown percentage of vertebrate deaths were the result of this catastrophe.

5. **The Cretaceous-Tertiary Extinction** *c.*65 million years ago
This is thought to have been aggravated, if not caused, by the impact of a huge asteroid that created the Chicxulub crater now hidden on the Yucatán Peninsula and beneath the Gulf of Mexico. Some scientists believe that this mass extinction was caused by gradual climate change or flood-like volcanic

eruptions of basalt lava from the Deccan Traps in west-central India. During this extinction, 16 per cent of marine families, 47 per cent of marine genera and 18 per cent of land vertebrate families, including the entire population of dinosaurs, went extinct.

6. The Eighteenth Century Onwards

Animals are currently going extinct 100 to 1000 times (possibly even 1000 to 10,000 times) faster than the normal background extinction rate, which is about ten to 25 species per year. Many researchers claim that we are in the middle of a mass extinction event worse than the Cretaceous–Tertiary extinction which wiped out the dinosaurs. Rather than a meteorite or large volcanic eruption, the alarming decline of biodiversity leading to the current mass extinction is the result of human activities. Firstly, habitat destruction including human-induced climate change is to blame. Human-induced climate change is the result of high amounts of greenhouse gas emissions (primarily carbon dioxide, methane and nitrous oxide) lodging in the atmosphere. Acting like a greenhouse, these gases trap heat from the Sun. Other human activities, such as habitat destruction, in combination with climate change are making the situation only worse. Increasing temperatures may force species to move towards their preferred, and generally cooler, climate range. If those habitats have already been destroyed, then the species are not be able to escape the effects of climate change and will go extinct. Destruction of the rainforests for palm oil, beef breeding, the cultivation of soya, building and similar activities are accelerating habitat destruction and species extinction. Human overpopulation has led to over-harvesting (hunting, fishing and gathering). Pollution is leading to species loss across the world, and invasive/alien species introduced into habitats by man displace native species through predation, competition and disease. In 2008, the Caribbean monk seal was officially declared extinct. In 2006, the West African black rhino was wiped out as its horn was sold to make Chinese aphrodisiacs. In 2008, the national symbol of Panama, the Panamanian golden frog, became extinct. All continents are impacted by this ongoing biological catastrophe. The completion of a comprehensive species inventory of Earth and efforts to save them from becoming extinct must be a world priority. Of the 40,177 species assessed using IUCN Red List criteria, 784 are known to be extinct and 16,119 are now listed as threatened with extinction. Many more species (thousands) still need to be assessed to know their status. When this is done, the number of extinct and threatened species is likely to be much higher than the current estimate.

it is caused by blooms of bacteria. Dinoflagellates, which cause red tides, flashing waves and sparkling wakes behind boats, need to be physically stimulated to produce their brief bright flashes. This type of display is intermittent and does not match the kind of display seen in milky seas. Bacteria, on the other hand, will glow with a continuous light under the right conditions. The light from a milky sea is sometimes described as white, but it is actually blue. It only appears white when detected by human night-time vision, as the rod photoreceptors in our eyes do not distinguish colours.

SEA SERPENT The Royal Navy frigate HMS *Daedalus* was cruising near the Cape of Good Hope on 6 August, 1848 when the officer of watch spotted an object in the sea. He drew the attention of the captain and several crew members on deck to a large sea snake, or sea serpent, that they estimated to be 60 feet (18 m) long, 15 inches (38 cm) in diameter, and moving through the sea with its head some 4 feet (1.2 m) out of the water. It moved quickly through the water with neither vertical nor horizontal undulation. The creature was dark brown, shading to yellow-white under the throat. On its back there seemed to be a seaweed-like mane. The *Daedalus* observed it for about 20 minutes. The SS *Tresco* was cruising 90 miles (145 km) south of Cape Hatteras in 1903 when Joseph Ostens Grey, the ship's second officer, spotted what he first thought was a derelict hulk in the water.

On closer examination, '*With a conviction that grew deeper, and ever more disquieting, we came to know that this thing could be no derelict, no object that hand of man had fashioned...*' reported Grey. He described a head that emerged out of water on a tall and powerful neck. It was '*dragon-like*' and accompanied a body some 100 feet (30 m) in length and 8 feet (2.4 m) across at the widest. The head was 5 feet (1.5 m) long and 18 inches (46 cm) in diameter. There was concern that the ship, running light without cargo, might be tipped and overturned if the creature attempted to clamber aboard. '*Presently I noticed something dripping from the ugly lower jaw,*' continued Grey. '*Watching, I saw that it was saliva, of a dirty drab colour, which dripped from the corners of the mouth.*' Eventually the creature turned away and the danger was averted. As years went by scientists scoffed at his story, which appeared under Grey's name in *The Wide World Magazine*. Then the *Tresco's* ship's log for Saturday 30 May 1903 was checked. It reads: '10 AM Passed school of sharks followed by a huge sea monster.'

There have been many reports from along the Pacific coast near Vancouver in Canada of several differently shaped creatures including a snake-like sea serpent. Further south more reports centre around the city of San Francisco. On 1 November 1983, a construction crew was working on Route 1 just north of the Golden Gate Bridge near Stinson Beach. Suddenly they spotted a creature, underwater, approaching the land. They estimated the creature's length at 100 feet (30 m) and its diameter at 5 feet (1.5 m). It appeared to have three humps. Using binoculars they watched it making coils, throwing its head about and whipping its body around. Two years later, in San Fransisco Bay, twins Robert and William Clark were sitting in a car near the sea wall. They watched two seals swimming extremely fast across the bay. Then they noticed a *'large black snake-like animal'* chasing the seals. They saw that the creature moved by forming its body into coils and wriggling up and down. The animal apparently also had small, translucent, fanlike fins that acted as stabilizers. There are many reports of 'sea serpents' from experienced mariners, including Captain Peter M'Quhae on HMS *Daedalus* in 1848, Lieutenant Hynes on the royal yacht *Osborne* in 1877, Captain Platt on the US Coast Survey steamer *Drift* in 1878, Captain George Drevar on SS *Pauline* in 1875, and several more.

SEA SUPERSTITIONS AND SAYINGS

Mention has already been made of the superstitions surrounding launching a ship with a bottle. Similar practices have been traditional for all of recorded history to help a ship into its new element for the first time. Flowers and wreaths of leaves were commonly part of the ceremony, and priests were often called upon to anoint and purify new vessels, blessing and consecrating them in the name of a patron saint. Some ships were even baptized. If anything went wrong during the launching ceremony – such as the bottle not breaking, or someone being injured while the supports were being removed or the ship remaining stationary when it should move down a slipway – it was usually perceived as a bad sign. In some cases, if anyone attending the ceremony refused to drink a toast to the launch, even that was considered a bad omen. No other calling has so many superstitions attached to it as seafaring. For instance, never start a voyage on the first Monday in April, as this is the day that Cain slew Abel, on the second Monday in August, as this is the day Sodom and Gomorrah were destroyed, or on 31 December, as this is the day Judas Iscariot hanged himself. Friday is the worst possible day because Christ was crucified on a Friday. Sunday is the best possible day because Christ's resurrection was on a Sunday, leading to the saying: *'Sunday sail, never fail'*.

Never say good luck or allow someone to say good luck to you unanswered – it is tempting fate. The only way to counter this omen is by drawing blood, such as by punching the person on the nose. Priests are unlucky on a ship as they dress in black and perform funeral services – black generally is the colour of death and indicative of the depths of the sea, so black travelling bags are bad luck. Flowers are unlucky onboard a ship – they could be used to make a funeral wreath. Church bells heard at sea mean that someone on the ship will die, and St Elmo's fire seen around a sailor's head means he will die within a day. When the clothes of a dead sailor are worn by another sailor during the same voyage, misfortune will befall the entire ship. Redheads and flat-footed people bring bad luck, which can only be averted if you speak to the redhead before they speak to you. For many sailors it was lucky to have tattoos, to wear gold hoop earrings, to throw an old pair of shoes overboard just after launch, for a child to be born on the ship and to touch the collar of a sailor – whether this is the origin of 'touching up' is unsure. It was also thought unlucky to name the ship with a word ending in 'a', to change the name of a boat, to sail on a green boat, to see rats leaving a ship, to have someone die on the ship, to whistle on board a ship, to cross an area where another ship had once sunk or to lose a bucket at sea. Women and clergymen as passengers brought bad luck to a voyage, and if a sailor met someone with cross-eyes on the way to the harbour, he was encouraged not to set sail. Sneezing was terrible luck, to be countered by saluting.

A bell ringing by itself on the ship is a death omen for one of the crew. Horseshoes on a ship's mast help turn away storms, and a ship without its figurehead will not sink. A ship will sail faster when fleeing an enemy and slower when carrying a dead body. Dead bodies mean that a storm could be brewing or there could be a haunting. Touching the deceased's possessions might cause their spirit to seek out the survivor for vengeance or mean that he would be destined to perish in the same way.

Drowned sailors were often rumoured to cause trouble for their former shipmates. Many superstitions are focused on stormy skies. Whistling may have the power to call up a storm. To help ward off the various dangers of storms, sailors have developed a number of superstitions. Hitting swords together in the shape of a cross could help against waterspouts, as could holding a black-handled knife and the Gospel of St John, or the clanging of drums and gongs. Tossing a stone over the left shoulder, throwing some sand into the air, swirling water into a hole, getting a piece of cloth wet and thrashing it against a stone all helped to ward off turbulent winds and bad weather. A ring around the Moon is thought to portend approaching rains, while a rising Moon during a storm means the skies will soon clear. If a partial Moon is tipped downward, rain is also on the way, with the reverse suggesting fair weather ahead. Disaster will follow if you step onto a boat with your left foot first, and never look back once your ship has left port as this can bring bad luck. A silver coin placed under the masthead ensures a successful voyage, as will pouring wine on the deck on a long voyage. The caul from the head of a new-born child is protection against drowning and will bring the owner good luck, and black cats will bring a sailor home from the sea. A stone thrown over a vessel that is putting out to sea ensures she will never return, and throwing stones into the sea on a voyage will cause great waves and storms, as it is a sign of disrespect to the sea. A dog seen near fishing tackle is bad luck. Swallows seen at sea and dolphins swimming with the ship are good signs, but curlews and cormorants are bad. A shark following the ship is a sign of inevitable death, as sharks are believed to be able to sense the presence of those near death. It is unlucky to kill a gull as, like albatrosses, they also contain the souls of sailors lost at sea. Handing a flag through the rungs of a ladder is bad luck, as is repairing a flag on the quarterdeck. Cutting your hair or nails at sea is bad luck. If the rim of a glass rings, silence it quickly or there will be a shipwreck; the feather of a wren slain on New Year's Day will protect a sailor from dying by shipwreck. Never say 'drowned' at sea.

SEA WITCHES The belief of sea witches has long been part of the experiences of seafarers. Women were thought to be able to raise wind and cause storms, a power which could send them to be burnt at the stake in times past. Sea witches were called upon to control the weather to ensure safe voyages. According to legends, witches were able to control the wind. One method was by tying three knots in a rope, or sometimes in a handkerchief. When the three knots were tied in the proper magical way, the wind was bound up in them. Witches gave, or sometimes sold, these magic knots to

sailors to help them enjoy safe voyages. The release of one knot brought a gentle southwesterly wind; two knots, a strong north wind; and three knots, a tempest. In the folklore of the Shetland Islands and Scandinavia, some fishermen were said to have commanded the wind in this way. The belief in controlling the wind by tying it up goes back to the legends of ancient Greece, when Odysseus received a bag of wind from Aeolus to help him on his journey. Sir Francis Drake is said to have sold his soul to the devil in order to become a skilled seaman and admiral. The devil allegedly sent Drake sea witches who raised a storm that helped him to defeat the Spanish Armada in 1588. The battle occurred near Devil's Point, overlooking Devonport, which is still considered to be haunted by witches.

THE SECRET OF THE IMPERIAL PURPLE OF ROME

The purple hue had special significance as the colour of Roman imperial power. Cleopatra also had the sails on her ship dyed purple. The pigment for imperial purple was derived from *Murex* shellfish, *'The murica is a sea snail, so called from its sharp point and rough surface; it is known by another name, concilium, because when you cut around it with an iron blade, it produces tears which are purple in colour, from which purple dye is made; from this comes the other name for purple, ostrum, because the dye is made from the fluid enclosed in the shell (in Greek, ostreon).'* (*The Aberdeen Bestiary c.*1200). However the recipe for the dye had been kept a secret in ancient Egypt and Rome. Recently, an amateur chemist has discovered how the ancient Romans dyed the togas of emperors, using a bacterium found in cockles available from a local supermarket. Retired engineer John Edmonds bought some, discarded the vinegar and placed several cockles with some of the purple pigment in a jam jar. The cockles are thought to harbour a bacterium that is crucial in reducing the dye. Wood ash was added to the container to ensure the mixture did not turn acidic, and it was then kept at 122° F (50° C) for about ten days. Wool dipped in the pigment turned green at first, but, eventually, in contact with light, it turned purple. This lost dyeing method has implications in that tons of chemicals are presently needed to reduce the dye for denim blue jeans, resulting in large quantities of sulphur waste. University of Reading scientists are trying to understand how the bacterium reduces indigo in order to develop a clean biotechnology, in order to replace the chemical process for indigo reduction in the future.

SHIP OF FOOLS - STULTIFERA NAVIS The ship of fools is an allegory that resonates in Western literature, music and art. It depicts a vessel populated by people who are deranged, frivolous, or oblivious and ignorant of their own direction. In the 15th and 16th centuries, this cultural motif of the 'ship of fools' also parodied the '*ark of salvation*' (referring to the Catholic Church). It originated as a satire in 1495 by Sebastian Brant (1458–1521), a conservative theologian. In 114 brief satires, illustrated with woodcuts, it includes the first commissioned work by the artist-engraver Albrecht Dürer. Much of the work was critical of the church, and the title turned on a pun on the Latin word '*navis*', which means both a ship and the nave of a church. Court fools were given licence to say what they wanted, and by writing his work in the voice of the fool, Brant could give vent to his criticism of

the church. Published only two years after Columbus's discoveries of the New World, it is the first literary reference to the lands beyond 'the Western Ocean' (the Atlantic):

'To lands by Portugal discovered
To golden isles which Spain discovered
With brownish natives in the nude
We never knew such vastitude.'

It was hugely successful, being translated into Latin as *Stultifera Navis*, and translated into English in 1509. The ship, laden with fools, sets sail for the *'fool's paradise'* of Narragonia. Brant identifies many examples of folly, including the corrupt judge, the drunkard and the untrained physician. The greatest painting of the ship is by Hieronymus Bosch (painted around 1500), where he imagines that the whole of mankind is voyaging through the seas of time on a small ship, that is representative of humanity. Every one of the representatives on board is a fool. Bosch tells us that this is how we live. We only spend our time eating, drinking, flirting, cheating, playing silly games and pursuing unattainable objectives. Meanwhile our ship drifts aimlessly and we never reach our destination. The concept has also been used many times in literature, most memorably by Douglas Adams in his *Hitch-Hiker's Guide to the Galaxy*. Golgafrincham is a red semi-desert planet that is home to a species of particularly inspiring lichen. Its people decided it was time to rid themselves of an entire useless third of their population, and so concocted a story that their planet would shortly be destroyed in a great catastrophe (under threat from a mutant star goat). The useless third of the population

(consisting of estate agents, politicians, judges, lawyers, committee junkies et al) were packed into the B-Ark, one of three giant Ark spaceships, and told that everyone else would follow shortly in the other two. The other two-thirds of the population, of course, did not follow and *'led full, rich and happy lives until they were all suddenly wiped out by a virulent disease contracted from a dirty telephone'*.

SIREN - PART WOMAN, PART BIRD, PART FISH Early sources described the siren as a female from the head to the navel, and bird from the waist down. Later sources say that the siren is fish from the waist down, like a mermaid, and usually has wings. In some cases sirens are described as having both bird's feet and a fish's tail. They charm men with their beautiful singing. In the *Odyssey* Odysseus has himself tied to the mast and his sailors stop their ears with wax so that he can experience the beauty of their song without falling under their spell. Sailors who are attracted to the singing sometimes fall asleep. Sirens then attack the men and tear their flesh. They sing when it is stormy, but weep when the weather is fair. *Sirene* is shown in heraldry as a mermaid with two tails. The Amari

family of Sicily have a white *sirene* on their heraldic shields. Isidore of Seville relates: '*Sirens have wings and claws because Love flies and wounds; they stay in water because a wave created Venus. It is imagined that there were three sirens, part woman, part bird, which had wings and claws. One of them played the lute, another the flute, while the third sang. They charmed sailors to cause shipwreck. This in untrue. They were actually prostitutes who led travellers into poverty.*' Isidore of Seville also mentions the *siren serpent*, which is so strong that its bite is followed by death before the pain of it is felt. In his 13th century *Bestiaire*, Guillaume le Clerc notes: '*The siren is a monster of strange fashion, for from the waist up it is the most beautiful thing in the world, formed in the shape of a woman. The rest of the body is like a fish or a bird. So sweetly and beautifully does she sing that they who go sailing over the sea, as soon as they hear the song, cannot keep from going towards her. Entranced by the music, they fall asleep in their boat, and are killed by the siren before they can utter a cry.*'

SPILLING SALT OR PEPPER

The reason why spilling salt or pepper is still seen as portending bad luck is as a result of the incredible historical cost of these spices, especially during Elizabeth I's reign. Pepper, particularly, had to be shipped extremely long distances to the tables of Europe and was highly valued.

THE 'SWARM OF EARTHQUAKES' MYSTERY

These were detected off the coast of central Oregon by scientists listening to underwater microphones (hydrophones) in 2008. More than 600 earthquakes were recorded during the first ten days in April by Oregon State University's Hatfield Marine Science Center. The 'swarm' is unique because it is occurring within the middle of the Juan de Fuca plate, away from the major regional tectonic boundaries. According to marine geologist Robert Dziak: '*We're not certain what it means… It looks like what happens before a volcanic eruption, except there are no volcanoes in the area.*' The crust of the Earth is made up of plates that rest on molten rock (magma), and these plates rub together up and down and side to side. If magma erupts through the crust, it creates volcanoes. This can happen even in the middle of a plate. When the plates bump against each other, they create earthquakes along the edges of the plates. At least three of the earthquakes have been of a magnitude of 5.0 or higher, and they have not followed the typical pattern of a major shock, followed by a series of diminishing aftershocks.

SWORDFISH - THE SHIP PIERCER

Isidore of Seville in the seventh century wrote: '*The swordfish (gladius) has a pointed beak with which it pierces and sinks ships*'. This predatory fish is named

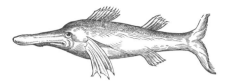

after its sharp beak resembling the flat blade of a sword, which together with its powerful, streamlined physique allows it to cut through the water with great ease. Contrary to popular belief, the 'sword' is not used to spear, but instead may be used to slash at its prey in order to injure the prey animal, making for an easier catch. However, the swordfish relies mainly on its great speed, up to 50 mph (80 kph), and agility in the water to catch its prey.

THOR HEYERDAHL and THE PROOF OF LEGENDS
In 1947 this remarkable Norwegian anthropologist sailed the balsa-wood raft *Kon-Tiki* 4300 miles (6920 km) from Peru to Polynesia, attempting to prove that the Polynesians originally came from South America. In 1970 he sailed the papyrus boat *Ra II* from Africa to the West Indies to demonstrate that Egyptians could have built the pyramids in South America. In 1977 he then sailed *Tigris*, a reed boat, from Iraq through the Persian Gulf to Pakistan and hence to the Red Sea, to show that Mesopotamia could have used sea routes to trade with the Indus Valley civilizations in India.

THE TILEFISH MYSTERY
In the 1860s a new and valuable food fish was found in huge quantities off New England. A member of the cod family,

the tilefish grew up to 50 pounds (23 kg) in weight, and was found at a depth of 50–100 fathoms (90–180 m) about 80 miles (130 km) offshore, preferring warm waters with temperatures of around 50° F (10° C). In 1882 ships reported seeing millions of dead tilefish covering the sea – an estimated 256,000 on each square mile of ocean. It was later found that there had been an increase in the strength of the Arctic current flowing south, which had shifted the warmer Gulf Stream. For over 30 years, not a single tilefish was landed or seen, until they returned in 1915, but not in their former numbers.

TORPEDO - THE ELECTRIC RAY
Isidore of Seville noted: '*The torpedo has its name because it becomes stiff (torpescere) when touched. Anyone who touch this fish, even with a long pole, becomes numb or paralyzed. It is so strong that even the breath from its body affects the limbs.*'

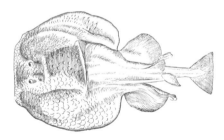

THE UNICORN OF THE SEAS - NARWHAL
This mysterious whale with a long spiral tusk (in fact, an incisor tooth that grows out of the upper jaw) is at risk from climate change. It is so narrow in its range of habitat and specific in its diet that it may be one of the least able of Arctic mammals to adapt to rapid warming. The narwhal population

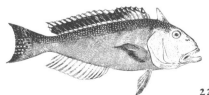

ranged farther south, and the last recorded sighting in British waters was in 1588. This was shortly before Queen Elizabeth I valued a horn, presented to her by the privateer Martin Frobisher, at ten times its weight in gold.

USÔUS - THE INVENTOR OF THE BOAT

According to the Greek translation of the Phoenician *Sanchuniathon* (*c*.700 BCE), Usôus cut the branches of a fallen tree, sat aside the log that remained, and paddled through water, thus inventing the boat. '*From the Wind, Colpia, and his wife Bahu* [Night] *were born Æon and Protogonus, mortal men so named; of whom one, Aeon, discovered that life might be sustained by the fruits of trees. Their immediate descendants were called Genos and Genea, who lived in Phoenicia, and in time of drought stretched forth their hands to heaven towards the sun; for him they regarded as the sole Lord of Heaven, and called him Baal-samin, which means "Lord of Heaven" in the Phoenician tongue, and is equivalent to Zeus in Greek. And from Genos, son of Æon and Protogonus, were begotten mortal children, called Phôs, and Pyr, and Phlox* [i.e. Light, Fire, and Flame]. *These persons invented the method of producing fire by rubbing two pieces of wood together, and taught men to employ it. They begat sons of surprising size*

is concentrated in a relatively small area between Baffin Island, Canada and Greenland. With a population of no more than 80,000 individuals, narwhals stick closely to established migratory patterns and are more narrowly distributed than the two other Arctic whales, the bowhead and beluga. Any change in the distribution of heavy winter pack ice is likely to adversely affect the whale, which feeds mainly in the cold and darkness of winter and can dive down in excess of 5000 feet (1500 m) in search of its favourite prey, the Greenland halibut, with a second-order preference for cod and squid.

The loss of sea ice is also making narwhal more vulnerable to killer whales which have in recent years ventured farther northwards with the retreat of the ice (killer whales tend to avoid water at or near freezing because they don't like to bump their unusually large dorsal fins against ice floes), but less so to polar bears which hunt narwhal in groups at the edge of the whales' breathing holes. The Inuit, who still harvest significant numbers of narwhal, have reported changes in their distribution and condition. During the last significant cooling period between the 12th and 19th centuries ('*the Little Ice Age*'), narwhals are believed to have

and stature, whose names were given to the mountains whereof they had obtained possession, viz. Casius, and Libanus, and Antilibanus, and Brathy. From them were produced Memrumus and Hypsuranius, who took their names from their mothers, women in those days yielding themselves without shame to any man whom they happened to meet. Hypsuranius lived at Tyre, and invented the art of building huts with reeds and rushes and the papyrus plant. He quarrelled with his brother, Usôus, who was the first to make clothing for the body out of the skins of the wild beasts which he slew. On one occasion, when there was a great storm of rain and wind, the trees in the neighbourhood of Tyre so rubbed against each other that they took fire, and the whole forest was burnt; whereupon Usôus took a tree, and having cleared it of its boughs, was the first to venture on the sea in a boat. He also consecrated two pillars to Fire and Wind, and worshipped them, and poured upon them the blood of the animals which he took by hunting. And when the two brothers were dead, those who remained alive consecrated rods to their memory, and continued to worship the pillars, and to hold a festival in their honour year by year.'
Things have moved on since.

A WOMAN ON BOARD BRINGS BAD LUCK It was traditionally believed that women were not as physically or emotionally capable as men, so had no place at sea. It was also observed that when women were aboard, men were prone to distraction or other vices that might distract them from their duties (and/or cause fighting). This, among other things, would anger the seas and doom the ship. However, while having a woman on board would anger the sea, having a 'naked' woman on board would calm the waves. This is why many vessels have a figure of a woman mounted on the bow of the ship, this figure almost always being bare-breasted. It was believed that a woman's bare breasts would 'shame' the stormy seas into remaining calm.

Strange Artefacts,
Buildings, Maps
and Writings

THE ALBERTINUS DE VIRGA WORLD MAP, 1411-15

This Venetian cartographer's map (which was stolen and lost since 1923) records a surprisingly accurate shape of Africa at a time when the continent had not yet been fully discovered by European explorers. Around 1415, the Portuguese were just beginning the '*Age of Discovery*', occupying Ceuta on the northern tip of Africa, and none of their sailors had ever ventured beyond the Canary Islands. (Even now, Ceuta is a Spanish enclave within Morocco). The source of the information on which the map is based is unknown, although it has been suggested that it could have come from descriptions supplied by Muslim traders, or possibly from Chinese mapmakers who sailed under Admiral Zheng He.

ANCIENT EGYPTIAN AND CENTRAL AMERICAN AIRCRAFT

An object looking like a modern aircraft, and thought to be a toy, was found in 1898 in a tomb at Saqquara, Egypt. It was dated as having been made around 200 BCE, thrown into a box marked as a 'wooden bird model' and stored in the basement of the Cairo Museum. In the later 20th century it was rediscovered, and considered so important by the Egyptian government that a special committee of scientists was established to study it. An exhibit was then set up in the main hall of the Cairo Museum with the little model as its centrepiece labelled as a 'model airplane'. It has the proportions of an advanced form of 'pusher-glider' that is able to stay in the air almost by itself. Even a very small engine will keep a pusher-glider operating at speeds as low as 55 mph (88 kph), with a large payload. This remarkable ability is because of the odd shape of wings, as tipping curving wings downward (a reverse-dihedral shape) can give an aircraft maximum lift. In Central and South America, pre-Columbian gold models or toys have been found, probably around 1000 years old. They do not resemble any known animal, bird or fish, but look more like modern aircraft or spacecraft. Structures just in front of the tail resemble a combination of ailerons and elevators with a slight forward curve. However, they are attached to the fuselage, not the wings. The wings viewed from the side are horizontal, but when seen from the front, they curve slightly downward. The elevators, which are behind the wings, are positioned on a slightly higher horizontal plane and are square-ended, giving a definite geometric shape. The tail is also unusual. No fish or bird has a single, upright and perpendicular flange, but this tail fin has the exact shape of fins on modern aircraft.

ANCIENT INDIAN SPACECRAFT AND THE ATOMIC BOMB

The *Mahabharata* and other Vedic epics such as *Bhagavata Purana* tell us of flying machines, *vimanas*, which were extensively discussed in *Vaimanika Shastra*. One of the great Indian epics, the *Ramayana*, includes a highly detailed story of a trip to the Moon in a vimana (or 'astra'), and details a battle there with an 'Asvin' ('Atlantean' airship). In old texts, some vimanas were double-decked circular aircraft with portholes and a dome, curiously like our current idea of a 'flying saucer'. They flew with the 'speed of the wind', making a 'melodious sound'. Four different types of vimanas were described, with some being saucer-shaped, and others like long cylinders. The Indians themselves were supposed to have manufactured the ships and have written their flight manuals. The *Samara Sutradhara* is a scientific treatise dealing with air travel in a vimana. A total of 230 stanzas describe the construction, take-off, cruising for thousands of miles, normal and forced landings, and even the possibility of collisions with birds. In 1875, the *Vaimanika Shastra*, a fourth-century BCE text based on even older texts, was rediscovered in a temple in India.

It dealt with the operation of vimanas, including information on their steering, precautions for long flights, protection of the airships from storms and lightning and how to switch the drive to 'solar energy' from a free energy source (which itself sounds like 'anti-gravity'). This text has eight chapters with diagrams, describing three types of aircraft, including apparatuses that could neither catch fire nor break. It also mentions 31 essential parts of these vehicles and 16 materials from which they are constructed, which absorb light and heat, so are considered suitable for the construction of vimanas.

According to the *Dronaparva*, part of the *Mahabharata*, and also the *Ramayana*, one vimana was shaped like a sphere and borne along at huge speeds on a mighty wind generated by mercury. It moved up, down, backwards and forwards as the pilot desired, a little like a Harrier jump-jet or a UFO. Some were even submersible. A passage in the *Ramayana* reads: '*The Puspaka car that resembles the Sun and belongs to my brother was brought by the powerful Ravan; that aerial and excellent car going everywhere at will... that car resembling a bright cloud in the sky... and the King [Rama] got in, and the excellent car at the command of the Raghira, rose up into the higher atmosphere.*' In another Indian source, the *Samar*, vimanas were '*iron machines, well-knit and smooth, with a charge of mercury that shot out of the back in the form of a roaring flame.*' In the *Mahavira of Bhavabhuti*, a Jain text of the eighth century taken from older texts, it states: '*An aerial chariot, the Pushpaka,* conveys many people to the capital of Ayodhya. The sky is full of stupendous flying-machines, dark as night, but picked out by lights with a yellowish glare.' The *Vedas*, ancient Hindu poems, describe vimanas of various shapes and sizes: the '*ahnihotra-vimana*' with two engines, the '*elephant-vimana*' with more engines, and other types named after the kingfisher, ibis and other animals.

It is possible that mercury had something to do with the propulsion, or more possibly, with the guidance system. The *Vaimanika Shastra* seems to describe the construction of what is now called a mercury vortex engine, the forerunner of the ion engines being made by NASA. More information on the mercury engines can be found in the *Samarangana Sutradhara*: '*Strong and durable must the body of the vimana be made, like a great flying bird of light material. Inside the circular air frame, place the mercury-engine with its solar mercury boiler at the aircraft centre. By means of the power latent in the heated mercury which sets the driving whirlwind in motion a man sitting inside may travel a great distance in a most marvellous manner. Four strong mercury containers must be built into the interior structure. When these have been heated by fire through solar or other sources the vimana* [aircraft] *develops thunder-power through the mercury… The movements of the vimana are such that it can vertically ascend, vertically descend, move slanting forwards and backwards. With the help of the machines human beings can fly in the air and heavenly beings can come down to earth.'*

Unfortunately, vimanas were ultimately used for war, because Atlanteans used their similar flying machines, '*vailixi*', to try and conquer the world. The Atlanteans were known as '*Asvins*' in Indian texts, and were even more technologically advanced than the Indians. Their vailixi were usually cigar-shaped and could operate underwater, in the air or in outer space. The *Mahabharata, Ramayana* and other texts tell us of the terrible war between Atlantis and Rama, 10–12,000 years ago. The epic tells of the awesome destructiveness of the war: '[the weapon was] *a single projectile / charged with all the power of the Universe. / An incandescent column of smoke and flame / As bright as the thousand suns rose in all its splendour… / An iron thunderbolt, / A gigantic messenger of death, / Which reduced to ashes / The entire race of the Vrishnis / And the Andhakas. /… the corpses were so burned / As to be unrecognizable. / The hair and nails fell out; / Pottery broke without apparent cause, / And the birds turned white. /… After a few hours / All foodstuffs were infected… /… to escape from this fire / The soldiers threw themselves in streams / To wash themselves and their equipment…*' Could this have been a nuclear war?

There is a thesis that with the wiping out of Rama's kingdom in a holocaust, and the sinking of Atlantis, the world collapsed back into a 'second Stone Age' with only remnants of an older, superior civilization remaining. A few thousand years after the terrible war, Alexander the Great invaded India and historians chronicled that he was attacked by '*flying, fiery shields*' which frightened his cavalry. Other civilizations recorded flying machines. The *Hakatha* (*Laws of the Babylonians*) state: '*The privilege of operating a flying machine is great. The knowledge of flight is among the most ancient of our inheritances. A gift from "those from upon high". We received it from them as a means of saving many lives.*' The ancient Chaldean text, the *Sifrala*, contains over 100 pages of technical details on building a flying machine, containing words which translate as graphite rod, copper coils, crystal indicator, vibrating spheres, stable angles, etc.

The *Mahabharata* describes Asura Maya having a vimana measuring twelve cubits in circumference, with four strong wheels. It describes weapons such as '*blazing missiles*' and '*Indra's Dart*', which acted via a circular 'reflector'. When the weapon operated, it produced a '*shaft of light*' which, when focused on any target, '*consumed it with its power*'. In one excerpt, the hero Krishna is pursuing his enemy, Salva, in the sky, when Salva's vimana is made invisible. Krishna immediately fired off a special weapon: '*I quickly laid on an arrow, which killed by seeking out sound*'. In the same narrative is recorded: '*Gurkha flying in his swift and powerful vimana hurled against the three cities of the Vrishis and Andhakas a single projectile charged with all the power of the Universe. An incandescent column of smoke and fire, as brilliant as ten thousands suns, rose in all its splendour. It was the unknown weapon, the Iron Thunderbolt, a gigantic messenger of death which reduced to ashes the entire race of the Vrishnis and Andhakas.*' Those killed were so burnt that their corpses were unidentifiable, and the crippled survivors saw their hair and nails to fall out.

ANTIKYTHERA MECHANISM - THE WORLD'S OLDEST SCIENTIFIC DEVICE

This was discovered with hundreds of valuable artefacts off the island of Antikythera (between Greece and Crete) in 1901. It came from a Greek cargo ship of 150–100 BCE. About a foot (30 cm) high, made of bronze and originally in a wooden frame, 30 of its 37 hand-cut bronze gear wheels survive. It was used for predicting the positions of the Sun and Moon. Three-dimensional surface-imaging indicates that it could not only predict planetary motions but also the 18-year Saros, the 54-day Exeligmos, the 19-year Metonic and the 76-year Callippic astronomical cycles. Artefacts of similar complexity did not appear again until well over a millennium later. Although only the size of a shoebox, the mechanism is too valuable to leave its museum in Athens, so a 7.5-ton X-ray tomography machine was sent there from England to examine the device. It

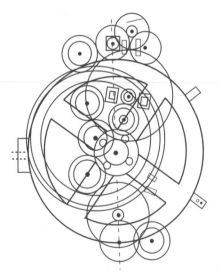

has enabled 932 characters to be read on the hidden inscriptions, compared to 180 'almost illegible' characters previously uncovered. In the first century BCE, Cicero mentions an instrument '*recently constructed by our friend Poseidonius, which at each revolution reproduces the same motions of the sun, the moon and the five planets.*' Archimedes is also said to have made a small planetarium, and two such devices were said to have been rescued from Syracuse when it fell in 212 BCE. The Antikythera reconstruction suggests that such references can now be taken literally. The amazingly complex and advanced Antikythera mechanism is the progenitor of our present scientific instruments.

ARK OF THE COVENANT

In Hebraic, it is called '*Aron Habrit*', with aron meaning an ark, chest or coffer. Along with the tablets of stone on which the Ten Commandments were inscribed, it is supposed to contain Aaron's Rod and manna. It is a symbol of God's permanent covenant with the Jewish people and others who believe in Judaic scriptures, such as Muslims and Christians. In the Pentateuch, the Ark was built at the command of God, following Moses' vision on Mt Sinai. God spoke to Moses from behind two cherubim, which are depicted on the cover of the Ark. God gave details for the construction of the Ark, and it was to be plated entirely with gold. Rings of gold were to be put into each of its four feet, and through these rings staves of acacia or shittah-wood, overlaid with gold, were to be inserted for carrying the Ark. These were not to be removed. A golden cover, adorned with golden cherubim, was to be placed above the Ark, and the Ark itself had to be hidden under a veil.

During the exodus under Moses of the Israelites from Egypt, the Ark was carried by priests 2000 cubits (about 3400 feet or 1000 m) in front of the people and their army. When the Ark was carried to the Jordan River, the waters parted for the Israelites to pass through. Jericho was captured with only a shout which caused the city walls to collapse, after the Ark had been paraded around them for seven days by seven priests sounding seven trumpets made of rams' horns. Returning to Jerusalem, Solomon's Temple was constructed with a special inner room, called Holy of Holies, to house the Ark. In 586 BCE, the Babylonians laid siege to Jerusalem, and destroyed the temple. The Ark may have been destroyed, or taken away by Nebuchadnezzar. The Second Book of the Maccabees and the Book of Revelation state that the Ark is no longer on present Earth.

However, there are many reports of its continued existence. According to Hebrew traditions, King Solomon, when building the Temple, had the Ark of the Covenant put on a platform which could be lowered down into a tunnel system if the Temple were ever taken. There have been modern excavations near the Temple Mount which have discovered the existence of secret tunnels. However, digging is heavily restricted because the major Islamic shrines, the Al-Aqsa Mosque and the Dome of the Rock, now stand where Solomon's Temple may have been. No mention was made of the Ark when the Temple was taken by Nebuchadnezzar, possibly because it had been hidden by Levite priests. The Ethiopian Orthodox Church claims possession of the Ark (or 'tabot') in Axum, where it is apparently kept under guard in a small treasury near the Church of Our Lady Mary of Zion. However, versions of the Axum tabot are kept in every Ethiopian church, each with its own dedication to a particular saint. A 13th-century document, the *Kebra Nagast*, states that the Ark was taken to Ethiopia by Menelik I with divine assistance, while he left a forgery in Jerusalem. Menelik

was the supposed son of King Solomon and the Queen of Sheba. The Armenian Abu Salih, writing in the last quarter of the 12th century, states: *'The Abyssinians possess also the Ark of the Covenant...'* and he describes it. The liturgy was celebrated upon the Ark four times a year: *'on the feast of the great Nativity, on the feast of the glorious Baptism, on the feast of the holy Resurrection, and on the feast of the illuminating Cross.'*

The Lemba people of South Africa and Zimbabwe claim that their ancestors brought it south, giving it the name of *'ngoma lungundu'* (the 'voice of God). They hid it deep in a cave in their spiritual home of the Dumghe Mountains. In his 2008 book *The Lost Ark of the Covenant*, Tudor Parfitt claimed that the Lemba ngoma was similar to the Ark, carried on poles, revered as the voice of God, not allowed to touch the ground, and used as a weapon to sweep enemies to one side. He believes that the Ark was taken to Arabia, possibly to Sena in Yemen, then to Africa by the Buba clan

of the Lemba. The Buba has a genetic signature which has a male Semitic link to the Levant, so it can also be postulated that they are one of the 'Lost Tribes' of Israel. The Lemba claim that at some time the Ark self-destructed, and priests made a replica, using a core from the original. This replica is now in Harare's Museum of Human Science and has been carbon-dated to 1350 CE, the time of the collapse of the Great Zimbabwe civilization.

Some Jewish sources believe that there were two Arks. The original simple wooden Ark of Moses was the 'Ark of War', while a later golden Ark was made by Bezalel to remain in the Temple, as described in the Book of Exodus. It is also claimed that the Ark's 'stones' are in Djaharya near a ruined temple of Ramses III. In legend, the Ark was taken to Languedoc after the Crusades by Knights Templar. Historical author Graham Phillips believes it was taken to the Valley of Edon near Mt Sinai by the Maccabees, then brought to England by the Templar, Ralph de Sudeley, and taken to his estates at Herdewyke in Warwickshire. Some believe that it was buried under the Hill of Tara in Ireland, and others in caves under Mt Tsurugi, in Shikoku, Japan.

THE AZTEC CALENDAR or SUN STONE

On 17 December 1760, a fabulous huge stone was discovered, which had both mythological and astronomical significance. The single block of basalt weighs almost 25 tons, has a diameter of just under 12 feet (3.7 m), and a thickness of 3 feet (90 cm). It was discovered buried in the 'Zocalo' (the main square) of Mexico City, the ancient Aztec capital then called Tenochtisan, and was subsequently embedded in the wall

of the western tower of the Metropolitan Cathedral, where it remained until 1885. It was then was transferred to the National Museum of Archaeology and History. It was carved during the reign of the sixth Aztec monarch in 1479, and dedicated to the principal Aztec deity, the Sun. Copies of it have been found across Mexico. The Aztec name for the huge basaltic monolith is *Cuauhxicalli*, Eagle Bowl, but it is universally known as the Aztec Calendar or Sun Stone. The Aztec calendar system was used not only by the Aztecs, but by other pre-Columbian peoples of central Mexico. It thus shares the basic structure of calendars that were prevalent throughout ancient Mesoamerica. They consisted of a 365-day calendar cycle called *xiuhpohualli* (year count) and a 260-day ritual cycle called *tonalpohualli* (day count). These two cycles together formed a 52-year 'century', sometimes called the '*calendar round*'. The *xiuhpohualli* or year count is considered to be the agricultural calendar, since it is based on the Sun. The *tonalpohualli* or calendar round is considered to be the sacred calendar.

Babylonian Devil Traps

These were terracotta bowls inscribed with magical texts and charms, used by the ancient Hebrews in parts of Mesopotamia. The inverted bowls were buried under the four corners of the foundations of buildings. Their magic provided protection against male and female demons, illnesses, curses and the 'evil eye'. These Babylonian devil traps were used between the third and first centuries BCE until the sixth century CE. As a surviving pagan custom, the bowls were technically prohibited by the Hebrew religion which proscribes magic in general. Probably to circumvent this religious law, the devil traps often also had inscriptions invoking the help of God, or quotations from Hebrew scriptures. One bowl from the third century BCE proclaims a 'bill of divorce' from the devil, and all of his night monsters, commanding them to leave the community forthwith.

THE BAGHDAD BATTERY

The Baghdad Battery, sometimes referred to as the Parthian Battery, is the common name for a number of artefacts created in Mesopotamia, possibly during the Parthian or Sassanid periods (the early centuries CE). Some ancient pots contained watertight copper cylinders that were glued into their openings with asphalt. Discovered in 1936 in excavations of a 2000-year-old village near Baghdad, Iraq, the artefacts came to wider attention in 1938 when Dr Wilhelm König came across them in the National Museum of Iraq, of which he was director. An archaeologist, König closely examined what had appeared to be an old clay pot. It was a 6-inch (15-cm) high vase of bright yellow clay, containing a cylinder of sheet-copper measuring 5 inches (13 cm) by 1.5 inches (4 cm). The edge of the copper cylinder was sealed with a 60-40 lead-tin alloy (a mix comparable to today's solder). The bottom of the cylinder was capped with a crimped-in copper disc, sealed with bitumen or asphalt. Another insulating layer of asphalt sealed the top and also held in place an iron rod suspended in the centre of the copper cylinder. The rod showed evidence of having been corroded by an acidic agent. In 1940 König published a paper declaring it to be an ancient galvanic cell battery, possibly used to electroplate gold onto silver. His 'battery', as well as others unearthed in Iraq, have all been dated to the Parthian occupation between 248 BCE and 226 CE. However, König also found copper vases plated with silver in the Baghdad Museum, excavated from Sumerian sites in southern Iraq, which dated back to at least 2500 BCE. When the vases were lightly tapped, a blue patina or film separated from the surface, which is characteristic of silver electroplated onto a copper base. It would thus appear possible that one of the earliest known civilizations, the Sumerians, passed on their knowledge of 'batteries' and electroplating to the Parthians.

In 1940 a General Electric engineer in Massachusetts made a replica of the battery and generated about half a volt of electricity using a copper sulphate solution. In the 1970s, a German Egyptologist also made a replica of the battery, filling it with freshly pressed grape juice to function as an electrolyte, as he speculated that the Parthians and Sumerians might have done. This generated almost 0.9 of a volt. He used the current from the battery to electroplate a silver statuette with gold, the electro-deposition process known as gilding. It is thus possible that electric batteries were used at least 1800 years, and possibly 4300 years before their modern invention by Alessandro Volta in 1799. Replicas can produce voltages from 0.8 to nearly two volts. Connected in series, a set of batteries could theoretically produce a much higher voltage.

THE BAYAN-KARA-ULA STONE DISCS

These mysterious stone discs may tell the story of a forced alien landing 12,000 years ago. Bayan-Kara-Ula is one of China's most remote regions near the Tibet border, with its mountains reaching from 7000 to 16,000 feet (2100 to 5000 m). In 1938, Chinese archaeologist Chi Pu Tei discovered graves arranged in rows in some mountain caves. He found small skeletons of beings with delicate frames, who nevertheless had disproportionately large skulls. On the walls of the caves were rock drawings which portrayed beings with round helmets. The stars, Sun

and Moon were also scratched on the rock and connected by groups of pea-sized dots. Chinese archaeologists knew that the Dropa and Kham (Kikang) tribes had once lived in the deserted region; they were pygmy people with an average height of around four feet two inches (1.27 m). Chi Pu Tei and his assistants managed to salvage 716 stone discs from the complex of caves, underground tunnels and storerooms. *'These tunnels are perfectly square and the walls, ceilings, and floors are highly glazed, as if somehow the passages and rooms were carved by a device emitting heat of such intensity that it simply melted its way into the mountains'*, according to Dr Zhou Guoxing of the Peking Natural History Museum. The discs, 9 inches (23 cm) in diameter and less than an inch (2.5 cm) thick, resemble modern-day vinyl records, with grooves and a hole in the centre. It was not until 1962 that Professor Tsum Um Nui of the Academy of Prehistoric Research in Peking was able to decipher parts of the incised script. At first the Academy prohibited Tsum Um Nui from publishing his work, because of his shocking findings. In cooperation with geologists he showed that the stone plates had a high cobalt and metal content. Physicists found that all 716 plates had a high vibration rhythm, which led to the conclusion that they had been exposed to very high voltages at some time. The scientists also learned that the grooves were actually a microscopic form of ancient writing.

'The discs are between 8,000 and 12,000 years old, which would make them the oldest known form of writing in the world' according to Dr Guoxing. *'Of the 716 discs, only five have been completely*

translated. *Four others have been partially deciphered.*' The translation tells the horrifying story of a catastrophe after two rival factions went to war. Around 12,000 years ago a group of alien people had crashed onto the 'third planet' (Earth) of this Solar System. Their aircraft no longer had enough power to leave this planet again. They had crashed in the remote and inaccessible mountains. There had been no means and materials for building a new craft. A survivor wrote that one faction authorized the use of a dreaded 'last weapon' to end the conflict. '*It was as if the elements had been unleashed… The sun spun around in circles. Scorched by the fearful heat of the weapon, the world reeled. Humans and animals were burned by the incandescent light. It was a ghastly sight to see. The corpses of the fallen were so mutilated that they no longer look like human beings. Never before have we seen such an awful weapon, and never before have we heard of such a weapon. It was as if the heavens cried out, flashing forth lightning and raining down death. Many who were near the centre of the conflict were turned to ashes.*' Dr Guoxing points out that the account is a perfect description of a nuclear holocaust.

The Chinese sagas of the Bayan-Kara-Ula region also tell of spindly yellow beings who came down from the clouds. The myth goes on to say that the alien creatures were shunned by the pygmy Dropa tribespeople because of their ugliness, and indeed that they were killed by the men in 'the quick way'. The Dropa believe that their ancestors came from space twice, the first time being 20,000 years ago.

THE BOOK OF THE DEAD

The real title of this Egyptian funerary work is '*Pert Em Hru*', meaning 'coming forth by day' or 'manifested in the light'. It consists of collections of spells to aid the dead in the crossing to the next life, and there are several versions, including examples from the priests at Heliopolis, Thebes and Salis. The spells were usually found inscribed on papyrus or leather scrolls in intimate association with the corpse. Usually they were placed next to it in the coffin, actually inside the mummy wrappings, or inside a small statue of a funerary deity. Probably, many of the spells were recited by priests at the funeral. Their proximity to the dead person meant that they were available when he or she faced the dangerous crossing to the next world. Papyri of sections from the Book of the Dead have been found in tombs, while inscriptions from it appear on tombs, pyramids and sarcophagi. Rich Egyptians from the earliest times were buried in substantial graves along with ornaments, weapons, cosmetics, clothes, food and drink. The earliest evidence of funeral liturgies are the 'Pyramid Texts' of around 2665–2155 BCE. They were concerned with protecting the mummified pharaoh and the royal family and courtiers buried in nearby tombs and helping them in the afterlife.

The Book of the Dead's Episode of Judgment

Part of the ritual involved in passing through to the afterlife in Ancient Egypt is revealed in chapter 125 of the Book of the Dead. In illustrations Osiris is shown enthroned, usually on the left, and facing four minor deities including the underworld goddess Ammut. She has the head of a crocodile, the trunk and forelimbs of a lion, and the hind part of a hippopotamus. She devours the bodies of the dead who are found unworthy. In the centre is a great set of scales with the heart of the deceased in one pan, and a feather representing truth in the other. The gods Horus and Anubis check the balance and the god Thoth records the result. To the right of the deceased, Maat, the goddess of truth, and 42 other deities sit in judgment around the hall. The deceased is required to make his own defence, first addressing Osiris in words that are part-hymn and part-spell. Then the deceased recites a general declaration of innocence, which is a denial of various evildoings and breaches of ritual customs. '*I have not oppressed dependents… I have not caused anyone to go hungry… I have not caused anyone to weep… I have not diminished the food offerings in the temples… I have not taken the cakes set aside for the blessed… I am pure*' etc. By doing this, he hopes to assure Osiris that he has lived a decent life on Earth, (and of course, that he has learned the litany for declaring his worthiness) and that his body is complete and ritually pure. Next he begins addressing the 42 deities, denying various faults to each. Again this requires a major feat of memory prior to death. It is at this point in his trial that he can gain credibility by speaking their secret names and places of origin, thus gaining control over them. Thus he needs to learn from the priests the powerful magic of the knowledge of the secret names and places of origin of Osiris and the other 42 deities. By such knowledge he can swing their judgment in his favour. Lastly the deceased addresses his heart, pleading with it not to bear witness against him. At this point in his trial the deceased loses all control of his defence. If the heart does not confirm the person's innocence, the person is lost. But when the heart confirms the person's innocence, then Horus leads the individual before Osiris who assigns the person a proper place in the realm of the blessed.

These texts, found on inner chamber walls of tombs, were expanded into the 'Coffin Texts' from around 2050–1755 BCE. This is when coffins were shaped in the form of mummies. The earliest examples of Books of the Dead date from the 18th Dynasty (1570–1300 BCE), and they incorporate and expand spells and liturgies found in the Pyramid and Coffin Texts. Sometimes plain black ink was used, but often the titles of spells and important words were written in red. Illustrations varied between black and white and full colour. The number and order of the spells varied greatly in the 18th and 19th Dynasty versions of the Book of the Dead, probably reflecting the commands of the noble commissioning the copy. Not until the Ptolemaic Dynasty in around 320 BCE was the number and order of the spells standardized in papyri, with sequential numbering of the spells. There are over 200 spells, but not all are contained in any one discovered papyrus.

A New Kingdom period book (1554–1075 BCE) entitled the *Book of What Is in the Netherworld* describes the Hereafter as a subterranean region completely devoid of light. It is an area divided into 12 regions, each called a 'cavern', and ruled by a king whose subjects are 'spirits'. For example, the sixth region was an agricultural area with canals ruled by Osiris. The many sections are connected by a great river similar to the Nile. Along this river, during the night, sails a boat of the Sun god bringing light and joy to the dwellers of the underground regions.

After death the Egyptian hoped to be free to return to the Earth during the day or be accepted as one of the blessed in the realm of Osiris. The Book of the Dead contains a variety of hymns, magic formulas, litanies, incantations, prayers and words of power which clearly were to be recited to help the deceased to overcome obstacles which might prevent them from achieving felicity in the afterlife. Various spells had specific objectives, e.g. spells 21–23 secured the help of several gods in 'opening the mouth' of the deceased, enabling him to breathe and eat. Spell 25 restored the deceased's memory, spell 42 put every part of the body under the protection of a god or goddess, spell 43 protected the body from decapitation, spell 44 prevented the deceased from dying a second time, and spells 130–131 enable the use the boats of sunrise and sunset. Spell 154 has an address to Osiris by the deceased that contains these words: '*I continue to exist, I continue to exist, alive, alive, enduring, enduring. I awake in peace untroubled. I shall not perish yonder… My skull shall not suffer, my ear shall not become deaf, my head shall not leave my neck, my tongue shall not be taken, my hair shall not be cut off, my eyebrows shall not fall off. No harm shall happen to my corpse. It shall not pass away, I shall not perish, from this land forever, and ever.*'

THE BOOK OF ENOCH - THE LOST BOOK OF THE BIBLE

This text was revered by Jews and Christians alike but fell into disfavour among early theologians, because of its controversial description of the nature and deeds of the fallen angels. Thus the Book of Enoch, along with others, such as the Books of Tobias, Esdras and others, were accepted into Biblical canon. Others were destroyed and the writings lost forever as they did not agree with current doctrines. The Book of Enoch was at one time considered to be among the biblical apocryphal writings by the early Church Fathers. The word apocryphal is derived from the Greek for 'hidden' or 'secret'. It was a complimentary term, and when applied to sacred books it meant that their contents were considered too exalted to be made available to the wider public. Gradually the idea was accepted that such books were only to be read by the 'wise', i.e. the controllers of belief. Thus the term 'apocrypha' began taking on a negative meaning. Believers felt they were being denied the teachings of these books, which were only available to small circles of powerful and influential men. Even the orthodox clergy were not permitted to read the hidden books, because they were thought not to be sufficiently enlightened. Over the centuries the church banned apocryphal material, deeming it heretical, thus forbidding anyone reading from it. The Book of Enoch was banned as heretical by later Church fathers, as the material infuriated some of them. As a result the book was conveniently lost for a thousand years. However, eventually it reappeared. Rumours of a surviving copy sent the Scottish explorer James Bruce to Ethiopia in 1773 in search of it. There he found that the Ethiopic church had preserved the book alongside other books of the Bible. In this work the spiritual world is minutely described, as is the region of Sheol, the place of the wicked. The book also deals with the history of the fallen angels, their relations with the human race and the foundations of magic. The book says: *'that there were angels who consented to fall from heaven that they might have intercourse with daughters of earth. For in those days the sons of men having multiplied, there were born to them daughters of great beauty. And when the angels, or sons of heaven, beheld them, they were filled with desire; wherefore they said to one another: "Come let us choose wives from among the race of man, and let us beget children".'*

Most scholars date the original writing of the Book of Enoch to the second century BCE, and it remained in circulation for at least 500 years. The earliest Ethiopic text was apparently made from a Greek manuscript, which itself was a copy of an earlier text. The original text appears to have been written in a Semitic language, now thought to be Aramaic. Though it was once believed to be post-Christian in date (the similarities to Christian terminology and teaching are striking), discoveries of copies of the book among the Dead Sea Scrolls found at Qumran prove that the book was in existence before the time of Jesus Christ. But the date of the original writing upon which the second century BCE Qumran copies were based will probably never be known. Nearly all the Fathers of the Christian church accepted the words of this Book of Enoch as authentic scripture, especially the part about the fallen angels and their prophesied judgment, including Irenaeus, Bishop of Lyons (115–85), Clement of Alexandria (150–220), Tertullian (160–230), Origen (186–255), and Lactantius (260–330). St Augustine (354–430) believed the work to be a genuine one of the patriarch. Many of the key concepts used by Jesus Christ himself seem directly connected to terms and ideas enunciated in the Book of Enoch, so it is thought likely that Jesus had studied the book, and elaborated on its specific descriptions of the coming kingdom and its theme of inevitable judgment descending upon 'the wicked'. Also, over a hundred phrases in the New Testament find precedents in the Book of Enoch.

THE BOOK OF SHADOWS This is a book of witchcraft, containing beliefs, rituals, uses of herbs, healing potions, laws and ethics, incantations, spells, dances and methods of divining the future. It is meant to be used by witches, and is adapted for use by different covens. Each witch or wizard usually had her or his own personalized copy. Some have been published, one of the first being Charles Godfrey Leland's *Ardia: or Gospel of the*

Witches in 1899. Leland claimed that the witch lore had been passed to him by an Etruscan practitioner. In 1949 Gerald B. Gardner, belonging to an hereditary coven of witches, published *High Magic's Aid*, containing material taken from Aleister Crowley. Rewritten, it was used and modified by Alexander Sanders to form the Alexandrian tradition of witchcraft. Traditionally a witch's book of shadows was burned upon the person's death.

CAUL This is a membrane which sometimes covers the head of a child at birth. It was once thought to be a preservative against drowning in the sea, so consequently the caul was much sought after by seamen. Roman midwives sold cauls as lucky charms to bring long life and happiness. They were also used for divination, and as recently as the 1870s newspaper advertisements were placed by prospective purchasers of cauls seeking to buy such items.

The Burning Bush

During the Exodus, God speaks to Moses from a burning bush, telling him '*I am come down to deliver* [the Israelites] *out of the hands of the Egyptians.*' Scientists hypothesize that the bush could have been growing over a natural gas vent, which was ignited by a spark from a nearby camp fire and kept burning fiercely. Others believe that it was the result of local volcanic action. A Norwegian physicist has studied the subsurface combustion of organic material in Mali and concluded that such events do happen in the natural world. Gardeners know that in certain conditions a pile of compost will burst into flame naturally.

CAULDRON The cauldron was the earliest iron cooking utensil, and was of immense importance in altering the quality of raw foods to make them edible and so help humankind survive. As such, in all primitive societies, it became a symbol of transmutation, germination and transformation. However, it importantly also symbolizes the womb, and became a Goddess or Earth Mother symbol. The symbolical connection with the womb of the Great Goddess arises from the concept that everything is born out of it and eventually returns to it. The original cauldron symbols were gourds, wooden vessels or large shells. Eventually the symbolism of metal cauldrons became linked to the hearth and home because they were used to cook meals. This latter aspect merged the Great Goddess with the Great Mother, as the image of the cauldron united them in a single deity. To Celts, it was the symbol of the Underworld. In Irish mythology the Daghda cauldron provided sufficient food for everyone, while the cauldron of Bran the Blessed in Welsh legend conferred rebirth. In Greek and Roman mythology the cauldron was always hidden in a cave. The Greek witch goddess Medea restored people to youth in a magic cauldron. Stemming from these origins, it became a mystery symbol of witchcraft.

The Cauldron and the Crone

In ancient Welsh legends, Cerridwen is the crone, representing the darker aspect of the Earth Mother. She can prophesy, and is the keeper of the cauldron of knowledge and inspiration in the Underworld. Cerridwen's cauldron was said to have a ring of pearls around its rim. It was located in the realm of Annwn (the Underworld) and, according to the Taliesin's poem *The Spoils of Annwn* the breath of nine maidens kindled the fire beneath it. Oracular speech reportedly came forth from the cauldron. This, of course, is a connection to the nine Muses that were associated with the oracle at Delphi. The vapours emanating from the volcanic pit below the oracle were said to bestow the gift of prophecy. Typical of Celtic goddesses, Cerridwen has two differing children. Her daughter Crearwy is fair and light, but her son Morfran (also called Afagddu) is dark, ugly and malevolent. In one tale in the wonderful *Mabinogion*, the cycle of Welsh myths, Cerridwen brews up a potion in her magical cauldron to give to Morfran. Included in the potion were yellow flowers known as Pipes of Lleu (cowslip), Gwion's silver (fluxwort), the berries of Gwion (hedge-berry), Taliesin's cresses (vervain) and mistletoe berries mixed with sea foam. She puts a young man Gwion in charge of guarding the cauldron, but

three drops of the brew accidentally fall upon his finger, blessing him with the knowledge held within. The furious and shape-shifting Cerridwen pursues the shape-shifting Gwion in animal and plant form through a cycle of seasons until, in the guise of a hen, she swallows Gwion, who is disguised as an ear of corn. Nine months later, she gives birth to Taliesin, the greatest of all the Welsh poets. Following the birth of Taliesen, Cerridwen plans to kill the infant but then changes her mind. She throws him into the sea, where he is rescued by a Celtic prince, Elffin. Taliesin becomes a bard in the court of Elffin, and when Elffin is captured by the Welsh king Maelgwn Gwynedd, Taliesen challenges Maelgwn's bards to a contest of words. Taliesen's eloquence ultimately frees Elffin from his chains. Through a mysterious power, he renders Maelgwn's bards incapable of speech, and frees Elffin from his bonds. Maelgwn Gwynedd became pendragon upon Arthur's death, and Taliesin became associated with Merlin in the Arthurian cycle.

In the Welsh legend of Bran the Blessed, the cauldron appears as a vessel of wisdom and rebirth. Bran, the mighty king of Wales, obtains a magical cauldron from Cerridwen (diguised as a giantess). She had been expelled from a lake in Ireland, which represents the otherworld. The cauldron can resurrect the corpses of dead warriors placed inside it. Bran gives his sister Branwen and her new husband Matholwch, the king of Ireland, the cauldron as a wedding gift, but when war breaks out Bran sets out to take the valuable gift back. He is accompanied by a band of a loyal knights with him, but only seven return home (as in Arthurian legend after the fatal Battle of Camlan). Bran himself is wounded in the foot by a poisoned spear, another theme that recurs in the Arthurian legend in relation to the Fisher King, the guardian of the Holy Grail. According to the *Mabinogion*, Queen Branwen died of grief at Aber Alaw after escaping the destruction of Ireland. On the banks of the Alaw at Llanddeusant in Anglesey, the cairn of Bedd Branwen (Branwen's Grave) was dug up in 1800, and again in the 1960s when several urns and

evidence of cremation were found. The stones have been carted away and the mound destroyed. All that remains of this ring cairn is kerb of surrounding stones and a small standing stone in the middle, close to a cist. In some Welsh stories, Bran marries Anna, the daughter of Ilid (Joseph of Arimathea). Bran was thought to be the father of Caradog (Caractacus), who spent seven years in exile with his son in Rome, where he became a Christian and met St Paul. Bran the Blessed brought Christianity back to Britain in the first century to Trefran, near Llanilid, which was said to be founded by Joseph of Arimathea. Bran travelled after his death to the otherworld, while Arthur makes his way to Avalon. There are theories that Cerridwen's cauldron, the cauldron of knowledge and rebirth, is in fact the Holy Grail for which Arthur spent his life searching.

CELTIC CROSS The historian Crichton E. M. Miller has theorized that the Celtic Cross was a scientific instrument as well as a sacred symbol, allowing navigation without a timepiece, and dating back to Neolithic times. He believes that it was used by Egyptians and Phoenicians to build complex structures and to navigate long distances. All construction requires surveying before work begins, and Miller examined the Pyramid of Cheops and the Giza complex in Egypt, Stonehenge, Avebury and Callanish in Scotland. Callanish is more than 5000 years old and is built in the form of a Celtic cross. Miller believes that the only appropriate instrument that could have been used by the architect, in the place of an uninvented theodolite, was a derivative of the cross with the addition of a plumb line. The Great Pyramid was an enormous undertaking of civil engineering, so using the simplest of materials and the accepted mathematics of the time, Miller assembled a theodolite that could carry out the tasks required. With the addition of a scale rule and a plumb line, the instrument became a Celtic Cross that was extremely accurate and fulfilled the set task, and much more. He has discovered that this incredibly simple instrument has the potential to measure angles and inclinations to an amazing accuracy of 1 minute of arc (1/60th of a degree), depending on the size of the instrument used. As a qualified yacht master, Miller also found that ancient mariners could determine latitude and longitude with the cross. He conducted experiments to prove that the ancients could find their position anywhere on Earth within 3 nautical miles (5.5 km) with a hand-held device. This discovery may help to prove that it was possible for sailors such as the Phoenicians to have made regular trading contact with the Americas in pre-Columbian times. Miller then went on to discover that the Celtic Cross could have been the basis upon which the sciences of geometry, mathematics, ancient astronomy, mapmaking and timekeeping were developed. It could be used in combination with a detailed knowledge of astronomy and monthly star positions, ecliptic and zodiac observations, so it would be possible to locate the position of any star at any time over any location on the Earth's surface. Today the prime meridian is at Greenwich but Crichton proposes that the original prime meridian was at Giza in Egypt from which all local times and distances were calculated. He also believes that the Mayan '*staff of power*', by which they measured the movement of the stars, was a Celtic Cross.

CHRIST'S BLOOD AND KNIFE
In 1270 Hailes Abbey in Gloucestershire was given a phial of Christ's blood, and thus became a hugely popular pilgrimage destination. It is, for instance, mentioned by the Pardoner in Chaucer's *Canterbury Tales*. When the monasteries were dissolved in the 16th century, the blood was declared to be a fake consisting of a mix of honey and saffron. The Basilica of the Holy Blood in Bruges, Belgium, also claims to have Christ's blood in the form of a phial which contains a cloth stained with his blood. It was reputedly brought to Bruges during the Second

Crusade of 1147–9. The knife that was claimed to have been used by Jesus during the Last Supper to slice bread was also worshipped. It was said to have been permanently exhibited in the logietta of St Mark's Campanile belltower in Venice, but the belltower and logietta collapsed in 1902 and were rebuilt. The knife was lost.

CHRIST'S FORESKIN Jewish boys must be circumcised upon the eighth day following their birth under Jewish religious law. In the Christian calendar the Feast of the Circumcision of Christ is celebrated on 1 January. The holy foreskin, or prepuce, has been claimed as an authentic relic by churches across Europe. It was supposed to have been saved in old spikenard (lavender) oil in an alabaster box. The holy foreskin first made an appearance in medieval Europe around 800, when King Charlemagne presented it as a gift to Pope Leo III. Charlemagne said it had been given to him by an angel. It was among the gifts sent by the Byzantine Emperor Alexius I Commenus around 1110 to King Henry I of England. It apparently went to Henry's tomb in Reading Abbey, but it was also claimed by France's Abbey of Coulomb and four cathedrals across Europe, making possibly seven different prepuces to be severed. No relic was more valuable than the holy foreskin since it was the only body part that the Bible specifically mentions being removed from Christ during his life, and which thus stayed behind on Earth after he ascended into Heaven. However, the 17th-century theologian Leo Allatius speculated in '*De Praeputio Domini*

Nostri Jesu Christi Diatriba' that the holy foreskin had ascended into heaven at the same time as Jesus, and had become the rings of Saturn. In the Middle Ages, holy prepuces began appearing in 21 different churches desirous of pilgrim revenues. Miraculous powers were attributed to them, for example, the protection of women during childbirth. The monks of San Giovanni in Laterano, Rome asked Pope Innocent III (1160–1216, pope from 1198) to rule on the authenticity of their foreskin. The monks of Charroux claimed their foreskin to be the only real one, pointing out that it apparently yielded drops of blood. Pope Clement VII (1523–34) declared theirs to be authentic. The Roman Catholic Church waited until 1900 until it declared that all the foreskins were fraudulent, and threatened excommunication to those who wrote or spoke further about the foreskin.

The Crystal Skulls of South America

Skulls are the foremost symbol of death, and at least 13 crystal skulls of apparently ancient origin have been found in parts of Mexico, Central and South America. Some of the skulls are believed to be between 5000 and 16,000 years old. One such skull, said to be of Aztec provenance, was bought by the British Museum from Tiffany's of New York for £120 in 1898.

The Anna Mitchell-Hedges 'Skull of Doom'

The so-called '*Skull of Doom*' is carved of pure quartz crystal, weighs 11 pounds 7 ounces (5.2 kg) and is said to be a relic of a lost American civilization. It was apparently found in the Mayan city of Lubaantun in British Honduras (now Belize) in 1924 by Mike Mitchell-Hedges and his daughter Anna. The jaw is detachable and was found a few months later. Mitchell-Hedges estimated that it would take 150 years of constant work to rub an immense block of rock crystal with sand to achieve the smooth skull shape. It is very similar in form to an actual human skull, even featuring a removable jawbone. Most known crystal skulls are of a more stylized design, often with unrealistic features and teeth that are simply etched onto a single skull piece. It appears, however, that the tale of the skull's discovery was entirely fabricated. Mitchell-Hedges apparently purchased the skull at an auction at Sotheby's in London in 1943. This has been verified by documents at the British Museum, which had bid against Mitchell-Hedges for the artefact. Researchers at Hewlett-Packard Laboratories in 1970 found that the skull had been carved against the natural axis of the crystal. Modern crystal sculptors always take into account the axis, or orientation of the crystal's molecular symmetry, because if they carve 'against the grain', the piece is bound to shatter, even with the use of lasers and other high-tech cutting methods. The scientists could find no microscopic scratches on the crystal which would indicate it had been carved with metal instruments. It is still in the possession of the family in Canada. One HP researcher is said to have remarked, 'The damned thing simply shouldn't be.'

The British Crystal Skull and the Paris Crystal Skull

There is a pair of similar skulls known as the *Aztec Skulls*. Both are said to have been bought by mercenaries in Mexico in the 1890s, possibly at the same time. They are so similar in size and shape that some have guessed that one was copied to produce the other. In comparison to the Mitchell-Hedges skull, they are made of cloudier clear crystal and are not as finely sculpted. The features are superficially etched and appear incomplete, without discretely formed jawbones. The British crystal skull is on display at London's Museum of Mankind, and the Trocadero Museum of Paris houses the Paris crystal skull. Using electron microscopes, researchers found that these skulls possessed straight, perfectly spaced surface markings, indicating the use of a modern polishing wheel. Genuine ancient objects would show tiny haphazard scratches from the hand-polishing process. Their report speculated that these skulls were actually made within the past 150 years.

The Mayan Crystal Skull and the Amethyst Skull

These were discovered in the early 1900s in Guatemala and Mexico, respectively, and were brought to the United States by a Mayan priest. The amethyst skull is made of purple quartz and the Mayan skull is clear, but the two are otherwise very similar. Like the Mitchell-Hedges skull, both of them were studied at Hewlett-Packard Laboratories, and they too were found to be inexplicably cut against the axis of the crystal.

Texas Crystal Skull

A skull known as 'Max' is a single-piece, clear skull weighing 18 pounds (8.2 kg). It reportedly originated in a Mayan tomb in Guatemala, then passed from a Tibetan spiritualist to Jo-Ann Parks of Houston, Texas. The Parks family allows visitors to observe Max and they display the skull at various exhibitions across the United States.

'Ami' - the Amethyst Crystal Skull

Its history is uncertain but it was part of a collection of crystal skulls held by the Mexican President Diaz from 1876–1910. It may be Mayan from the Oaxaca area of Mexico.

The 'ET' Skull

'ET' is a smoky quartz skull found in the early 20th century in Central America. It was given its nickname because its pointed cranium and exaggerated overbite make it look like the skull of an alien being.

Rose Quartz Crystal Skull

The only known crystal skull that comes close to resembling the Mitchell-Hedges skull is this, which was reportedly found near the border of Honduras and Guatemala. It is not clear in colour and is slightly larger than the Mitchell-Hedges, but displays a comparable level of craftsmanship, including a removable jaw.

Brazilian Crystal Skull

This 13.8-pound (6.25-kg) life-size skull was donated to the museum's Section of Minerals by a Brazilian gem dealer in 2004.

'Compassion' - the Atlantean Crystal Skull

A newly discovered crystal skull, said to be 'Atlantean' by a Mayan shaman and elder at a crystal skull conference held on 9 September 2009.

THE CURSE OF 'THE DIAMOND OF DEATH'

The Hope Diamond was allegedly stolen from a temple in Burma or India from the forehead (or eye) of a statue of the Hindu goddess Sita. Throughout its history, it has had the reputation of being cursed. The priest who took it was said to have been tortured to death. It is known that in 1642 Jean Baptiste Tavernier (1605–86), a French jeweller, visited India and bought a 112 carat (23 g) blue diamond, believed to have come from the Kollur mine in Golconda, India. Only the Great Mogul could sell diamonds, so whether is was bought legally or smuggled out is unknown. Tavernier arrived back in France in 1668, and Louis XIV bought the large, blue diamond as well as 44 other large diamonds and 1122 smaller diamonds. Tavernier was made a nobleman and died at the age 84 in Russia. According to legend, Tavernier was torn apart by wild dogs on this trip to Russia. In 1673, Louis XIV decided to recut the diamond to enhance its brilliance. The newly cut gem was 67 carats (13.4 g). It was officially named the '*Blue Diamond of the Crown*' and he would often wear the gem on a long ribbon around his neck. Louis XIV allowed his favourite mistress, the Marquise de Montespan, to wear it also, but she was publicly disgraced shortly after and fell from his favour. Nicholas Fouquet, the French finance minister who was guardian of the crown jewels, supposedly wore the diamond for a festive occasion and was later disgraced, imprisoned and executed by order of the King in 1680. Louis XIV himself died in agony of gangrene, his empire in ruins.

In 1749, Louis XV was king and ordered the crown jeweller to make a decoration for the *Order of the Golden Fleece*, using the blue diamond and the Côte de Bretagne (a large red spinel thought at the time to be a ruby). The resulting decoration was extremely ornate and large. It was later a favourite gem of Marie Antoinette, the wife of King Loius XVI, who was beheaded in the French Revolution. According to the malign legend, Marie Antoinette and Louis XVI were killed because of the blue diamond's curse. The Princess de Lamballe, a member of the court, had briefly worn the diamond and she was torn to pieces by a French mob. During the French Revolution, the crown jewels (including the blue diamond) were taken from the royal couple after they attempted to flee France in 1791. The jewels were placed in the royal storehouse but were not properly guarded. Though most of the crown jewels were soon recovered, the blue diamond was not.

Somehow the Dutch diamond-cutter Wilhelm Fals obtained it, recut the diamond and was then robbed by his own son, Hendrik. Wilhelm was said to have been ruined and died of grief, and Hendrik Fals committed suicide in 1830. Before Hendrick Fals killed himself, he had apparently given the diamond in payment of a debt. He had not dared to acknowledge the debt to his father, so had robbed him of it. The man who took the diamond from Fals was named Francis

Beaulieu, who travelled from Marseilles to London to sell it. He fell terribly ill from gaol fever, and died in a poor lodging-house. Just before his death, he had arranged for a London jewel dealer, Daniel Eliason, to buy the diamond, but when Eliason went to pay, Beaulieu was dead, so the money never changed hands. Somehow Eliason got possession of the diamond. There is documentation that a large blue diamond of almost 45 carats (9 g) was owned in 1812 by Daniel Eliason, 'a diamond merchant'. The diamond was described and sketched in colour by an English jeweller, John Francillon, in a legal memorandum that he signed and dated London, 19 September 1812. Daniel Eliason killed himself in 1824. There is some evidence that indicates that George IV of England bought the blue diamond from Eliason, and upon George IV's death in 1830, the diamond was sold to pay off his massive debts. It was bought by the banker Henry Philip Hope. It is said that Hope gave £18,000 to £20,000 for it, although it had been valued at £30,000, but this was all the money he would pay for it. His nephew, Henry Thomas Hope, owned the diamond from around 1839 after his uncle's death and suffered a long series of misfortunes, including the death of his only son. Lord Henry Francis Hope inherited the diamond and suffered scandal, a collapsed marriage and financial ruin. His wife died in poverty. Because of gambling and profligate spending, Francis Hope requested permission from the court in 1898 to sell the Hope diamond.

(Francis was only given access to the life interest on his grandmother's estate). His request was denied. In 1899, an appeal case was heard and again his request was denied. In both cases, Francis Hope's siblings opposed selling the diamond. In 1901, on an appeal to the House of Lords, Francis Hope was finally granted permission to sell the diamond. It was known now as the Hope diamond, the finest and largest blue diamond in the world. It only weighed 44 carats (8.8 g) instead of 67 (13.4 g) but was enormously improved in appearance by its recutting. Lord Henry Francis Hope's wife, who was well known as the actress May Yohe, used to wear it. He divorced her in 1902 and the diamond was sold. She died in poverty.

A merchant in Hatton Garden, named Adolph Weil, bought the diamond, and transferred it almost at once to an American trader named Simon Frankel. From the moment Frankel took possession of it, he had financial troubles, and had to get rid of the diamond in desperation in 1907 in the hope of saving his fortune. In 1908 it was in the possession of a French dealer named Jacques Colot, who almost at once sold it to a Russian prince, Ivan Kanitovski, who lent it to his mistress, a beautiful actress named Mademoiselle Lorens Ladue. She wore it at the Folies Bergère. She was wearing it when Prince Ivan Kanitovski shot her with a revolver. Two days afterwards he was battered to death by Russian revolutionaries. Jacques Colot, who had never received the whole of the purchase price, went mad, and a week after this event he committed suicide. Before Kanitovski died he had transferred the diamond to a French dealer, who fell downstairs and broke his leg. The French dealer sold it to a Greek jewel broker named Montharides or Maoncharides, who took it to Athens. Shortly afterwards he was captured by thieves, thrown over a cliff and killed, along with his wife and his two children. Another version of the story recounts that he drove his carriage off a cliff, killing himself, his wife and one child. He had just sold the stone for $400,000 to the 34th Sultan of the Ottoman empire, Abdul Hamid II (1842–1918), but it is not certain that the sultan ever actually had the diamond in his possession. The sultan lost his empire in an army revolt in 1909. The diamond had been given to a servant named Abu Sabir to be polished. Abu Sabir said he had never received it, so was flogged, tortured and thrown into a dungeon for some months. The diamond was found in the possession of the gaoler. He was discovered strangled. It next appeared in the possession of one of the eunuchs of the sultan's household named Kulub Bey, who was captured in the streets of Istanbul and hanged by a mob from a lamp-post. Jehver Agha, an official of the sultan's treasury, attempted to steal the diamond and was hanged. Meantime, the sultan's favourite concubine, a beautiful French girl, had got hold of the diamond. She had assumed a Turkish name and was known as Salma Zubayba. She was wearing it when the revolutionaries broke into the sultan's palace, and when she was killed, the diamond was on her breast. Thence it came into the possession of a Turkish or Persian diamond merchant

named Habib Bey, a jewel merchant in Istanbul (Constantinople). He perished in the shipwreck of a French steamer in the Moluccas, and it seemed that the tragic the story of the jewel had reached a conclusion.

However, he had left the diamond in Paris, and it came into the possession of the jeweller Pierre Cartier of Messrs. Cartier, who exhibited it in the Haymarket, London. It was sold in Paris on 22 June 1910 at the Habib sale by Bailly & Appert for £16,000. A French dealer who bought it for £28,000 sold it to Mr. Edward B. McLean in America for £60,000 ($180,000). He gave it to his wife, who was born Evalyn Walsh, the daughter of a wealthy American mine owner. Edward Beale McLean had one son, Vincent Walsh, who was believed at one time to be the richest child in the world because

he was to succeed to the fortunes of his two grandparents, John McLean, the owner of the *Washington Post* and of the *Cincinnati Inquirer*, and Thomas E. Walsh, the Colorado mining king. The child's full name was Vincent Walsh McLean, and from the time of his birth he was subject to very special security precautions as his parents had been warned that he would be kidnapped. The house and grounds where he lived were surrounded with steel fences and there were guards to protect him in all circumstances. One day the 9-year-old boy slipped out of the security gates, ran down the street, and was killed by a passing motorcar. Both his parents were away from the house at a racecourse in Kentucky. The McLeans suffered another major loss in 1946 when their daughter committed suicide aged 25. Evalyn McLean's husband left her for another woman, became alcoholic and was declared insane, being confined to a mental institution until his death in 1941. Evalyn was forced to sell the family newspaper, the *Washington Post*, and died soon after her daughter's death. On Evalyn's death in 1947 the Hope Diamond passed into the collection of the Smithsonian Institution. James Todd was the mail worker who delivered the Hope Diamond to the Smithsonian. He crushed his leg in a truck accident, injured his head in an automobile accident and then lost his home in a fire. Though Evalyn McLean had wanted her jewellery to go to her grandchildren when they were older, it was put on sale in 1949, two years after her death, in order to settle debts from her estate. It was taken from the Smithsonian and bought by Harry Winston, a New York jeweller. Winston did not believe in the curse and was unaffected by it. He exhibited it for a time and then donated the Hope diamond to the Smithsonian Institution in 1958 to be the focal point of a newly established gem collection.

DAVID - THE GREATEST STATUE OF THE RENAISSANCE

Prior to Michelangelo's work on the statue, the authorities in Florence planned to commission a series of 12 massive Old Testament sculptures for the façade of the Cathedral of Santa Maria del Fiore. Two had been created independently by Donatello and his assistant Agostino di Duccio. In 1464 Agostino was commissioned to create a sculpture of David. An immense block of Carrara marble was provided, but with the death of Agostino's master Donatello in 1466, another sculptor, Antonio Rossellino, was commissioned to take up where Agostino had left off. The contract was quickly terminated, however, and the great block of marble remained neglected for 25 years, lying exposed to the elements in the yard of the cathedral workshop. In 1501, the church authorities ordered the block of marble, called '*The Giant*', to be 'raised on its feet' so that a master experienced in this kind of work might examine it and express an opinion. Leonardo da Vinci and others were consulted, but it was the 26-year-old Michelangelo who convinced the authorities that he deserved to take on the incredibly difficult commission. He worked on it for three years, and in 1504 a committee of artists including Leonardo and Botticelli met to decide on an appropriate site for its display. It took four days to move the statue from Michelangelo's workshop onto the Piazza della Signoria. Michelangelo's David is not depicted, as was normal practice, with the head of the slain Goliath, but rather as a warrior tense and ready for the battle. His veins bulge out of his lowered right hand and the twist of his body conveys the feeling that he is in motion, David has become perhaps the most recognized work of Renaissance sculpture, standing as a symbol of both strength and youthful human beauty. It is now in Florence's Accadamia Gallery, while a replica stands in the Piazza della Signoria. The larger-than-life size statue is an utterly breathtaking work of art.

There is a plaster cast of David in London's Victoria and Albert Museum, with a detachable plaster fig leaf displayed nearby. It was created for visits by Queen Victoria, when it was hung on two strategically placed hooks to hid the statue's naked genitals. The fig leaf was chosen because of its appearance in the story of the 'Fall' of Adam and Eve in the Garden of Eden after Eve persuaded Adam to eat an apple from the Tree of Knowledge: '*And the eyes of them both were opened, and they knew that they were naked; and they sewed fig leaves together, and made themselves aprons.*' (Genesis 3:7). This suggests that statues should be 'clothed' with aprons, rather than a single large leaf. Before 1500, depictions of 'private parts' were hardly

ever obscured in pictures and sculptures, but with the rise of Protestant preachers like Luther and Calvin denouncing the sinfulness of human flesh, we begin to see the use of strategically placed gauze, clouds, branches and leaves. The Catholic Church then tried to outdo its Protestant counterpart in terms of piousness, and the Council of Trent issued an edict explicitly forbidding the depiction of genitals, buttocks and breasts in sacred art. In 1557, Pope Paul IV issued a bull to reduce the amount of nudity on public display, and fig leaves began being placed everywhere. In the case of Michelangelo's vast mural '*The Last Judgment*', folds of drapery or extra branches of foliage were added. On the giant statue of Mercury in the Vatican, a huge fig leaf was commissioned and stuck over the offending article.

ELECTRIC LAMPS IN ANCIENT EGYPT
Sculptured reliefs, which have been interpreted as lamps, can be seen in the Temple of Hathor at Dendera, around 40 miles (64 km) north of Luxor. A Norwegian electrical engineer noticed that an object on the reliefs might work as a lamp, and a colleague was able to construct a working model. There appeared to be a bulb, with two arms reaching into it near

its thick end, and a type of cable at the other end, from where a snake is leaping out to touch the arms on the other side. The whole appearance is of a lamp. Perhaps electricity was known and used in antiquity, a theory supported by the discovery of the Baghdad Battery in Iraq, and early Indian writings. People have tried to prove that there were electric lamps used during the construction of the pyramids, as they claim that in none of the many thousands of subterranean tombs and pyramid shafts was a single trace of soot found. Many tombs are full of colourful wall paintings, and the argument is that light sources such as candles and oil lamps would leave carbon traces. Reflected light from mirrors was not an option, as the burnished copper plates of the time were not sufficiently reflective. Others argue that there are traces of soot, e.g. in the Red Pyramid of Dahschur. It also appears that the great chambers of the Red Pyramid, and the passages in the Great Pyramid, were built in full daylight. Until the last ceiling block was positioned years after the chamber was begun, all tasks like polishing and furnishing the walls and roof beams could be performed in natural daylight.

THE EMERALD TABLET

Also called the *Emerald Table* or *Tabula Smaragdana*, this is a crucial part of the *Hermetica*, and is a revered magical document in Western occultism, which views it as a founding text in the art of alchemy. It was a stone said to have been discovered in a cave tomb, clutched in the hands of the corpse of Hermes Trismegistus, a fabulous figure who combined the natures of the Great god Hermes and the Egyptian god Thoth.

Hermes is portrayed in art as holding an emerald, upon which he inscribed the entire Egyptian philosophy. The discovery was said to have been made by either Sarah, wife of Abraham, Alexander the Great or by the Greek philosopher Apollonius of Tyana. The stone was inscribed in Phoenician, and revealed the magical secrets of the universe. After several Arabian translations, a Latin translation appeared in 1200. The opening sentences read '*That which is above is like that which is below and that which is below is like that which is above, to achieve the wonders of the one thing.*' Therefore, '*This is the foundation of astrology and alchemy: that the microcosm of mankind and the earth is a reflection of the macrocosm of God and the heavens.*' However, translations differ and the rest of the text makes little sense. Most of the works of the *Hermetica* have disappeared or been destroyed over the centuries, but it is said that the entire system of magic was inscribed upon the emerald tablet in cryptic wording.

The Eye of Horus

The all-seeing Eye of Horus was a common amulet in Egypt, featuring a highly stylized eye of the falcon-headed, solar and sky god Horus. Horus was associated with regeneration, health and prosperity. The eye has become a significant symbol in esoteric and occult love. Horus was the son of Osiris and Isis, and he lost an eye in a fight with his murderous uncle, Seth. The eye was reassembled by the magic of Thoth, and Horus gave the eye to Osiris who experienced rebirth in the underworld. As an amulet, the Eye of Horus appears in three versions: a left eye, a right eye and two eyes. The Eye of Horus is embellished with a typical Egyptian cosmetic extension and subtended by the markings of a falcon's cheek. In ancient Egypt the eye was used as a funeral amulet as protection against evil and to help rebirth in the underworld, and for decorating mummies, coffins, and tombs, as described in *The Book of the Dead*.

FAIRY FLAG OF DUNVEGAN

This fragment of faded brown silk is owned by Clan McLeod and preserved at Dunvegan Castle on the Isle of Skye, Scotland. It is supposed to provide salvation for the clan in the event of a disaster, and some believe it to be Norse in origin, taken when the Viking King Harold Hardrada was killed in battle at Stamford Bridge in 1066. The Danish king's most treasured possession was his *Landoda* (Land Ravager), and he said '*With this banner, I can never be defeated in battle.*' The Chief of the Clan McLeod, however, asserted in the 1920s that it had been given to his clan by fairies, and could only be used three times. The first time it was used, in 1490, the Fairy Flag was brought out in a desperate battle against the MacDonalds and the tide turned in the favour of the McLeods. In 1520, the McLeods were hopelessly outnumbered by the MacDonalds at Waternish, but they unfurled the banner and beat off the attack.

FETISH A fetish is an object representing a god or spirit, and it is used to establish a bond between a human being and the supernatural. They have been common throughout history and are worn or possessed by people as a means of gaining protection, luck, love, health or money or to ward off evil, or bring down curses on enemies. Typical fetishes range from dolls, carved images and stones to animal hair, claws or bones. The 'corn dolly' is a survival in England of a pre-Christian fetish used as part of harvest customs. It was believed that the spirit or god of the corn lived with the essential crop, and that harvesting would make it homeless. Across all of Europe there were customs relating to the last harvested sheaf of corn or other cereal crops. Hollow shapes were fashioned from the sheaf, to contain the corn spirit to be brought into the home for the winter. The corn 'dolly' was then ploughed into the first furrow of the new season to ensure a new crop. Dolly may well be a corruption of idol, and an amazing variety still are made, such as the Norfolk Lantern, Anglesey Rattle, Welsh Long Fan, Stafford Knot and Barton Turf Dolly.

GOLDEN BOUGH and SILVER BRANCH The golden bough is mystical tree in a Graeco-Roman myth. Aeneas consulted the prophetess who was one of the Sybils at Cumae. He was told to break a branch from a certain tree that was sacred to Proserpina. Then Aeneas was led to the entrance of the Underworld into which he descended.

Aeneas approached the Stygian lake but Charon the boatman would not ferry him across because he was not dead. The Sybil who accompanied Aeneas then produced a *Golden Bough* that allowed Aeneas entrance into the Underworld. In Celtic legend, Bran is guided by a female fairy bearing the *Silver Branch*, through which he gains admittance to the Fairy Realm.

GOLDEN CALF In the Old Testament the golden calf was a figure made by Aaron while waiting for Moses to return from the mountain where he had gone to seek advice from God. The Israelites became anxious about their leader's long absence during the Exodus from Egypt. They pleaded with Aaron to make them gods that might go before them and lead them home to Israel. Before returning to his people, Moses had been told by God that his people had corrupted themselves. When Moses descended from the mountain, with the tablets upon which God had written his commandments, Moses immediately saw the golden calf and the people dancing about it. In rage, Moses broke the tablets, then smashed the calf, burned it in a fire, ground it to pieces and scattered it upon water which he forced the children of Israel to drink.

THE GOLDEN RECTANGLE

The Golden Rectangle is a rectangle that is based upon the Golden Mean, which is a number that is represented by the Greek Letter phi (F) or represented decimally as 1.6180339887499 etc. The dimensions of a Golden Rectangle are approximately in the proportion of 1: 1.618, for example, 13 feet by 8 feet. In nature the numbers contained within the Golden Mean occur again and again in many diverse things. If you start with the numbers 0 and 1, then make a list where each number is the sum of the previous two you create a list like this: 0, 1, 1, 2, 3, 5, 8, 13, 21, 34, 55, 89, 144 and so on to infinity. These numbers are called a Fibonacci series, after Fibonacci, an Italian mathematician who, while studying the way plants grew, realized they followed the above sequence perfectly. After a plant had grown one flower, it would have to grow one more, then two more, and so on, following the pattern exactly. Other examples of this numerical series that occur in nature are found in the way a nautilus constructs its seashell, each time growing larger on a spiral conforming to the phi ratio. A sunflower has 55 clockwise spirals overlaid on either 34 or 89 anti-clockwise spirals, again following the Fibonacci series perfectly. In architecture, the Golden Mean has been used widely throughout history. Originally discovered by Pythagoras, the Greeks constructed their temples to fit the Golden Mean, for example the Parthenon in Athens. The Golden Mean was used in architecture because the ratio was very easy to reproduce accurately without requiring highly technical methods of calculation. After the fall of Rome, knowledge of the Golden Mean was lost until the Renaissance, when Italian painters rediscovered the ratio, using it to create perspective in their paintings, and to construct plans for buildings.

The Golden Mean is also known as the golden ratio, golden section, divine section, divine proportion, golden proportion, golden cut, golden number, medial section and mean of Phidias, being an irrational mathematical constant to the value of approximately 1.6180339887, which has been called '*the world's most astonishing number*' by Mario Livio. For around 2400 years, it has fascinated many of the world's greatest mathematicians such as Pythagoras, Euclid and Kepler. Not only mathematicians and architects have debated its importance, but also biologists, artists, musicians, historians, architects and psychologists have been involved in researching and using the golden mean.

THE GORDIAN KNOT

Gordium is a city 50 miles (80 km) southwest of Ankara in Turkey, and it was the capital of Phrygia under the famously wealthy King Midas (725–675 BCE). Its fortress guarded the only practicable trade route between Troy and Antioch, where it crossed the Sangarius River. To trade with Asia, one had to pay taxes to pass the citadel of Gordium. Phrygia was left without a king, and its council, on consulting the oracle, heard that the next man to appear riding an ox and cart would become the king. Midas, a poor landowner, thus became king and dedicated his ox and cart to

Zeus. The new king secured the cart's yoke to a beam with an intricate knot. An oracle predicted that whoever could solve the knot and untie it would become the ruler of all Asia. Many people tried with no success, but in 333 BCE, Alexander the Great faced the challenge. When he could find no end to the knot to untie it, he simply sliced it in half with a stroke of his sword, producing the required result. To get a quick result is now known as an '*Alexandrian solution*'.

GOSPEL OF ST JOHN The Gospel of St John is the exorcist's defence against the devil, sending the possessing demon into fits. The medieval demon could not stand to hear it read aloud. The Gospel of St John was supposedly used during exorcism because it was believed that the idea of God becoming incarnate in Christ was something which the devil and demons abhorred. The Gospel begins: '*In the beginning was the Word, and the Word was with God, and the Word was God. The same was in the beginning with God. All things were made by him; and without him was not any thing made that was made. In him was life; and the life was the light of men. And the light shineth in darkness; and the darkness comprehended it not.*'

THE GREAT PYRAMID OF GIZA – HOW WAS IT BUILT?

The tallest structure in the world until the building of the Eiffel Tower, the Great Pyramid of Giza is said to be a tomb for the Pharaoh Khufu, who ruled for just 23 years between 2589 and 2566 BCE. Many question whether there was such a pharaoh, and speculate that it may have been built much earlier. Civilization only arose in Egypt in around 3100 BCE, and we still do not understand how these early builders could have created such a structure. The pyramid, its causeway and two associated temples, mastabas (tombs), four lesser pyramids and six boat pits have a combined volume of over 95 million cubic feet (2.7 million m³).

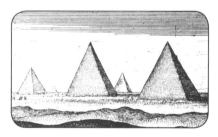

To build the complex in Khufu's reign would have required his workmen to quarry, dress and set 11,360 cubic feet (320 m³) of stone every hour of every day for 23 years without a break. This is the equivalent of quarrying, dressing, transporting and laying an average pyramid block of 2.5 tons (2540 kg) every two minutes. The Indiana Limestone Institute estimated that just to quarry and ship enough stone to build the Great Pyramid would take 81 years, using explosives, power tools, cranes and diesel transport. The effort of actually building the pyramid, an incredibly complex task, was not taken into account. Almost as incredible is the fact that the 13 acres (5.3 ha) of a rocky plateau had to be levelled to less than an inch difference in height. The Egyptians levelled the bedrock and filled in depressions with the sort of fantastic precision that would need laser measurement today. The pyramid was originally faced with 22 acres (9 ha) of polished limestone casings, transported 20 miles (32 km) from Aswan. Most has gone to build mosques, but some are left at the very apex of the pyramid. They weighed up to 15 tons (15.2 tonnes) each, and had to be placed with extreme precision. A playing card cannot be slid between them as they deviate from absolute true by less than 1/100th of an inch. Once placed in position, these limestone blocks could not subsequently be moved slightly to face up to the next block. There is no known way that they could be placed so precisely by manpower alone.

GRIS-GRIS The *gris-gris* developed among the African-American slave culture in the southern United States as talismans to attract good luck or to ward off evil. Generally they were charm bags filled with magical powders, herbs, spices, bones, stone, feathers or other ingredients. Gris-

gris became traditional in New Orleans, the home of voodoo magic in the United States, and were used for attracting money and love, stopping gossip, protecting the home, maintaining good health etc. A gris-gris was (and still is) ritually made at an altar containing the four elements of salt (representing earth), incense (air), water and a candle flame (fire). The number of ingredients placed in the gris-gris always comes to 1, 3, 5, 7, 9 or 13. Stones and coloured objects are chosen for their occult and astrological meanings. The New Orleans voodoo queen Marie Laveau said her gris-gris contained bones, coloured stones, graveyard dust, salt and red pepper. One of her '*wangas*' to bring bad luck reputedly was a bag made from a shroud of a person who had been dead for nine days. It contained a dried one-eyed toad, the little finger of a black person who had committed suicide, a dried lizard, a bat's wings, a cat's eyes, an owl's liver and a rooster's heart. If such a gris-gris were hidden in the victim's handbag or under their pillow, he or she would die. A red flannel bag holding a lodestone or magnet was a gambler's favourite gris-gris, supposed to guarantee good luck. In the days of slavery, those who mistreated their slaves sometimes found gris-gris filled with black pepper, saffron, salt, gunpowder and pulverized dog manure in their vicinity.

THE HAIR OF A DOG IS NOT WHAT IT SEEMS
We know the sayings '*give me a hair of the dog that bit me*' or '*the hair of a dog*' that are used to signify a drink of alcohol to alleviate the effects of a hangover. In the Middle Ages, the burnt hair of a mad dog was supposed to cure rabies or the effects of a dog bite,

when applied to the wound. The phrase 'the hair of the dog' was in print in 1546, in *A dialogue containing the number in effect of all the proverbs in the English tongue: 'I pray thee let me and my fellow have / A hair of the dog that bit us last night – / And bitten were we both to the brain aright. / We saw each other drunk in the good ale glass.'* A hangover is the symptom of withdrawal from alcohol poisoning. Drinking a small amount of alcohol will help the body feel better temporarily, but eventually it will make the hangover even worse.

A little-known use of 'the hair of a dog' is recorded in the life of Lord George Byron. Scores of women used to send the 'mad, bad and dangerous to know' poet locks of their hair with their love letters. The archives of his

Hermetica

These 42 sacred books of wisdom were traditionally written by Hermes Trismegistus (Thrice Great Hermes), and combine the wisdom of the Greek god Hermes and the Egyptian god Thoth (see THE EMERALD TABLET). They appeared between the first and third century CE, and have always influenced Western magic and occultism. They were supposedly originally written on papyrus, and the Christian theologian Clement of Alexandria stated that 36 of the books contained the entire Egyptian philosophy. Four books were devoted to astrology; ten books called the *Hieratic* were authorities on law, ten books concerned sacred rites and observances, two were on music, and the rest on writing, cosmography, geography, mathematics and measurement and the training of priests. Six remaining books concerned medicine and the body, discussing diseases, medical instruments, the eyes and women. Most of the Hermetic books, along many with others, were lost during the burning of the royal libraries in Alexandria. The surviving books were secretly buried in the desert. What remains has been passed down through generations. The most important and oldest is *The Divine Pynander*, consisting of 17 fragments containing the way to divine wisdom and the secrets of the universe as they were revealed to Hermes.

Mysterious Pyramids

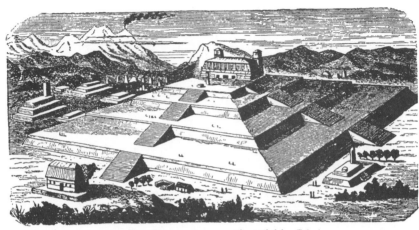

A teocalli - Mesoamerican pyramid - at Cholula, Mexico

Pyramids of Egypt

One of the pyramids of Meroe, Ethiopia

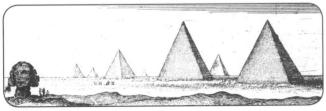

Pyramids of Egypt

262

The Sphinx and Great Pyramid of Giza, Egypt

The pyramid of Cestius, Rome

publisher, John Murray, contain more than 100 locks from women whom he had seduced, including Lady Caroline Lamb. When he halted their relationship, she had her long hair cropped short so she resembled a Cambridge choirboy who was one of Byron's conquests at the time. In return for locks of his lovers' hair, Byron would often send the clippings from his beloved Newfoundland dog, Boatswain, on the pretext that it was his own. If he had employed his own hair, he would have been virtually bald, which would undoubtedly have played havoc with his love-life.

HERO'S ENGINE Hero (or Heron) of Alexandria (*c*.10–70 CE) was a Greek lecturer, mathematician and engineer who lived in the Roman province of Egypt. He was considered to be the greatest experimenter of antiquity. Many of his designs have been lost, but others have been preserved in Arabic manuscripts. Many appear to be his lecture notes on pneumatics, mathematics, physics and mechanics, copied from originals in the great Library of Alexandria. Hero published a description of an *aeolipile* or a steam-powered engine. This device spins when heated, and is the first recorded reaction steam turbine or steam engine. Aeolipile comes from the Greek words meaning '*the ball of Aeolus*', Aeolus being the god of wind. The water is heated in a simple boiler, which forms part of a stand for a rotating vessel. The boiler is connected to the rotating chamber by a pair of

pipes that also serve as the pivots for the chamber. In another design, the rotating chamber may serve as the boiler, and this arrangement greatly simplifies the pivot/bearing arrangements, as they then do not need to conduct steam. Hero also invented a 'windwheel', the first method of harnessing wind on the land, and a wind-powered organ. Another amazing invention was the world's first vending machine. When a coin was dropped via a slot on the top of the machine, a set amount of holy water was dispensed. When the coin was deposited, it fell upon a pan attached to a lever. The lever opened up a valve which let some water flow out. The pan continued to tilt with the weight of the coin until it fell off, at which point a counterweight would snap the lever back up and turn off the valve. Hero also invented many mechanisms for the Greek theatre and a stand-alone fountain operating under hydrostatic energy. He designed different types of syringe, and his force pump was used in a fire-engine. A millennium before anyone else, Hero formulated the 'Principle of the Shortest Path of Light', and wrote down the Babylonian method of calculating square roots. Hero's (Heron's) Formula is used to find the area of a triangle from its side lengths.

HEX This word designating a witch's spell has an historical association with the number six. Christian authorities labelled six 'the number of sin'. A triple six, 666, in the Book of Revelations was '*the number of the Beast*' and has been referred to as '*Satan's number*'. However, Egyptians considered 3, 6 and 7 to be the most sacred numbers: 3 represented the Triple Goddess, 6 meant her union with God, and 7 represented the seven Hathos (goddesses of fate), seven planetary spheres, the seven-gated holy city, seven-year reigns of kings, and so on. Egyptians believed that the total number of all deities had to be 37, because of that number's magical properties. It combined the sacred numbers 3 and 7. Also 37 multiplied by any multiple of 3 (up to 27) gave a triple digit or 'trinity': 111, 222, 333, 444, 555, 666 etc. The number 666 itself is the product of 3 x 6 x 37. Traditionally, hex signs were painted on barns and houses for protection against lightning, to ensure fertility and to protect animal and human occupants alike from becoming bewitched. Various hex signs have a distinct meaning, with some of the symbols and designs such as the swastika dating back to the Bronze Age.

The Holy Chalice and the Holy Grail

At the last supper, Jesus used this vessel to serve wine to his disciples. Some churches have claimed to hold the chalice, e.g. the Santo Càliz (Holy Chalice) de Valencia – found at Valencia Cathedral in Spain. Recently both Pope John Paul II and Pope Benedict XVI have venerated it, but neither has pronounced it to be authentic. The chalice itself has given rise to the legend of the Holy Grail, that was sought by the knights of King Arthur and is the subject of hundreds of books. Some have postulated that the grail is a symbol for the bloodline of Christ, who fathered children, rather than a physical object.

HOLY NAILS AND OTHER
RELICS Relics are the material remains of a Christian saint after death, and the sacred objects associated with Christ and the saints. At the Second Council of Nicaea in 787 CE, the church leaders Jerome and Augustine promoted reverence for relics and icons, and the Council ruled that no church should be constructed without them. During the Crusades, huge quantities of relics were brought back to Europe, then kept in reliquaries (often elaborate, decorated vessels of formularized shape), that were carried in processions and credited with miraculous powers. Relics of martyrs were placed under all altar stones in Roman Catholic churches until 1969. In the fourth century CE St Helena of Constantinople, the mother of Constantine the Great, travelled to Palestine to gather relics, such as fragments of the *True Cross*. The staircase ascended by Jesus for his trial at Pontius Pilate's praetorium, the *Scala Sancta*, was supposedly brought by St Helena to Rome. She also brought back *Holy Nails*, of which there are now at least 30 venerated across Europe. They are found in church treasuries at Santa Croce in Rome, Venice, Aachen, Escorial in Spain, Nuremberg and Prague. However, church authorities still cannot decide whether Christ was crucified using three or four nails. Other relics include the Iron Crown of Lombardy and the Bridle of

Constantine, both said to be made from nails used during the Crucifixion. Trier Cathedral in Germany and Argenteuil Church in France both claim to house the *Holy Coat*, or *Seamless Robe*, the tunic of Christ for which soldiers drew lots after the Crucifixion. Argenteuil claims that it was taken there by Charlemagne. Relics of the *Gifts of the Magi* are at St Paul's Monastery on Mount Athos, Greece. In Croatia, Dubrovnik Cathedral has the *Swaddling Clothes* which baby Jesus wore during his presentation at the Temple. Many churches have relics of the *Crown of Thorns*, placed upon Jesus' head at the Crucifixion. A segment of the *Column of the Flagellation*, which Jesus was tied to during his flogging, is in Rome's Basilica of St Praxedes.

The *Holy Sponge* used during the Crucifixion is at the Basilica of Santa Croce in Gerusalemme in Rome. Also in this church is a part of the *Titulus Crucis*, the panel which was hung on the cross; two thorns of *Christ's Crown*; an incomplete nail; some fragments of the grotto of Bethlehem; a large fragment of the Good Thief's cross; the bone of an index finger said to be the finger of St Thomas that he placed in the wounds of the Risen Christ; and three small wooden pieces of the True Cross. A much larger piece of the cross was taken from Santa Croce to St Peter's Basilica on the instructions of Pope Urban VIII in 1629, and can be seen near a huge statue of St Helena. There is also a single reliquary containing small pieces of: the Scourging Pillar (to which Christ was tied as he was beaten), the Holy Sepulchre (Christ's tomb), and the crib of Jesus. All of the relics were once in the ancient St Helena's Chapel at the basilica, which is partly under ground level. Here the founder of the church had some earth from the Crucifixion site at Calvary dispersed, from which derived the name Gerusalemme of the basilica. Medieval pilgrim guides noted that the chapel was considered so holy that entry by women was forbidden. *The Spear of Destiny*, or *Holy Lance*, or *Spear of Longinus* was used to pierce the side of Jesus on the Cross to ensure that he was dead, and fragments of it are kept in various holy places.

IRON PILLAR OF DELHI

In the centre of the Qutb complex of monuments in Delhi, this dates to the fourth century CE, and bears an inscription that it was erected as a flagstaff in honour of the Hindu god Vishnu, and in the memory of the Gupta King Chandragupta II (375–413). It is composed of 98 per cent wrought iron and has stood for 1600 years without rusting or decomposing. Around 24 feet (7.3 m) tall, it weighs approximately 6.5 tons (6.6 tonnes), and was manufactured by forged welding. Not until 2002 did scientists solve the secret of the non-corrosion of the iron column despite Delhi's harsh weather conditions. They discovered that a thin layer of 'misawite', a compound of iron, oxygen and hydrogen, had protected the cast iron pillar from rust. The protective film began to form within three years of the erection of the pillar and has been growing extremely slowly since then. After 1600

years, the film has grown to just one-twentieth of a millimetre thick. The protective film was formed catalytically by the presence of high levels of phosphorous in the iron, as much as 1 per cent compared to less than 0.05 per cent typical in today's iron, i.e. around 20 times as much. The high phosphorous content is a result of a unique iron-making process, which reduced iron ore into steel in one step by mixing it with charcoal. Modern blast furnaces use limestone in place of charcoal, yielding molten slag and pig iron, which is later converted into steel. In the modern process most phosphorous is carried away by the slag. The pillar demonstrates remarkable metallurgical knowledge, and a model developed for predicting growth of the protective film may also be useful for modelling long-term corrosion behaviour of containers for nuclear storage applications.

THE KATZENKLAVIER - THE CATS' CHORUS

The word means 'cats' piano' and it was a musical instrument designed by the German Jesuit scholar and polymath Athanasius Kircher (1602–80). Pet-lovers of a nervous disposition, please move on to the next entry now. The invention consisted of a row of cats in cages, arranged by vocal tone. They were then 'played' using a keyboard which jabbed nails into their tails and caused them to howl. This author has developed a similar invention for politicians and bankers. Considered the '*founder of Egyptology*', Kircher discovered the link between micro-organisms and plague, and invented the megaphone, automata and a magnetic clock. However, it may be that Kircher only updated this ghastly instrument.

Jean-Baptiste Weckerlin (1821–1910) noted in his book *Musicana*: '*When the King of Spain Felipe II was in Brussels in 1549 visiting his father the Emperor Charles V, each saw the other rejoicing at the sight of a completely singular procession. At the head marched an enormous bull whose horns were burning, between which there was also a small devil. Behind the bull, a young boy, sewn into a bearskin, rode on a horse whose ears and tail had been cut off. Then came the Archangel Saint Michael in bright clothing, carrying a balance in his hand. The most curious was on a chariot that carried the most singular music that can be imagined. It held a bear that played the organ; instead of pipes, there were sixteen cat heads each with its body confined; the tails were sticking out and were held to be played as the strings on a piano, if a key was pressed on the keyboard, the corresponding tail would be pulled hard, and it would produce each time a lamentable meow. The historian Juan Cristobal Calvete noted the cats were arranged properly to produce a succession of notes from the octave (chromatically, I think). This abominable orchestra arranged itself inside a theatre where monkeys, wolves, deer and other animals danced to the sounds of this infernal music.*' The 'cats' piano' was also described by the German physician Johann Christian Reil (1759–1813) as a way of treating patients who had lost the ability to focus their attention. Reil believed that if they were forced to see and listen to this instrument, it would inevitably capture their attention and they would be cured. The instrument

was recreated using squeaky toys by Sound Sculptor Henry Dagg at a garden party held by Prince Charles at Clarence House in 2010. The tune 'Over the Rainbow' was played, to the prince's evident amusement.

LUCKY CHICKEN MANURE

Harry Edwards, head of the Australian Skeptics Society, wrote a letter to his local newspaper in St James, New South Wales, Australia, on 8 March 2004. His pet chicken often perched on his shoulder, leaving a 'deposit' there. He correlated these occurrences with subsequent events such as winning the lotto, receiving unexpected money etc and concluded that the bird brought good luck. One day the chicken left its mark on Edwards's son's jacket who then found wallets, wrist watches etc., which he returned to their owners. Edwards wrote that he then took some of his chicken's feathers to a 'past lives reader' who confirmed the chicken was a reincarnated philanthropist and that Edwards '*should spread the luck around by selling the product*'. Edwards ended his letter offering to sell his 'lucky chicken crap'. Edwards received two orders and $20 for his lucky manure.

THE MAHABHARATA AND EVIDENCE OF SPACEFLIGHT

The *Mahabharata* and *Ramayana* are the national epics of India. They are probably the longest poems in any language. The *Mahabharata*, attributed to the sage Vyasa, was written down from around 540 to 300 BCE, and it relates the legends of the Bharatas, one of the Aryan tribal groups. Even by the time the complete literal English translation had been published, in the years 1886–90 (by Kisari Mohan Ganguli) no aircraft had ever flown, and the first combustion engine was still a few month earlier. However, the following description from the *Mahabharata* seems to indicate the flight of spaceships: '*After the Lokopalas had gone away, Arjuna – that slayer of all foes – began to think, "O monarch, of the car of Indra!" And as Gudakeca, gifted with great intelligence, was thinking of it, the car endowed with great effulgence and guided by Matali, came dividing the clouds and illuminating the firmament and filling the entire welkin with its rattle, deep as the roar of mighty masses of clouds. Swords, and miscrias of terrible forms, and maces of frightful description, and winged darts of celestial splendour, and lightnings of the brightest effulgence, and thunderbolts, and Tutagudas furnished with wheels and worked with atmospheric expansion and producing sounds, loud as the roar of great masses of clouds, were on that car. And there were also on that car fierce and huge-bodied Nagas with fiery mouths, and heaps of stones white as the fleecy clouds. And the car was drawn by ten-thousand horses of golden hue, endowed with the speed of the wind.*

The Mandylion – the Image of Edessa

According to Christian legend, this is the first icon; it is a piece of cloth with an image of Jesus upon it. This was allegedly sent by Jesus himself to King Abgar V of Edessa in Iraq to cure him of leprosy, with a letter declining an invitation to visit the king. Over the centuries, the image has reportedly been lost and reappeared several times. Today two images claim to be the Mandylion. One is the Holy Face of Genoa kept at the Church of St Bartholomew of the Armenians in Genoa, Italy. The other is the Holy Face of San Silvestro kept in the Church of San Silvestre in Capite (Rome) up until 1870, which is now located in the Matilda Chapel of the Vatican Palace.

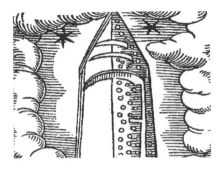

And furnished with prowess of illusion, the car was drawn with such speed that the eye could hardly mark its progress. And Arjuna saw on that car the flag-staff called Vaijayanta, of blazing effulgence, resembling in hue the emerald or the dark blue lotus, and decked with golden ornaments, and straight as the bamboo. And beholding a charioteer decked in gold seated on that car, the mighty-armed son of Pritha regarded it as belonging to the celestials... Matali, the charioteer of Cakra, hearing these words of Arjuna, soon mounted the car and controlled the horses... Arjuna, blazing like the sun itself, ascended the celestial car. And the Kuru prince, gifted with great intelligence, with a glad heart, coursed through the firmament on that celestial car effulgent as the sun and of extraordinary achievements. And after he had become invisible to the mortals of the earth, he beheld thousands of cars of extraordinary beauty. And in that region there was no sun or moon or fire to give light, but it blazed in light of its own, generated by virtue and ascetic merit. And those brilliant regions that are seen from the earth in form of stars, like lamps – so small in consequence of their distance, though very large – were beheld by the son of Pandu, stationed in their respective places, full of beauty and effulgence and blazing with splendour all their own... "These, O son of

Pritha, are virtuous persons, stationed in their respective places. It is these whom thou hast seen, O exalted one, as stars from the earth!"

THE MAYAN BRIDGE Yaxchilan is a Mayan ruin situated on the River Usmacinta in the jungle about 8 miles (13 km) from Bonampak in Mexico. It has been studied by archaeologists for more than a century. In 1989, a civil engineer, James O'Kon noticed a mysterious mound of rocks which he thought were part of a bridge. To prove his thesis, he used computers to integrate archaeological studies, aerial photos and maps to develop a three-dimensional model of the site and determine the exact positioning and dimensions of the bridge. He discovered that the Maya had constructed the longest bridge span in the ancient world in the seventh century CE. It was 600 ft (183 m) long, and consisted of a hemp rope suspension structure with two piers and three spans. The bridge connected

Yaxchilan in Mexico with its agricultural domain in the Peten, which is now Tikal in Guatemala. What archaeologists had assumed to be a pile of rubble were the remains of a pier 12 ft high and 35 ft (3.6 by 10.6 m) in diameter. Aerial photos have located a twin support pier on the opposite side of the river.

THE MAYAN CALENDAR and THE END OF THE WORLD

The 365-day Mayan calendar year that was used in the pre-Columbian Mayan civilization of Mesoamerica was more precise than the Gregorian calendar that we use today. It is still unclear how they came to understand such a complex phenomenon as the 'precession of the equinoxes'. They devised three different calendrical systems: the *tzolkin* (sacred calendar), the *haab* (civil calendar), and *the long count*. The tzolkin is a cycle of 260 days (13 months of 20 days each) and the haab is the solar cycle. These two tzolkin and haab calendars were combined in an interlocking fashion to produce a cycle of *c.*52 years (18,980 days), which was known as a 'calendar round'. Each day had a particular glyph and meaning ascribed to it and at the end of the 52-year cycle, a renewal ceremony was performed. The long count period of 100 calendar rounds ended after 5200 years. This was equivalent to an age. According to the Maya, humanity was in the fourth Sun or age. That would end 5200 years from the beginning of their calendar. The start of the Mayan calendar (long count cycle) was 10 August 3113 BCE. The end of the Mayan calendar

(long count cycle) is thus 21 December 2012, and many people are predicting the end of the world upon that date (see page 108). The longest cycle in Mayan cosmology is the *grand cycle* of 26,000 years, which corresponds to the precession of the equinox (the amount of time it takes for the Earth's axis of rotation to complete one cycle of change and return to its original position, see below). There is another 5200 year cycle left to complete the grand cycle since five long count cycles to make one grand cycle, and we are only nearing the end of the fourth. The combination of a long count date and a tzolkin/haab date occurs only once every 136,656,000 days (approximately 374,152 years or 73 Mayan eras).

The Mayan calendar lost only one day in 6000 years. Their predictions of solar and lunar eclipses were incredibly accurate. The date that they believed would be the end of the world, translates to our calendar, as 21 December 2012. This date marks the time in the precessional cycle of the Earth that we will move out of the constellation of Pisces and into the Age of Aquarius. In the Age of Pisces, the Sun rises on the vernal equinox in the direction of the constellation of Pisces in the sky. However, due to precession, after every 2160 years on the vernal equinox the Sun rises in a different constellation. The Earth spins on its axis while it revolves around the Sun. The Earth's axis is not perfectly vertical, but rather is tilted at an angle of about 23.5 degrees. However, the axis is not always inclined this way, as it slowly varies from about 24.5 degrees to 22.1 degrees, making a complete cycle every 41,000 years. While it is moving in this way, due to varying gravitational forces, the axis precesses (wobbles in layman's terms) in a clockwise circle. The angle of the Earth stays the same (or somewhere within its three-degree variance), but the direction in which it points changes. For example, our current North Star is Polaris (or Ursa Minor), as the north pole points towards this star. However, around 13,000 years ago, the north pole would have pointed towards the star Vega, and it will do so again in about another 13,000 years. It takes about 25,776 years to complete a complete precessional cycle.

THE MAYAN ROAD MYSTERY

The Mayan civilization is famous for its pyramids, many of which were constructed in their jungle empire.

The pyramids were coated with stucco, so their smooth exteriors would have gleamed in the sunshine and by the light of a full moon (as did the Egyptian pyramids). Despite their advanced knowledge of astronomy, mathematics and architecture, the Maya are still regarded as a 'Stone Age' or Neolithic culture as they did not use metal tools. However, the nearest iron ore deposits were 1500 miles (2400 km) away, so the Mayan people used jade for tools (and weapons) instead, which was harder than iron. The Romans had a crude mathematical system compared to that of the Maya, and unlike the Maya had no concept of zero, but no-one considers Rome to be a Neolithic culture. The achievements of Mesamerican civilizations have never been fully recognized by our Eurocentric system of history (nor have the impressive advances of China, India and the rest of Asia over a millennium ago). The '*sacbe*' was the system of flat white roads interconnecting Mayan holy sites and cities, built up with rocks, and levelled and paved over with limestone cement. The roads vary in width from 8 to 30 feet (2.4 to 9 m). However, the Mayan people appear to have had no wheeled vehicles, and nor did they drive herds of domesticated animals between population centres. Reports from the early Spanish conquistadores, e.g. Bishop Diego de Landa, tell us of an elaborate network of all-weather roads that linked Mayan urban sites. Why these roads were built remains a mystery.

THE MAYPOLE This was a central feature in the pre-Christian Beltane festivities, which are still celebrated by neo-pagans, and it also plays a harmless part in the social fabric of some English

The Nagant Revolver and Russian Roulette

Many have wondered why the Russian officer corps was so willing to attempt to play 'Russian roulette', i.e. placing one bullet into the multiple bullet chamber of a revolver, spinning the chamber, pointing the muzzle at their heads and pulling the trigger. The Nagant M1895 was the standard firearm issued to Russian officers between 1895 and 1933, and was still in use throughout the Second World War. As it had a gas seal, the gun is rumoured to be the only revolver capable of being silenced, and it is known that the various Soviet secret police forces used them in this clandestine manner. The seven-shot revolver had to be reloaded one cartridge at a time through a loading gate, and each of the used cartridges had to be manually ejected, making reloading laborious and time-consuming. In the 'game' of Russian roulette, two players take turns spinning and firing the revolver so that each successive spin results in an equal 7-1 probability of the player being killed. Sometimes up to seven men would play, without spinning the chamber, so that the first man had a one in seven chance of dying, the second man a one in six chance etc. If all the first six players survived, the seventh man would obviously have a 1 in 1 chance of dying. Not good odds. Sometimes a gambler would take bets from his fellow officers to play Russian roulette. With the Nagant M1895, a single cartridge would be loaded into the drum before it was spun. The heavy bullet tended to settle in the lower chamber, so a player could be reasonably confident that an empty bullet hole would be aligned with the hammer. A recent study showed that about 80 per cent of the victims of Russian roulette were white, all of them were male, the average age was 25 years, and alcohol drinking played a much bigger role than in other cases of suicide by shooting.

villages. Beltane is a fertility festival celebrated on May Eve, from which the maypole receives its name. The maypole was usually a newly cut birch tree, although oak and elm were also used. These trees have always been associated with fertility, and the maypole is a phallic symbol. Trees have always played a major part in animistic and pagan rituals to ensure the fertility of women, cattle and crops. The cutting of the maypole was accompanied by celebrations with dancing and singing, and it was erected in the centre of the local village, stripped of its branches and decorated with garlands of flowers. Long coloured ribbons were attached to its crown, the ends of which were taken by young men and women alternately, who then danced around the tree in opposite directions. The ribbons were braided over and under, until the tree was entirely wrapped. These May dances were common across Europe and the United States. Orris dances similarly served to help the harvest weather. Today most poles are burned and a new pole is cut and dressed again at the next Beltane festival. In the past villagers kept a permanent maypole on the village green and dressed it each year.

NUMBER 7 Across many cultures, this is a 'lucky' number. The New Testament Book of the Apocalypse, or Revelation, refers frequently to the mystic sacredness of the number seven. In the book St John addresses himself to seven churches in Asia, greeting them from the Lord and from the seven spirits which are before His throne. John describes his vision on the island of Patmos, when he saw one like the Son of Man, in the midst of seven golden candlesticks, and holding in his right hand seven stars. The golden candlesticks are explained as being the seven churches, and the seven stars the angels of those churches. In following visions, a throne is set in heaven, and in the right hand of Him that sat on it is a book sealed with seven seals. Then a lamb with seven horns and seven eyes, which are the seven spirits of God sent forth into all the Earth, takes the book and opens the seven seals one after another. When the seventh seal is opened, seven angels appear with seven trumpets, which they blow one after another. Before the

seventh angel sounds his trumpet, there are seven bursts of thunder. Afterwards there appears a dragon with seven heads and ten horns, and seven crowns upon his heads. Then a beast rises up out of the sea, also with seven heads and ten horns, but with ten crowns upon his horns. The seven angels, pour out one after another the seven vials of God's wrath upon the Earth. Then there is seen a woman seated on a scarlet coloured beast which has seven heads, these being seven mountains on which the woman sits. It is added that there are seven kings, of whom five are fallen, and one is reigning, and one is yet to come. In the last vision, that of the heavenly Jerusalem, the prevailing number is not seven but 12, derived probably from the 12 tribes of Israel. However, with this exception seven is the prevailing number of the Book. Von Hammer-Purgstall observes that, there

are two sevens in the Book's greeting; seven churches and seven spirits. In the body of the Book there are found besides two sevens of sevens: first are described seven candlesticks, stars, seals, horns, eyes, trumpets and thunders; and second, seven angels, heads, crowns, plagues, vials, mountains and kings.

THE OLMEC STONE HEADS

With the discovery of a colossal stone head in 1869, an unknown advanced civilization came to light, which preceded the Maya and Aztecs of Mexico and Central America. The representations of its people seemed unmistakably to resemble black Africans. They were named Olmecs by archaeologists, and after a great deal of dispute, it was suggested that they represented the earliest 'Mother Civilization' of Mesoamerica, dating back to around 1500 BCE. They flourished from 1500–400 BCE, around Veracruz and Tabasco in what is today southwest Mexico. They constructed permanent city-temple complexes, where luxury artefacts made of magnetite, obsidian and jade have been found. The Great Pyramid at La Venta was the largest Mesoamerican structure of its day, rising 110 feet (33.5 m) about the plain. Over 1000 tons (1016 tonnes) of serpentine blocks, mosaic pavements and deposits of jade and haematite mirrors have been found there. Olmec artworks are considered masterpieces today. Seventeen huge basalt stone heads have so far been discovered, carved with African features. Thought to be depictions of rulers, they were carved from single blocks of stone and the largest is 12 feet (3.6 m) tall. Other sculptures, altars, thrones, jade face masks and stelae with representations of figures have been found. Olmecs are the civilization in the Americas thought to have begun writing, formed inscriptions, ballgames and bloodletting. Some believe they practised human sacrifice. However, there are no representations of human sacrifice, and we should recall that bloodletting was used until recently in the West to cure illnesses. They may also have invented the compass, the concept of zero and the Mesoamerican or Mayan calendar with its 'long count'. The long count calendar required the use of a zero. The Olmec may have been the first Western hemisphere civilization to invent a writing system. Finds in 2002 and 2006 predate the oldest Zapotec writings of around 500 BCE.

THE PHAISTOS DISC

Since 1900, archaeological excavations have uncovered the magnificent Minoan palace of Phaistos on Crete, with its royal courts, great staircases and theatre. According to mythology, Phaistos was the seat of King Radamanthis, brother of King Minos. It was also the city that gave birth to the great wise man and soothsayer Epimenides. The first palace was built *c.*2000 BCE, but was destroyed *c.*1700 BCE by an earthquake. Rebuilt, in even more luxurious style, it was destroyed again *c.*1400 BCE. The disc of Phaistos is the most important example of hieroglyphic inscription from Crete.

It was discovered in 1908 in a small room near the depositories of the archive chamber of the palace. It was next to a 'Linear A' tablet and pottery dated to 1850–1600 BCE. Although many inscriptions were found by the archaeologists, they are all in Linear A code which is still un-deciphered. It is a roundish clay disc, with symbols stamped into it. The text consists of 61 words, 16 of which are accompanied by a strange 'slash' mark. There are 45 different symbols occurring 241 times. These symbols portray recognizable objects like human figures and body parts, animals, weapons and plants. Since the text of the disc is so short, decipherment by the statistical cryptographic techniques employed in cracking the Linear B code were impossible. However, it is thought that another ancient writing system,

Proto-Byblic script (named after Byblos in Lebanon), provides the key to reading the Phaistos Disc. The mysterious 'slash' on 16 of the words seem to be numerals counting commodities recorded on the disc, similar to the majority of Linear B texts. The impressions on the clay were made using reusable seals, making this a possible precursor of moveable type. In 2008 Dr Jerome M. Eisenberg claimed that the disc was a fake, but Greek authorities will not allow it to be moved from its display case for examination because of its fragility.

THE PHILOSOPHER'S STONE

Originally the philosopher's stone was believed to be the chemical that changed base metals into silver or gold, and often it was termed the *Power of Projection*. First mentioned by the alchemist Zosimos

the Theban (*c.*250–300 CE), it has taken on huge powers and occult significance. Some think that it holds the secret of life and health. In the 13th century alchemists had to follow strict devotional ritual and purification before being thought worthy to perform their activities. The philosopher's stone came to signify the force behind the evolution of life, and the universal binding power which unites minds and souls in a human oneness. It now represents the purity and sanctity of the highest realm of pure thought and altruistic existence.

THE PIRI REIS MAP AND THE MYSTERY OF THE LOST PEOPLE

In 1929, historians found a map drawn on a gazelle skin. It had been created in 1513 by Piri Reis, a famous admiral of the Turkish fleet. His high rank within the Turkish navy allowed him to have privileged access to the Imperial Library of Constantinople, so he could have sourced lost maps dating back to the fourth century BCE or earlier. The Piri Reis map shows the western coast of Africa, the eastern coast of South America and the northern coast of Antarctica. It is the oldest surviving map to show the Americas. We do not know how Piri Reis managed to draw such an accurate map of the Antarctic region 300 years before it was discovered, or how the map shows the actual northern Atlantic coastline which is up to a mile under the ice. Many believe that the admiral must

have used knowledge obtained from and earlier civilization. Piri Reis himself admitted he based his map on much older charts. The Piri Reis map shows the northern part of Antarctica before the ice covered it. We now know that the last period of ice-free conditions in the Antarctic began about 13,000–9000 BCE and ended about 4000 BCE. The first civilization developed in the Middle East around 6500 BCE, to be followed within a millennium by those of the Indus valley and China. Somehow, a map was drawn that is only now possible with the application of modern technology.

In 1953, a Turkish naval officer sent the Piri Reis map to the US Navy Hydrographic Bureau. To evaluate it, the Chief Engineer of the Bureau asked Arlington H. Mallery, an authority on ancient maps, to help. Mallery discovered the projection method used, by making a grid and transferring the Piri Reis map onto a globe. The map was accurate, and Mallery stated that the only way to draw a map of such accuracy was by aerial surveying. Also the spheroid trigonometry used to determine longitudes was supposedly a process not known until the mid-18th century. It was seemingly copied from mapmakers who knew that the Earth was round, and also had knowledge of its true circumference to within 50 miles (80 km). On 6 July 1960 the US Air Force responded to Prof. Charles

H. Hapgood of Keene College, and specifically with regard to his request for an evaluation of the ancient Piri Reis Map:

Dear Professor Hapgood,

Your request of evaluation of certain unusual features of the Piri Reis map of 1513 by this organization has been reviewed. The claim that the lower part of the map portrays the Princess Martha Coast of Queen Maud Land, Antarctic, and the Palmer Peninsular, is reasonable. We find that this is the most logical and in all probability the correct interpretation of the map. The geographical detail shown in the lower part of the map agrees very remarkably with the results of the seismic profile made across the top of the ice-cap by the Swedish–British Antarctic Expedition of 1949. This indicates the coastline had been mapped before it was covered by the ice-cap. The ice-cap in this region is now about a mile thick. We have no idea how the data on this map can be reconciled with the supposed state of geographical knowledge in 1513.

Harold Z. Ohlmeyer Lt. Colonel, USAF Commander

PORTOLANI AND UNNATURAL PRECISION

In the Middle Ages sailing charts were called *portolani*. They were accurate maps of the most common sailing routes, showing coastlines, harbours, straits, bays, etc. Most portolani focused on the Mediterranean and the Aegean seas, and other known routes, for example the 'sailing book' of Piri Reis noted above. *Dulcert's Portolano* of 1339 gives the perfect latitude of Europe and North Africa, and the longitudinal coordinates of the Mediterranean and of the Black Sea are approximated to half a degree. Even more incredible in accuracy is *Zeno's Chart*, of 1380. It shows a huge area in the north, stretching as far as Greenland. Professor Charles Hapgood in *Maps of the Ancient Sea Kings* stated, *'It's impossible that someone in the fourteenth century could have found the exact latitudes of these places, not to mention the precision of the longitudes…'* Another amazing chart is that of the Turkish Hadji Ahmed, 1559, in which he shows a land strip, about 1000 miles (1600 km) wide, joining Alaska and Siberia. Such a natural bridge had been covered by seawater at the end of the glacial period, so could he have used ancient maps?

Mathematician and cartographer Oronteus Fineus represented the Antarctic with no ice-cap, in 1532. There are also maps showing Greenland as two separated islands, and this was confirmed by a polar French expedition which found out that there is a thick ice cap joining what it is actually two islands. Professor Hapgood also discovered a cartographic document copied by an older source, that had been carved on a rock column in China in 1137. It revealed the same high level of scientific accuracy as the other western charts, the same grid method and the same use of spheroid trigonometry.

THE PYGMY TUNNELS OF MONTE ALBÁN

The Zapotec civilization flourished in southwest Mexico from around 200 BCE until the Spanish conquistadores arrived in 1519. In their art and architecture, mathematics and calendrical science, the Zapotecs reveal clear affinities with the earlier Olmec and Mayan civilizations to the south, but history shows no migration from that area. Their capital was at Monte Albán, 7 miles (11 km) from Oaxaca, situated on an artificially levelled mountain promontory. At its centre lay a huge plaza measuring 1000 feet by 650 feet (300 by 200 m), flanked by terraces and courtyards. Systematic excavations began in 1931, and treasures of gold, jade, rock crystal and turquoise were soon found in several of the city's tombs. However, the most remarkable discovery was a complex network of stone-lined tunnels, far too small to be used by adults or children of average stature. The first of these tunnels, explored in 1933, was just 20 inches (50 cm) high and 25 inches (64 cm) wide. It is so small that the excavators could make their way along it only on their backs. After they had inched through it for 195 feet (60 m), they came upon a skeleton, an incense burner and funeral urns. There were also ornaments of jade, turquoise and stone, and a few pearls. A little way beyond this the tunnel was blocked, and to enter it again the explorers had to dig a shaft down from the surface beyond the blockage. Worming along the next stretch, they found even smaller passages, no more than 1 foot (30 cm) high, branching off from the main tunnel. Leading down into one of these was a tiny flight of steps. At a distance of 320 feet (100 m) from the main entrance, the archaeologists found another skeleton, and a few yards beyond this, at the edge of the northern terrace of the great plaza, the tunnel came to an end. Further excavations revealed two similar tunnels, both packed with clay. Finally, to the east of tomb number seven, where the richest treasures had been found, a complex network of miniature tunnels was discovered, all lined with stone with some being less than a foot high. Smoke was blown into these in an effort to trace their course and purpose and it 'revealed a number of unexpected exits'. The excavators' initial thought that the tunnels had been a drainage system was abandoned. They also dismissed the idea that the tunnels had been a network of emergency escape routes, or had been of any other service to humans of ordinary size. Their purpose remains a mystery.

THE SANCTA CAMISIA - THE CLOAK OF THE BLESSED VIRGIN MARY

Chartres Cathedral in France is one of the greatest achievements in the history of architecture, almost perfectly preserved in its design and details. Its extensive cycle of portal sculpture remains fully intact and its superb 170 stained-glass windows are all original. It is possibly the only cathedral

it is said to have housed the tunic of the Blessed Virgin Mary since 876 CE when an earlier church stood on the site. Some sources maintain that it was worn by Mary when Gabriel announced the coming birth of Christ (the Annunciation), while other assert that it was worn by Mary when she gave birth to Christ. The Byzantine Empress Irene gave the holy cloak to Charles the Bald, king of the Franks, in 876 CE. The Holy Cloak drew many pilgrims to Chartres, including the English King Henry V. After the first cathedral burnt down in 1020, a glorious new Romanesque basilica with a massive crypt was built, but in 1194 lightning ignited a great fire that destroyed all but the west towers, the façade and the crypt.

that conveys an almost perfect image of how it looked when it was built. It has long been a centre of pilgrimage as

The Seven Tablets of Creation

The Babylonian *Epic of Creation* (*Enuma Elish*) is written in cuneiform script on seven tall clay tablets, each being between 115 and 170 lines long. The tablets describe the views and beliefs of the Babylonians and Assyrians about the Creation. They were discovered among the ruins of the Palace and Library of Ashur-bani-pal (668–626 BCE) at Nineveh in Mesopotamia, between the years 1848 and 1876. George Smith first published these texts in 1876 under the title *The Chaldean Genesis*. The Babylonian god finished his work within the span of six tablets of stone. The seventh stone exalted the handiwork and greatness of the deity's work. Thus the inference can be made that the story of the seven days of creation found in the Bible borrowed its theme from the Babylonians, as they did in turn from the Sumerians. It supposedly was written no later than the reign of Nebuchadnezzar I (1125–1103 BCE), but there is little doubt that this story was first composed much earlier, during the time of the Sumerians, c.5000 BCE.

The clergy despaired when it seemed that the Sancta Camisia had perished in the fire, but three days later it was found unharmed in the treasury, which the bishop proclaimed was a sign from the Virgin Mary herself that another, even more magnificent, cathedral should be built in Chartres. Donations came from all over France and rebuilding began almost immediately. By 1220 the main structure was complete, with the old crypt, the west towers and the west façade incorporated into the new building. Dedicated in the presence of King Louis IX, it is now a World Heritage site. The stone floor still bears the ancient Chartres Labyrinth (1205), used for walking contemplation by monks and still used for the purpose of meditation by Christian pilgrims. There is just one path through the labyrinth and it is 964 feet (294 m) long.

SILVER BULLETS AND THE BEAST OF GÉVAUDAN In folklore,
a silver bullet is supposed to be the only kind of weapon that will kill a werewolf, witch or some monsters. Sometimes the silver bullet is also meant to be inscribed with Christian religious symbolism, such as a cross or the initials '*J.M.J*' (Jesus, Mary and Joseph). It is said that the werewolf's vulnerability to silver dates back to the legend of the Beast of Gévaudan, in which a gigantic wolf was killed by a hunter called Jean Chastel. Man-eating wolf-like animals terrorized the Margeride Mountains in southern France from 1764 to 1767, over a huge area stretching 50 miles (80 km) square.

The creatures were consistently described as having formidable teeth, immense tails, fur with a reddish tinge and they gave off an unbearable odour. They killed their victims by tearing at their throats with their teeth. There were an estimated 210 attacks, resulting in 113 deaths and 49 injuries. Ninety-eight of the dead were partly eaten. The beasts seemed to target people in preference to farm animals; many times one would attack someone while cattle were in the same field. In 1765 King Louis XV personally sent professional wolf-hunters, with eight bloodhounds trained in wolf-hunting, but the attacks continued. The king next sent his personal Lieutenant of the Hunt, François Antoine who killed a large grey wolf measuring 5 feet 6 inches (1.7 m) long, 2 foot 7 inches (79 cm) high and weighing 130 pounds (59 kg). It was agreed to be larger than the normal wolf, but dozens more deaths continued to be reported. The killing of the creature that eventually marked the end of the attacks is credited to a local hunter, Jean Chastel. Upon being cut open, in a grisly discovery the animal's stomach was shown to contain human remains.

In 2009, a documentary called *The Real Wolfman* was shown on The History Channel. Travelling to Gévaudan, the researchers studied contemporary accounts, met the direct descendants of Jean Chastel, examined Chastel's rifle and studied wolf behaviour. Extensive forensic testing of the reported 'silver bullets' used versus normal bullets revealed their inability to accurately and effectively kill anything. Wolves could not have been the culprits, as they are physically incapable of exerting enough bite pressure to cut swiftly through bone, or to decapitate or shear off limbs, as was reported in the original archives. They also discovered that there is a written record of a dead Asian hyena being presented to the king, and that this coincided with the end of the killings. Local archive descriptions of the beast accurately depicted an Asian hyena – hyenas are one of the few animals with powerful enough bite pressure to slice easily through human bone. The investigation concluded that the 'Beast' was an Asian hyena, a long-haired species of Hyaenidae which is now extinct. Jean Chastel was a bitter outcast from the community, and he was probably the hyena's caretaker. This would explain why Jean Chastel was able to supposedly kill the animal with a silver bullet, which would be only possible with a shot at very close range and by striking it in a vital area. The Gévaudan attacks were not considered isolated events. A century earlier, similar killings occurred in 1693 at Benais, during which more than 100 victims, almost all of them women and children, were claimed by a creature described as exactly resembling the Gévaudan beasts. During the events in Gévaudan, another beast was sighted at Sarlat, a prehistoric cave region just outside Gévaudan, on 4 August 1767.

The use of a silver bullet in the Caribbean, however, predated this European example. This author transcribed the factional account of *The Journal of Penrose, Seaman,* written by William Williams in America in the 1760s. Here Williams relates how his alter-ego, Lewellin Penrose, is frightened in the Nicaraguan littoral rainforest: '*My present uneasiness proceeded from a noise I often heard late on moonlit nights. This was a hollow treble tone, as thus: Yaoho, Yaoho, repeated perhaps three or four times together. Some other like sound always answered this at a distance; this was always to the westward of me in the high land and at a great distance. [This must have been a howler monkey]. Now the chief cause of my terror originated thus. While I remained in Providence Island* [Nassau in the Bahamas]*, I had frequent converse with an old Negro man, a native of the Island of Jamaica, who in his younger days had been acquainted with many of the buccaneers, had sailed with them, and knew many of their haunts, but had come in by the Queen's Act of Grace* [Queen Anne reigned from 1702–14, so the relevant Act of Grace dated from this time]*. He then followed the piloting trade, or went out to hunt after wrecks about the coast. This white-headed old fellow, although he could read and write and was well-versed in the Scriptures, had been in England, France, Spain, and all over the coast of the Spanish Main, but was yet full of superstition. Now this old man, whose name was William Bass, related to me among other stories one concerning a sort* *of Nocturnal Animal, who walked upright as a Man and the same size, that they were black and wonderfully swift of foot, and that they sucked the blood of all the animals they caught, and left them dead. He observed also that by the track of their feet, one would think that their heels were placed foremost, and that their cry was as above related. He observed likewise that nothing but a bullet made of silver could kill one of those creatures, such credit did he give those romantic notions.'* In Caribbean voodoo lore, vampires can only be killed with a silver bullet. Penrose's nocturnal creature also can only be killed with a silver bullet, and William Williams may have known about such legends from his own time in Jamaica. In 1804, Jean-Jacques Dessalines became the first ruler of an independent Haiti and he believed that he could only be killed by a silver bullet. Some of his disaffected officers bayoneted him to death. His successor, King Henri-Cristophe, killed himself with a silver bullet in 1820. The 'silver bullet' legend thus seems to have its origins rooted in the traditions of the West Indies.

THE STARCHILD In the 1930s, at the back of a mine tunnel about 100 miles (160 km) southwest of Chihuahua, Mexico, a complete human skeleton, and a smaller skeleton that appeared to be holding the larger one's arm, were discovered. In late February 1999, Lloyd Pye was first shown the smaller *Starchild* skull by its owners. It showed strange anomalies, mainly in that the skull's symmetry was astonishing, far more so than that of the average human. All of its bones, most of which had human counterparts, were beautifully shaped.

There were striking differences between the depth of the eye sockets and the shape of temporal area just behind outer edges of eyes. The American couple who own it, Ray and Melanie Young, believe that the skull is that of an alien being rather than a child with genetic abnormalities.

THE SUDARIUM OF OVIEDO
This bloodstained cloth is identified as the one described in John's Gospel as having covered Christ's head in the tomb. It measures around 33 by 21 inches (84 by 53 cm), and is kept in the Cámara Santa of the Cathedral of San Salvador in Oviedo, Spain. A 1999 study investigated the relationship between the Turin Shroud and the Sudarium. Based on history, forensic pathology, blood chemistry and stain patterns, it was concluded that the two cloths covered the same head at two distinct, but close, moments of time. Another analysis indicated that the pollen grains in the Sudarium match those of the Shroud, coming from the same timeframe in Palestine. Both blood stains were from the same group, AB, common in the Middle East, but rare in medieval Europe. The Sudarium is

displayed to the public three times a year: on Good Friday, the Feast of the Triumph of the Cross on 14 September and its 'Octave' on 21 September. The cloth is soiled and crumpled, with dark flecks that are symmetrically arranged but form no image. The most important physical evidence of a connection between the two relics is that the material of the cloth is identical, although there are differences in the manner of weaving.

TESLA'S WEAPON TO END WAR

Nikola Tesla (see page 52) sought a technological way to end warfare, presciently thinking that throught the application of science war could be converted into *a mere spectacle of machines.* In 1931 he announced at a press conference that he was on the verge of discovering an entirely new source of energy... *'The idea first came upon me as a tremendous shock... I can only say at this time that it will come from an entirely new and unsuspected source.'* On 11 July 1934 the *New York Times* headline read, *'TESLA, AT 78, BARES NEW DEATH BEAM'.* The article reported that it would *'send concentrated beams of particles through the free air, of such tremendous energy that they will bring down a fleet of 10,000 enemy airplanes at a distance of 250 miles.'* Tesla stated that the death beam would make war impossible by offering every country an *'invisible Chinese wall'.* He approached the banker J.P. Morgan to finance a prototype, but was

unsuccessful. With war looming in 1937 he sent elaborate technical papers on his 'peace beam' (also called a 'peace ray' or 'teleforce') to Allied nations including the United States, Canada, Britain, France, the Soviet Union and Yugoslavia. His paper was entitled *New Art of Projecting Concentrated Non-Dispersive Energy Through Natural Media*, and provided the first technical description of what is today called a charged particle beam weapon, such as were being developed by the USA and Soviet Union during the Cold War. His system required a series of power plants located along a country's coast that would scan the skies in search of enemy aircraft. Since the beam was projected in a straight line, it was only effective for about 200 miles (320 km), which is the distance that is unobstructed by the curvature of the Earth.

Peacetime applications for Tesla's invention included the transmission of power without wires over long distances. The macroscopic particle beam projector was based upon a large Van de Graaff generator and a special type of open-ended vacuum tube, allowing a system for the acceleration of very small charged metallic particles to extremely high velocity of about 48 times the speed of sound. The particles were projected out of the tube by means of electrostatic repulsion. The tube was designed to project a single row of highly charged particles to a great distance, with no dispersion.

THE TRIUMPHAL QUADRIGA - THE FOUR HORSES OF ST MARK'S

These four 'bronze' horse statues were originally part of a monument depicting a quadriga (a four-horse carriage used for chariot racing), and they were set into the façade of St Mark's Basilica in Venice in 1254. These wonderful sculptures have been attributed by some to the fourth century BCE Greek sculptor Lysippos. Although called 'bronze horses', they are at least 96 per cent copper. High purity copper was chosen to give a more satisfactory mercury gilding. The horses and quadriga had been displayed for centuries at the Hippodrome of Constantinople (Istanbul). They are possibly the *'four gilt horses that stand above the Hippodrome'* which *'came from the island of Chios under Theodosius II'* mentioned in an eighth- or ninth-century Byzantine text. In some accounts the horses once adorned the Arch of Trajan in Rome. In 1204, they were looted by Venetian forces as part of the Sack of Constantinople during the Fourth Crusade. It should be mentioned that this 'crusade' actually attacked the capital of the Christian Byzantine Empire. Crusades were meant to fight the 'infidel' followers of Islam and retain the Holy Land for Christianity. The Fourth Crusade fatally weakened Christian control of eastern Europe and the Near East. The Doge of Venice sent the horses to be installed on the terrace of the façade of the basilica. In 1797, Napoleon removed the horses and transported them to Paris, where they were used in the design of the Arc du Triomphe du Carrousel, together with a new quadriga. After his defeat at Waterloo in 1815 the horses were returned to Venice. They remained in place on the basilica until the early 1980s, when damage from growing air pollution forced their replacement with replicas. The originals are now on display just inside the basilica.

THE TRUE CROSS

Many fragments of wood are claimed as relics of the cross upon which Jesus was crucified. Tradition attributes the discovery of the True Cross to St Helena, mother of Constantine the Great, who travelled to Palestine during the fourth century in search of Christian relics. Eusebius of Caesarea was a contemporary who wrote about Helena's journey in his *Life of Constantine*. He did not mention the finding of the True Cross, although he stated that she found the site of the Holy Sepulchre. Pieces of the purported True Cross, including half of the INRI inscription tablet, are preserved at the Basilica of Santa Croce

The Turin Shroud

'The Holy Face of Jesus' is supposed to be imprinted on the cloth of his burial shroud that is now housed in Turin Cathedral. This is the best-known relic of Christ and receives visits from millions of pilgrims. Controversy still rages about the authenticity of the 14 feet (4.25 m) by 45 inches (114 cm) linen fabric, with some contending it to be a 1000-year-old forgery while others believe it to be contemporary with the Crucifixion. The impressive negative image was first observed on the evening of 28 May 1898, on the reverse photographic plate of an amateur photographer called Secondo Pia who had been allowed to photograph it. If it was a medieval forgery, it seems odd that this image was only discovered in 1898. The twin wrist wounds seem to indicate that the body had been crucified. If nailed through the hands, the victim would die too quickly of suffocation from a collapsed chest. There is also evidence of an upward gouge in the side penetrating into the thoracic cavity, possibly evidence of the wound caused by the lance of Longinus. Small punctures around the forehead and scalp indicate the possibility of a Cross of Thorns. There are scores of linear wounds on the torso and legs, indicative of the distinctive wounds caused by a Roman flagrum or whip. Swelling of the face from severe beatings can be seen. Streams of blood down both arms seem to be consistent with the angle that the arms would adopt during Crucifixion.

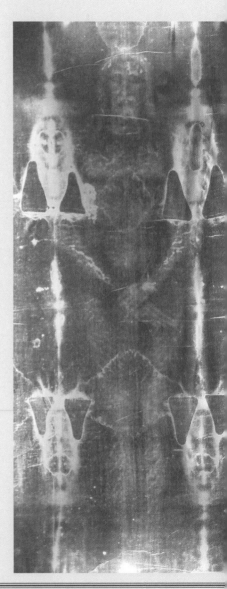

There is no evidence of either leg being fractured, but large puncture wounds in the feet can be seen, as if they were pierced by a single spike. The image of the man has a beard, moustache and shoulder-length hair parted in the middle.

A second face has been found imprinted on the opposite side of the Shroud, matching that on the front. It is a superficial image, not caused by paint, so it seems that the fabric was wrapped twice around the face and that there was a chemical reaction between a body and the cloth. Whereas reports of a smaller shroud known as the Image of Edessa (see Mandylion on page 265) have circulated since the fourth century, the first reliable records of the Turin Shroud come from France in 1357. The smaller shroud was presented to King Agbar V (of Edessa in Iraq) by a disciple, then was in Constantinople until that city was sacked in the Fourth Crusade. A burial cloth, which some historians maintain was the Turin Shroud, was owned by the Byzantine emperors, but disappeared during the Sack of Constantinople in 1204 The religious charges against the Kights Templar in 1307 included the allegation that they worshipped an 'idol' in the form of a red, monochromatic image of a bearded man imprinted on linen or cotton. On 6 April 2009, the *Times* newspaper reported that an official Vatican researcher had uncovered evidence that the Shroud had been kept and venerated by the Templars since the Sack of Constantinople. According to the account of one neophyte member of the order, veneration of the Shroud appeared to be part of the initiation ritual. Historical records indicate that a shroud bearing an image of a crucified bearded man was in the possession of a French Crusader called Geoffroy de Charney around the years 1353 to 1357. He put it on display in Lirey, France which became a place of pilgrimage. The House of Savoy then owned it and it was moved to Turin Cathedral in 1578. Radiocarbon dating of a sample of the cloth to 1260–1390 is contentious because it seems to have been carried out on a repaired non-representative piece of the linen cloth, with additional carbon content because of fire damage suffered in 1532. Fourteen large triangular patches and eight smaller ones were sewn onto the cloth by nuns from the Order of St Clare in that year to repair the damage caused by a fire in the chapel in Chambéry, France. Also the seams on the shroud are of the style used in the first century CE or before. Pollen and the imprints of thorns have been identified as rock rose, bean caper plant and a species of tumbleweed, a combination found only in Palestine. In 2002, the Holy See had the shroud restored. The cloth backing and 30 patches were removed, making it possible to photograph and scan the reverse side of the cloth, which had previously been hidden from view. A ghostly part-image of the body was found on the back of the shroud in 2004. The Shroud was placed on public display (for the eighteenth time in its history) in Turin from 10 April to 23 May 2010, and more than 2,100,000 visitors queued to see it.

in Gerusalemme in Rome. Tiny pieces of the True Cross are preserved in hundreds of other churches in Europe and inside crucifixes.

THE VEIL OF VERONICA

According to legend, this cloth was used to wipe the sweat from Jesus' brow as he carried the cross towards the place of Crucifixion, and is said to bear the likeness of his face. Several images claim to be the Veil of Veronica, for instance one preserved in St Peter's Basilica in Rome. Very few inspections of the cloth are recorded in modern times and there are no detailed photographs. There is a copy of the Veronica image in the Hofburg Palace in Vienna that was made in 1617. The image at the Monastery of the Holy Face in Alicante, Spain was acquired by Pope Nicholas V from relatives of the Byzantine emperor in 1453. It was given by a Vatican cardinal to a Spanish priest who took it to Alicante in 1489. The Cathedral of Jaén in Spain has a copy known as the Santa Rostro, originating from Siena in Italy, which dates from the 14th century.

THE VOYNICH MANUSCRIPT

This is a medieval document written in an unknown language. Author Robert Burmbaugh has dubbed it, 'the most mysterious manuscript in the world'. It contains illustrations that suggest the book is in six parts: herbal, astronomical, biological, cosmological, pharmaceutical and recipes. It was probably written in central Europe at the end of the 15th or during the 16th century and is named after the Polish-American antiquarian bookseller, Wilfrid M. Voynich, who acquired it in 1912. Described as a magical or scientific text, nearly every page contains botanical, figurative and scientific drawings of a provincial (but lively) character, drawn in ink with vibrant washes in various shades of green, brown, yellow, blue and red. It resists all efforts at translation. Based on the evidence of the calligraphy, the drawings, the vellum and the pigments, Voynich estimated that the manuscript was created in the late 13th century. The manuscript is small, 7 by 10 inches (18 by 25 cm), but thick, running to around 240 vellum pages. It is written in an unknown script of which there is no other known instance in the world. It is abundantly illustrated with coloured drawings of unidentified plants, what seem to be herbal recipes, tiny naked women playing in bathtubs connected by intricate plumbing, strange charts which contain astronomical objects or live cells seen through a microscope, charts with an odd calendar of zodiacal signs populated

by tiny naked people in rubbish bins, and so on. From a piece of paper which was once attached to the Voynich manuscript, it is known that the manuscript once formed part of the private library of the 22nd General of the Society of Jesus or Jesuit order.

It is written in an alphabetic script, variously reckoned to have from 19 to 28 letters, none of which bear any relationship to any English or European letter system. There is evidence for two different 'languages' and more than one scribe, probably indicating an ambiguous coding scheme. It is known that it was in the possession of Emperor Rudolph II of Bohemia (1552–1612) in 1586 and is now in Yale University Library. Accompanying the manuscript was a letter that stated that it was the work of the Englishman Roger Bacon, who flourished in the 13th century and who was a noted pre-Copernican astronomer. Only two years before the appearance of the Voynich Manuscript, John Dee, the great English navigator, astrologer, magician, intelligence agent and occultist, had lectured in Prague on Bacon. In 1987, Dr Leo Levitov wrote that the manuscript is the only surviving primary document of the *Great Heresy* that arose in Italy and flourished in Languedoc in France, until eliminated by the Albigensian Crusade in the 1230s. The tiny women in baths are supposed to be partaking in a Cathar suicide ritual, the *Endura*, or '*death by venesection* [cutting a vein] *in order to bleed to death*

in a warm bath'. The plant drawings are not botanically identifiable, but Levitov stated: '*There is not a single so-called botanical illustration that does not contain some Cathari symbol or Isis symbol. The astrological drawings are likewise easy to deal with. The innumerable stars are representative of the stars in Isis' mantle. The reason it has been so difficult to decipher the Voynich Manuscript is that it is not encrypted at all, but merely written in a special script, and is an adaptation of a polyglot oral tongue into a literary language which would be understandable to people who did not understand Latin and to whom this language could be read. Specifically, a highly polyglot form of medieval Flemish with a large number of Old French and Old High German loan words.*' His thesis is still not accepted by the academic community.

WITCH BOTTLES In 2004 the first of more than 200 stoneware 'witch bottles' was found in Greenwich, England. It still had its contents intact. Dating from the last quarter of the 17th century, it contained a small heart-shaped piece of leather pierced by a nail, more iron nails, eight brass pins, a pinch of navel fluff, nail clippings and a pint of human urine. By placing bodily fluids and items in a witch bottle, an evil spell could not only be diverted, but also could rebound on the witch. There were traces of brimstone and sulphur in the navel fluff, the nail parings were from an adult and the urine contained nicotine. Other charms were placed in houses to ward off evil spirits, including dead cats and children's shoes, up until the early 20th century.

THE WITCHES' HAMMER - MALLEUS MALEFICARUM

This was a witch-hunter's manual dating from the Middle Ages and Renaissance, with complete instructions on the prosecution of witches. It was written by Heinrich Kramer and Jakob Spreyer, both Catholic inquisitors, and was first published in Germany in 1487 then disseminated across Europe, being used in witch trials on the continent for almost 200 years. The authors were empowered by Pope Innocent VIII in 1484 to prosecute witches throughout northern Germany. The pope wanted to squash Protestant opposition to the Inquisition and to solidify the case made in 1258 for the prosecution of witches as heretics. It was the pope's opinion that civil courts were not punishing witches severely enough. Both priests were later implicated for forging notarized documents, and using fraudulent tactics to frame people as witches, by torturing them into making confessions. By 1485 the priests, both later promoted within the church, had drafted a comprehensive manual on witchcraft that evolved into the *Malleus Maleficarum*. The basis of the book is the injunction in Exodus: *'Thou shall not suffer a witch to live'*, and both Protestant and Catholic civil and ecclesiastical judges quickly adopted its thesis and punishments. Even not to believe in the existence of witchcraft is deemed a heresy, since God acknowledged witches. Although the book states that both men and women can become witches, women are more susceptible, *'Because the female sex is more concerned with things of the flesh than men'*. As women were formed from a man's rib they were *'only imperfect animals'* and *'crooked'*, but man belonged

to the privileged sex from which Christ emerged. The priests warned against the *'spitefulness of womankind'*.

Part I of the book describes how the Devil and his witches cooperate to perpetrate many evils on men and animals including tempting them with the demons of the night called incubi and succubi. They instilled hatred, obstructed or destroyed fertility and metamorphosized men into beasts. Part II describes witches casting spells and practising their *maleficia*, and shows how such actions might be prevented or remedied. The Devil's Pact, an agreement signed between the witch and the devil, is described in detail. The witch renounces Christ, to whom she has belonged to since her baptism, and signs her immortal soul over to Satan, who in return makes all forbidden things available to her. This act was blasphemous and a betrayal of God. The evidence of witches and their *maleficia* was derived from confessions obtained under torture during inquisitions conducted by the two priests, and from material on witchcraft written by other ecclesiastical writers. This evidence consisted of instances of casting spells, pacts, sacrificing of children and copulating with the devil.

Pope Innocent VIII in his 1484 Bull that gave the priests inquisitorial powers relates that men and women could have sexual relationships with demons. Part III deals with the legal procedures for prosecuting a witch. This includes rules for taking testimony, admitting evidence, procedures for interrogation and torture and guidelines for sentencing. Hostile witnesses were permitted to testify as everyone feared witches. If the accused did not confess after a year or so in prison, then torture could be used as an incentive. Confessions obtained by torture were deemed valid. Judges were permitted to lie to the accused, promising leniency if they confessed, because such duplicity was done in the best interests of society and the state. Most of the instructions on sentencing recommended death. Eliminating heretics was one way to strengthen church control and it also enriched the church by the confiscation of the victim's property. Usually the confiscated property was divided three ways between the Inquisition members, the church officials and the state treasury. Even the dead were not safe. If a suspicion arose that a dead person might have been a heretic, the body could be dug up and burned. His or her property was then confiscated. Records show that many women and children were left penniless because of such confiscation. In addition, the church and state kept strict accounts of the prisoner's incarceration, trial and execution costs. If the value of confiscated property was not enough to cover these costs, then the victim's heirs had to pay the difference. The families of the victims were often also prosecuted.

ZODIAC KILLER CYPHER

The Zodiac Killer was active in northern California for ten months in the late 1960s, killing at least five people, and injuring two others. He committed the first murders of two young people with a pistol, just inside the Benecia city limits. In his second shooting in Vallejo, he again attempted to kill two people, but the young man survived despite gunshots to the head and neck. Forty minutes later the police received an anonymous phone call from a man claiming to be their killer and admitting to the murders of the previous two victims. One month later three letters were sent to newspapers in California containing a cypher that the killer claimed would give his name. It was decrypted to read: 'I LIKE KILLING PEOPLE BECAUSE IT IS SO MUCH FUN IT IS MORE FUN THAN KILLING WILD GAME IN THE FORREST BECAUSE MAN IS THE MOST DANGEROUE ANAMAL OF ALL TO KILL SOMETHING GIVES ME THE MOST THRILLING EXPERENCE IT IS EVEN BETTER THAN GETTING YOUR ROCKS OFF WITH A GIRL THE BEST PART OF IT IS THAE WHEN I DIE I WILL BE REBORN IN PARADICE AND THEI HAVE KILLED WILL BECOME MY SLAVES I WILL NOT GIVE YOU MY NAME BECAUSE YOU WILL TRY TO SLOI DOWN OR ATOP MY COLLECTIOG OF SLAVES FOR MY AFTERLIFE EBEORIETEMETHHPITI'
The last eighteen letters have not been decrypted. The Zodiac murders have not been solved.

Witches' Compendium Maleficarum

CHAPTER 7
Tales *of* Secret Treasure

THE AMBER ROOM PANELS

Construction of the *'Eighth Wonder of the World'* began in 1701 in Prussia following a design by the German baroque sculptor Andreas Schlüter. It was given by the Prussian King Friedrich Wilhelm I to Tsar Peter the Great in 1716 to decorate the Catherine Palace near St Petersburg. It was a decorated chamber of carved amber panels, backed with gold leaf and mirrors. Covering 592 square feet (55 m²) and weighing 6 tons, it was later looted by the Nazis, and removed to Königsberg in Prussia from where it has subsequently vanished from history. During the Second World War in 1943 and 1944, the shore of Lake Toplitz, 60 miles (100 km) from Salzburg in the western Austrian Alps, was used as a Nazi naval testing station. It was only accessible on foot along a hazardous mile-long path through mountainous forests. It is thought that the Germans may have stashed vast quantities of gold and other priceless items around there, including the stolen panels from the Amber Room. After the war, former SS members employed divers to try and salvage a number of sealed tubes from the depths of the lake, which were said to contain details of secret Nazi bank accounts in Switzerland. Millions of counterfeit pound notes were also dumped in the lake after *Operation Bernhard*, a plan designed to destabilize the British economy, was never put into action. American documentary makers using a mini-submarine have managed to recover some of the banknotes from the lake. But the fate of the Amber Room panels remains a mystery.

THE BEALE SECRET CIPHERS

In January 1820, a handsome, sun-tanned stranger calling himself Thomas Jefferson Beale rode into Lynchburg, Virginia, and checked into the Washington Hotel. He checked out in March, but returned two years later, spending the winter in the hotel and leaving in the spring of 1822. He left a locked iron box in the safekeeping of the hotel owner, Robert Morriss, containing *'papers of value and importance'*, but never returned. In 1845, assuming that Beale was dead, Morriss broke open the iron box. Inside was a note written by Beale in plain English, and three sheets full of numbers. The note revealed that in April 1817, Beale and 29 others had embarked on a journey across America, arriving in Santa Fé, New Mexico, before heading north in search of buffalo. Then, according to the note, they found gold (and some silver) which they mined for the next 18 months. The group agreed to move their new wealth to a secure place, a secret location in Virginia. Beale traded some of the gold and silver for jewels, and in 1820 he travelled to Lynchburg, and buried the treasure. This is when he first met Morriss, after which he returned to join his men, who had stayed working the mine. The note said that in the event of his sudden death, Beale had chosen Morriss to look after the secret of the whereabouts of the jewels, gold and silver, to pass on to relatives if the men did not appear again. Beale's note stated that the key required to decipher the three sheets of numbers would be posted to Beale by a third party, but it never materialized.

For 20 years Morriss struggled to decipher the codes, until aged 84 in 1862 he confided the secret to a friend.

A pamphlet was published containing the whole Beale story, including the Beale ciphers and Morriss's account of the events. There was a breakthrough in deciphering the second code of 800 numbers, as each number was found to correspond to a word in the Declaration of Independence. Decoded, it read: *'I have deposited in the county of Bedford, about four miles from Buford's, in an excavation or vault, six feet below the surface of the ground, the following articles, belonging jointly to the parties whose names are given in number three, herewith: The first deposit consisted of ten hundred and fourteen pounds of gold, and thirty-eight hundred and twelve pounds of silver, deposited Nov. eighteen nineteen. The second was made Dec. eighteen twenty-one, and consisted of nineteen hundred and seven pounds of gold, and twelve hundred and eighty-eight of silver; also jewels, obtained in St. Louis in exchange for silver to save transportation, and valued at thirteen thousand dollars. The above is securely packed in iron pots, with iron covers. The vault is roughly lined with stone, and the vessels rest on solid stone, and are covered with others. Paper number one describes the exact locality of the vault, so that no difficulty will be had in finding it.'* It seems that the other ciphers must also be based upon published documents or books. Today's value of the treasure described stands at around $50 million; the numbers that make up ciphers 1 and 3 can easily be found by treasure seekers upon the many Beale-related websites.

BLACK BART'S EMERALD CROSS

The teetotaller Black Bart Roberts (1682–1722) was the greatest and most successful pirate of all time, taking over 400 ships and bringing transatlantic shipping to a standstill. Virtually alone among pirates, he took on opposing naval warships. One of his greatest exploits was to successfully venture, with a single ship, into the middle of the mighty 42-strong Portuguese treasure fleet at night off Bahia, Brazil, and take the richest ship, even though he was pursued by two men of war. Legend persists that Black Bart hid his treasure inside a cave on Little Cayman Island. He took at least 40,000 gold coins, and a huge emerald cross which had been commissioned for the king of Portugal. Roberts wore the cross with a scarlet satin outfit whenever he went into battle. When his drunken crew was surprised off the coast of Africa by the Royal Navy, Roberts was

wearing the cross when he was killed. His crew wrapped him in chains as he had requested, and tipped him into the sea, complete with the priceless cross. On 28 March 1722, there followed the greatest pirate trial in history. Ninety-one of Roberts's men were found guilty and 74 acquitted. Captain Skyrme and most members of Roberts's 'House of Lords' were found 'Guilty in the Highest Degree', and the president of the court, Captain Herdman, pronounced: '*Ye and each of you are adjudged and sentenced to be carried back to the place from whence you came, from thence to the place of execution without the gates of this castle, and there within the flood marks to be hanged by the neck till you are dead, dead, dead. And the Lord have mercy on your souls*'...'*After this ye and each of you shall be taken down, and your bodies hung in chains.*' (Source: *Records of the High Court of the Admiralty*). The men hung in chains included Israel Hands, who had previously served with Blackbeard and features in the famous novel *Treasure Island*. Captain Herdman sentenced 52 of Bart Roberts's crew to death, 20 men to an effective death sentence in the Cape Coast mines, and sent another 17 to imprisonment in London's Marshalsea Prison. Of these 17, 13 died in the passage to London. The four survivors were eventually pardoned while in Newgate Prison. Two 'guilty' sentences were 'respited'. Of the 52 pirates hanged at Cape Coast, nearly half were Welsh or West Countrymen, and most of the others indentured servants or poor white colonists. Fifteen pirates had died of their

wounds on the passage to Cape Corso Castle, and four in its dungeons. Ten had been killed in the *Ranger*, and three in the *Royal Fortune*. Thus 97 of Roberts's crew had died. The 70 blacks on board the pirate ships were returned to slavery. This greatest pirate trial of all time is scarcely known by the general public, nor is the career of the remarkably fearless Roberts. The king of Portugal's fabulous emerald cross lies somewhere on the ocean floor about a mile offshore at Cape Lopez, Gabon, tangled up for almost 300 years in Roberts's skeleton and chains.

THE BUZZARD'S BOOTY

Olivier le Vasseur was variously known as la Buse or la Bouze (the Buzzard) or la Bouche (the Mouth). He was a pirate captain sailing out of New Providence (Nassau) in the Bahamas from 1716. He accompanied other pirate ships captained by Benjamin Hornigold, Samuel Bellamy and Paul Williams. In spring 1719, la Bouze joined up with captains Howell Davies, Thomas Cocklyn and Edward England off the coast of Africa. He next sailed alongside John Taylor from 1719 in the seas around Madagascar. Off Réunion Island, they took vast treasure off the *Virgem do Cabo*. In the bishop of Goa's treasure ship they found '*rivers of diamonds, a large quantity of gold bars, cascades of gold coins and cases and chests of sacred church vessels*'. It included the diamond-encrusted, golden 'Fiery Cross of Goa', an opulent crucifix which, it is said, it took three men to lift. During his ten-year pirate career it is said that le

Vasseur took spoils estimated at around £300 million in today's money. He was eventually captured by the French man-of-war *La Méduse*, was tried and sentenced to death. On the scaffold at Réunion in 1730, he flung a coded message into the crowd, crying '*Find my treasure he who can!*' The Buzzard's code seems to have surfaced in the Seychelles, 1100 miles (1770 km) north of Réunion, soon after the First World War. In 1948 Reginald Cruise-Wilkins bought the cryptogram, believing that it showed la Bouze's treasure to be buried at Bel Ombre Bay on Mahé, the main island in the Seychelles. He spent the rest of his years searching for the booty, finding what he thought was an 18th-century pirates' graveyard and dozens of artefacts contemporary with la Bouze. The Seychelles were uninhabited until the middle of the 18th century. On his death-bed in 1977, Cruise-Wilkins claimed that he was only a few feet away from finding the loot. In 1988, his son John resumed the search upon hearing that a metal object the size of a table had been traced by a remote survey of Bel Ombre. Cruise-Wilkins has found three skeletons, and is still searching for the treasure, which he believes is worth in excess of $200 million in today's value.

THE CACHE OF DEATH'S HEAD RINGS

The silver SS Honour Ring (or Death's Head Ring) was given to members of the Nazi SS as an award for bravery. Upon the death of the recipient, the ring had to be returned to Wewelsburg Castle, the 'spiritual home' of the SS in North Rhine-Westphalia, north Germany. As the Second World War drew to a close, SS chief Heinrich Himmler

ordered that all of the 9280 rings that had been returned to the castle should be hidden in a nearby cave and the entrance to the cave sealed forever with explosives placed to protect it from future fortune hunters. At current market values, the rings would be worth around £50 million.

CAPTAIN KIDD'S SECRET ISLAND MAP

The so-called '*Kidd–Palmer charts*' were discovered in 1929 by retired lawyer Hubert Palmer, when he bought a number of items of furniture that were said to have belonged to the executed pirate Captain Kidd (1645–1701). A heavy oak bureau bore the inscription '*Captain William Kidd, Adventure Galley 1669*', and in a secret compartment Palmer discovered a hand-drawn map of a secret island. It bore the initials *W.K.*, the words *China Sea* and was dated *1699*. Many believe that the island depicted is not in the China Sea, but is instead Oak Island off the coast of Nova Scotia, the inscription being a deliberate attempt to mislead treasure hunters. Palmer and his brother Guy also claimed to have found two sea chests and a wooden box that belonged to Kidd,

with further maps of the same unknown island in all three of them, inscribed with varying levels of detail. After Palmer's death, all four maps were bequeathed to his housekeeper, Elizabeth Dick. She took them to the British Museum to be authenticated by map expert R.A. Skelton. Skelton believed all of the maps to be 17th century in origin, which he confirmed to author Rupert Furneaux in 1965 (as reported in Furneaux's book *Money Pit – The Mystery of Oak Island*, 1976). Elizabeth Dick sold all four faded maps in 1950 to an Englishman who later moved to Canada.

In 1698, Kidd had captained the *Adventure Galley* when taking the valuable Armenian ship *Quedagh Merchant* and its cargo of gold, silver, silks and merchandise. The island in the Kidd–Palmer charts resembles Gardiners Island, which lies just off the coast of Suffolk County, Long Island, New York State. Kidd definitely concealed treasure in the Cherry Tree Field area of Gardiners Island in June 1699, shortly before his arrest for piracy. These items of value were recovered and returned to England by New York Governor Bellomont, and used as evidence at Kidd's trial. The recovered treasure consisted of gold and silver bars, gold dust (over 1000 troy ounces of gold and more than 2000 troy ounces of silver), rubies, other precious stones, silks and 57 valuable bags of sugar. The goods were sold off in November 1704 for a total of £6437, the money being used to help found Greenwich

Hospital. This is only a fraction of the loot taken from the *Quedagh Merchant*, so many people are convinced that more treasure is to be found on the 5-square-mile (13 km²)island. However, it is private property. Many believe that Kidd's missing treasure is in the Oak Island Money Pit, which has already claimed the lives of several treasure hunters. Other places which are thought to resemble the island in Kidd's maps have also been searched for his treasure. They include Charles Island in Milford, Connecticut; Thimble Islands, Connecticut; Money Cove on Grand Manan Island, Bay of Fundy, Canada; Block Island off Rhode Island; Takarajima (Treasure Island) in the Tokara archipelago south of Kagoshima, Japan; and Phu Quoc, the largest Vietnamese island.

THE ROBINSON CRUSOE ISLAND HOARD

Juan Fernández Island, in an archipelago off the coast of Chile, was where Scottish sailor Alexander Selkirk was marooned. Selkirk was later immortalized by Daniel Defoe in his novel *Robinson Crusoe*, and the island chain was renamed the Robinson Crusoe Archipelago, in the hope of attracting tourists. In 2010 it was announced that Wagner Technologies, a Chilean company that had developed a robotic exploration vehicle, had found an estimated 600 barrels of gold coins and Inca jewels on Selkirk's island. Its lawyer, Fernando Uribe-Etxeverria, estimated the value of the buried treasure at £5.6bn, saying '*The biggest treasure in history has been located.*' The company claimed half the treasure was theirs and that they would donate it to non-profit-making organizations, but the Chilean government ruled that they had no share to donate. Chilean newspapers were filled with reports that the treasure includes ten papal rings and original gold statues from the Spanish looting of the Inca empire. The hoard is supposedly buried 50 feet (15 m) deep on the island, and for centuries treasure hunters had scoured the island for loot reportedly buried there in 1715 by Spanish sailor Juan Esteban Ubilla y Echeverria.

The story took a new twist in October 2005 after Wagner Technologies renounced all claims to the treasure during a meeting with government officials in Valparaíso, in what had been expected to be a contentious debate over the rights to the fortune. According to Uribe-Etxeverria, the company did not believe it was capable of excavating the treasure, implying that all it wanted was publicity for their robot vehicle that had made the discovery.

YAMASHITA'S GOLD Yamashita's Gold is the name given to the gold, platinum, jewellery and other precious items stolen by the forces of Japanese General Tomuyuki Yamashita '*The Tiger of Malaya*' (1885–1946). The treasure came from all over Asia and was taken to finance Japan's military effort during the Second World War. It had to be transported from the continent back to Japan by sea. Most of the stolen treasure from Southeast Asia was first shipped to the port of Singapore, from where it was then relayed to the Philippines. From the Philippines, it was intended that the treasure would be shipped

to the Japanese home islands. Many treasure hunters believe that Yamashita's loot is still concealed somewhere in the Philippines. He is said to have ordered the concealment of the treasure as he retreated from advancing US forces, breaking the treasure, said to have been carried on several trucks, into many smaller hoards that were hidden along the line of his retreat on the island of Luzon. The bulk of the loot is said to be concentrated in the mountainous area where Yamashita made his last stand against the invading US forces, before his eventual surrender on 2 September 1945. Convicted of war crimes, Yamashita and some of his officers were executed in Manila on 23 February 1946.

ZORRO'S TREASURE Joaquin Murrieta (1829–53) became known as *Mexico's Robin Hood* during the 1850s' California Gold Rush, and was the inspiration for the character of Zorro. He was the leader of a band known as *The Five Joaquins*, who were notorious for cattle rustling, robberies, and murders in the Sierra Nevada from 1850–3. His men had stolen treasure from one of the northern gold mines, but a group of Native Americans attacked them and stole the gold. The Native Americans hid the treasure in an old burial grave underneath a cliff ledge. Murrieta had also buried some of his stolen treasure somewhere between Burney, California and Hatcher Pass, close to Highway 299. Another cache is said to consist of $200,000 of gold dust, believed to be hidden near Highway 36 between Susanville and Freedonyer Pass. One of his gang members was Manuel Garcia, 'Three-Fingered Jack', who stole a strongbox from a stagecoach believed to contain 250 pounds (113 kg) of gold nuggets, which at the time would have been worth $140,000. He and Murrieta buried that treasure along the banks of the Feather River, close to Paradise, California. None of his gold has ever been found. Murrieta's supporters claim that he was not a bandit, but was a patriot working to finance the recovery of the part of Mexico lost to the United States (Upper California and New Mexico) by the Treaty of Guadelupe Hidalgo which was drawn up at the end of the Mexican–American War (1846–8). In 1853, the California State Legislature passed a bill to hire a company of 20 California Rangers for three months to hunt down the 'Five Joaquins' (Murrieta, Botellier, Carrillo, Ocomorenia, Valenzuela) and their accomplices. On 25 July 1853 Three Fingered Jack and another Mexican, said to be Murrieta, were killed in a stand-off at Pacheco Pass by the Rangers.

CHAPTER 8

The Reality
of Legends
and Myths

THE ABOMINABLE SNOWMAN - THE YETI

On the borders of Nepal and Tibet, over 20,000 feet (6100 m) up in the Himalayas, many Sherpas believe that a creature called the Yeti exists. Sightings agree that it is larger than a man, has arms down to its knees, walks upright and is covered with reddish-black hair. The mountaineer Eric Shipton took photographs of Yeti footprints in the snow in 1951, with an ice-pick laid alongside them to confirm their size. An American expedition in 1972 and one organized by Lord Hunt in 1973 took more pictures, all confirming a footprint size of 14 by 7 inches (36 by 18 cm), made by a large creature with well-defined toes. Plaster casts show a longer second toe, like humans rather than other primates or bears. Dr W. Tschernezky, a London zoologist at London's Queen Mary College, ruled out human, gorilla or langur monkey footprints, saying that the Yeti prints were made by a heavily built bipedal primate similar to the fossil *Gigantopithecus*. The creature makes howling yelps, like no other creature encountered at these heights. Sherpas claim that there are three different types of Yeti. The *Dzu Teh* (Big Thing) is around 7–8 feet (2.1–2.4 m) tall, attacks and eats cattle and has a shaggy pelt. This is almost certainly the Tibetan blue bear (*Ursus arctos pruinosus*), a subspecies of the brown bear, found on the eastern Tibetan plateau. It is also known as the Himalayan blue bear, Himalayan snow bear, Tibetan brown bear or the horse bear. Its Tibetan name is *Dom gyamuk*, and it is one of the rarest subspecies of bear in the world. It was first classified in 1854, and may even be extinct, with very few reported sightings. The blue bear is known in the west only through a small number of fur and bone samples. Sir Edmund Hillary's 1960 expedition to search for evidence of the Yeti returned with two scraps of fur, identified by locals as 'Yeti fur', that were later scientifically identified as being portions of the pelt of a blue bear. The Tibetan name '*Yeti*' means 'rock bear'. The second type of Yeti identified by the Sherpas is the *Thelma*, or *NichTeh* (Little Thing) a 'small man' of 3–4 feet (0.9–1.2 m) that runs around collecting sticks and eats frogs – this could conceivably be a gibbon. Sherpas would probably know what langur monkeys look like, but gibbons have not been recorded this far north of India. The third Yeti is our so-called 'Abominable Snowman', the 5 to 6 feet (1.5–1.8 m) tall *Mih Teh* of stocky build with red or black hair. They resemble orang-utans, and are omnivorous. When the snows retreat, the area is covered by dense forest, the home of yaks, ibex, lynx and woolly wolves. These animals are hardly ever seen by Himalayan expeditions, so perhaps there is a remnant population of *Gigantopithecus* still in existence. It was not until 2010 that tigers were found living as high as 16,000 feet (4875 m) in Bhutan, far higher than thought possible. The *Daily Mail* of 18 August 2010 reported that hairs recovered from jungle near the India-Pakistan border are said to have come from no known common wild animals in the area, and are hypothesized to be those of a Yeti. The hairs are up to 1.7 inches (4.3 cm) long and are long, thick, wiry and curved.

AHOOL - THE GIANT MONKEY BAT of JAVA

With a population of roughly 136 million Java is the most populated island in the world, and its rainforests have been severely depleted in recent times. The remnants of Java's once great rainforests still support a wonderful array of wildlife, however, including more than 200 bird species and 500 forms of plant life. The native population of these remaining forests believe it is also home to a large unidentified winged creature known as the Ahool. It is said to live in the deepest rainforests of Java, and was first described in 1925 by the naturalist Dr Ernest Bartels while he was exploring the volcanic Salak mountain range. Bartels was exploring a waterfall on the slopes of the mountains when a giant unknown bat flew directly over his head. Two years later he was lying in bed, inside his thatched house close to the Tjidjenkol River in western Java, when he suddenly heard a very different sound coming from almost directly over his hut. The loud cry sounded like '*A Hool!*' Grabbing his torch Dr Bartels ran out of his hut following the direction in which the sound seemed to be heading. Less than 20 seconds later he heard it again, a final '*A Hool!*' at a considerable distance downstream. As he

would recall many years later, he was transfixed by the sound because he had heard of the legendary Ahool. The creature is named after this call, and is said by islanders to be a bat-like creature, the size of a one-year-old child, with a massive wing span. It is reported to be covered in short, dark grey fur, have large, black eyes, flattened forearms supporting its leathery wings and a monkey-like head, with a flattish, man-like face. It has been seen squatting on the forest floor, at which times its wings are closed and pressed against its body, its feet appearing to point backwards. It is thought that the Ahool is nocturnal, spending its days concealed in caves located behind or beneath waterfalls; its nights are spent skimming across rivers in search of large fish.

Is it a giant unknown bat? It is said to have a gigantic wingspan of 10–12 feet (3–3.65 m). The largest known bat in the world, the Bismarck flying fox, has a wingspan of around 6 feet (1.8 m). It is certainly a more likely theory than that it is the world's first known flying primate. Recent expeditions have found several new species, such as a giant rat, a pigmy possum and a tiny wallaby, in the forests of Indonesia.

Is it a pterosaur? Some researchers have suggested that the Ahool may be part of a surviving population of flying reptiles thought to have gone extinct around the time of the dinosaurs, 65 million years ago. The description of the Ahool matches what we currently know about some pterosaur species, including large forearms supporting leathery wings. Most pterosaurs seem to have had wings that were covered with a downy fluff to prevent heat loss. One speculation is that the Ahool it may be a relative of Kongamato (see page 342) in Africa.

Is it an owl? Two large earless owls exist on the island, the spotted wood-owl (*Strix seloputo*) and the Javan wood-owl (*Strix (leptogrammica) bartelsi*). They are 16–20 inches (41–51 cm) long and have a wingspan of perhaps 4 feet (1.2 m). Despite this size discrepancy, wingspans are usually overestimated when flying animals are being observed. The Javan wood-owl seems a reasonable candidate: it has a conspicuous flat face with large dark eyes exaggerated by black rings of feathers and a beak that protrudes only a little, and it appears greyish-brown when seen from below. Its call is characteristic – a single shout, given intermittently, and sounding like 'HOOOOH!' Like most large owls, it is highly territorial in the breeding season and will frighten away intruders by engaging in mock attacks from above and behind. Its flight, as with other owls, is nearly completely silent. The Javan wood-owl is extremely rare and elusive, hiding during daylight. It is found only in remote forest, and does not tolerate human encroachment, logging or other disturbances.

The Orang-Bati of Indonesia

These are strange human/bat monsters living on the island of Seram. According to folklore they are often seen flying about at night when they may abduct small children. They return every morning to an extinct volcano, where the children are devoured. They are described as looking like humans with reddish skin, bat wings and a long tail, both wings and tail being covered with a dense black fur. The orang-batis are sometimes reported from other islands in the same area, but they only seem to kill people on Seram. The creature has also been described as looking like a naked woman covered with a coat of short black fur, this fur also covering the wings. Researchers have suggested that the orang-bati may be a giant bat, with a monkey-like face as has been reported for the Ahool. Islanders believe that the orang-bati might be a monkey-eating bat, like the monkey-eating eagles that are some of the world's largest flying birds. Since Seram has no monkeys, it is thought that the orang-bati mistakenly preys on young children instead, but that it finds plenty of monkeys on other islands which explains why it doesn't kill humans in other places.

ALMAS In the Caucasian Mountains, the Russian steppes, the Altai Mountains, the Gobi Desert of Mongolia and Siberia, tales abound of a creature similar to the Yeti (Abonimable Snowman) or Sasquatch (Bigfoot). Reports say that it is more man-like than the ape-like creatures of the Himalayas and North America. It was first recorded in Nikolai Przhevalski's expedition of 1879, which also discovered the wild camel and the wild Mongolian horse. Almas are said to eat small animals, such as marmots, and plants, and are believed by some to be the last survivors of Neanderthal man, supposedly wiped out around 40 millennia ago.

AMPHITERE and JACULUS (JAVELOT)

'Amphitere' is a term used to describe a type of legless winged serpent, usually feathered, that is found in European heraldry. It is based upon the *Jaculus*, the winged snake that guarded the frankincense trees of southern Arabia. Frankincense is the extremely valuable resin of the *Boswellia sacra* tree, found in Yemen and Oman. Frankincense burns with a white, fragrant smoke and was thought to carry prayers to heaven. The Greeks and Romans burned it as an offering to their gods, and the Egyptians buried it in their royal tombs. Apart from being insect-repellent incense, frankincense was also used as a diuretic, to cleanse the kidneys, to stop internal and external bleeding, to aid in fat elimination and to cure forgetfulness, and it is still harvested in Yemen. The historian Herodotus (*c.*485–*c.*425 BCE) reported

that the gum was dangerous to harvest because of the venomous snakes that lived in the trees. He claimed that '*the bushes that grow frankincense are guarded by tiny winged snakes, of dappled colour, and there are great numbers of them around each bush.*' He described the method used by the Arabs to solve the problem by burning the gum of the Styrax tree, the smoke of which would drive the snakes away.

In the first century CE Lucan wrote in *The Pharsalia*: '*Upon branchless trunk a serpent, named / By Libyans Jaculus, rose in coils to dart / His venom from afar. Through Paulus' brain / It rushed, nor stayed; for in the wound itself / Was death…*' Jaculus means '*thrown*' in Latin, and Lucan explains that it is the wound caused by the Jaculus hitting the victim that causes death, not its venom. It was thus known as the '*Javelin-Snake*'. Also in the first century, Pliny the Elder in his *Natural History* noted: '*Frankincense occurs nowhere except Arabia… The jaculus darts from the branches of trees; and it is not only to our feet that the serpent is formidable, for these fly through the air even, just as though they were hurled from an engine* [a siege catapult].' In the seventh century, Isidore of Seville in *Etymologies* wrote: '*The jaculus is a flying snake. They jump from trees and dart onto passing animals, from which they get their name, darter (jaculi).*'

In Madagascar, legend tells of a snake called the fandrefiala, which will fall tail first from a tree like a spear and stab animals and people that pass underneath. It is the most feared snake on the island,

and is known to science as *Ithycyphus perineti* or the Perinet night snake. It has V-shaped head markings which resemble a spearhead, and unusual coloration. The front of the body is yellowish, and the rear and tail are red, leading islanders to believe that it hangs from trees tail-first, falling to impale passers-by on its tail. Before doing so, it chooses to warn its victims by dropping a particular number of leaves (either three or seven) before making the fatal attack. An islander explained how clever it was: *'If you stop under his tree it will drop three leaves, one at a time, onto your head. It does this to check the trajectory. Then it drops out of the tree and springs its body straight like a spear to kill you.'* However, despite this colourful and bloodcurdling story, all snakes on Madagascar are known to be harmless.

ASP, DEAF ADDER AND OUROBOROS The asp was said to block its ear with its tail so as not to hear a music charmer, and this tale may be the origin of the Ouroboros (see page 85). It was supposed to guard a tree that dripped balsam; to get the balm one had to first put the asp to sleep by playing or singing to it. It was also supposed to have the precious gem, the carbuncle, inside its head. Certain words have to be uttered by the enchanter to obtain the stone.

The Yemeni Chameleon

Also known as the veiled chameleon, *Chamaeleo calyptratus*, it is found in the mountainous regions of Yemen and Saudi Arabia. They are expert tree climbers and tree dwellers, with feet specially adapted to grasp limbs and branches. The green base colour is marked with stripes and spots of yellow, brown and blue. Adult male veiled chameleons can reach a length of 24 inches (61 cm), and the species has a tall decorative growth called a casque on its head. They have a prehensile tail that acts as a fifth appendage and aids in climbing. Veiled chameleons are ambush predators and are capable of lying still for very long periods of time waiting for an unsuspecting locust to wander by. The veil suggesting the appearance of a dragon, the front legs and the snake-like tail, allied to their tree-dwelling habits, may mean that this chameleon was the origin of the myth of the *Jaculus*.

Animals Back From the Dead

THE COELACANTH

The coelacanth predates the dinosaurs. It has been part of this world for 410 million years, but is now near extinction. It is the 410 million-year-old *'living fossil'* fish. *Latimeria chalumnae* was long thought to be extinct but was rediscovered in 1938 off the coast of Africa. Another species, *Latimeria menadoensis*, was discovered off Indonesia only in 1999. The coelacanth is sadly threatened with extinction, with an estimated remaining population of just 500. In actuality, the coelacanth is not a 'living fossil' but what is known as a *'Lazarus taxon'* – a species thought to be extinct that suddenly reappears in nature (or in the fossil record). A 'living fossil' is a species that has not changed over a very long time. Some living fossils are species that were known from the fossil record before living representatives were discovered, e.g. the coelacanth and the dawn redwood tree (*Metasequoia*) found in a remote Chinese valley. Others include types of lobsters, wasps and beetles. Some are a single living species with no close living relatives, but which is the sole survivor of a large and widespread group in the fossil record, e.g. the *Gingko biloba* tree.

MEGALODON - 'BIGTOOTH' - THE MEGATOOTH SHARK

Relatively recent findings of the colossal squid, coelacanth and megamouth shark (see below) have led some people to hope that the extinct shark called *Megalodon* may still exist in deep waters. The popular press a few years ago claimed that a catch was the long-lost megalodon, a giant shark that lived from about 16 to 1.5 million years ago, and which was the apex predator of its time. It 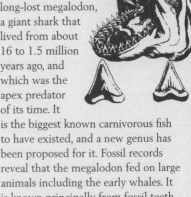 is the biggest known carnivorous fish to have existed, and a new genus has been proposed for it. Fossil records reveal that the megalodon fed on large animals including the early whales. It is known principally from fossil teeth and a few fossilized vertebrae. As with other sharks, its skeleton was formed of cartilage, not bone, resulting in the poor fossil record as cartilage does not fossilize. The teeth are in many ways similar to great white shark teeth, but are much larger and can measure more than 7 inches (18 cm) in length. The teeth indicate that this creature could actually have been over 56 feet (17 m) long. However, the animal caught was a giant Pacific sleeper shark. Several whale vertebrae and bones have been found with clear signs of large bite marks made by teeth that match those of megalodon. The teeth of the megalodon were serrated, which would have helped in tearing the flesh of prey with great efficiency. It appears that a megalodon would focus its attack on the middle of the body of a whale, crushing the ribs and lungs along with the pectoral fins in a single attack.

MEGAMOUTH - THE NEW SHARK
The megamouth shark, *Megachasma pelagios*, is an extremely rare and unusual species of deepwater shark. Discovered only in 1976 by the US Navy, only a few have ever been seen, with 44 specimens known to have been caught or sighted since then. It grows to 18 feet (5.5 m) in length and is distinctive for its large head with rubbery lips. It is so unlike any other type of shark that it is classified in its own family Megachasmidae, though it may belong in the family Cetorhinidae of which the basking shark is currently the sole member. Like the endangered whale shark and basking shark, it is a filter-feeding shark, swimming with its enormous mouth wide open, filtering water for plankton and jellyfish.

OTHER RECENT DISCOVERIES
Until the 1870s, the **ivory-billed woodpecker** (*Campephilus principalis*) was widespread in the lowland primary forests of the southeastern United States. It was thought to be extinct in the 1920s but ornithologists observed the first wild individual in Arkansas in 2004.

The **Madagascar serpent eagle** (*Eutriorchis astur*), a species that had not been seen in 60 years, was observed again in 1993. Currently, at least 75 breeding pairs live in the wild. This bird occupies dense and humid evergreen forests in northeastern and east-central Madagascar.

The **Laotian rock rat** (*Laonastes aenigmamus*) was believed to have been extinct for 11 million years. It is a member of a family that, until now, was only known from the fossil record. Scientists noticed a dead squirrel-like rodent on sale at a market in Laos in 2005 that later was identified as the Laotian rock rat. In 2006 David Redfiled, an academic from Florida State University, released video footage of a specimen that he had captured in Laos.

No specimens of the **Bavarian pine vole** (*Microtus bavaricus*) had been oberved since 1962 and it was thought to be extinct. However, a population apparently belonging to this species was discovered in 2000 in Northern Tyrol, just across the German-Austrian border.

Wollemia nobilis is a conifer, the sole species in the genus *Wollemia*, only discovered in 1994 in gorges in the Blue Mountains around 100 miles (160 km) northwest of Sydney, Australia. The oldest fossil of so-called **Wollemi Pine** has been dated to 200 million years ago.

The wonderfully named **Jellyfish Tree** (*Medusagyne oppositifolia*), is the only species of the family Medusagynaceae, thought to be extinct until a few individual specimens were discovered in the 1970s on Mahé island in the Seychelles. This critically endangered tree is thought to have originated on the old continent of Gondwana.

The **Lord Howe Island stick insect**, *Dryococelus australis*, was thought to be extinct by 1930, only to be rediscovered in 2001. Extinct in its largest habitat, Lord Howe Island, it has been called 'the rarest insect in the world'; less than 30 live on the tiny islet of Ball's Pyramid.

The **La Palma giant lizard** (*Gallotia auaritae*) is a giant wall lizard living near La Palma in the Canary Islands. Believed extinct for 500 years, it was rediscovered in 2007. Other giant lizards of the Canary Islands, the El Hierro giant lizard and the La Gomera giant lizard, were also rediscovered only recently in 1974 and 1999 respectively. The Tenerife speckled lizard was only discovered for the first time in 1996.

The **woolly flying squirrel** (*Eupetaurus cinereus*) is the sole species in its genus, and until 1994 scientific knowledge was limited to 11 skins collected in the late 19th century. The largest known gliding mammal, it is now known still to exist in Kashmir.

The exotically named **Gilbert's potoroo** (*Potorous gilbertii*) is sometimes called a rat-kangaroo. It is about the size of a rabbit and is critically endangered in Western Australia. Less than 40 of these marsupials remain. Discovered in 1840 by John Gilbert, it was considered extinct for 120 years until rediscovered in 1994. Their main diet is truffles.

The **Caspian pony** (*Equus ferus caballus*) is a small horse native to Iran, thought to be descended from Mesopotamian horses. It supposedly became extinct in the seventh century, but was rediscovered in the 1960s.

The **Takahe** (*Porphyrio hochstetteri*) is a New Zealand flightless bird of the sail family. It was thought extincts after the last four known specimens were taken in 1898. It was refound in 1948 on South Island, but a related species on North Island is extinct.

There were no known sightings of the **night parrot** (*Pezoporus occidentalis*) of Australia made between 1912 and 1979, leading to speculation that it was extinct. Sightings since 1979 have been extremely rare and the bird's population size is unknown. The last sighting was in 2006, when an individual was found dead, having crashed into a barbed wire fence in Queensland.

The **Cuban kite** (*Chondrohierax wilsonii*) is critically endangered with a current population of an estimated 50 mature birds. There was a confirmed sighting in 2001 and in 2009 a photograph was taken of one individual.

The **Cuban Solenodon** (*Solenodon cubanus*) is a small mammal with, unusually for a mammal, venomous saliva. It was discovered in 1861 and since then only 36 have been caught. By 1970 it was thought to be extinct, but in 1974 and 1975 three specimens were captured. Its last sighting was back in 2003.

There are thousands of other species close to extinction, while new species are still being found, for example the biggest rat in the world that was discovered in Indonesia in 2010. Overwhelmingly the cause of species extinction is the effect of global overpopulation by humans.

In Christian allegory, the asp represented the wealthy and worldly, who keep one ear open to earthly desire, but whose other ear is blocked by sin. They are mentioned in Psalm 58 in the Bible: '… *they are like the deaf adder that stops her ear; which will not hearken to the voice of charmers, charming never so wisely'*. In the first century CE, Pliny wrote: *'When the neck of an asp swells up, the only remedy for its sting is to immediately amputate the bitten part.'* Around the same time, Lucan tells us: *'First from the dust was raised a gory clot / In guise of Asp, sleep-bringing, swollen of neck: / Full was the blood and thick the poison drop / That were its making; in no other snake / More copious held. Greedy of warmth it seeks / No frozen world itself, nor haunts the sands / Beyond the Nile; yet has our thirst of gain / No shame nor limit, and this Libyan death, / This fatal pest we purchase for our own… Haemorrhois huge spreads out his scaly coils, / Who suffers not his hapless victims' blood / To stay within their veins… Greedy Prester swells / His foaming jaws… a Prester's fang / Nasidius struck, who erst in*

Marsian fields / Guided the ploughshare. Burned upon his face / A redness as of flame: swollen the skin, / His features hidden, swollen all his limbs / Till more than human: and his definite frame / One tumour huge concealed. A ghastly gore / Is puffed from inwards as the virulent juice / Courses through all his body… On Tullus great in heart, / And bound to Cato with admiring soul, / A fierce Haemorrhois fixed. From every limb, / (As from a statue saffron spray is showered / In every part) there spouted forth for blood / A sable poison: from the natural pores / Of moisture, gore profuse; his mouth was filled / And gaping nostrils, and his tears were blood. / Brimmed full his veins; his very sweat was red; / All was one wound'.

Augustine of Hippo in the fifth century CE described the asp blocking its ears to prevent the enchanter from drawing it out of its cave, and Isidore of Seville in the seventh century agreed: *'The asp (aspis) kills with a venomous bite, and from this it gets its name, for the Greek word for poison is* ios *(as). When an enchanter calls an asp out of its cave by incantations and it does not want to go, it presses one ear to the ground and covers the other with its tail, so it cannot hear the enchantment. There are many kinds of asp, but not all are equally harmful. The dipsas is a kind of asp, called in Latin* situla *because one bitten dies of thirst. The hypnalis is a kind of asp that kills in sleep, as Cleopatra was freed by death as if by sleep when bitten by one. The haemorrhois is called an asp because anyone bitten by it sweats blood; for the Greek word for blood is* haima. *The prester (or praester) is a kind of asp that always runs with its steaming mouth open; one bitten becomes distended for rot follows the* bite.' Around 1200, the *Aberdeen Bestiary* noted: *'The emorrosis is an asp, so called because it kills by making you sweat blood. If you are bitten by it, you grow weak, so that your veins open and your life is drawn forth in your blood. For the Greek word for 'blood' is emath… The prester is an asp that moves quickly with its mouth always open and emitting vapour… If it strikes you, you swell up and die of gross distention, for the swollen body putrefies immediately after… There is a kind of asp called ypnalis, because it kills you by sending you to sleep. It was this snake that Cleopatra applied to herself, and was released by death as if by sleep.'*

Asp is the Anglicization of the word *aspis* (Greek for viper), which formerly referred to any one of several venomous snakes found around the Mediterranean and in the Nile region. Perseus, after killing the Gorgon Medusa, flew over Egypt to transport her head to Mt Olympus. Some of her blood fell to the ground, and was transformed into asps. According to Plutarch, Cleopatra tested various deadly poisons on condemned persons and animals for daily entertainment. She decided that the bite of the asp was the least terrible way to die, as the venom brought sleepiness without spasms of pain. Some believe this asp was probably *Naja haje* (the Egyptian cobra), *haje* being the Arabic for snake or viper. A stylized Egyptian cobra was the symbol of sovereignty for the pharaohs, who incorporated it into their diadem. *Vipera aspis* is a venomous viper found across southwestern Europe. Bites are more severe than those delivered by the European adder (*Viper berus*), but only about 4 per cent of all untreated bites are fatal.

AUROCHS - THE RECREATION OF A DEAD MONSTER BULL

The coat of arms of the noble Moravian family of Pernstein bore on a white shield a black aurochs' head *'couped affonty'* i.e. with no neck visible and facing the viewer. According to family legend, the founding father of the Pernsteins was an extraordinarily strong charcoal burner named Vénava. He caught a wild aurochs and took it to the court of the king at Brno, where he cut its head off with a single blow of his axe. The king was so impressed that he gave the charcoal burner huge estates and the right to bear the aurochs' head on a coat of arms. The family seat at Pardubice has a sculptured wall relief showing the feat. The aurochs or urus (*Bos primigenius*), the ancestor of domestic cattle, was a type of huge wild ox which is now extinct. Once they roamed over Europe, Asia and North Africa, but the last one died in Poland in 1627. They stood 6 feet 6 inches (2 m) at the shoulder and weighed almost a ton.

Difficult to herd, they were hunted to extinction for food. Aurochs are shown in many Paleolithic European cave paintings, and were worshipped in the Near East as the Lunar Bull. Julius Caesar wrote: *'…those animals which are called uri. These are a little below the elephant in size, and of the appearance, colour, and shape*

of a bull. *Their strength and speed are extraordinary; they spare neither man nor wild beast which they have espied. These the Germans take with much pains in pits and kill them. The young men harden themselves with this exercise, and practise themselves in this sort of hunting, and those who have slain the greatest number of them, having produced the horns in public, to serve as evidence, receive great praise. But not even when taken very young can they be rendered familiar to men and tamed. The size, shape and appearance of their horns differ much from the horns of our oxen. These they anxiously seek after, and bind at the tips with silver, and use as cups at their most sumptuous entertainments.'* Their mystique means they remain as the symbol of several states and cities in Europe, having figured prominently in Teutonic folklore. Italian scientists are hoping to use genetic expertise and selective breeding of modern wild cattle to recreate the fearsome beasts. Breeds of large cattle which most closely resemble *Bos primigenius*, such as Highland cattle,

Vaynol Welsh wild cattle and the white Maremma breed from Italy, are being crossed with each other in a technique known as 'back-breeding'. Scientists have created a map of the aurochs' genome from preserved bone material to breed animals nearly identical to aurochs. The first round of crosses, between three breeds native to Britain, Spain and Italy, has recently been carried out. The last time there was an attempt to recreate the animal was on the express orders of Hitler. The Nazis directed a pair of German zoologists to recreate the aurochs as part of the Third Reich's belief in racial superiority and eugenics. Herman Goering hoped to use the aurochs to populate a vast hunting reserve which he planned to create in the conquered territories of Eastern Europe.

BARNACLE GOOSE - THE BIRD BORN FROM A SEA SHELL

Sir John Mandeville wrote in his 14th century *Travels*: '*I told them of as great a marvel to them, that is amongst us, and*

that was of the Bernakes. For I told them that in our country were trees that bear a fruit that become birds flying, and those that fell in the water live, and they that fall on the earth die anon, and they be right good to man's meat. And hereof had they as great marvel, that some of them trowed [believed] *it were an impossible thing to be.*' However, another school of thought until around 1800 held that barnacle geese originated from barnacle shells which encrusted the wooden hulls of sailing ships in huge numbers. They attracted weed and significantly slowed down ships. In English, the term 'barnacle' originally referred only to this species of goose and it was only later applied to the crustaceans. The natural history of the barnacle goose was long tied up with a legend claiming that they were born of driftwood. In 1187, the chronicler Gerald of Wales wrote: '*Nature produces* [Bernacae] *against Nature in the most extraordinary way. They are like marsh geese but somewhat smaller. They are produced from fir timber tossed along the sea, and are at first like gum. Afterwards they hang down by their beaks as if they were a seaweed attached to the timber, and are surrounded by shells in order to grow more freely. Having thus in process of time been clothed with a strong coat of feathers, they either fall into the water or fly freely away into the air. They derived their food and growth from the sap of the wood or from the sea, by a secret and most wonderful process of alimentation. I have frequently seen, with my own eyes, more than a thousand of these small bodies of birds, hanging down on the sea-shore from one piece of timber, enclosed in their shells, and already formed. They do not breed and lay eggs like other birds, nor do they ever* hatch any eggs, nor do they seem to build nests in any corner of the earth.*' This belief probably came about because the geese were never seen in summer – they were actually breeding in remote Arctic regions. Supposedly they developed underwater in the form of barnacles. Because of this, some Irish clerics considered barnacle goose flesh to be acceptable food for fast days, a practice that was criticized by Gerald of Wales: '*…Bishops and religious men in some parts of Ireland do not scruple to dine off these birds at the time of fasting, because they are not flesh nor born of flesh… But in so doing they are led into sin. For if anyone were to eat of the leg of our first parent although he was not born of flesh, that person could not be adjudged innocent of eating meat.*' In 1215, Pope Innocent III prohibited the eating of these geese during Lent, arguing that despite their unusual method of reproduction, they lived and fed like ducks and so were of the same nature as other birds.

THE BASILISK - THE JESUS LIZARD

The legend of the basilisk (see also page 70) possibly originated in India by way of travellers' and merchants' tales. It might have derived from the appearance of the horned viper, or more likely the hooded cobra. Indeed, in the first century CE Pliny the Elder describes it merely as a snake with a golden crown. However, by the Middle Ages it had become a snake with the head of a cock, and sometimes with the head a human, and a potent symbol of evil. There are four known species of basilisk today, all spectacular lizards found in Central and South America. The males grow up to 3 feet (90 cm) long, including the tail. Male basilisks have fins, and live in trees near water. Extremely wary, a frightened basilisk will drop from a branch overhanging a pool of water and run for shelter. The lizards have specialized scales on the bottoms of their rear feet, so are able to run upright across the surface of water for some distance, using their tails as rudders. When they eventually break the surface tension of the water, the basilisks then swim quickly away to escape. Thus they have been nicknamed the 'Jesus Lizard' as they can apparently 'walk on water'.

THE BAT IS A BIRD In the first century CE Pliny the Elder wrote: '*The bat is the only flying creature that bears live young and feeds them with its milk; it also carries its children in its arms as it flies.*' Isidore of Seville in his seventh century *Etymologies* noted: '*The bat, unlike other birds, is a flying quadruped, resembling a mouse. It has its name* (vespertilio) *from the time when it flies, after twilight. It flies about driven by precipitate motion, hangs from fragile branches, and makes a sound like a squeak.*' Medievalist writers recorded that bats gathered together and hung from high places like a bunch of grapes. They believed that if one bat fell from its roost, all the rest also fell. It is now known that bats cannot take off from the ground, and need to climb to a height from which they can unfold their wings to glide before they start flying.

BEARS LICK THEIR CUBS INTO SHAPE (LITERALLY) In the 13th century *De Proprietatibus Rerum*, written by the Franciscan monk Bartholomaeus Anglicus states: '*Avicenna says that the bear brings forth a piece of imperfect and evil shapen flesh, and the mother licks the lump, and shapes the members with licking… For the whelp is a piece of flesh little more than a mouse, having neither eyes nor ears, and having claws… and so this lump she licks, and shapes a whelp with licking.*' He seems to have obtained his information from the ubiquitous Pliny the Elder, whose first century *Natural History* tells us: '*Bears mate at the beginning of winter, after which the male and female retire to separate caves. The cubs are born thirty days later, in a litter of no more than five. Newborn cubs are a shapeless lump of white flesh, with no eyes or hair, though the claws are visible. The mother bear gradually licks her cubs into their proper shape, and keeps them warm by hugging them to her breast and lying on them, just as birds do with their eggs. In the winter, male bears remain in hiding for forty days, and females for four months; during this time they do not eat or drink, and for the first fourteen days are so soundly asleep that not even wounds can wake them. When they emerge from their caves they eat an herb to loosen their bowels and rub their teeth on tree stumps to get their mouths ready. To cure the dimness of their eyes they go to bee hives and allow the bees to sting their faces. A bear's weakest part is the head; some say the brains of bears contain a poison that if drunk drives a man bear-mad. When a bear fights a bull, it hangs from the bull's horns and mouth, and so the weight of*

the bear tires it… Bears produce young that are unfinished at birth, and shape them by licking them. In this they are like lions and foxes. The breath of bears is pestilential; no wild animal will touch anything a bear has breathed on, and things so tainted quickly go bad.' If injured, it was thought that a bear could heal itself by touching the herb phlome or mullein. The fiercest bears were said to be found in Numibia.

THE BEAVER'S PAINFUL ESCAPE MECHANISM

This author lives in the Teifi Valley, a few hundred yards from the river where the last beavers in England and Wales were found. In the early 12th century, Gerald of Wales wrote *The Journey Through Wales*, in which he informs us: '*The Teifi has another singular particularity, being the only river in Wales, or even in England, which has beavers; in Scotland they are said to be found in one river, but are very scarce. I think it not a useless labour, to insert a few remarks respecting the nature of these animals – the manner in which they bring their materials from the woods to the water, and with what skill they connect them in the construction of their dwellings in the midst of rivers; their means of defence on the eastern and western sides against hunters; and also concerning their fish-like tails. The beavers, in order to construct their castles in the middle of rivers, make use of the animals of their own species instead of carts, who, by a wonderful mode of carnage, convey the timber from the woods to the rivers. Some of them, obeying the dictates of nature, receive on their bellies the logs of wood cut off by their associates, which they hold tight with their feet, and thus with transverse pieces placed in their mouths, are drawn along backwards, with their cargo, by other beavers, who fasten themselves with their teeth to the raft. The moles use a similar artifice in clearing out the dirt from the cavities they form by scraping. In some deep and still corner of the river, the beavers use such skill in the construction of their habitations, that not a drop of water can penetrate, or the force of storms shake them; nor do they fear any violence but that of mankind, nor even that, unless well armed. They entwine the branches of willows with other wood, and different kinds of leaves, to the usual height of the water, and having made within-side a communication from floor to floor, they elevate a kind of stage, or scaffold, from which they may observe and watch the rising of the waters. In the course of time, their habitations bear the appearance of a grove of willow trees, rude and natural without, but artfully constructed within. This animal can remain in or under water at its pleasure, like the frog or seal, who show, by the smoothness or roughness of their skins, the flux and reflux of the sea. These three animals, therefore, live indifferently under the water, or in the air,* and have short legs, broad bodies, stubbed tails, and resemble the mole in their corporal shape. It is worthy of remark, that the beaver has but four teeth, two above, and two below, which being broad and sharp, cut like a carpenter's axe, and as such he uses them. They make excavations and dry hiding places in the banks near their dwellings, and when they hear the stroke of the hunter, who with sharp poles endeavours to penetrate them, they fly as soon as possible to the defence of their castle, having first blown out the water from the entrance of the hole, and rendered it foul and muddy by scraping the earth, in order thus artfully to elude the stratagems of the well-armed hunter, who is watching them from the opposite banks of the river.

When the beaver finds he cannot save himself from the pursuit of the dogs who follow him, that he may ransom his body by the sacrifice of a part, he throws away that, which by natural instinct he knows to be the object sought for, and in the sight of the hunter castrates himself, from which circumstance he has gained the name of Castor; and if by chance the dogs should chase an animal which had been previously castrated, he has the sagacity to run to an elevated spot, and there lifting up his leg, shews the hunter that the object of his pursuit is gone. Cicero speaking of them says, "They ransom themselves by that part of the body, for which they are chiefly sought." … Thus, therefore, in order to preserve his skin, which is sought after in the west, and the medicinal part of his body, which is coveted in the east, although he cannot save himself entirely, yet, by a wonderful instinct

and sagacity, he endeavours to avoid the stratagems of his pursuers. The beavers have broad, short tails, thick, like the palm of a hand, which they use as a rudder in swimming; and although the rest of their body is hairy, this part, like that of seals, is without hair, and smooth; upon which account, in Germany and the arctic regions, where beavers abound, great and religious persons, in times of fasting, eat the tails of this fish-like animal, as having both the taste and colour of fish.'

Both St Bernard and Juvenal stated that beavers had this unusual habit, and in the sixth century BCE *Aesop's Fables* we find: 'The beaver, a four-footed animal that lives in pools, knows that he is hunted for his testicles, which are used to cure ailments. When pursued, the beaver runs for some distance, but when he sees he cannot escape, he will bite off his own testicles and throw them to the hunter, and thus escape death.' Pliny in the first century CE said in his *Natural History*: 'Beavers in the region of the Black Sea (Pontici) know that they are hunted for the oil produced by their testicles (castoreum), so when they are in danger from hunters they castrate themselves. The beaver has the tail of a fish, and soft fur on its otter-like body. They have a strong bite, cutting down trees as if with steel, and if they bite a man they will not let go until the bones are heard grinding together.' The fable of the beaver was used as a religious lesson. For man to live purely, he must cut off all his earthly vices and hurl them in the face of the devil. The devil will see that man has nothing belonging to him, and leave man alone.

BEITHIR This large, serpentine monster features in Scottish mythology, and there have been several recent sightings. It is said to have a head about 2 feet (60 cm) long, bulky in shape and with what appear to be pointed ears or horns. It has a body which appears humped, like a caterpillar's, when it moves, and it seems to drag its belly along with difficulty. It is said to be about 20 feet (6 m) long.

BIGFOOT AND SASQUATCH

Bigfoot, also known as the Sasquatch, is depicted as an ape-like man who inhabits forest areas of the Pacific northwest and parts of the Canadian province of British Columbia. Over the years there have been many sightings and photographs of Bigfoot but no conclusive proof exists to verify his existence. Most experts on the matter consider the Bigfoot legend to be a combination of folklore and hoaxes, but there are a number of authors and researchers who do believe that the stories could be true. There is some speculation that, like the Loch Ness monster, Bigfoot may be a living survivor from an earlier age – specifically a *Gigantopithecus blacki*, a supersize ape. The earliest accounts of Bigfoot date from 1924 though reports of a similar type of creature did appear as early as the 1860s.

This is the North American version of the Abominable Snowman of the Himalayas. In Canada it is usually called 'Sasquatch'.

The word is derived from several native names for the creature used by tribes in the northwest coastal area North America. Sasquatch is supposed to be at least 6 foot 9 inches (2.05 m) tall, rising to an incredible 11 foot 5 inches (3.5 m). Its footprints have been measured at 16–20 inches (40–50 cm) long by 7 inches (18 cm) wide. It has long arms, an ape-like face with a flat nose and thick hairy fur, and is said to live in caves and hidden valleys. Westerners first encountered it in 1811, since which time there have been hundreds of reported sightings, but no scientific proof of its existence. Several have postulated that it is a remnant population of *Homo erectus* or 'Java Man', and the depth of its footprints indicate it weighs between 300 and 1000 pounds (136 and 454 kg). (Java Man is the name given to fossils discovered in 1891 in East Java, Indonesia, one of the first known specimens of *Homo erectus*.) Foot casts confirm that the creature is not a bear, as there are no traces of claws, and trails of up to 3000 footprints are said to have been followed, which would be almost impossible to fake.

BOA - THE MILK SUCKER AND CHILD-SWALLOWER
Pliny the Elder recorded: '*The boa is a serpent of Italy, that is so large it can swallow a child whole. Their chief food is milk sucked from cows; from this they derive their name.*' If such a snake ever existed, it is unknown at present. Boa is a common name for a non-poisonous snake of the boa and python family that numbers some 70 species. Like pythons, boa kill their prey by constricting (squeezing) them to death and then

worldwide. Large snakes have been reported in Mediterranean areas which were 9 feet (2.75 m) in length or more. The largest European snake is now the *green whip snake*, which reaches 6 feet (1.8 m) in length and which may be the remnant populations of pythons. Before the Sahara became a huge desert, pythons and many other animals ranged right up into northernmost parts of Africa.

CATOBLEPAS (KATOBLEPS) - the BUFFALO WITH FATAL BREATH

The Roman author Claudius Aelianus, in his second century CE *On the Nature of Animals* recounts: '*Libya is the parent of a great number and a great variety of wild animals, and moreover it seems that the same country produces the animal called the Katoblepon. In appearance it is about the size of a bull, but it has a more grim expression, for its eyebrows are high and shaggy, and their eyes beneath are not large like those of oxen but more narrow and bloodshot. And they do not look straight ahead but down on to the ground: that is*

swallowing the body whole. While a large boa might easily kill an average-size person, it would have difficulty in swallowing the body, and is generally not considered a threat to humans. Boas give birth to live young, while pythons lay eggs; pythons are confined mostly to the Old World, whereas boas are found

Hungry White Python Was Italian Cocaine Guard

Reuters international news agency reported on 12 August 2010: '*Italian police seized a rare albino python in Rome yesterday in a raid on a group of drug traffickers who used the snake to guard cocaine and intimidate customers who owed them money. The 10-ft reptile attacked police when they burst into the dealers' apartment. "When we went in,*

we found the animal right behind the door waiting for us, just like a proper guard dog," said Lieutenant Luca Gelormino. "We were surprised to find 200 grams of very pure cocaine under the snake." The animal had been starved for a week to make it aggressive, but it calmed down after it was given a helping of chicken.'

why it is called 'down-looking' [from kata and blepo]. *A mane that begins on the crown of its head and resembles horsehair, falls over its forehead covering its face, which makes it more terrifying when one meets it. It feeds upon poisonous roots. When it glares like a bull it immediately shudders and raises its mane, and when this has risen erect and the lips about its mouth are bared, it emits from its throat pungent and foul-smelling breath, so that the whole air overhead is infected, and any animals that approach and inhale it are grievously afflicted, lose their voice, and are seized with fatal convulsions. This beast is conscious of its power; and other animals know it too and flee from it as far away as they can.'* The catoblepas is thought to be based on encounters with downward-looking 'bulls', which had the body of a buffalo and the head of a swine. These were probably wildebeest or gnu.

However, many sources state that it was a small animal, or had a scaly back. Around 1245, Bartholemaeus Anglicus wrote in *De Proprietatibus Rerum*: '*Among the Hisperies and Ethiopians is a well, that many men believe is the head of Nile, and there beside is a wild beast that is Catoblefas, and hath a little body, and nice in all members, and a great head hanging always toward the earth, and else it were greatly annoying to mankind. For all that see his eyes, should die anon, the same kind* [of eyes] *has the cockatrice*' He is describing a small animal, as did Leonardo da Vinci in *The Notebooks*: '*It is found in*

Ethiopia near to the source Nigricapo. It is not a very large animal, is sluggish in all its parts, and its head is so large that it carries it with difficulty, in such wise that it always droops towards the ground; otherwise it would be a great pest to man, for any one on whom it fixes its eyes dies immediately.' Edward Topsell in his 1607 *The Historie of Foure-Footed Beastes* also reminds us that before Aelianus described what seems to be a wildebeest or gnu: '*Pliny calls this beast Catablepon, because it continually looks downwards, and says all the parts of it are but small excepting the head, which is very heavy, and exceeds the proportion of his body, which is never lifted up, but all living creatures die that see his eyes. By which there arises a question whether the poison which he sends forth, proceeds from his breath, or from his eyes. Whereupon it is more plausible, that like the cockatrice, he kills by seeing, than by the breath of his mouth, which is not compatible to any other beasts in the world.*' The Roman Pliny the Elder travelled between Ethiopia and Egypt, and in his first century *Natural History* tells us: '*In Western Ethiopia there is a spring, the Nigris, which most people have supposed to be the source of the Nile... In its neighbourhood there is an animal called the Catoblepas, in other respects of moderate size and inactive with the rest of its limbs, only with a very heavy head which it carries with difficulty – it is always hanging down to the ground; otherwise it is deadly to the human race, as all who see its eyes expire immediately.*'

Because of the scaly back, small size and downwards-facing large head, the animal in question may be the pangolin, or scaly anteater. It can curl up into a ball when threatened, with its overlapping, razor-sharp scales acting as armour and its face tucked away from danger under its tail. The front claws are so long that they are unsuited for walking, and so the animal walks with its fore paws curled over to protect them, and its head lowered to the ground searching for insects. Pangolins can also emit a noxious smelling acid from glands near the anus, just like the spray of a skunk. The noxious smell may be that of the 'catoblepas'. Pangolins have short legs, and grown from 12 to 39 inches (30 to 100 cm) long, dependent upon species. Their sharp claws are used for burrowing into ant and termite mounds.

The Extinction of Catoblepas

Pangolins are hunted across Africa for bush-meat. Pangolins are also in great demand in China because their meat is considered a delicacy, and many Chinese believe pangolin scales promote blood circulation and help breast-feeding women to produce milk. Coupled with habitat loss through deforestation, the effects of humanity mean that all species of pangolin are now threatened. As a result of increasing demand, the pangolin populations of China, Vietnam, Laos and Cambodia have been wiped out. With traders moving further and further south, the animal is declining even in its last Asian habitats in Java, Sumatra and the Malaysian peninsula. They are being smuggled out of Africa, where the Chinese have an increasing presence. In 2007, Thai customs officers rescued over 100 live pangolins from one consignment being smuggled to China. One raid on a restaurant in Guanghzou found 118 pangolins, 132 pounds (60 kg) of snakes and 880 pounds (400 kg) of toads. *The Guardian* newspaper (10 November 2007) provided a gruesome description of the trade: '*A Guangdong chef interviewed last year in the Beijing Science and Technology Daily described how to cook a pangolin: "We keep them alive in cages until the customer makes an order. Then we hammer them unconscious, cut their throats and drain the blood. It is a slow death. We then boil them to remove the scales. We cut the meat into small pieces and use it to make a number of dishes, including braised meat and soup. Usually the customers take the blood home with them afterwards."*'

CENTAURS AND CAVALRY

Isidore of Seville recorded in his seventh century *Etymologies* that '*Centaurs are fabulous animals that are part man and part horse. Some say that this idea came from the horsemen of the Thessalians, because in battle on horseback they appear to be one body, horse and man.*' The Thessalians, of Celtic origin, were superb horsemen whereas early Greek armies were infantry-based. When Spanish horsemen were first seen in South and Central America, some Indians believed that man and horse were a single animal.

CHICKCHARNEY - THE RED-EYED ELF of THE BAHAMAS

This fabulous creature reputedly lives in the forests of Andros Island in the Bahamas. Andros was called by the Spanish 'the Isle of the Holy Spirit' and also lays claim to a Loch Ness type of monster, and a sea-dragon called the Lusca (see page 204). Andros is the largest of the Bahama chain, being 104 miles (167 km) long and 40 miles (64 km) wide at its widest point. Many of its creeks, lakes and headlands are uncharted and its coastline was incorrectly plotted even as late as 1963. The tiny population of around 8000 people is spread out across villages and settlements, mainly on the east coast. The west coast, which faces many square miles of shallow water known as 'The Mud', and the mysterious interior are hardly known. A band of Cuban exiles, having made their way across the interior from the west coast to Fresh Creek in 1962, told of seeing '*the fires of unknown settlements*' and of '*innumerable deer and rookeries of flamingos*' that were hitherto unrecorded.

Chickcharnies were supposed to be forest-dwelling red-eyed elves resembling birds, furry or feathered and ugly-looking. Their nesting sites were constructed by joining the tops of the tallest two pine trees in the remotest forest. Their piercing eyes are said to be red. They have three fingers, three toes and a tail, which they use to suspend themselves from the trees. Folk wisdom recommends that visitors carry flowers or pieces of brightly coloured cloth to charm the chickcharnies. At least one islander says he has seen them: '*It has a black ring around its neck, and it look like a dove. It makes nests you can see in the trees. I don't say nothing against them.*' In legend, if a traveller meets a chickcharney and treats it well, he will be rewarded with good luck for the rest of his life. Treating a chickcharney badly will result in hard times, sometimes resulting in having one's head forcibly turned around backwards.

The story about turning the head around 360 degrees brings to mind an owl, and it is believed that the origin of the legend was in fact a large, three-toed, burrowing owl which once lived in the forests, but became extinct in the 16th century. This 2-feet (600cm) tall flightless owl was called *Tyto pollens*, a remote cousin of the smaller common barn-owl (*Tyto alba*), and it is known from fossil records on the island. It may be that it was territorially aggressive and coexisted with humans. There are variations in eyewitness accounts of what they look like but, generally speaking, chickcharnies are considered tree spirits, somewhat like frigate birds, feathered and fearsomely red-eyed. They hang from cottonwood branches by their three toes, and it is not always easy to tell when they are right side up.

The chickcharnies were blamed for the failure of prime minister Neville Chamberlain's sisal plantation at Mastic Point in 1897, when he cut down their homes. A *Reader's Digest* travelogue in 1956 recalled the creatures: '*strange, half-human, half-animal creatures with magic powers to work ill or harm… The Chickcharnies are knee-high, have big ears and huge, owlish eyes. Birdlike, they build nests at the juncture of three tall trees that touch at the top. They inflict a lifelong curse on anyone who molests their abodes. Legend has it that all the misfortune that befell the late British Prime Minister, Neville Chamberlain, was the work of the Chickcharnies. The story is that Chamberlain, as a young man, came across a Chickcharnie nest while clearing ground for a sisal plantation here. When native workmen fled in terror at his order to tear down the home of the aerial elves, Chamberlain chopped down the trees himself. Elderly leaders* [on the island] *still blame Chamberlain's failure at Munich on the Chickcharnie curse, and say Britain would never have won the war if he hadn't been succeeded by Churchill.*'

EL CHUPACABRA - THE GOAT SUCKER El Chupacabra is mostly associated with Latin American communities in the USA, Mexico and Puerto Rico (where it was first reported). It is supposedly a heavy creature, the size of a small bear, with a row of spines reaching from its neck to the base of its tail. It takes its name from the fact that it is supposed to attack animals and drink their blood – especially goats. While the legend began around 1987, there are many similarities to the *Vampire of Moca* (see page 370), the name given to an

The Legend of the Chick Charney (from The Rum Portal 2002)

Like the Irish Leprechaun,
The Chick Charney is our sprite.
He brings good luck to man and woman;
sleep in silk cotton tree come night.

Some say Chick Charney save de slaves,
Some say he jus a guess,
Some claim he live in Andros,
Das why he take no mess!

Chick Charney like tiny bird,
He gat dem great big eyes.
Sometimes he make some mischief–
Depends on what he spy!

So be careful! Watch your back!
An don cha do no wrong,
Cause when Chick Charney ready,
He sure could do you harm!

unknown creature that killed animals all over the small town of Moca in the 1970s. The Vampire of Moca left the animals completely devoid of blood which had apparently been drained from the body by a series of small circular wounds. The most common description of the Chupacabra refers to a lizard-like creature with leathery or scaly greenish-grey skin and sharp spines or quills running down its back. It stands approximately 3 to 4 feet (90 to 120 cm) tall, and moves in a fashion similar to a kangaroo. In at least one sighting, the creature hopped 20 feet (6 m) in one bound. This variety is said to have a dog or panther-like nose and face, a forked tongue protruding from it, large fangs and to hiss and screech when alarmed, as well as leave a sulphuric stench behind. When it screeches, some reports note that the chupacabra's eyes glow an unusual red that cause the witnesses nausea. To some people, it appeared with bat-like wings.

In Canóvanos, Puerto Rico, Luis Guadalupe and his brother-in-law fled for their lives from the ugly demon, and Luis reported: '*It was about four or five feet tall and had huge elongated red eyes… A pointy, long tongue came in and out of his mouth. It was gray but his back changed colors. It was a monster.*' Madelyne Tolentino said she stared at the chupacabra as it jumped like a kangaroo down a Canóvanas street and paused by her window. She said it exuded such a sulphur-like stench that her eighteen-month-old, who was in the car with her during a second sighting, was still coughing from it. Two dozen other people swear that they have seen this vampire-like predator that has killed scores of animals. However, Dr Hector J. Garcia, head of the Agriculture Department's veterinary services, was sceptical, believing that the attacks were made by feral dogs. Francisco F. Monge, a Canóvanas construction worker who lost five sheep worth about $500, said all five showed the trademark neck perforations. He had raised animals since he was nine years old and found the deaths highly unusual. '*Dogs have never attacked my animals*', he said. The Mayor of Canóvanas, Jose Soto, a former police detective, led search parties of more than 200 people through thick mountain foliage. More than 100 animals had died in his jurisdiction, creating mass hysteria, he said. The Mayor's pleas to government agencies for help with the hunting efforts were ignored.

In 2004, a rancher near San Antonio, Texas, shot 'the *Elmendorf Beast*' a hairless, dog-like creature which had been attacking his livestock. It was a coyote. In 2006 a farmer in Coleman, Texas, killed a strange creature, a cross between a dog, a rat and a kangaroo, which had been attacking his chickens and turkeys, but threw it out with his rubbish. Around the same time a rodent-like creature with fangs was found dead alongside a road in Turner, Maine, but the carcass had been picked clean before it coud be examined. Phyllis Canion took a picture of a strange animal found dead after killing 30 of her chickens in Cuero, Texas by sucking their blood. A state veterinarian thought it was a grey fox suffering from extreme mange.

Some Legendary Horned Creatures

A single-horned onager, or wild ass, of legend

A legendary horned animal, possibly mistakenly based on a hyena

A mythical sheep or goat with two straight, sharply pointed horns

A yale, or centicore, a mythical antelope-like animal with large horns that can be swivelled in any direction

The alicorn was thought to cure many diseases and have the ability to detect poisons

An onager aldro, a mythical wild ass with the horns of a rhinoceros

CROCODILE TEARS AND FACE-PACKS In medieval bestiaries the dung of the *Nile crocodile* was recommended to enhance a person's beauty: the excrement was meant to be smeared on the face and left there until sweat washed it off. It was said that only two animals could kill it. '*Fish with sawtooth backs*' (dolphins) could cut the crocodile's stomach, and the '*hydrus*' or '*ichneuman*' could crawl into the crocodile's mouth and kill it from the inside. Crocodiles would always weep after eating a man. In the fifth century BCE the Greek historian Herodotus wrote: '*During the four winter months they eat nothing; they are four-footed, and live indifferently on land or in the water. The female lays and hatches her eggs ashore, passing the greater portion of the day on dry land, but at night retiring to the river, the water of which is warmer than the night-air and the dew. Of all known animals this is the one which from the smallest size grows to be the greatest: for the egg of the crocodile is but little bigger than that of the goose, and the young crocodile is in proportion to the egg; yet when it is full grown, the animal measures frequently seventeen cubits and even more. It has the eyes of a pig, teeth large and tusk-like, of a size proportioned to its frame; unlike any other animal, it is without a tongue; it cannot move its under-jaw, and in this respect too it is singular, being the only animal in the world which moves the upper-jaw but not the under. It has strong claws and a scaly skin, impenetrable upon the back. In the water it is blind, but on land it is very keen of sight. As it lives chiefly in the river, it has the inside of its mouth constantly covered with leeches; hence it happens that, while all the other birds and beasts avoid it, with the trochilus it lives at peace, since it owes much to that bird: for the crocodile, when he leaves the water and comes out upon the land, is in the habit of lying with his mouth wide open, facing the western breeze: at such times the trochilus goes into his mouth and devours the leeches. This benefits the crocodile, who is pleased, and takes care not to hurt the trochilus.*'

Pliny the Elder recorded: '*It allows a small bird to enter its mouth to clean its teeth; if it falls asleep with its jaws open while this is happening, the ichneuman jumps down its throat and gnaws its way out through the belly… Dolphins also attack crocodiles, using the sharp fin on their backs to cut open the crocodile's soft belly. Crocodiles have poor sight in the water but very good sight when out of it. It is said that the crocodile is the only animal that continues to grow all its life, and that it can live four months in a cave without food in the winter.*' In his 13th century *Bestiaire*, Guillaume le Clerc noted: '*Never was seen another such a beast, for it lives on land and in water. At night it is submerged in water, and during the day it reposes upon the land. If it meets and overcomes a man, it swallows him entire, so that nothing remains. But ever after it laments him as long as it lives. The upper jaw of this beast is immovable* when it eats, and the lower one alone moves. No other living creature has this peculiarity. The other beast of which I have told you [the water-serpent], which always lives in the water, hates the crocodile with a mortal hatred. When it sees the crocodile sleeping on the ground with its mouth wide open, it rolls itself in the slime and mud in order to become more slippery. Then it leaps into the throat of the crocodile and is swallowed down into its stomach. Here it bites and tears its way out again, but the crocodile dies on account of its wounds.'

DOGS AS WITNESSES In the early 12th century, Gerald of Wales (Giraldus Cambrensis) wrote in his *The Journey Through Wales'*: 'A dog, of all animals, is most attached to man, and most easily distinguishes him; sometimes, when deprived of his master, he refuses to live, and in his master's defence is bold enough to brave death; ready, therefore, to die, either with or for his master. I do not think it superfluous to insert here an example which Suetonius gives in his book on the nature of animals, and which Ambrosius also relates in his Exameron. A man, accompanied by a dog, was killed in a remote part of the city of Antioch, by a soldier, for the sake of plunder. The murderer, concealed by the darkness of the morning, escaped into another part of the city; the corpse lay unburied; a large concourse of people assembled; and the dog, with bitter howlings, lamented his master's fate. The murderer, by chance, passed that way, and, in order to prove his innocence, mingled with the crowd of spectators, and, as if moved by compassion, approached the body of the deceased. The dog, suspending for a while his moans, assumed the arms of revenge; rushed upon the man, and seized him, howling at the same time in so dolorous a manner, that all present shed tears. It was considered as a proof against the murderer, that the dog seized him from amongst so many, and would not let him go; and especially, as neither the crime of hatred, envy, or injury, could possibly, in this case, be urged against the dog. On account, therefore, of such a strong suspicion of murder (which the soldier constantly denied), it was determined that the truth of the matter should be tried by combat. The parties being assembled in a field, with a crowd of people around, the dog on one side, and the soldier, armed with a stick of a cubit's length, on the other, the murderer was at length overcome by the victorious dog, and suffered an ignominious death on the common gallows. Pliny and Solinus relate that a certain king, who was very fond of dogs, and addicted to hunting, was taken and imprisoned by his enemies, and in a most wonderful manner liberated, without any assistance from his friends, by a pack of dogs, who had spontaneously sequestered themselves in the mountainous and woody regions, and from thence committed many atrocious acts of depredation on the neighbouring herds and flocks. I shall take this opportunity of mentioning what from experience and ocular testimony I have observed respecting the nature of dogs. A dog is in general sagacious, but particularly with respect to his master; for when he has for some time lost him in a crowd, he depends more upon his nose than upon his eyes; and, in endeavouring to find

Dogs With Two Noses

Following a 1913 expedition to the South American rainforests, Colonel Percy Fawcett (see page 114) supposedly claimed to have seen dogs with double noses. The double-nosed Andean tiger hound is a rare breed which has been seen in Bolivia. The 'double nose' appears to be a normal dog's nose, but with the nostrils separated by a band of skin and fur dividing the nose all the way to the dog's upper lip. There were sightings in 2006 and 2007. The dogs may be genetic anomalies within the strain of Andean tiger hounds. 'Tiger' in their name is a reference to the South American jaguar, not to Asian tigers. The Andean tiger hound may be descended from the *Pachon Navarro*,

a type of dog probably introduced to the Americas by the conquistadores. The Pachon Navarro is a Spanish hunting dog, also known as an old Spanish pointer, which has the unusual feature of a split or double nose. It is believed that this unusual nose gives this dog an especially keen sense of smell, a primary reason it was chosen as a hunting dog.

him, he first looks about, and then applies his nose, for greater certainty, to his clothes, as if nature had placed all the powers of infallibility in that feature. The tongue of a dog possesses a medicinal quality; the wolf's, on the contrary, a poisonous: the dog heals his wounds by licking them, the wolf, by a similar practice, infects them; and the dog, if he has received a wound in his neck or head, or any part of his body where he cannot apply his tongue, ingeniously makes use of his hinder foot as a conveyance of the healing qualities to the parts affected... In this wood of Coleshulle, a young Welshman was killed while passing through the king's army; the greyhound who accompanied him did not desert his master's corpse for eight days, though without food; but faithfully

defended it from the attacks of dogs, wolves, and birds of prey, with a wonderful attachment. What son to his father, what Nisus to Euryalus, what Polynices to Tydeus, what Orestes to Pylades, would have shewn such an affectionate regard? As a mark of favour to the dog, who was almost starved to death, the English, although bitter enemies to the Welsh, ordered the body, now nearly putrid, to be deposited in the ground with the accustomed offices of humanity.'

THE DONKEY-CENTAUR

'There is a certain creature which they call an Onokentaura, and anybody who has seen one would never have doubted that the race of Kentauroi once existed... But this creature of which my discourse set out to *speak, I have heard described as follows. Its face is like that of a man and is surrounded by thick hair. Its neck below its face and its chest are also those of a man, but its teats are swelling and stand out on the breast; its shoulders, arms, and forearms, its hands too, and chest down to the waist are also those of a man. But its spine, ribs, belly and hind legs closely resemble those of an ass; likewise its colour is ashen, although beneath the flanks it inclines to white. The hands of this creature serve a double purpose, for when speed is necessary they run in front of the hind legs, and it can move quite as fast as other quadrupeds. Again, if it needs to pluck something, or to put it down, or to seize and hold it tight, what were feet become hands; it no longer walks but sits down. The creature has a violent temper. At any rate if captured it will not endure servitude and in its yearning for freedom declines all food and dies of starvation.'* The Roman writer Aelian, who included this description in *On Animals*, is probably describing a chimpanzee.

DRAGONS OF KOMODO

The dragon was originally considered the greatest of all serpents, with a scaly body and wings and often depicted as bat-like. Its head was horned and tufted, and its tail thorny and pointed. The Welsh Dragon is the oldest national flag in the world, and possibly copied from that of the Roman legions. The British (Welsh) war-leader was known as the '*pendragon*' (pen meaning 'head' in Welsh). Maelgwn Gwynedd, the sixth-century pendragon of the British, succeeding

Arthur, was also known as '*the island dragon*' because of his lands on the island of Anglesey. The dragon has long featured in Chinese mythology, as well as in Roman, Greek and other ancient cultures. Dragons were believed to live in caves or deep in the Earth's core, where fire was their constant companion, so they came to breathe fire themselves. In British heraldry, the four-legged dragon is a late development, as before the 15th century it just had two legs. In heraldry the two-legged dragon now tends to be called a *wyvern* or *basilisk*. The dragon possibly had its origins in travellers' tales of the Komodo dragon, or in unearthed fossils of huge prehistoric beasts.

The Komodo dragon (*Varanus komodoensis*) is a massive monitor lizard found on some Indonesian islands. It grows to 10 feet (3 m) long and 11 stone (70 kg) in weight. They are representative of a relic population of very large varanid lizards that once lived across Indonesia and Australia, most of which died out after contact with modern humans. Although Komodo dragons mainly eat carrion, they will also hunt and ambush prey. Komodo dragons have been known to attack humans. On 4 June 2007 a Komodo dragon attacked an eight-year-old boy on Komodo Island, who

later died of massive bleeding from his wounds. Natives blamed the attack on environmentalists outside the island who had prohibited goat sacrifices, so denying the Komodo dragons their expected food source. Many natives of Komodo Island believe that Komodo dragons are the reincarnation of fellow kinspeople and should thus be treated with reverence. On 24 March 2009, two Komodo dragons attacked and killed fisherman Muhamad Anwar on Komodo. Anwar was attacked after he fell out of a sugar-apple tree and was left bleeding badly from bites to his hands, body, legs and neck. In 2001, actress Sharon Stone's husband, Phil Bronstein, had to have emergency surgery to his foot when attacked by a Komodo dragon in Los Angeles Zoo.

EAGLE REJUVENATION

Psalm 105 says '*youth will be renewed like the eagle's*'. Pliny the Elder recorded: '*The eagle is the strongest and most noble bird. There are six kinds of eagles. Only the sea-eagle forces its unfledged young to look at the rays of the sun; if any of them blinks or has watering eyes, those ones are thrown out of the nest. Some kinds of eagles have a stone called the eagle-stone built into their nests; this stone can survive fire without loss of virtue, and is useful in many cures. The stone is large and has another stone inside it, which can be heard to rattle when shaken. Eagles drive their young from the nest when they tire of feeding them, and chase them far away so they do not compete for food. Eagles do not die from old age or sickness; when they are old they die of hunger, because their upper beak grows so large and hooked that they cannot open their mouths to feed. Some kinds of eagles do battle with stags; they roll in dust to gather it on their feathers, then perch on the stag's horns and shake the dust into its eyes, and beat the stag's head with their wings until it falls. Eagles also fight with a great serpent which tries to eat their eggs; the serpent can defeat the eagle by wrapping itself around the eagle's wings so that it falls to the ground.*' St Antony of Padua compared the saints to eagles. '*The eagle is so called from the acuteness of its sight, because she can behold the sun with unflinching eyes. Wherefore it is said concerning it in books of natural history, that she is of very sharp sight, and compels her young ones to look at the sun before they are fully fledged. To this end she strikes them and turns them towards the sun, and, if the eyes of any one of them water, she kills him, and pays attention to the others. It is said also that she lays three eggs and throws out the third. It is asserted, moreover, that she places an amethyst in the nest with her young ones, that by its virtue serpents may be driven away. In the eagle the subtle intelligence of saints and their sublime contemplation is set forth; for they turn towards the aspect of the true Sun, to the light of wisdom, their young, that is, their works, in order that if any thing which becomes not their extraction should be* concealed there, it may be brought to light by the splendour of the sun. For all iniquity is made manifest by the light. Whence, if they see that any work of theirs cannot rightly look at the sun, and is confounded by its rays and weeps, they immediately slay it… And note that the three eggs of the eagle are the three kinds of love which exist in a righteous man; the love of God, of his neighbour, and of himself. Which, last love he is bound to expel altogether from the nest of his conscience…'

In his 13th century Bestiaire, Guillaume le Clerc wrote: 'The eagle is the king of birds. When it is old it becomes young again in a very strange manner. When its eyes are darkened and its wings are heavy with age, it seeks out a fountain clear and pure, where the water bubbles up and shines in the clear sunlight. Above this fountain it rises high up into the air, and fixes its eyes upon the light of the sun and gazes upon it until the heat thereof sets on fire its eyes and wings. Then it descends down into the fountain where the water is clearest and brightest, and plunges and bathes three times, until it is fresh and renewed and healed of its old age. The eagle has such keen vision, that if it is high up among the clouds, soaring through the air, it sees the fish swimming beneath it, in river or sea; then down it shoots upon the fish and seizes and drags it to the shore. Again, if unknown to the eagle its eggs should be changed and others put into its nest, when the young are grown, before they fly away, it carries them up into the air when the sun is shining its brightest. Those which can look at the rays of the sun, without blinking, it loves and holds dear; those which cannot stand to look at the light, it abandons, as base-born, nor troubles itself henceforth concerning them.'

ECHENEIS - THE FISH WHICH HALTS SHIPS

From the first to the 13th century the idea held sway that this fish delayed ships. Pliny the Elder noted: 'The echeneis is a small fish that is often found on rocks. It has the ability to slow the passage of ships by clinging to their hulls. It is also the source of a love-charm and a spell to slow litigation in courts, and can be used to stop fluxes of the womb in pregnant women and to hold back the birth until the proper time. This fish is not eaten. Some say this fish has feet; Aristotle says it does not, but that its limbs resemble wings.' Isidore of Seville observed: 'The echinais has its name because it clings to a ship and holds it fast (echei-naus). It is a small fish, about six inches long, but when it attaches to a ship the ship cannot move, but seems rooted in the sea, despite raging storms and gales. This fish is also called "delay" (mora) because it causes ships to stand still.'

Barthlomaeus Anglicus wrote: 'Enchirius is a little fish half a foot long: for though he is little of body, nonetheless he is most of virtue. For he cleaves to the ship, and holds it still steadfastly in the sea, as though the ship were on ground therein. Though winds blow, and waves arise strongly… that ship may not move… And that fish holds not still the ship by no craft, but only cleaving to the ship. It is said of the same fish that when he knows and feels that tempests of wind and weather be great, he comes and taketh a great stone, and holds himself fast thereby, as it were by an anchor, lest he be smitten away and thrown about by waves of the sea. *And shipmen see this and beware that they be not overset unwarily with tempest and with storms.'*

The echeneis is the *remora*, (family Echeneidae), sometimes called a *suckerfish* or *sharksucker*. It grows from 1-3 feet (30 to 90 cm) long. Its distinctive first dorsal fin is modified into a sucker, with slat-like structures that open and close to create suction and take a firm hold against the skin of larger marine animals. By sliding backwards, the remora can increase the suction, or it can release itself by swimming forwards. Remoras sometimes attach themselves to small boats. The remora benefits by using the host as transport and protection and also feeds on materials dropped by the host. They swim well on their own, with a sinuous, or curved, motion. Some cultures use remoras to catch turtles. A cord or rope is fastened to the remora's tail, and when a turtle is sighted the fish is released from the boat; it usually heads directly for the turtle and fastens itself to the turtle's shell, and then both remora and turtle are hauled in. Smaller turtles can be pulled completely into the boat by this method, while larger ones are hauled within harpooning range. In Latin remora means 'delay', while the genus name *Echeneis* comes from Greek *echein* ('to hold') and *naus* ('a ship'). Pliny the Younger blamed the remora for the defeat of Mark Antony's fleet at the Battle of Actium in 31 BCE, by slowing down his ships.

ELEPHANTOI - THE EXTINCT ELEPHANTS OF HANNIBAL

Elephants were reasonably well-known in the ancient world, in particular the (now extinct) sub-species that was then common in Mauretania (northwest Africa). Hannibal took 37 elephants across the Alps to attack Rome, and they were the smaller Mauretanian elephant, *Loxodonta africanus* var. *berberica*. They were often used in warfare by the Carthaginians, e.g. outside Carthage in the First Punic War, when Xanthippus routed the Roman legions of Regulus. However, the deployment of 80 war elephants could not prevent Hannibal's defeat at Zama by Scipio Africanus in 202 BCE. The animal was also known as the Atlas elephant as it lived around the Atlas Mountains, but it had almost disappeared by the second century. At the time Roman mosaics in Tunis showed the huge variety of wildlife that existed before the desertification of North Africa. They feature elephants, lions, bears, wild boars, ostriches and leopards. All have now disappeared except for the wild boar, which is hunted for game. The last Atlas lion was killed in 1920 in Morocco. These animals were all taken for gladiatorial sports in Rome and elsewhere across the Roman empire.

ELEPHANTS HAVE NO KNEES

There are many weird and wonderful stories that have been reported about elephants over the centuries, while products made from elephants' body parts have been used medicinally and cosmetically. For instance, a salve was made of ivory, ground up and applied to spots and lines on the face, and was used for whitening the teeth. The blood was drunk to cure a haemorrhage. If the skin or bones of an elephant were burned, the smoke would drive out serpents. The *Book of Maccabees* records: '*And they showed the elephants the blood of grapes, and mulberries to provoke them to fight.*' Pliny the Elder wrote: '*The elephant is the closest of all animals to humans in intelligence. It understands the language of its own country, and can therefore understand and obey orders. Elephants are wise and just, remember their duties, enjoy affection, and respect religion. They know that their tusks are valuable, so when a tusk falls off they bury it. Elephants are gentle, and do no harm unless provoked. Females are more timid than males. Male elephants are used in battle, carrying castles full of armed soldiers on their backs. The slightest squeal of a pig will frighten them, and African elephants fear to look at Indian elephants. They hate mice and will refuse to eat fodder that has been touched by one. Their period of gestation is 2 years and they never bear more than one child at a time. They become adults at the age of 60 years, and live between 200 and 300 years. They love rivers but cannot swim. Elephants constantly feud with the large serpents of India, which can encircle an elephant in their coils. When this happens, the elephant is strangled and dies, but in falling crushes the serpent and kills it. Another way these large serpents kill elephants is by submerging themselves in a river and waiting for an elephant to come and drink; coiling around the elephant, the serpent bites its ear and drains all its blood. The elephant in dying falls on the serpent and kills it. The largest elephants are from India, though Ethiopian elephants rival them in size, being 30 feet high... The breath of elephants attracts snakes out of their holes.*'

St Ambrose (340–397 CE) tells us that the elephant does not bend its knees, as it has need of rigid legs like pillars in order to support so great a fabric of limbs. The result is that it cannot lie down. He describes how tame elephants '*are propped up with great beams, so that when asleep they can to some extent recline without danger of falling. But wild elephants, which lean against trees when rubbing their sides or sleeping, not infrequently fall down by the tree giving way, and there they lie and perish, or betray themselves by trumpeting, so that the hunter comes up and kills them. And the hunters take advantage of this habit to cut a slit partly through the tree, so that it gives way under the elephant's weight, and so they are captured.*' Ambrose calls them '*walking towers*' and explains how everything goes down before their onset. Like high buildings, elephants are supported on very firm foundations, and it is owing to their legs being in proportion with their size that they are able to enjoy a lifespan of 300 years or more. '*So their joints are close-set, but in the case of men, if they stood long or ran very fast, or continually walked about, how soon would their knees and the soles of their feet ache!*' He compares their tusks to natural spear-points, and says that whatever they roll up in their trunk they break and whatever they trample underfoot they crush the life out of as if it were crushed by the fall of a building. After further observations about their habits, he concludes by pointing to elephants as an object lesson to us that nothing superfluous has been created in nature; '*and yet this beast of so great size is subject to us, and obeys the commands of man.*'

ELEPHANTS AND MASTERS

The Roman statesman and writer Cassiodorus (*c*.485–*c*.585 CE) recorded '*The living elephant, when it is prostrate on the ground, as it often is when helping men to fell trees, cannot get up again unaided. This is because it has no joints in its feet; and accordingly you see numbers of them lying as if dead till men come to help them up again. Thus this creature, so terrible by its size, is really not equally endowed by Nature with the tiny ant. That the elephant surpasses all other animals in intelligence is proved by the adoration which it renders to Him whom it understands to be the Almighty Ruler of all. Moreover it pays to good princes a homage which it refuses to tyrants. It uses its proboscis, that nosed hand which Nature has given it to compensate*

for its very short neck, for the benefit of its master, accepting the presents which will be profitable to him. It always walks cautiously, mindful of that fatal fall [into the hunter's pit] *which was the beginning of its captivity. At its master's bidding it exhales its breath, which is said to be a remedy for the human headache. When it comes to water it sucks up in its trunk a vast quantity, which at the word of command it squirts forth like a shower. If anyone have treated it with contempt, it pours forth such a stream of dirty water over him that one would think a river had entered his house. For this beast has a wonderfully long memory, both of injury and of kindness. Its eyes are small, but move solemnly. There is a sort of kingly dignity in its appearance, and while it recognises with pleasure all that is honourable, it seems to despise scurrilous jests. Its skin is furrowed by deep channels, like that of the victims of the foreign disease named after it, elephantiasis. It is on account of the impenetrability of this hide that the Persian Kings used the elephant in war.*'

Isidore of Seville states in his *Etymologies*: '*The elephant takes its name from the Greek word for "mountain"* [lophos] *because its body is large like a mountain. This beast is useful to the military; Indians and Persians fight from wooden turrets placed on the backs of elephants, and shoot arrows from there. Elephants have a strong memory and intelligence, travel in herds, are afraid of mice greet the sun with movements of their bodies, and live three hundred years.*

They give birth, after a gestation period of two years, to a single child at a time. They give birth in secret and send their young to water or islands to protect them from their enemy the dragon which kills elephants by binding them. Elephants once lived in Africa and India, but now only live in India.' This favourable view of elephants is confirmed in the *Aberdeen Bestiary* (c.1200): '*Whatever elephants wrap their trunks around, they break; whatever they trample underfoot is crushed to death as if by the fall of a great ruin. They never fight over female elephants, for they know nothing of adultery. They possess the quality of mercy. If by chance they see a man wandering in the desert, they offer to lead him to familiar paths. Or if they encounter herds of cattle huddled together, they make their way carefully and peacably lest their tusks kill any animal in their way. If by chance they fight in battle, they have no mean [intent to] the wounded. For they take the exhausted and the injured back into their midst.'*

ELEPHANT MATES and MICE

The British Library's Harley MS 3244 of c.1260 – a bestiary written by an unknown author – records the elephant's mating habits: '*There is an animal, which is called "elephant", which possesses no desire for sexual intercourse. The Greeks imagine that it is called "elephant" from the great size of its body, because it resembles a mountain. For in Greek a mountain is called "Eliphio". But among the Indians it is called "barrus" from its trumpeting. So also its trumpeting is called "barritus" and its teeth "ebur". Its snout is called "promuscis", because it puts food into its mouth with it; and it is like a snake and is guarded by a rampart of ivory. No bigger animal is to be seen... For the Indians and Persians, stationed in wooden towers placed upon them, fight with darts, as if from a wall. They are possessed of a vigorous intelligence and memory. They move about in herds (they salute with such movements as they are capable of), are afraid of a mouse, and are disinclined to breed. They bring forth after two years, and they do not produce young more than once, and then not several but only one. They live 300 years. Now if the elephant wishes to beget children it goes to the East to paradise; and there is a tree there which is called Mandragora, and it goes with its female, who first takes of the fruit of the tree and gives it to her male. And she beguiles him until he eats, and immediately she conceives; and when the time for bringing forth has come, she goes into a pool so deep that the water comes up to the udders of the mother. But the [male] elephant guards her while giving birth because of the dragon which is the enemy of the elephant. Now if it should find a serpent it kills it, trampling it underfoot until it is dead. The elephant is a source of terror to bulls but fears the mouse. It has such a nature that if it has fallen down it cannot get up. Now it falls down when it leans against a tree to sleep, for it has no joints in its knees. Then the hunter makes a cut partly through the tree, so that the elephant when it has leant against it may fall down together with it.*

But as it falls, it cries out loudly, and at once a great elephant appears, but is not able to lift it up. Then both cry out, and there come twelve elephants, but they are not able to raise that which was fallen. Thereupon they all cry out, and immediately there comes a little elephant which places its mouth with its trunk under the big elephant and lifts it up. Now the little elephant has this nature that, where a fire is made of its hair and bones, no evil thing will come nor dragon. Now elephants break whatever they roll up in their trunks, and whatever they tread upon is crushed as it were by the fall of a vast building. They never fight about the females, for none of them have promiscuous intercourse. They have the good quality of gentleness. Indeed should they chance to see a man wandering in the desert, they offer themselves as an escort to the high road; or if they should fall in with a flock of sheep, they make the way clear for themselves gently and quietly with their trunks, lest they should kill with their tusk any animal that comes in the way. And when they happen to be engaged in battle with a band of enemies, they take no small care of the wounded, for they place the tired and wounded in the middle.'

THE FIERY SERPENT OF THE BIBLE Moses led the Children of Israel into the hills of Edom after their harrowing journey across the Sinai Desert. In a difficult journey through what is thought to be the rocky Araba (Arava) Valley, the Israelites revolted against Moses' leadership. Here, they experienced deadly venomous snakes which later became became symbolic of opposition

The Serpent on the Staff

In the Bible, Numbers 21:6 we read: '*the Lord sent fiery serpents among the people, and they bit the people, and many people of Israel died…*' Numbers 21:8-9 tells us: '*After the people repented, the Lord instructed Moses, "make thee a fiery serpent, and set it upon a pole, and it shall come to pass that every one that is bitten, when he looketh upon it, shall live. And Moses made a serpent of brass, and put it upon a pole, and it came to pass, that if a serpent had bitten any man, when he beheld the serpent of brass, he lived".*'

to Christianity. It has been postulated that the snakes may have been Egyptian cobras, which are deadly, but which are no longer present in the Araba Valley. The horned viper is deadly and inhabits the Araba Valley, but the most likely candidate appears to be the Israeli saw-scale viper. This snake is 'fiery', i.e. pinkish or reddish in colour, lives in rocky terrain in the valley (but not in the Sinai Desert) and is one of the world's deadliest snakes.

THE FLY The fly was a predominant symbol of the soul in many ancient religions. It was believed that flies possessed the souls of deceased people, perhaps because of the appearance of flies around corpses. By swallowing a fly a woman might conceive children. Virgin mothers of Celtic heroes such as Culchulainn conceived in this manner. The Greeks believed that souls travelled from one life to the next in insect form. Their word for soul, 'psyche', meant a butterfly. In the Middle East, Baal-Zebub or Beelzebub is now thought of as 'Lord of Flies' whereas his title originally meant 'Lord of Souls'.

THE GEESE WHICH SAVED ROME It was thought that geese could smell the odour of people better than any other animal could, so they were often used as sentries to warn against night attacks. Pliny the Elder wrote in his *Natural History*: '*Geese keep careful watch; the cackling of geese warned of an attack at the Capitol in Rome. Geese may have the power of wisdom, as shown by the story of a goose which was the companion of the philosopher Lacydes and refused to leave his side. Geese are valued for their liver, which is a great delicacy, and for their feathers, especially the soft inner down. Geese come on foot to Rome from Gaul; if one gets tired it is moved to the front, so that it is forced to continue by the press of the geese behind it. Medicine can be made by mixing goose fat with cinnamon in a bronze bowl, covering it with snow and letting it steep. Only the ostrich reaches a greater size than the goose. Geese kept in a fishpond lose their flavor, and stubbornly hold their breath until they die.*' Isidore of Seville recorded: '*The goose* [anser] *took its name from its similarity to the duck* [ans], *or because it swims frequently. Geese watch at night and give warning with their noise; they can smell humans better than any other animal can. Geese warned Rome of attack by the Gauls.*' In Europe, the original domesticated goose was derived from the greylag goose (*Anser anser*). When Aphrodite first came ashore she was welcomed by the Charites (Roman 'Graces'), whose chariot in legend was drawn by geese.

The warning of an attack on the Capitol came after the Battle of the Allia, which was a battle during the first Gallic invasion of Rome in *c*.387 BCE. The Senones, a Celtic tribe, had crossed the Appennines looking for new land to

settle. The Roman historian Livy records that they were tricked by three Roman ambassadors, who killed one of their leaders. The Senones marched 90 miles (145 km) from Clusium to Rome to take revenge for the treachery. Livy describes their journey: '*Contrary to all expectation the Celts did them* [the people of the countryside] *no harm, nor took aught from their fields, but even as they passed close by their cities, shouted out that they were marching on Rome and had declared war only on the Romans, but the rest of the people they regarded as friends.*' The battle took place at the Allia River near Rome, with about 24,000 men on each side. The Senones, under Brennus, fought the Roman army about 12 miles (19 km) north of the city. When they attacked, the Roman flanks were routed leaving the Roman centre to be surrounded and slaughtered. The remnants of the army fled back to Rome. Livy states: '*all hastened to Rome and took refuge in the Capitol without closing the gates*' and the citizens then barricaded themselves on the Capitoline Hill. The Senones noticed a steep path leading up onto the hill. According to legend the defenders were alerted to the attack at night by the noise of the sacred geese of Juno. The rest of Rome was plundered and the Romans negotiated an end to the siege by agreeing to pay one thousand pounds of gold. The Celts used heavier and better-made long swords and full body shields, which they interlocked as a defensive measure. This tactic was later named the *testudo* (tortoise) and adopted in battle by the Roman legions.

Hedgehogs as Weather Forecasters

The 'hedge pig' or hedgehog was cooked to make medicine and as food. Pliny the Elder wrote: '*To prepare for winter, hedgehogs roll on fallen apples to stick them to their spines, then taking one or more in their mouths, carry the load to hollow trees. Hedgehogs foretell a change in wind direction from north to south when they retire to their lairs. When hunted, they roll up into a ball so that it is not possible to pick them up without touching their spines.*' Isidore of Seville tells us: '*The hedgehog is covered with quills, which it stiffens when threatened, and rolling itself into a ball is thus protected on all sides. After it cuts a bunch of grapes off a vine it rolls over them so it can carry the grapes to its young on its quills.*' Other medieval writers insisted that hedgehogs would only take apples or figs from orchards.

GOATS AND DIAMONDS

The he-goat was accounted a lascivious beast, known for its lust. This nature made the male-goat so hot that its blood could dissolve a diamond.

HYENAS and SEX CHANGE

In Aesop's *Fables* from the sixth century BCE, we read: '*It is told that hyenas change their sex, one year being male and the next year female. One day a male hyena tried to perform an unnatural sex act with a female, who told him to remember that what he did to her this year would be done to him next year.*' Pliny the Elder wrote: '*The Hyaena is popularly believed to be bisexual and to become male and female in alternate years, the female bearing offspring without a male; but this is denied by Aristotle. Its neck stretches right along the backbone like a mane, and cannot bend without the whole body turning round. A number of other remarkable facts about it are reported, but the most remarkable are that among the shepherds' homesteads it simulates human speech, and picks up the name of one of them so as to call him to come out of doors and tear him in pieces, and also that it imitates a person being sick, to attract the dogs so that*

it may attack them; that this animal alone digs up graves in search of corpses; that a female is seldom caught; that its eyes have a thousand variations and alterations of colour; moreover that when its shadow falls on dogs they are struck dumb; and that it has certain magic arts by which it causes every animal at which it gazes three times to stand rooted to the spot.' Aelian in *On Animals* recorded: '*It seems that the Hyaina and the Korokottai, as they call it, are viciously clever animals. At any rate the Hyaina prowls about cattle-folds by night and imitates men vomiting. And at the sound dogs come up, thinking it is a man. Whereupon it seizes and devours them.*' Some early commentators considered that there was a stone in the hyena's eye (or in the stomach of its young) that gave a person the ability to predict the future if the stone was placed under the person's tongue. Hyenas would circle a house at night, calling out words with the voice of a man. Anyone who was deceived and went out to investigate would be eaten. A dog that crossed a hyena's shadow would lose its voice. The hyena's spine was thought to be rigid, so to turn it had to move its whole body. The result of a mating between a hyena and lioness was a beast known as the *leucrota*.

ICHNEUMON - PHARAOH'S RAT

Pliny the Elder recorded in his *Natural History*: '*The ichneuman is known for its willingness to fight to the death with the snake. To do this, it first covers itself with several coats of mud, drying each coat in the sun to form a kind of armor. When ready it attacks, turning away from the blows it receives until it sees an opportunity, then with its head held sideways it goes for its enemy's throat. The ichneuman also attacks the crocodile in a similar manner.*' It was also the enemy of the dragon. Those who believed it was the enemy of the crocodile may be confusing it with the *hydrus*. Confusingly, Isidore of Seville noted: '*That which is produced from the smell of this beast is both healthful and poisonous in food.*' The Greek word ichneumon was the name used for 'Pharaoh's rat' or the Egyptian mongoose which attacks snakes, but it can also mean otter. The scientific name of the Egyptian mongoose is *Herpestes ichneumon*.

KONGAMATO - BREAKER OF BOATS

Kongamato means '*breaker of boats*', and the name refers to a pterodactyl-like creature said to exist in Zambia, Cameroon, Angola, Tanzania, Namibia, Kenya and Congo. In Kenya the creature is called *Batamzinga* and in Cameroon, *Olitu*. It is described by the Kaonde tribe as a huge red lizard with membranous wings, lacking feathers and like a huge bat with teeth in its long beak. It has a reputation for capsizing canoes and causing death to anyone who merely looks at it. Its main sightings have been in the Jiundu swamps in western Zambia, near the borders of Congo and Angola. Frank Melland in his 1923 book *In Witchbound Africa* describes it as living along certain rivers, and as being very dangerous, often attacking small boats. It was red, with a wingspan of 4 to 7 feet (1.2 to 2.1 m). Members of the local Kaonde tribe identified it as a pterodactyl after being shown a picture of one from Melland's book collection.

Pterosaurs (meaning 'winged lizards') are often referred to as pterodactyls, from the Greek *pterodaktulos* (meaning 'winged finger'). They were flying reptiles, existing for hundreds of millions of years up to 65 million years ago. Their wings were formed by a membrane of skin, muscle and other tissues stretching from the hindlimbs to a greatly lengthened fourth finger on the forelimb. Early species had long, fully-toothed jaws and long tails, while later forms had a highly reduced tail, and some lacked teeth. Some had furry coats made up of hair-like filaments and they spanned an extremely wide range of adult sizes.

The Kaonde people of the northwestern province of Zambia used to carry charms called '*muchi wa Kongamato*' to protect them at certain river crossings from the Kongamato. In 1925, a newspaper correspondent, G. Ward Price, was travelling with the Prince of Wales (later Edward VIII) on an official visit to Rhodesia (now Zambia). He reported that a civil servant told them of the wounding of a man who had entered a feared swamp in Rhodesia. The man entered the marsh to prove his bravery as it was supposedly full of demons. He returned badly injured with a great wound in his chest, saying that a strange bird with a long beak had attacked him. The civil servant showed the man a picture of a pterodactyl, a flying dinosaur, from a book of prehistoric animals, and the man screamed in terror and fled from the civil servant's home. The evidence for it being a pterodactyl is that the natives could describe it accurately when unprompted, and that they all agreed about its appearance. Melland wrote: *'The natives do not consider it to be an unnatural thing like a mulombe* [demon] *only a very awful thing, like a man-eating lion or a rogue elephant, but infinitely worse… I have mentioned the Jiundu swamp* [northwestern Zambia] *as one of the reputed haunts of the kongamato, and I must say that the place itself is the very kind of place in which such a reptile might exist, if it is possible anywhere.'*

In 1932–3 the Percy Sladen Expedition journeyed to West Africa for the British Museum under the direction of Ivan T. Sanderson (1911–73), a zoologist and writer. In the Assumbo Mountains in the Cameroons, they made camp in a wooded valley, near a steep banked river. One evening, as the team was hunting near the river, Sanderson shot and killed a large fruit-eating bat, and when the animal fell into the water, Sanderson began to make his way over to retrieve it from the fast-moving current. He accidentally lost his balance and fell. When regaining his balance, his companion suddenly shouted in horror *'Look out!'* as a monster swooped at him. Sanderson described the following events: *'Then I let out a shout*

also and instantly bobbed down under the water, because, coming straight at me only a few feet above the water was a black thing the size of an eagle. I had only a glimpse of its face, yet that was quite sufficient, for its lower jaw hung open and bore a semicircle of pointed white teeth set about their own width apart from each other. When I emerged, it' was gone… And just before it became too dark to see, it came again, hurtling back down the river, its teeth chattering, the air "shss-shssing" as it was cleft by the great, black, dracula-like wings.' He later referred to it as *'the grand-daddy of all bats'*.

In 1942 Colonel C.R.S. Pitman reported stories told by the natives of a large bat/bird type creature that lived in Northern Rhodesia (now Zambia) in a dense swampy region. Supposedly even to look upon it meant death. Tracks of the creatures were seen, with evidence of a large tail dragging along the ground behind. These reports were not limited to Zambia, but also came from other locations in Africa such as Mt Kilimanjaro and Mt Kenya. Dr J.L.B. Smith (famous

for his investigation into the living fossil, the coelacanth) wrote in his 1956 book *Old Fourlegs* about flying dragons that lived near Mt Kilimanjaro, Tanzania: '... *one man had actually seen such a creature in flight close by at night. I did not and do not dispute at least the possibility that some such creature may still exist.*' A game warden, A. Blaney Percival, was stationed in Kenya and noted that a huge creature whose tracks only revealed two feet and a heavy tail was believed by the Kitui Wakamba tribe to fly down to the ground from Mt Kenya every night (recounted in Karl Shuker, *In Search of Prehistoric Survivors*, 1995). In 1956 an engineer, J.P.F. Brown, said that he saw the creature at Fort Rosebery near Lake Bangweulu, Zambia. It was reported in the 2 April 1957 edition of the *Rhodesia Herald*. Brown was driving back to Salisbury from a visit to Kasenga in Zaire, and had stopped at Fort Rosebery, just west of Lake Bangweulu, to get his canteen of water from the boot. At about 6 p.m. he saw two creatures flying slowly and silently directly overhead. He stated that they looked prehistoric, with a long tail and narrow head. He estimated a wingspan of about 36 to 42 inches (90 to 107 cm). One opened its mouth in which he saw a large number of pointed teeth.

In 1957, at a hospital also at Fort Rosebery, a patient came in with a severe chest wound. The victim claimed that a massive bird had attacked him in the Bangweulu swamps. When asked to sketch the bird, the native drew a picture of a creature that resembled a pterosaur. Soon afterwards the Zambezi valley was flooded as a result of the Kariba Dam hydroelectric project. A *Daily Telegraph* correspondent Ian Colvin was at the scene, and he took a controversial photograph of what might be a pterosaur. In 1988, Professor Roy Mackal led an expedition to Namibia where there had been reports of a strange flying creature with a wingspan of up to 30 feet (9 m). According to eye witnesses, it usually glided through the air, but also was capable of true flapping flight. It was generally seen at dusk, gliding between crevices between two hills about a mile apart. The expedition was unsuccessful in collecting solid proof, but one team member, James Kosi, reportedly saw the creature from about 1000 feet (300 m) away. He described it as like a giant glider in shape, black with white markings. In 1998 Steve Romandi-Menya, a Kenyan exchange student living in Louisiana, declared that the Kongamato is still known to the bush-dwelling people in his country. The creatures are said to feed on decomposing human flesh, digging up bodies if they are not buried to a sufficient depth.

Suggested identities for the Kongamato include a modern-day survivor of the genus *Rhamphorhynchus*, a type of long-tailed pterosaur with needle-like teeth in its jaw. It probably fed on fish. Others believe it is a giant unknown bat, possibly now extinct through the effects of habitat loss. Some sceptics believe that African locals and travellers have been confusing Kongamato with two different species of very large storks native to the region, the shoebill and saddleback. The shoebill stork is a dark coloured bird with an 8-feet (2.4 m) wingspan and a prehistoric appearance. They have become rare, and can only be found in the deep swamps in Zambia and neighbouring countries. However, there is no evidence of shoebill storks behaving aggressively towards humans. Their bills are large, but not pointed, and like all birds, they have no teeth. The saddle-billed stork has a wingspan of up to 8½ feet (2.6 m), a long red bill and an overall coloration of iridescent black and white with a black head, and featherless red feet. The beak is long and pointed.

LEOPARD - THE ILLEGITIMATE CAT

The leopard was said to be the illicit offspring of a lion and a 'pard'. Isidore of Seville said it was: '*the degenerate offspring of the adulterous mating of a lion (leo) and a pard*', hence its name leopard. The Franciscan monk Bartholomaeus Anglicus in the 13th century wrote: '*The leopard is a beast most cruel, and is gendered in spouse-breach of a pard and of a lioness, and pursues his prey by startling and leaping and not running, and if he takes not his prey in the third leap, or in the fourth, then he stints for indignation, and goes backwards as though he was overcome. And he is less in body than the lion, and therefore he dreads the lion, and makes a cave*

under earth with a double entry, one by which he goes in, and the other by which he goes out. And that cave is full wide and large in either entering, and more narrow and straight in the middle. And so when the lion comes, he flees and falls suddenly into the cave, and the lion pursues him with a great rese, and enters also into the cave, and weens there to have the mastery over the leopard, but for greatness of his body he may not pass freely by the middle of the den which is full straight, and when the leopard knows that the lion is so let and held in the straight place, he goes out of the den forwards, and comes again into the den in the other side behind the lion, and resets on him behind with biting and with claws, and so the leopard has often in that way the mastery of the lion by craft and not by strength, so the less beast has often the mastery of the strong beast by deceit and guile in the den, and dare not set on him openly in the field, as Homer says in the book of the battles and wiles of beasts.'

Because of the connotations with illegitimacy, a leopard in heraldry can indicate that the first bearer of the arms was born as a result of adultery. Nicholas Upton, a 15th-century writer on heraldry, said that the '*Leopard is a most cruel beast engendered wilfully of a Lion and a beast called a Parde*' and advises that it is to be painted with '*his whole face shewed abroad openly to the lookers on*'. The arms of Richard the Lionheart had three gold leopards after 1195, a possible allusion to his grandfather, William the Conquerer, who was also known as 'the Bastard'.

Some Curious Horned Creatures

Giraffes

Rhinoceros

Ibex

Bison or Buffalo

Mountain Goat

LEOPARDS, PARDS, PARDALES, PANTHERS, LIONS AND CHEETAHS

There is much confusion in old bestiaries between these species. Recently some commentators have surmised that what were known in earlier times as leopards were in fact cheetahs, and that pards were leopards. Others argue that 'pards' are panthers. 'Pardales' were also leopards. Scientifically, the genus *Panthera* belongs to the Felidae (feline) family which contains the four 'big cats' – lions, tigers, leopards (but not the snow leopard) and jaguars. Only these four *Panthera* cat species have the anatomical structure which enables them to roar. The leopard is *Panthera pardus*. As ancient and medieval writers knew nothing of the Americas, we can discount jaguars. The picture is further confused by the extinction of species such as *Panthera gombaszoegensis* (European jaguar); *Panthera toscana* (Tuscany lion or Tuscany jaguar); *Panthera leo spelaea* (Eurasian cave lion); *Panthera leo europaea* (European lion); *Panthera pardus sickenbergi* (European leopard) and *Panthera tigris virgata* (Caspian tiger). *Panthera leo leo*, the Barbary lion, is extinct in the wild. The lion is *Panthera leo*, and the Asiatic lion is *Panthera leo persica*. The Persian leopard is *Panthera pardus saxicolor*, and the Anatolian leopard is *Panthera pardus tulliana*. The tiger is *Panthera tigris*, the Bengal tiger is *Panthera tigris tigris* and the Siberian tiger is *Panthera tigris altaica*. The cheetah (*Acinonyx jubatus*) is another member of the cat family that is unique in its speed, while lacking real climbing abilities. It is the only living member of the genus *Acinonyx* and is the fastest land animal, reaching speeds between 70 and 75 mph (113 to 120 kph) in short bursts over distances of up to 1500 feet (460 m). Subspecies include the Asiatic cheetah (*Acinonyx jubatus venaticus*) and the Northwest Africa cheetah (*Acinonyx jubatus hecki*).

Ancient Egyptians often kept cheetahs as pets, and also tamed and trained them for hunting. They were not domesticated, but bred under human supervision. They were also known as hunting leopards. The cheetahs would be taken to hunting fields in low-sided carts or by horseback, while hooded and blindfolded, and kept on leashes while dogs flushed out their prey. When the prey was near enough, the blindfolds were taken off and the cheetahs were released. The tradition was passed on to the Persians, then taken to India, where the practice was continued by princes into the 20th century. Charlemagne, Genghis Khan and other kings and princes kept cheetahs in their palace grounds. Akbar the Great, the Indian Mughal emperor from 1556–1605, kept as many as 1000 cheetahs. Even in the 1930s Emperor Haile Selassie of Ethiopia was often photographed leading a cheetah on a lead. Apart from pumas, cheetahs are the only large cats that purr. Many cheetah cubs are killed by a lack of food or by their natural enemies, lions and hyenas. An old African legend says that the tear-stain marks on the cheetah's face are caused by the mother weeping for her lost cubs.

LEUCROTA - THE BEAST WITH THE GRIN FROM EAR TO EAR

Different sources say that this beast lived in India, Libya or Ethiopia, and that its head was like that of a badger or a horse. It was said to be the result of a mating between a hyena and a lioness, but the Greek historian and philosopher Strabo thought it was the progeny of a wolf and a dog. Also known as the *crocotta*, *leucrocotta*, or *yena*, this creature was a mythical dog-wolf, linked to the hyena and said to be a deadly enemy of men and dogs. Pliny the Elder recorded it thus: *'The leucrocota is the size of an ass, and has the neck, tail and breast of a lion, the haunches of a stag, cloven hooves, a badger's head, and a mouth that opens from ear to ear, with ridges of bone instead of teeth. It is the swiftest of wild animals, and is said to be able to imitate the human voice.'* Photius, the ninth-century Byzantine scolar, said: *'In Ethiopia there is an animal called crocottas, vulgarly kynolykos [dog-wolf], of amazing strength. It is said to imitate the human voice, to call men by name at night, and to devour those who approach it. It is as brave as a lion, as swift as a horse, and as strong as a bull. It cannot be overcome by any weapon of steel.'* The crocotta was reported to have appeared in the Roman arena, when in 148 CE the Emperor Antonius Pius presented one. Cassius Dio said that the Emperor Septimius Severus took one to Rome: *'[this] Indian species…was then introduced into Rome for the first time, so far as I am aware. It has the colour of a lioness and tiger combined, and the general appearance of those animals, as also of a dog and fox, curiously blended.'* In the bestiaries, the eyes of a crocotta were striped gemstones that gave the possessor the power of foresight when placed under the tongue.

The spotted hyena bears a species name of *Crocuta crocuta*, derived from the mythological crocotta, and there are some similarities in the description. Hyenas have very powerful teeth and jaws, can digest a wide range of foods, are known to dig up human bodies for food and can make human-like cries, such as their laugh. Folklore about hyenas often attributes to them powers such as gender switching (probably because males and females are difficult to distinguish), shape shifting and human speech. Thus the hyena may have contributed to the original myth of the crocotta. Another candidate for the leucrota is the African wild dog (*Lycaon pictus*). It is the only extant species in the genus *Lycaon*, with one ancestral species, *Lycaon sekowei* being extinct.

LEVIATHAN - THE SEA MONSTER

Leviathan is the great sea monster referred to in the Bible, and its name has become synonymous with any large marine monster or sea dragon. Leviathan and similar serpent-demons have a long history in ancient mythology, with a hero-god having defeated a seven-headed serpent being recorded as early as the third millennium BCE. In Psalm 74 God is said to *'break the heads of Leviathan in pieces'* before giving his flesh to the people of the wilderness. In Isaiah 27:1 Leviathan is called the '*wriggling serpent*' which will be killed at the end of time. Chapter 41 of the Book of Job seems to be describing a large whale when describing Leviathan:

1: Canst thou draw out leviathan with a hook? Or his tongue with a cord which thou lets down?
2: Canst thou put a hook into his nose? Or bore his jaw through with a thorn?
3: Will he make many supplications unto thee? Will he speak soft words unto thee?
4: Will he make a covenant with thee? Will thou take him for a servant for ever?
5: Will thou play with him as with a bird? Or will thou bind him for thy maidens?
6: Shall the companions make a banquet of him? Shall they part him among the merchants?
7: Canst thou fill his skin with barbed iron? Or his head with fish spears?
8: Lay thine hand upon him, remember the battle, do no more.
9: Behold, the hope of him is in vain: shall not one be cast down even at the sight of him?

10: None is so fierce that dare stir him up: who then is able to stand before me?
11: Who hath prevented me, that I should repay him? Whatsoever is under the whole heaven is mine.
12: I will not conceal his parts, nor his power, nor his comely proportion.
13: Who can discover the face of his garment? Or who can come to him with his double bridle?
14: Who can open the doors of his face? His teeth are terrible round about.
15: His scales are his pride, shut up together as with a close seal.
16: One is so near to another, that no air can come between them.
17: They are joined one to another, they stick together, that they cannot be sundered.
18: By his neesings a light doth shine, and his eyes are like the eyelids of the morning.
19: Out of his mouth go burning lamps, and sparks of fire leap out.
20: Out of his nostrils goes smoke, as out of a seething pot or caldron.
21: His breath kindles coals, and a flame goes out of his mouth.
22: In his neck remains strength, and sorrow is turned into joy before him.
23: The flakes of his flesh are joined together: they are firm in themselves; they cannot be moved.
24: His heart is as firm as a stone; yea, as hard as a piece of the nether millstone.
25: When he raises up himself, the mighty are afraid: by reason of breakings they purify themselves.
26: The sword of him that lays at him cannot hold: the spear, the dart, nor the habergeon.
27: He esteems iron as straw, and brass as rotten wood.
28: The arrow cannot make him flee: slingstones are turned with him into stubble.

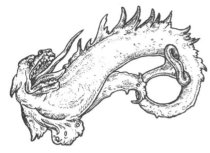

29: Darts are counted as stubble: he laughs at the shaking of a spear.
30: Sharp stones are under him: he spreads sharp pointed things upon the mire.
31: He makes the deep to boil like a pot: he makes the sea like a pot of ointment.
32: He makes a path to shine after him; one would think the deep to be hoary.
33: Upon earth there is not his like, who is made without fear.
34: He beholds all high things: he is a king over all the children of pride.

LION LORE The lion has always been regarded as 'the king of the beasts', and thus is usually the first animal described in the medieval bestiaries. Lions were native to Ancient Greece itself, as well as to Asia Minor, the Middle East and North Africa. In the sixth century BCE, one of Aesop's most famous fables concerns the lion: *'The lion was complaining to Prometheus that while the god had made him big and strong, he was still afraid of the cockerel. The lion felt foolish because of this lack of courage. He went to talk to the elephant, and found him being tormented by a gnat. When the lion asked him about his trouble, the elephant said that he was afraid of the gnat, because if it got into his ear he would surely die. The lion, hearing that, felt much better about his own courage, since a cockerel is much more frightening than a gnat.'...'An ass and a cockerel were together* one day, when a lion attacked the ass. The cockerel began to crow, and the lion ran away, since lions are afraid of the crowing of the cockerel. The ass, believing the lion was fleeing through fear of him, gave chase, but as soon as the lion was far enough from the cockerel so that its crowing could not be heard, he stopped running and killed the ass.' Herodotus in the fifth century BCE recorded: *'The lioness, on the other hand, which is one of the strongest and boldest of brutes, brings forth young but once in her lifetime, and then a single cub; she cannot possibly conceive again, since she loses her womb at the same time that she drops her young. The reason of this is that as soon as the cub begins to stir inside the dam, his claws, which are sharper than those of any other animal, scratch the womb; as the time goes on, and he grows bigger, he tears it ever more and more; so that at last, when the birth comes, there is not a morsel in the whole womb that is sound.'*

Pliny the Elder noted in his *Natural History* (first century CE) the belief that the lioness only gave birth once, because her womb is injured by the claws of the cub, but he refuted it: *'The lioness bears five cubs the first year, four the next, and one less each following year, until she becomes barren after the fifth year. The cubs are born as mere lumps of flesh the size of weasels, do not move at all in their first two months of life, and cannot walk until six months old. Lions are found in Europe only between the rivers Achelous and Mestus; these lions are stronger than those of Syria and Africa. There are two kinds of lions: a timid kind, with curly manes; and a long-haired kind that is bold. They drink infrequently, and eat only every other day, sometimes fasting for three days after a large meal. If a lion* eats too much, it will reach down its throat with its claws and pull out the meat from its stomach. The lion is the only animal that spares people who prostrate themselves before it. When angry it attacks men, not women, and only attacks children when extremely hungry. A lion's greatest strength is in its chest, and its blood is black. When a mother lion is defending her cub from hunters, she looks at the ground so as not to be intimidated by the sight of the hunter's spears. Lions are frightened by turning wheels, empty chariots, crowing cocks, and fire. A lion which has lost its appetite for food can cure itself by tasting the blood of a monkey… Lions produce young that are unfinished at birth, and shape them by licking them. In this they are like bears and foxes… The lion's breath contains a severe poison.'

Isidore of Seville tells us: 'The lion is the king of all beasts, thus its name in Greek means "king" in Latin. The kind of lion with a curly mane is weak, but the ones with straight hair are larger and more violent. Their courage is seen in their front and tail; their endurance is in the head; and their strength is in the chest. If they are surrounded by hunters with spears, they look at the ground so as not to become frightened. They are afraid of the sound of wheels but even more so of fire. They sleep with their eyes open. When lions walk, they erase their tracks with their tail so hunters cannot follow them. When they give birth to a cub, it is thought to sleep for three days and nights, until the place where it sleeps is shaken by the roar of the father, which wakes it. Lions can fight with their claws and their teeth even while they are cubs. Lions will only attack a man when they are extremely hungry; otherwise they are so gentle that they cannot be provoked unless they are struck. They spare anyone who prostrates himself and allow captives to return home.'

Guillaume le Clerc's 13th-century verse bestiary entitled *Bestiaire* informs us: 'It is proper that we should first speak of the

Lizard Blindness Cure

Isidore of Seville recounted in the seventh century CE: 'The lizard (lacertus) is so called because it has arms. As it ages it goes blind; as a cure it goes to an opening in a wall that faces east and looks at the sun, and gets light.'

nature of the lion, which is a fierce and proud beast and very bold. It has three especially peculiar characteristics. In the first place it always dwells upon a high mountain. From afar off it can scent the hunter who is pursuing it. And in order that the latter may not follow it to its lair it covers over its tracks by means of its tail. Another wonderful peculiarity of the lion is that when it sleeps its eyes are wide open, and clear and bright. The third characteristic is likewise very strange. For when the lioness brings forth her young, it falls to the ground, and gives no sign of life until the third day, when the lion breathes upon it and in this way brings it back to life again.' The lion is one of the most popular animals in heraldry, representing nobility and bravery for it will only attack if attacked, or in great need of food. It is most often depicted *rampant* (standing upright on its hind legs, with its fore legs, claws extended, held in front of its chest), but sometimes *passant* (standing on all four feet or lying down).

LOCH NESS MONSTER Loch Ness is the most voluminous freshwater lake in Great Britain. The earliest account of its monster comes from the seventh-century *Life of Saint Columba* by the abbot of Iona, Adomnán. It describes how the missionary Irish monk was staying in the land of the Picts when he came across the burial of a man near the River

Ness. Locals explained that the man had been swimming in the river when he was attacked by a 'water beast' that had dragged him under. They tried to rescue him in a boat, but were able only to drag up his mauled corpse. Hearing this, Columba stunned the Picts by sending his follower Luigne moccu Min to swim across the river. The animal came after him, but Columba made the sign of the Cross and commanded: 'Go no further. Do not touch the man. Go back at once.' The monster halted as if it had been 'pulled back with ropes' and fled. Columba's companions and the pagan Picts praised God for the miracle.

The term 'monster' was supposedly used for the first time on 2 May 1933 by Alex Campbell, the water bailiff for Loch Ness, in a report in the *Inverness Courier*. However, worldwide interest was stimulated after a 22 July 1933 sighting, when Londoner George Spicer and his wife saw '*a most extraordinary form of animal*' cross the road in front of their car. They described the creature as having a large body (about 4 feet [1.2 m] high and 25 feet [7.6 m] long), and long, narrow neck, slightly thicker than an elephant's trunk and as long as the 10 to 12 feet (3 to 3.7 m) width of the road; the neck had a number of undulations in it. They saw no limbs because a dip in the road obscured the animal's lower portion.

Nessie and an Anagram

The late naturalist and artist Sir Peter Scott was a great believer in the Loch Ness monster, so much so that he coined a new scientific Latin name for it, *Nessiteras rhombopteryx*, meaning something like 'the inhabitant of Ness with the diamond-shaped fins'. He was very pleased with the name he had invented, until the politician Nicholas Fairbairn pointed out that an anagram of it is '*Monster hoax by Sir Peter S*'.

It lurched across the road towards the loch some 20 yards (18 m)away, leaving only a trail of broken undergrowth in its wake. On 4 August 1933, the *Inverness Courier* published this as a full news story claiming that Spicer and his wife, while motoring around the loch, had seen '*the nearest approach to a dragon or pre-historic animal that I have ever seen in my life*', carrying '*an animal*' in its mouth. Many other letters followed reporting claimed sightings, speaking of a 'dragon', 'sea serpent' or 'monster fish'. On 6 December 1933 the first purported photograph of the monster, taken by Hugh Gray, was published, and shortly after the secretary of state for Scotland ordered the police to prevent any attacks on it. In 1934 came the famous 'surgeon's photograph' showing a head and neck emerging from the water. It has since proved to be a hoax. In 1938, Inverness Chief Constable William Fraser penned a letter stating that it was beyond doubt the monster existed. His letter expressed concern regarding a

hunting party that had arrived armed with a specially-made harpoon gun that was determined to catch the monster 'dead or alive'. He believed his power to protect the monster from the hunters was 'very doubtful'. The letter was released by the National Archives of Scotland on 27 April 2010. There have been other sightings but no concrete evidence of anything untoward living in the loch. The belief that it may be a plesiosaur that survived the extinction of the rest of the dinosaur population is not tenable. It may be a seal or even just wave movement. Modern technology has been harnessed in several expeditions, but all to no avail.

LYNX AND THE PRECIOUS URINE The Greek philosopher Theophrastus in the fourth century BCE wrote in his treatise *On Stones*: '[Lapis lyncurius – the stone created by a lynx's hardened urine] *has the power of attraction, just as amber has, and some say that it not only attracts straws and bits of wood, but also copper and iron, if the pieces are thin, as Diokles used to explain. It is cold and very transparent, and it is better when it comes from wild animals rather than tame ones and from males rather than females; for there is a difference in their*

food, in the exercise they take or fail to take, and in general in the nature of their bodies, so that one is drier and the other more moist. Those who are experienced find the stone by digging it up; for when the animal makes water, it conceals this by heaping earth on top.' In the first century CE, Ovid repeated the claim: '*Vanquished India gave lynxes to Bacchus of the clustered vines, and they say that whatever their bladder emits, changes to stone, and solidifies on contact with air.*' Pliny tells us, in the same century: '*The lynx, which has the shape of a wolf and leopard's spots, was first displayed in the games of Pompey the Great* [55 BCE]*... Ethiopia produces lynxes in great numbers... The urine of lynxes solidifies into drops like carbuncles, coloured*

like flame; this substance is called "lynx-water" (lyncuriam)*. Lynxes know that this happens, so they cover their urine with earth to make it solidify more quickly.*'

THE MAMMOTH OF THE SOUTH AMERICAN RAINFOREST This author had the great pleasure of receiving the Everett Helm Visiting Fellowship Award of Indiana University, in order that he could transcribe *The Journal of Llewellin Penrose – Seaman*. It is a factional story of William Williams's marooning among the Rama Indians of the Nicaraguan coast in the 1760s. It was published as *The First American Novel: The Journal of Penrose, Seaman by William Williams, & The Book, the Author and the Letters in the Lilly Library* (2007). Apart from describing some species of flora and fauna for the first time, and discovering hieroglyphics inscribed upon basalt columns 200 years before they were rediscovered, he wrote the following remarkable passages: '*One day this year, being out about half a mile back from our home, I proposed for us to make our way back into the country to see what we could discover, and on the next day we armed ourselves for the purpose. For some time our passage proved exceedingly*

hard and difficult. At length we made our way so far that we came to an opening of the ground well grown with fine lofty trees, and after that to a bare country. There we spied three deer running swiftly; and our dogs put after them but soon lost them. We then came to a place where there was a kind of morass, on the other side of which was to be seen a long range of broken banks. Here we saw multitudes of wild parrots flying over our heads.

Now, as the scene was quite new to us, we were the more curious, and Somer observed at the foot of the bank a monstrous skull of some beast or other. It was as much as he could lift. The jaw teeth were many of them but still in the head, quite sound, but could be drawn out easily. Going a little further on, I pulled out of the bank a rib of monstrous size. We then found more bones pertaining to the same kind of beast. Now what species of animal it could be I knew not, but Somer insisted it must have been an elephant, having seen one, but I never had. However, we came off with three of the teeth, and we also found that all the bits of wood, or sticks that had fallen into this water were petrified. We then decided to mount the bank, from whence we could see far around us. After we had so far satisfied our curiosity, we returned. When we got home a council was held again about the teeth, but all were ignorant. Only Harry had heard the old folks say that they had found such when hunting. And thus it rested, nor could we make any more of the matter…

I then took the opportunity to ask Owagamy his opinion concerning the teeth that we had found. After the Indians had handed them from one to the other, and conferred notes together in their tongue, Owagamy told Harry that both he and his father had seen them, and that they knew of a deep valley wherein there were many of them, but it was far to the south. He said that he could never learn if any of their old people had seen one of those animals alive, saying they knew those creatures had long white horns as long as an Indian, for some old people related that they had seen them – instancing old Wariboon, a great hunter, who had kept one of them a long time by him, but as they lived a great distance from him they had never seen it.

Upon this, an Indian whose name was Kayoota, and present at the time said his father had seen it so many times – holding up his fingers; from all we gathered the beast then talked of must have been an elephant, and that those horns he mentioned came with the teeth of the animal. But how the whole race became extirpated remained to us a riddle unless the natives, in time out of mind, had unanimously joined to destroy them. Yet one should imagine that the task was of such a copious undertaking that they could never have succeeded. As the continent being so extensive, all the natives could never have joined by mutual consent as they were separated thousands of miles asunder, and quite unintelligent of each others' existence. But I leave it to the learned to put what constructions on this great mystery they think proper.

These prehistoric mammoth bones must have been recently washed out of the bank by Nicaragua's torrential rains. This is the first record by a writer of such a discovery in the Americas, but mammoths ranged the American continent as far south as Nicaragua. Importantly, an American team has just discovered the skeletal remains of a mammoth near Santa Isabel, halfway between Lake Maracaibo and the Pacific coast. It is estimated that about 10,000 years ago they migrated from North to South America, so Williams is right that they were in this area. If his Indian sources were correct, it means that they lingered in Nicaragua long after their supposed extinction.

The hunter Wariboon is mentioned as having kept a tusk of a mammoth. If Kayatoo's father had seen a mammoth, there may well have been a remnant mammoth population in the rainforest. In 2009, the journal *Science* claimed '*diamond proof*' that a massive comet struck the atmosphere somewhere above North America in 11,000 BCE, raining down fire and death. It made extinct the early Paleo-Americans (also known as Clovis people), the American lion, sabre-toothed cat, American camel, the ground sloth, short-faced bear, mastodon and woolly mammoth. The last mammoths in the Siberian turndra died out about 3600 years ago, and with the summer melting of the tundra, people are now finding tons of mammoth ivory. It is reported that Michelle Obama wears jewellery made from mammoth tusk ivory. Sadly, illegally poached elephant ivory is being passed off as legal mammoth ivory, and elephants from both Africa and Asia are still being slaughtered for their tusks.

MANDRAKE - THE HUMANOID PLANT This is the most magical plant in history, the Mandragora, also called Mandragloire. It is a plant with human-shaped roots, which shrieks when it is pulled from the earth. It was used in medicine, but anyone who heard the plant's cry died or went mad. Therefore a starving dog was tied to the plant, with a tempting piece of meat dangled beyond its reach. To get at the meat, the dog tugged at the cord and dragged up the plant. It was said to grow in the East, near Paradise. In order to conceive, the female elephant had to eat some mandrake root. In the British Library, the 12th-century herbal that is identified as Harley MS 4986 states: '*If you want to gather the mandrake because of its great health-giving qualities, you shall gather it in this way. It shines at night like a lamp, and when you see it mark it round quickly with iron less it escape you. For so strong is this power in it, that if it sees an unclean man coming to it, it runs away. So for this reason mark it round with iron and dig about it, taking care that you do not touch it with the iron; but remove the earth from it with the utmost care with an ivory stake, and when you have seen the foot of the plant and its hands, then you shall at once bind the plant with a new rope,*

ΛΑϹ ΜΑΝΔΡΑΓΟΡΑ ΑΡΓϹ Λ ΙΑΝΔΡΑΓΟΡΑΘΗΛ

and you shall tie the same round the neck of a hungry dog, and in front of it place food at a little distance, so that in its eagerness to get the food it may pull out the plant. Again you may get it out in another way. Make an apparatus like a mangonel instead and fix in it a tall rod, to the top of which you shall tie a new rope to which also the plant is tied; and you shall make it work as a kind of mousetrap from a distance, when the rod springing back pulls out the plant by its own force. And when you have got it unbroken in your hands, presently store the juice of the leaves in a glass jar, and so will you keep it as a remedy for human beings.'

There are six cures described in this herbal, the first being for a headache which prevents sleep. For this a salve is made with the juice and applied to the forehead as a plaster, 'when the pain in the head is soon relieved, and sleep will come again quickly'. The second cure is for pain in the ears. The juice must be mixed with oil of nard and the mixture poured into the ears, 'when the patient will be cured with wonderful quickness'. The third is for a severe attack of gout. You take a scruple each of the right hand and the right foot of the mandrake and grind it to powder, and administer in wine for seven days, when the patient will be quickly cured. It causes not only the swelling but also the contraction of the muscles to recover themselves, and so 'both these troubles are cured in a wonderful way as has been proved by the author's experiments'. The fourth cure is for epileptics, for persons who have fallen in fits or who suffer from spasms. One scruple of the body of the plant is

ground up and given to the patient in hot water, 'as full as the vessel can hold, and immediately he will be cured'. The fifth is for cramp and contraction of the muscles. 'Make a powder, very fine, of the body of this plant and mix it with sweet oil, and smear it upon those persons who have the troubles mentioned'. The sixth cure is used 'if a cold in the head, of a particularly virulent kind, has appeared in the house, the mandrake plant – however little they have of it inside the house – drives away all the infection'.

Pliny the Elder in his *Natural History* tells us that there were two varieties, the white mandragora which is generally thought to be the male plant, and the black, which is considered to be the female. 'It has a leaf narrower than that of the lettuce, a hairy stem, and a double or triple root, black without and white within, soft and fleshy, and nearly a cubit in length. Both kinds bear a fruit about the size of a hazel-nut... The leaves of the female plant are broader than those of the male.' In the same century (the first CE) Dioscorides described the root as a maker of love medicines. The human shape of the mandrake root is possibly the origin of the belief that the plant springs from the bodily secretions of a man hanged on a gallows. In Germany the plant was called the *Little Gallows Man*. When a hereditary thief, born of a family of thieves, or one whose mother stole while he was in her womb, was hanged on a gallows, and his semen or urine fell on the ground, the mandrake or little gallows man sprouted on the spot. Another version is that the human progenitor of the plant must be not a thief, but an innocent and chaste youth who has been forced by torture falsely to declare himself a thief and has consequently ended his days on a gallows. Mandrake is the common name for plants in the genus *Mandragora* belonging to nightshade family (Solanaceae). It contains hallucinogenic and delirium-inducing alkaloids. The roots sometimes are split causing them to resemble human figures, so the roots have long been used in magic and occult rituals. All parts of the mandrake plant *Mandragora officinarum* are poisonous. It is native to southern and central Europe and in lands around the Mediterranean. Its globular red berries were known as 'love apples' and its Hebraic name means 'love plant'. Hebrews and Asian cultures believed that it could help barren women to conceive.

THE MANTIKHORAS (MANTICORE, BARICOS) IS A TIGER?

The name manticore was reputedly derived from a Persian word meaning man-eater, and this creature had the body of a lion, the face of a man and a spike-tipped arrow-shooting tail. In the fourth century BCE, the Greek historian Ctesias related: '*The Martikhora is an animal found in this country* [India]. *It has a face like a man's, a skin red as cinnabar, and is as large as a lion. It has three rows of teeth, ears and light-blue eyes like those of a man; its tail is like that of a land scorpion, containing a sting more than a cubit long at the end. It has other stings on each side of its tail and one on the top of its head, like the scorpion, with which it inflicts a wound that is always fatal. If it is attacked from a distance, it sets up its tail in front and discharges its stings as if from a bow; if attacked from behind, it straightens it out and launches its stings in a direct line to the distance of a hundred feet. The wound inflicted is fatal to all animals except the elephant. The stings are about a foot long and about as thick as a small rush. The Martikhora is called in Greek Anthropophagos* [man-eater], *because, although it preys upon other animals, it kills and devours a greater number of human beings. It fights with both its claws and stings, which, according to Ktesias, grow again after they have been discharged. There is a great number of these animals in India, which are hunted and killed with spears or arrows by natives mounted on elephants.*' However, Pausanias in the second century CE tells us: '*The beast described by Ktesias in his Indian history, which he say is called Mantikhoras by the Indians and man-eater by the Greeks, I am inclined to think is the tiger. But that it has three rows of teeth along each jaw and spikes at the tip of its tail with which it defends itself at close quarters, while it hurls them like an archer's arrows at more distant enemies.*' The Roman author Aelian noted that '*the Indians hunt the young of these animals while they are still without stings in their tails, which they then crush with a stone to prevent them from growing stings. The sound of their voice is as near as possible that of a trumpet.*' The shape of the manticore in illustrations varies, but they can be readily identified by their human faces. The Caucasian or Hyrcanian tiger was the third largest of the living types of tiger, after the Siberian and Bengal tigers. It was found throughout Afghanistan, Turkey, Mongolia, Iran, northern Iraq and Russia. The Red Army was ordered to kill all tigers around the Caspian Sea, and by their extreme efficiency all Caucasian tigers were extinct by 1959.

MONOCERUS - THE UNICORN?

A fierce beast with a single long horn, this may be modelled on the rhinoceros. Pliny does not distinguish between the monocerus and the unicorn, but some consider them to be different beasts, with the monocerus described as having the head of a stag, the body of a horse, the feet of an elephant, the tail of a boar, and a single very long black horn growing from its forehead. It makes deep lowing sounds, is the enemy of the elephant, and when fighting it aims at the belly of its opponent.

Martlet – the Bird With No Feet

A *martlet* has tufted feathers instead of feet, and a *merletten* has no feet or beak in heraldic designs. These birds, like swifts, were believed never to land. Stories were told of them by Crusaders returning from the Holy Land. The martlet was given as an heraldic charge to younger sons of the English nobility as a reminder to '*trust to the wings of virtue and merit, and not to their legs, having no land of their own to put their feet on.*' Martlet is the diminutive of martin, but swifts were also called martlets. They have such short legs that they were believed to have none at all. The heraldic device must be based upon some kind of swift, which finds it difficult to take off if it lands on the ground, and consequently spend most of its time in the skies. Swifts never settle voluntarily on the ground, perching instead on vertical surfaces. There are several species of swift, and they are among the fastest fliers. In a single year the common swift can cover at least 125,000 miles (200,000 km) in the course of its migration.

MORAG - SCOTLAND'S NUMBER TWO MONSTER

Morag or Mòrag is the best known loch monster in Scotland after 'Nessie', and it reputedly lives in Loch Morar. There have been more than 30 sightings since 1887, 16 of which involved multiple witnesses. In 1948 *'a peculiar serpent-like creature about 20 feet long'* was reported by nine people in a boat, in the same place as the 1887 sighting took place. In 1969, Duncan McDonnel and William Simpson, in a speedboat, accidentally struck the creature, and it hit back at them. McDonnel retaliated with an oar, and Simpson opened fire with his rifle, whereupon it sank slowly out of sight. They described it as being brown, 25–30 feet (7.6 to 9.1 m) long, and with rough skin. It had three humps rising 18 inches (46 cm) above the lake's surface, and a head a foot (30 cm) wide, held 18 inches (46 cm) out of the water. As with Nessie, there seems little logical explanation of the sightings and the evidence for its existence remains anecdotal.

THE MOTHMAN

Mothman is the name given to a strange creature reported in the Charleston and Point Pleasant areas of West Virginia between November 1966 and December 1967. The creature was sporadically reported to have been seen before and after those dates, with some sightings occurring as recently as 2007. Most observers described the Mothman as a winged man-sized creature with large reflective red eyes. It often appeared to have no head, with its eyes set into its chest. The Mothman was first spotted in 1926 by a young boy. At the same time three men were digging a grave in a nearby graveyard when they saw a brown human shape with wings soaring out from behind trees. Both incidents were reported independently of each other. There have been numerous sightings of Mothman, though no photographic evidence exists.

MOUSE PROCREATION

Pliny the Elder writes in his *Natural History*: *'Some kinds of mice gnaw at iron by instinct; in the country of the Chalybes they also gnaw at gold in mines, and when their bellies are cut open stolen gold is always found. The appearance of white mice is a good omen. Shrew-mice do not associate with mice from another forest, but fight with them to the death. When their parents are old, they feed them with remarkable affection. Mice hibernate in winter; this is the time when the old ones die… Mice are the most prolific of animals; they conceive by licking rather than by coupling, or by tasting salt. The mice in Egypt walk on two feet, as do the Alpine mice.'* Isidore of Seville expands thus: *'The mouse is a small animal; some say it is born from earth. A mouse's liver gets larger at the time of the full moon… Dormice sleep all winter, remaining motionless as though dead, but revive in the summer.'*

OXEN CAN PREDICT THE WEATHER

Sacred in some cultures, early authorities thought that oxen could predict the weather, refusing to leave their stalls when they knew it was about to rain. An ox wanted to be with its usual partner when pulling a plough, and would roar if separated. In India there lived a particularly cruel type of ox with one horn, that could not be tamed. Isidore of Seville noted that '*the dung of an ox cures the bite of a water snake called hydros*'. Pliny the Elder related in *Natural History*: '*Indian oxen are said to be as tall as camels and to have horns up to four feet wide. Among the Garamantes oxen only graze while walking backwards. A tale is told of an ox that is worshipped as a god in Egypt.*'

PANTHER – THE SWEET-SMELLING ENEMY OF THE DRAGON

Pliny the Elder relates in Book 8 of his *Natural History*: '*Panthers are light-coloured but have small spots like eyes. Their wonderful smell attracts all four-footed creatures, but the savagery of their heads frightens the creatures away. Therefore, to catch prey, panthers hide their heads as their smell attracts the prey animals within reach. Some people say that panthers have a mark on their shoulder that resembles a crescent moon. Panthers occur most frequently in Africa and Syria.*' Isidore of Seville noted: '*The panther (pantera) takes its name from the Greek word for "all" (pan), because the panther is the friend of all beasts other than the dragon. They are covered with black and white circles that look like eyes. Female panthers can only give birth once, because the cubs, in their eagerness to escape the womb, tear at their mother with their claws so she can no longer conceive.*' Philip de Thaun's *Bestiaire* of around 1121 states: '*That is a curious beast, wonderously beautiful, of every hue such men tell, persons of Holy Spirit, that Joseph's tunic was of every tinge in colours varying, of which each more bright, each more exquisite than other shone to the sons of men. Thus this beasts hue, pale, of every change, brighter and fairer wonderously shines; so that more curious than every other yet more unique and fairer it exquisitely glistens ever more excellent. When the bold animal rises up gloriously endowed on the third day suddenly from sleep a sound comes of voices sweetest, through the wild beasts mouth; after the voice an odour comes out from the plain a steam more grateful, sweeter and stronger than every perfume, than blooms of plants and forest leaves, nobler than all earths ornaments.*'

In Christian allegory, the panther represents Christ, who drew all mankind to him. The dragon represents the devil,

who feared Christ and hid from him. The many colours of the panther symbolize the many qualities of Christ. After Christ was sated with mockery and abuse, he fell asleep in death and entered the tomb. Descending into hell he bound the dragon. After three days Christ left the tomb and roared out his triumph over death. The sweet breath of the panther that drew all animals to it is a symbol of the words of Christ that draw all to him, Jews and Gentiles alike.

THE PYGMAEI or PYGMIES

They were described as tiny, black-skinned men who grew to a height of one 'pugmê' tall, a pugmê being the length from a man's elbow to his knuckle bone (about 18 inches/46 cm). The pygmies were variously located by the ancients in India and subSaharan Africa, two regions which were believed to lie in the farthest south along the shore of the great Earth-encircling River Okeanos, the 'Ocean-stream'. Pygmies, according to Homer's *Iliad*, had every spring to sustain a war against the cranes on the banks of Oceanus. '*The clamour of cranes goes high to the heavens, when the cranes escape the winter time and the rains unceasing and clamorously wing their way to streaming Okeanos, bringing the Pygmaioi men bloodshed and destruction: at daybreak they bring on the baleful battle against them.*' Later writers usually situate them near the sources of the Nile, whither the cranes are said to have migrated every year to take possession of the fields of the pygmies. When Heracles came into their country, they climbed with ladders to the edge of his goblet to drink from it; and when they attacked the hero, a whole army of them made an assault

upon his left hand, while two others made the attack on his right hand. Aristotle did not believe these fabled accounts of the pygmies, but thought that they were a tribe living in Upper Egypt, who had exceedingly small horses, and lived in caves. We also have mention of Indian pygmies, who lived under the earth on the east of the River Ganges. The name first appears in Homer. Pygmy is a term now used for various ethnic groups worldwide whose average height is unusually low. It is defined as any group whose adult men grow to less than 4 feet 11 inches (1.5 m) in average height. The best-known groups of pygmies are in Central Africa. The story of Indian pygmies may have a basis of truth. It was only in the 20th century that reports emerged of a tribe of pygmy Tibeto-Burman speakers, the T'rung, in Southeast Asia, on the borders of India, Tibet and Burma. Only a few individuals now survive.

QUAILS AS SHIP-SINKERS In the

first century CE Pliny the Elder wrote: '*Quails prefer to remain on the ground, though they arrive on migration by flying. They are sometimes a danger to sailors; arriving near land at night, they land on the sails of ships and cause them to sink. As protection against hawks, quails try to obtain an escort of other birds, including the tongue-bird [glottis], eared owl [otus] and ortolan [cychramus]. When they fly they prefer a north wind to carry them, since they are weak and become tired; this fatigue is why they give a mournful cry while flying. If they encounter a wind blowing against them, quails pick up small stones or fill their throats with sand to serve as ballast. Quails like to eat poison seeds; for this reason quails are not eaten. This bird is the only creature other than man to have epilepsy, so as a charm against the illness it is customary to spit at the sight of the bird.'* Isidore of Seville agreed: *'The quail [coturnices] is named from the sound of its voice. The Greeks, having first seen them on the island of Ortygia, call them ortugai. They cross the sea at a fixed time. The quail [ortygometra] is so named because it leads the flock. When a hawk sees the first one coming toward land it siezes it, so they try to get an escort of a different kind of bird to avoid being first. They like to eat poison seed, so the ancients said they could not be eaten.'* The

Greeks called the quail *ortygas* because they were first found on the island of Ortygia (Delos). Thus the leader of the quail flock is ortygometra, or 'mother of quails'. Quails seek a leader from another species of bird, because when the leading ortygometra is near the ground, it is often attacked by a hawk.

RAVEN The largest of the crow family, the black raven features throughout history as an intelligent bird. Pliny the Elder related: *'When raven chicks are strong enough to fly, their parents drive them far away from the nest, so that in small villages there are never more than two pairs of ravens. Ravens experience 60 days of poor health due primarily to thirst, before the figs ripen in autumn. Some say that ravens mate or lay eggs through the beak, and as a consequence if a pregnant women eats raven eggs or has such eggs in the house, she will experience a difficult birth; but Aristotle says this is not true. Ravens are the only birds that understand the meaning they convey in auspices, and it is a particularly bad sign*

Ram

Pliny the Elder tells us: *'The wildness of rams can be curbed by drilling a hole in the horn near the ear. Female sheep will be produced if a string is tied around the right testicle of the ram; if put on the left, males will be produced.'*

if a raven gulps down its croak as though it was choking... When Tiberius was emperor, there was a raven in Rome that always greeted him by name. Another raven was seen dropping stones into an urn of water, causing the water to rise high enough for it to drink.'

Bartholomaeus Anglicus wrote: '*The raven beholds the mouths of her birds when they yawn. But she giveth them no meat ere she knows and sees the likeness of her own blackness, and of her own colour and feathers. And when they begin to wax black, then afterward she feeds them with all her might and strength. It is said that ravens' birds are fed with dew of heaven all the time that they have no black feathers by benefit of age. Among fowls, only the raven has four and sixty changings of voice.'* Like most carrion eaters, when it comes across a corpse, the raven first pecks out the eyes so that it can feed on the nutritious brain. The allegory is that as the raven first pecks out the eyes, so the devil first destroys the ability to judge correctly, leaving the mind open to attack. As the raven will not feed its chicks until it recognizes them as its own, so the teacher should not tell his students of the inner mysteries until he recognizes that they are ready to receive them, when they have grown dark with repentance.

ROC - BIRD OF THE SUN The
origin of the myth of the roc may stem from eyewitness reports of the power of an eagle that could carry away a newborn lamb. It is possible, however, that the myth originated from accounts of an actual huge bird, perhaps the enormous *Aepyornis* or *elephant bird* of Madagascar, an extinct 10-feet (3-m) tall flightless

bird. Its eggs were 3 feet (90 cm) in circumference and it only went extinct in the 17th century. Another theory is that the existence of rocs was postulated from the sight of an ostrich, which because of its flightlessness and unusual appearance, was mistaken for the chick of a much larger species. Yet another theory suggests that the roc was inspired by a bird-like form seen within the Sun's corona during some total solar eclipses. Perhaps this gigantic coronal 'Bird of the Sun' is the source of inspiration for the phoenix and other mythical birds that are closely associated with the Sun. The total solar eclipse theory is supported by the fact that the roc is described as being white (the colour of the Sun's corona) and is described in the *Arabian Nights* as, '*A bird of enormous size, bulky body* [possibly the darkened moon] *and wide wings* [possibly the corona's equatorial streamers], *flying in the air; and it was this that concealed the body of the sun and veiled it from the sun* [causing a total solar eclipse].'

Through the 16th century the existence of the roc was accepted as fact by Europeans. In 1604 the poet Michael Drayton envisaged the rocs being taken aboard the Ark:

'*All feathered things yet ever knowne to men,*
From the huge Rucke, unto the little Wren;
From Forrest, Fields, from Rivers and from
*   Pons,*
All that have webs, or cloven-footed ones;
To the Grand Arke, together friendly came,
Whose severall species were too long to
*   name.'*

The Salamander and the Goldsmith

This extract is from the *Life of Benvenuto Cellini* (1500–71), the autobiography of the superb Italian sculptor and goldsmith: '*When I was about five years of age, my father, happening to be in a little room in which they had been washing, and where there was a good fire of oak burning, looked into the flames and saw a little animal resembling a lizard, which could live in the hottest part of that element. Instantly perceiving what it was, he called for my sister and me, and after he had shown us the creature, he gave me a box on the ear. I fell a-crying, while he, soothing me with caresses, spoke these words: "My dear child, I do not give you that blow for any fault you have committed, but that you may recollect that the little creature you see in the fire is a salamander; such a one as never was beheld before to my knowledge." So saying he embraced me, and gave me some money.*' There are 500 species of the amphibians known as salamanders. Many salamanders tend to dwell inside rotting logs. When placed into a fire, the salamander would attempt to escape from the log leading to the belief that salamanders were created from flames.

SNAKES FLEE FROM NAKED MEN

There are thousands of tales across the world involving snakes and serpents, many involved with Creation myths. The following are examples of some of them. When a snake grows old, it begins to lose its sight, which it can regain by eating fennel. To renew its youth, it fasts until its skin becomes loose, then it crawls through a narrow crack and sheds its old skin. When a snake goes to a river to drink, it spits its venom into a hole and retrieves it later. Snakes attack clothed men but flee from naked men. If a snake is attacked, it will protect its head. A snake that tastes the spit of a fasting man dies. It is the enemy of the mongoose, the stork and the stag, and the smoke from burning stag antlers is deadly to snakes.

THE SPHINXES AITHIOPIKOI – HALF WOMAN, HALF LION

These were a legendary breed of half-lion, half-woman creatures native to Ethiopia (subSaharan Africa). They are cited in Pliny the Elder's *Natural History* and probably derived from travellers' accounts of a species of African baboon, just as the Onokentaura probably derives from a description of a chimpanzee.

SPIDER RAIN-MAKERS

Like snakes, it was said that if the spider tasted the saliva of a fasting man, it died. Pliny the Elder recounted: '*Forecasts are made by observing spiders: when spiders weave many webs it is a sign of rain, and when rivers are going to rise spiders raise their webs higher. It is said that the female weaves and the male hunts, thus fairly dividing their labour.*'

STORKS - BILL RATTLERS

Pliny the Elder related how: '*Storks use the herb marjoram as a drug when they are sick. No one knows where storks go or where they come from during migration; they depart and arrive only at night. When they are preparing to leave they all gather at a fixed place and depart together as if the appropriate date was fixed in advance. Some say storks have no tongue. They are highly valued in some places for their ability to kill snakes. Storks return to the same nest each year, and care for their parents in their old age.*' Isidore of Seville tells us: '*Storks [ciconiae] are named after the noise they make, which is not from their voice but from the rattling of their beaks. Storks are the heralds of spring, the enemies of snakes and the companions of society. They fly in line across seas to Asia, preceded by two crows who they follow like an army. They take extraordinary care of their young, even to the extent of losing their feathers through constant brooding; but later their young feed them for as long as they spent raising their children.*'

SWALLOW OCULISTS

According to Pliny the Elder in his *Natural History*: '*Swallows use the herb celandine to treat the sore eyes of their chicks… Swallows do not go far when they migrate, but only to sunny valleys in the mountains. They will not enter the city of Thebes because it has been captured so often. It is known that swallows always return to the same nest; this trait has allowed them to be used as messengers. The swallow has a swift and swerving flight, and only feeds while in the air… Swallows build their nests from straw and clay; if there is a lack of clay, they wet their wings with water and sprinkle it on dust. The parents apportion food to their young with great fairness, and keep the nest clean. There is a kind of swallow that nests in holes in river banks* [the sand martin]; *if the river rises and threatens the nests, the swallows leave many days in advance. The chicks of this kind of swallow, when burned to ash, make a medicine for a deadly throat illness.*'

TIGERS WITH SPOTS

In his Etymologies Isidore of Seville related: '*The tiger [tigris] has its name after the word the Persians and Medes use for "arrow", because tigers are so fast. The Tigris River is named after the tiger because it is the fastest of all rivers. Tigers have many spots and are admired for their strength and speed. Most tigers live in Hyrcania… In India female dogs are tied up in the forest at night, where wild tigers mate with them; dogs born in this way are fierce and can overcome lions.*'

UCU - THE BIGFOOT OF SOUTH AMERICA The Ucu, sometimes called Ucumar or Ukumar-zupai, is a reported Bigfoot-like creature thought to live in the mountainous regions in and around Chile and Argentina. The Ucu is described as the size of a large dog and walking erect; it is also thought to prefer the more tropical regions of the Andes mountain range. According to natives, the Ucu likes to eat payo, a plant with an inside similar to cabbage, and emits a sound like *uhu, uhu, uhu*, which the naturalist and cryptozoologist Ivan T. Sanderson compared to the noises reported by Albert Ostman, who claimed to have been held captive by a family of Sasquatch in 1924.

UNICORN The word is based on the Hebrew word *re'em* (horn), which in early versions of the Old Testament was translated as 'monokeros', meaning 'one horn', which then became 'unicorn' in English. The creature is possibly based on the rhinoceros or the narwhal, the whale with one horn. In 398 BCE the Greek historian Ctesias wrote that unicorns lived in India, describing them as *'wild asses which are as big as a horse, even bigger. Their bodies are white, their heads dark red and their eyes are deep blue. They have a single horn on their forehead which is approximately half-a-metre long.'* This description seems to combine a mixture of an Indian rhinoceros, a Himalayan antelope and a wild ass. Perhaps the horns of the African or Asian oryx were also an influence. The horn was believed to possess healing qualities. Dust filed from the horn was thought to protect against poison, and many diseases. It could even resurrect the dead. Among royalty and nobility in the Middle Ages, it became quite fashionable to own a drinking cup

The Hippoi Monokerata – One-horned Horses

These were the swift-footed unicorns of the East. They were magnificent snow-white horses with a single, brightly coloured horn rising from the middle of their foreheads. The Greeks also referred to them as Onoi Monokerata (One Horned Asses). Pliny the Elder describes them differently: *'the fiercest animal is the Monocerotem, which in the rest of the body resembles a horse, but in the head a stag, in the feet an elephant, and in the tail a boar, and has a deep bellow, and a single black horn three feet long projecting from the middle of the forehead. They say that it is impossible to capture this animal alive.'*

made of the horn of an unicorn, not least because it was supposed to detect poison. During the last significant cooling period between the 12th and 19th centuries ('*the Little Ice Age*'), narwhals are believed to have ranged farther south than they do now, and the last recorded sighting in British waters was in 1588. This was shortly before Queen Elizabeth I valued the gift of a narwhal horn, presented to her by the privateer and explorer Martin Frobisher, at ten times its weight in gold.

UNKNOWN SNAKES The *snow snake*, reported in native legends of eastern North America, is supposedly a very poisonous snake with pure white skin. It is alleged to spend much of its time in hiding, biting anything that approaches it. The early colonists also believed in its existence. If it does exist, this could be a pit viper of some kind, as pit vipers can survive in latitudes that other snakes would not be able to tolerate. In the same region, the *hoop snake* is alleged to stiffen its body, curve into a hoop shape, and roll down a hill when it needs to escape. In New Mexico,

Arizona and Mexico, the *pichu-cuate* was described by Charles Fletcher Lummis in his book *The King of the Broncos* a century ago. Lummis claimed that it was the only true viper in America. It was very small, being the width and length of a typical pencil and having a head smaller than a man's thumbnail. It was the most fearless, ferocious and venomous snake in North America, lead-grey on top, rosy red underneath, with a distinctly triangular head and tiny horns. Indians were said to worship rattlesnakes and have no fear of them, but were scared of the tiny pichu-cuate. This little snake may well be extinct now. There are not supposed to be any pythons in North Africa, yet people often see giant snakes in Morocco and Tunisia that can only be identified as pythons. Before the Sahara suffered desertification, pythons were present throughout Africa, but they died off as the climate changed probably leaving only a few scattered populations in small oases. *N'guma-monene* is described as a large, snake-like animal in the Congo that, while not a snake, looks like a dinosaur without any legs.

VALKYRIES - THE CHOOSERS OF THE SLAIN

In Viking mythology, valkyries are ranked as minor female deities, described as 'battle-maidens' who rode in the ranks of the gods. Their role was to choose the most heroic of those who had died in battle and to carry them off to Valhalla where they became *einherjar*. This was necessary because Odin needed warriors to fight at his side at the preordained battle at the end of the world, Ragnarök. It is now believed that the original valkyries were the priestesses of Odin who officiated at sacrificial rites in which prisoners were executed ('given to Odin'). These priestesses sometimes carried out the sacrifices themselves, which involved the use of a ritual spear.

THE VAMPIRE OF MOCA

Coinciding with a large number of cattle mutilations that occurred in the United States, in February 1975 a Puerto Rican newspaper ran one of the very first headlines concerning the wave of mysterious animal deaths that centred on the small town of Moca in Puerto Rico. 'The Moca Vampire' started killing in Barrio Rocha, Moca, where it took the lives of a number of animals in a grisly manner never seen before. Fifteen cows, three goats, two geese and a pig were found dead with bizarre perforations on their hides, suggesting that a sharp instrument had been inserted into the bodies. Autopsies showed that the animals had been thoroughly drained of blood, as if it had been consumed by some predator. On 7 March 1975, a cow belonging to Rey Jiménez was found dead in Moca's Barrio Cruz. It had deep, piercing wounds on its skull and a number of scratches around the wounds on its body. Jiménez's cow was added to the growing list of victims, which now totalled well over 30. María Acevedo, a Moca resident, claimed that a strange animal had landed on her home's zinc rooftop in the middle of the night. The animal pecked at the rooftop and at the windows before taking flight, issuing a terrifying scream. More animals were killed, and on 18 March 1975 two goats belonging to Hector Vega, a resident of Moca's Barrio Pueblo, were found drained of blood. Puncture marks on the goats' necks were the unmistakable sign of the attack. The animal returned to Vega's farm the following night to finish off ten more goats and wound another seven. Twenty years later the Chupacabra visited the same area.

THE VEGETABLE LAMB OF TARTARY

The full name for the legendary plant was '*Planta Tartarica Barometz*' – 'barometz' being the Tartar word for 'lamb'. It was believed to bear sheep as its fruit. The fruit of the *vegetable lamb* was cotton, but travellers from Europe knew nothing about cotton, so reasoned that the material must be wool. Since wool came from sheep, they thought that the plant was some kind of hybrid, and that the puffs of cotton were tiny sheep attached to the plant by their navels. It was thought that the plant bent to let the sheep graze on the grass beneath it, and that when all the grass was gone, the sheep dropped from the plant and ran off, the plant then dying. In reality, it is a species of fern *Cibetium* barometz. The 'body' of the *vegetable lamb* is the root of the plant. In another tale, on the front of John Parkinson's 17th-century manual *Paradisi in Sole*, we see a picture of 'the Vegetable Lamb'. It grew in Tartary and the seed developed into what looked like a large melon, carried on a stalk 2 feet (60 cm) above the ground. When the melon ripened and split, a creature looking like a woolly lamb appeared, which rotated around the stalk and grazed upon the grass immediately within reach. When the grass was all eaten, the vegetable lamb died.

VIPER ROMANCE The fifth-century BCE Greek historian Herodotus included this description of vipers mating in Book 3 of his *History*: '*It is found that when the male and female come together, at the very moment of impregnation, the female seizes the male by the neck, and having once fastened, cannot be brought to leave go till she has bit the neck entirely through. And so the male perishes; but after a while he is revenged upon the female by means of the young, which, while still unborn, gnaw a passage through the womb, and then through the belly of their mother, and so make their entrance into the world.*'

WEASEL - THE BASILISK KILLER Medieval bestiarists regarded the weasel a dirty animal that must not be eaten. It was held to conceive at the mouth and give birth through the ear. If the birth took place through the right ear, the offspring would be male; if it was through the left ear, a female would be born. Pliny the Elder related: '*A weasel's hole can be easily found because of the foulness of the ground around it. If a basilisk is thrown into a weasel's hole, the stench of the weasel will kill the basilisk, though the weasel will also die… If a weasel is injured in a fight with mice while hunting them, it cures itself with the herb rue.*'

WHALES AS ISLANDS Isidore of Seville noted in Book 12 of his *Etymologies*: '*Whales [ballenae] conceive through coition with the sea-mouse. Whales are immense beasts, with bodies equal to mountains. They have their name from emitting water, for the Greek ballein means emit; they raise waves higher than those of any other sea beast. They are called monsters [cete] because of their horribleness. The whale that swallowed Jonah was of such size that its belly resembled hell; as Jonah says: "He heard me from the belly of hell".*' In the 13th century Guillaume le Clerc recorded: '*In the sea, which is mighty and vast, are many kinds of fish, such as the turbot, the sturgeon, and the porpoise. But there is one monster, very treacherous and dangerous. In Latin its name is Cetus. It is a bad neighbour for sailors. The upper part*

of its back looks like sand, and when it rises from the sea, the mariners think it is an island. Deceived by its size they sail toward it for refuge, when the storm comes upon them. They cast anchor, disembark upon the back of the whale, cook their food, build a fire, and in order to fasten their boat they drive great stakes into what seems to them to be sand. When the monster feels the heat of the fire which burns upon its back, it plunges down into the depths of the sea, and drags the ship and all the people after it. When the fish is hungry it opens its mouth very wide, and breathes forth an exceedingly sweet odour. Then all the little fish stream thither, and, allured by the sweet smell, crowd into its throat. Then the whale closes its jaws and swallows them into its stomach, which is as wide as a valley.'

WILD ASS - NOT A ROLE MODEL FATHER Pliny the Elder
related, 'Each male wild ass is the lord of his own herd of females. Because he is jealous of rivals, he watches his females and castrates with a bite any male foals that are born. To prevent this, the females try to give birth in secret. The wild ass indulges in a great deal of sexual activity.' Isidore of

Seville backed up Pliny's findings: 'The wild ass is called onager because "ass" in Greek is onus and "wild" is agrion. The wild asses of Africa are large and wander in the desert. A single male is lord over a flock of females. Being jealous of newborn males, the male lord bites off their testicles; in fear of this, the females hide their young in secret places.' It was also said that upon 25 March the onager brays 12 times to signal the spring equinox. He brays both at night and during the day, and the number of brays marks the hour.

WOLVES AND WEREWOLVES
In Book 8 of his *Natural History* Pliny the Elder describes wolves: 'If a wolf looks at a man before the man sees the wolf, the man will temporarily be unable to speak. The wolves of cold regions are cruel and fierce, but those of Africa and Egypt are weak. It is not true that men can be turned into wolves and back into men (werewolves), though the Greeks believed it. If a wolf while eating looks away from its food, it forgets what it is eating and goes to look for something else. The tail of the wolf

contains a love potion in a small tuft of hair, which is only effective if the tuft is plucked from the wolf while it is still alive; for this reason a wolf when caught will shed the tuft of hair, rendering it worthless. Wolves breed only twelve days of the year. It is considered to be the finest of omens if a wolf eats large mouthfuls of earth when barring the way of travellers who come upon it on their right hand side.' In Rome, prostitutes were called she-wolves (*lupae*) because they laid waste their lover's riches.

WOODPECKER SOOTHSAYERS

Pliny the Elder tells us in Book 8 of his *Natural History*: '*Woodpeckers are used for taking auguries. Some climb straight up a tree, like a cat; others cling to the tree upside down. They can feel there is food under the bark by the sound it makes when they strike it. Woodpeckers are the only birds that raise their young in holes. A common belief has that when shepherds drive wedges into a woodpecker's hole, the birds use a type of grass to make them slip out. If a wedge or nail is driven into a tree where a woodpecker nests, when the bird perches in the tree the nail immediately comes out, no matter how hard it was driven in.*'

References

Books

Bellingham, D., Whittaker, C. & Grant, J., *Myths and Legends*, New Burlington Books 1992, London

Breverton, T.D., *Breverton's Nautical Curiosities – A Book of the Sea*, Quercus 2010, London

Breverton, T.D., *The First American Novel – The Journal of Penrose, Seaman*, Glyndwr Publishing 2007, Glamorgan

Breverton, T.D., *The Pirate Dictionary*, Pelican 2004, New Orleans

Breverton, T.D., *Wales – A Historical Companion*, Amberley Publishing 2009, Stroud

Spencer, John and Anne, *The Encyclopaedia of the World's Greatest Unsolved Mysteries*, Headline Book Publishing 1995, London

Welfare, Simon & Fairley, John, *Arthur C. Clarke's Mysterious World*, William Collins, Sons and Co. Ltd. 1981, London

Useful Websites

http://bestiary.ca
A medieval bestiary site of beasts, manuscripts, digital texts etc.

http://monsters.monstrous.com
Mythological monsters, and well researched items about topics from aliens to zombies.

http://sacred-texts.com
Freely available archive of online books about religion, mythology, folklore and the esoteric.

http://world-mysteries.com
Source of information about strange artefacts, mystic places, ancient writings and science mysteries.

http://www.monstropedia.org
Calls itself the 'original open-source bestiary', with more than 2100 articles ranging from angels to shapeshifters.

http://www.theoi.com
A thorough A–Z of Greek mythology.

http://www.timelessmyths.com
A compendium of classical, Celtic, Norse and Arthurian mythology.

Index

N

O

Quercus Publishing Plc
21 Bloomsbury Square
London
WC1A 2NS

First published in 2011

A catalogue record of this book is available
from the British Library

UK and associated territories
ISBN: 978-0-85738-337-2

Canada
ISBN: 978-1-84866-145-5

Printed and bound in China

10 9 8 7 6 5 4 3 2 1

Text by Terry Breverton
Edited by Philip de Ste. Croix
Designed by Paul Turner and Sue Pressley,
    Stonecastle Graphics Ltd
Index by Philip de Ste. Croix